Sowing

LEGENDARY FARMER BOOK 3

Print book ISBN 978-1-7376510-4-8

Ebook ISBN 978-1-7376510-5-5

First edition, September 2022

This is a work of fiction. Names, characters, places, and individuals either are the product of the author's imagination or are used fictitiously, and any resemblance to actual persons, living or dead, businesses, companies, events, or locales is entirely coincidental.

For my wonderful husband, Dave, who's always supportive, and actually believes I'll someday be able to buy him his own airplane.

Book Three: Sowing

sow /sō/ *verb*

gerund or present participle: sowing

1. plant (seed) by scattering it on or in the earth.
2. be thickly covered with.
3. cause to appear or spread.

Chapter One

Rouge

Zoey got to work early on Monday. Her dad had some big meeting first thing in the morning, so it was either go in early, or take the bus to work all the way from home. One thing Zoey had discovered was that buses weren't as reliable as it seemed like they really *should* be, what with the fact that a lot of people took them to work. Going home, it wasn't a big deal, because if she missed her connecting bus, she just had to read or people-watch until the next one.

Going *to* work, though, was a whole other story. If you missed a connecting bus (and for some reason, a bus would get to the stop and then leave *early*, so you would chase after it, yelling, but never, ever catch it) then you were late, even though it was the bus's fault.

Worse, if you had more than one connection, like she did, you inevitably missed the other buses in a horrible slow-motion trickle-down effect of *doom*, and then you were an *hour* late, and you had to go to HR and talk to your rep, and get an official warning in your file, and no matter how many times Zoey had been *perfectly polite* to Georgia McKeene when passing her in the halls, the woman was still a *snake*, and…

It all added up to Zoey going in early with her dad, because either leaving *before* he did or else taking the chance of missing one or more of her buses was. Not. Worth. It.

So, at 7:23am on Monday, Zoey found herself sitting on her single, reliable, quiet bus as it left the college campus and headed for Veritas Corp and other Parts Unknown. She was still tired from the excitement of the weekend, and she quickly found herself drowsing as she thought over everything that had happened. Finally reaching North Goose, finding the abandoned farm, rescuing Millie, then saving Struthio, Aspen's friend Manuela (*just* a friend?), and Mai Ley, priestess of Atae, aka *Emily*! Mai Ley? An anagram of Emily? Yeah, okay, she'd added an 'a' (for AI?), but apparently the whole thing about computers not having much imagination was true.

When Rouge had Stealthed her way over to check out the two people chained to the wall, she'd never, *ever* expected one of them to suddenly sit up and start talking to her. Much less have everyone else act like they couldn't hear or see them. She was vaguely aware that Aspen was talking quietly to the person on the stone table, but, as in Bloodhaven, everything outside herself and Emily went kind of fuzzy and silent.

Plus, that weird emotionless voice Emily did. That was kind of Atae's thing, supposedly, though Rouge hadn't ever been in one of Atae's temples, because she was more of a Dark Races goddess, but she'd heard it was pretty grim.

So, seeing the black-robed figure sit up straight like some kind of creepy possessed thing had freaked Rouge out. She'd totally screamed like a girl, which she *was*, but she didn't usually go all stereotypical, but seriously, the avatar looked like one of those sinister dolls with the staring eyes that opened and closed when you moved them around.

"Are you ready to fulfill our bargain, Rouge the Rogue?" she'd asked, and Rouge had caught on pretty quickly. At least, her brain had caught on. It took a bit longer for her heart-rate and the massive adrenaline surge to take the hint.

"Holy cats, Emily! What are you doing here?"

The AI tilted her head quizzically, though her expression barely changed. "I told you I would join your party using one of the test accounts. This one is known as Mai Ley. I thought that joining you in this manner would be more acceptable than simply showing up and asking your companions to include me. Was I incorrect?"

Rouge looked around at the grim room in which they found themselves, Struthio's gaunt form on the ground nearby, and the hazy shapes of her friends. "No, I just... What if we hadn't found you?"

"Given your propensity for accepting random side quests, and Aspen's new [Life Sense], the odds of that were fairly small. This path leads to the greatest chance of your successfully completing your secret quest, though there is a 42% chance Aspen will die within the next ten minutes-"

Rouge raised a hand to halt the dispassionate recitation. "Whoa, wait, what? Why would Aspen die?" She felt her heart-rate start picking back up as she clutched her Mambele.

"The owner of this domicile has returned. You failed to notice an alarm on the door leading down to this area, so he is moving quickly and bringing assistance."

Rouge started to spring up, but halted as a cool, satin-gloved hand came to rest on her arm. "I suggest you release me and the quest NPC. Your odds of surviving this encounter will increase by-"

She was already using her lockpicks to pop the simple locks on the manacles that 'trapped' the AI and Struthio. As she released the poor man's last shackle, she felt as though cotton balls had just been removed from her ears and realized that Emily had dropped the Somebody Else's Problem Field that had surrounded them.

She turned to her farmer friend, who was helping the female prisoner stand up. ::Aspen?::

❧ ❧ ❧

Zoey's eyes popped open as she felt the bus pull to a stop, and heard her device play a soft chime. She glanced down at the screen.

GPS and the public bus system indicate you have reached your destination. Please exit the vehicle.

She stood, stretching and yawning as she glanced at the time. Still more than an hour before work was supposed to start, though she could see other people already entering the building. She sighed and climbed down from the bus, jumping the last step to the pavement.

The tiered building with its glossy façade was familiar to her now, and she went straight to the front doors without pausing to gawk, walking in on the heels of a tall older man with a grim expression and a stride so stiff she was a little surprised to see that he was actually bending his knees. The man went up to Sam, who was already hard at work, with an unusually solemn expression as they watched the doors and their monitors.

The man leaned in, speaking so softly that Zoey could only hear because the lobby music was barely audible. Maybe it adjusted to the ambient sound level, and the lobby was so quiet right now that it didn't need to be very loud? Or maybe whoever controlled it just didn't feel like listening to it before they had to?

"…everything ready in the clinic?" the man was asking Sam.

The guard nodded. "I'm very sorry for your loss, sir."

The older man's stiff shoulders sagged briefly. "Thank you, Sam. You may continue." He lifted a hand in farewell (or maybe dismissal?) as he continued on through the gate. Oddly, he didn't use a card to get through, and he didn't have to have his briefcase checked on the way in. He just pressed his whole hand to the scanner and then walked on in like he owned the place.

She stepped up to the desk, smiling. "Hey, Sam. My dad had to go to work early today, so I just came on in. Do I need to wait out here in the lobby until closer to 9, or can I go in and hang out in the cafeteria or something?"

Sam's round face brightened a little. "Good morning, Zoey! It's all right, you can go in. You'll have to stay in the general admittance areas, like the gym, the clinic, and the outside concourse until 8:30. The offices won't be open until then, even though some folks are already in there. If the door is closed and your pass won't let you in, just wait. Lots of people come in early to swim or work out though."

Zoey made a face. "Not my idea of a good time, but..." she shrugged, then glanced after the vanished man. "What's going on in the clinic?"

Sam's eyes widened. "You didn't get the memo? I wonder if they didn't include interns, since you guys never would have met her. The owner's daughter, Amy, died last week. She was involved in a hit and run in January, and had been in a coma ever since. Her passing wasn't exactly a surprise at this point, but it's still sad. She was a really nice lady. She was a researcher and worked in the labs in the clinic building. They set up a memorial table there so people could leave cards and flowers."

Zoey's eyes widened, and she flashed back to Sara telling her about Dr. Joe's 'family member' who had died. Was she referring to Amy, or someone else? Zoey remembered Nina mentioning that Dr. Joe had been engaged to Amy at one point, but they'd broken up, right? Still, just because you broke up with someone didn't mean you had to stop caring about them.

She pointed after the man who had just waltzed through security. "So that was...?"

Sam nodded. "Carl Landon himself. He-"

A quiet but meaningful clearing of a throat came from nearby, and Zoey and Sam both looked toward the other guard sitting at the desk. The man was studiously examining the screens in front of him and not watching them at all, but it was pretty clear that that little cough had been for them. Gossip time was over.

Zoey sighed, and smiled at Sam. "Thanks. I'll, uh, go pay my respects then."

She waved and walked over to security, where another guard stood by the gates, watching.

ᔕ ᔕ ᔕ

The large table set up in the clinic lobby took the place of several chairs, which had been moved to make room. A gorgeous damask tablecloth draped perfectly to the floor on all four sides, and a large holo of a woman's face grinned out at Zoey. Her long, light brown hair was center parted and brushed smooth, and pretty greenish eyes twinkled as she looked to the left, smiled as if seeing someone she knew, and then the holo returned to the beginning of the loop. She wore just a touch of makeup, and her oval face had round cheeks and a slightly snub nose. She looked like someone Zoey would have liked.

The table around the holo was already piled high with cards and flowers, probably from family and business contacts, delivered over the weekend. A stack of blank white cards sat next to some fancy pens, ready to receive the condolences of those who hadn't thought to bring their own card. Absently, Zoey flipped through a few cards, trying to figure out what to say.

Most of the expensive looking pre-printed cards said the kinds of things people always said, not because they weren't really sad, but because they didn't know what else *to* say.; 'I'm sorry for your loss', 'We'll miss her too', or 'With deepest sympathy'.

In a glass bowl nearby sat a few lonely, hand-printed cards; the first of the ones written by co-workers and friends. Hoping to get an idea what to write on her own card (and totally not because she was just nosy), Zoey glanced around, and then pulled them out.

The first one, in heavy block letters, read, 'Amy. I miss you. I'd do anything to change that night.'

The second, in equally firm script, said, 'This isn't over. I promise they'll pay.'

Zoey stared down at the cards, wide eyed. Those were *not* sentiments she'd expected to see. What night? What had happened that someone wanted to change? More importantly, *what* wasn't over, and *who* was going to pay? Because that was totally ominous!

Behind her, Zoey heard the click of shoes on the tile in the hallway coming from the labs. She dropped the cards back in the bowl as if they'd burned her fingers, and shot a panicked look around. Then, without making a conscious decision to do so, she dove under the table, letting the heavy tablecloth fall back down behind her, completely concealing her presence. The instant the cloth touched the floor, she remembered she *wasn't* in the game, and she was *Zoey*, not Rouge about to be caught stealing the family silver, but it was far too late to take it back.

Zoey gulped, eyes huge in the near blackness under the table. A dim hint of light at the floor-line was the only illumination, and (not for the first time) she desperately wished for Rouge's [Darkvision]. She realized she was holding her breath, and forced herself to let it out slowly, before she had to gasp for air and gave herself away.

In the lobby, the sound of the shoes passed by her hiding place, then paused. They turned back, and came so close that Zoey realized the person must be standing in front of the table, right where she herself had been a moment before.

A quiet shuffling came, as someone handled the cards on the table, and there was the *tink* of metal on glass. A ring tapping the glass bowl, maybe? In the silence of the room, she heard a soft tearing sound, and two small, dark shadows obscured the line of light in front of the crouching girl. Suddenly, there was a soft thud, and the table shook. Zoey swallowed hard as she realized that someone had just hit the tabletop with an open hand.

"It *is* over," a quiet voice hissed. "Rot in hell, Amy Landon."

Then there was a soft *shoosh* of shoes as the speaker turned in place, and an instant later the sound of clicking shoes began receding again. The door opened, then hissed shut, and the room was silent.

Zoey reached out with shaking fingers and lifted the edge of the tablecloth. The room was empty, but on the floor lay two halves of a white card. One side, facing up, read, 'This isn't,' and when Zoey turned over the other piece, she saw, 'over. I promise they'll pay.'

Carefully, Zoey crawled out of the dark hollow beneath the table, suddenly feeling very grateful for whatever instinct had led her to lunge for it instead of standing there. Whoever the person was who just left, Zoey was absolutely certain she hadn't wanted to meet them face to face.

Zoey spent the next forty-five minutes or so sitting on the bench she and Nina usually occupied while they ate lunch. She wished her friend was there so they could talk about what had just happened, but Zoey was at least able to relax in the familiarity of 'their' space. Finally, at about 8:40, she figured it should be safe to head on up to the office. She would still be about ten minutes earlier than she usually was, but she was sure that Jazmin, at least, would already be there.

Sure enough, when she reached Design, she could see that the light was on inside, and when Zoey peeked in, she could see Jazmin seated at her desk. However, she wasn't alone, and while Zoey would normally have breezed on in, after her close call that morning, she was feeling a little jittery, so she hesitated.

It didn't take long for the girl to realize that she'd made the right decision. While she couldn't see the face of the woman speaking to Jazmin, she'd know that screechy nasal voice anywhere. It was Zoey's least favorite Veritas Corp employee, the woman who went out of her way to make Zoey's life a little more miserable every time she saw her, good ol' Georgia McKeene.

The snake lady was leaning over Jazmin's desk, staring at the screen intently. After a moment, her French-tipped claw stabbed out, pointing at something. "There," she said triumphantly, "that's definitely a false claim. Who needs two bags of pet litter at an office?"

Jazmin's face was as neutral as Zoey had ever seen it as she said, "That's for the hamster. They use it as a life model for all the in-game rodents. It's a work-related expense."

Georgia sounded frustrated as her finger moved down the screen. "This, then. Eight 'Zen gardens'? What are *those*?"

"It's part of Harris' work flow. He encourages his team members to use them to assist in entering a more creative mind frame." Jazmin's hand crept up to touch the cross that was hidden beneath her high-necked gold blouse. Zoey could practically hear her praying to God for patience.

The HR rep visibly gritted her teeth. "Miss Andrews really knows about and approves these expenses?"

"Yes, Ms. McKeene," Jazmin said stiffly, and Zoey just couldn't stand it anymore. Drawing in a bracing breath, she pushed the door open wide.

"Good morning, Jazmin!" she said, as cheerfully as she could under the circumstances. She let her eyes widen as if in surprise. "Oh! Ms. McKeene! I didn't realize you were here." Very deliberately, she did not extend her 'good morning' to the viper in their midst.

Georgia McKeene stood up straight, tugging at the slim skirt of her black suit. Her blonde hair was pulled back in its usual tight bun, and her thin lips pulled into a hard smile as she looked at Zoey. "Oh, Miss Williams. I see you made it to work on time today."

Zoey's smile locked up, but she kept it pinned to her face. "I did. I just love work so much that I couldn't wait to get here this morning."

The older woman's smile slipped into a sneer that looked much more natural than her fake smile. "Too bad you only have a few more weeks before your internship is over. Though that may be all for the best, since you can only get one more red mark on your record before you're no longer eligible for the position. Or, in fact, *any* position at Veritas Corporation. Ever."

Zoey's shoulders pulled together like someone had tightened the world's biggest rubber band between her shoulder blades. "Yes. You mentioned that when you had me come down so you could write me up for being three minutes late."

The snake waggled a slim finger at Zoey. "Punctuality is the foundation of a solid work ethic. You'll thank me for helping you understand that if you go on to college."

If. Zoey gritted her own teeth. Sure, she might choose not to get a four-year degree, but she was certain the woman meant that Zoey wouldn't be accepted to any college. What *was* it with this lady?

Jazmin stood up abruptly, towering over the other woman by a good six inches, especially in her honey-colored heels. Her voice was cool as she stepped around her desk, passing by Zoey to open the door. "Thank you so much for the reminder, Ms. McKeene. I almost forgot we have an all-hands meeting this morning promptly at nine. I'm certain you wouldn't want us to be late."

Georgia McKeene walked stiffly past them, her low-heeled matte black shoes scuffing the carpet. "I'm certain that's true, Jazmin." She speared the assistant with a meaningful look as she turned to walk away. "Do remember to let me know if you see anything *concerning* in the coming days, will you? You know how important it is for all of us to communicate." With that, she turned away and strode off down the hall, undoubtedly already looking for the next peon to torment.

Zoey turned to Jazmin as soon as the door was closed behind the HR rep. "What is *with* her? I feel like she's had it in for me since the day I got here."

Jazmin sighed and brushed at the creases of her black slacks, her expression distant and a little angry. "Don't take it personally. She was a childhood friend of Harkness Landon. She got the position here because she knows him and Mr. Landon, not because of her job skills." The tall woman's eyes focused, and she slapped a hand over her mouth. "I'm so sorry! I shouldn't have said that. It was inappropriate."

Zoey just grinned. "I won't tell if you don't. It's actually good to know that she's like that with other people, too."

Sighing again, Jazmin sat down at her desk again, touching her ValPAC screen to adjust the angle as she did. "You're definitely in good, and plentiful, company. She's written me up more than once, too." The older woman's smile was tight, and she pushed the small name plate that was already perfectly centered on her desk to the right half an inch. Then she pushed it back where it had been.

Looking up, she seemed to shake off her residual anger and offered Zoey a more genuine smile. "In any case, you should head back to the big conference room. There really is an all-hands meeting in about five minutes."

"Oh! Um," Zoey looked around, "that's the one at the end of the hall that no one uses, right?"

Jazmin chuckled. "It is. Meetings like this are the only time it's needed, so maybe two or three times a year. Come on back when the meeting is over, and I'll let you know what your job tasks are for the rest of the day."

Zoey paused, already several feet down the hall. "Aren't you coming?"

The other woman shook her head. "Bridget already briefed me. I'll be covering everyone's calls and any urgent requests. Go on, now."

Zoey nodded and, seeing other people emerging from offices and the smaller meeting rooms ahead of her, she picked up her pace. After all, 'punctuality was the foundation of a solid work ethic'. Zoey rolled her eyes so hard she thought they might pop out and bounce down the hallway ahead of her.

🐛 🐛 🐛

When she reached the conference room, she found the door wide open and the space already filled with most of the Design department's employees. Several people were sipping beverages, and there was a box of croissants open on the table to one side. Zoey started drifting toward them, because while they weren't cinnamon rolls, they did at least qualify as a breakfast pastry, at least in her mind, and she could definitely use something to distract her brain (and stomach) from the events of that morning so far.

When she had acquired a flaky, buttery, crescent-shaped bread roll, and had just shoved half of it in her mouth, she heard a throat clearing in the front of the room. She looked up, chewing quickly, and saw Bridget standing there. The department head looked exhausted, with pale lips and dark circles under her eyes. Her hair was pulled back in a messy bun, and her plain black dress was a far cry from the many shades of blue that she usually wore.

Bridget waved a hand toward the chairs arrayed around the room. "Thank you for coming, everyone. If you would take a seat, please, I'll try to keep this short."

There was a long minute of rustling and quiet chatter as everyone shuffled into a seat. When they were done, Zoey was amused to see that they had formed into smaller groups according to their teams. Cliques were alive and well in corporate America.

Once everyone had settled down, Bridget smiled wanly. "Thank you." She looked down, visibly struggling to maintain her composure. "As most of you know, Amy Landon…" she swallowed hard, "passed away last week. While it was not unexpected, after her unfortunate accident earlier this year, it was still heart-breaking for all of us who knew her."

Bridget's small hands clutched at the sides of her skirt convulsively. "As most of you also know, Amy is," her voice broke, "*was* my best friend. We've known each other since college, and she was integral to the development of VR. We joined Veritas Corp together, at her father's request, and we had almost five years together here."

She looked up again, and now there was no denying the tears standing in her eyes. "What you may *not* know is that our initial contract with Veritas is set to expire at the end of five years, which is just a few months away. Unfortunately, between some upcoming changes in the management structure of the company and Amy's… loss, I will not be renewing my contract."

A sudden murmur of voices replaced the respectful silence that had filled the room, and Bridget allowed it to swell as she gathered herself again. Finally, she raised a hand, and the room fell silent. "Obviously, that will leave a gap in our team here, and I'd like to encourage any of you who feel that you would like to fill that gap to apply. Carl intends to open interviews to the entire company starting next week, but I told him that I would like to see one of you in my place when I go. He has promised to seriously consider whoever I recommend."

Several people, including most of the team leads, raised their hands, but Bridget waved them down. "Jazmin is sending you all a document listing the job requirements, as well as my personal suggestions for areas that you may want to brush up on before the interview process begins. Anyone who wishes to apply will need to follow the standard application process. I will, however, be glad to look over your resume and cover letter and give you my feedback before you submit it."

Everyone settled back into their seats, but Zoey could practically feel the room humming with a suppressed mixture of excitement and concern. She bit her lip, wondering how much her own quest in *Veritas Online* was affecting, and affected by, Bridget's decisions. She just wished she could speak to the other woman about it.

As if reading her mind, Bridget looked over and met Zoey's eyes, giving her a small, painful smile. Then the other woman looked around at the others in the room, clapping her hands firmly once. "I'll let you all get back to work. Some of you have some thinking to do, and others, I suspect," Bridget's blue eyes touched on each of her team leads, "will be touching up your resumes. Also, if you knew Amy at all, please take a moment sometime over the next few days to go down to the clinic and pay your respects. Thank you."

Nodding, Bridget waved to the group and made her way toward the door. As she passed Zoey, she touched the girl's shoulder and murmured softly. "Please come to my office in a few minutes, if you would, Zoey?"

Zoey blinked and nodded. Bridget had gone above and beyond for the last several weeks to make sure that there was no chance for anyone to think Zoey was anything to her other than a particularly young intern. Obviously, Amy's death and Bridget's decision had changed something. Zoey couldn't help but feel excited, though guilt followed rapidly on the heels of her excitement as she saw a tear fall from Bridget's eye as the woman hastily left the room.

Zoey waited five minutes before following Bridget. The first minute wasn't bad. She watched everyone talking, some of them intensely, while others had the air of inveterate gossips having a wonderful day. The second minute of waiting allowed Zoey to start picking out those whose expressions contained darker emotions; anger, sadness, frustration. In the third minute, she found the two people who were staring after Bridget with expressions of real concern: Dot (aka 'Granny', for no apparent reason), and Harris. Dot's face had nothing in it but sadness and worry, but the anxiety in Harris' expression was definitely threaded with… greed? Desire? Nothing quite as simple as the naked ambition on several other faces.

In the fourth minute, Zoey found herself edging toward the door. She kept glancing at her screen, then at the exit, and then back to her screen. The seconds crawled. When they finally ticked over into the fifth minute, she gave in and took a big step toward Out. One more step, and she was pulling the door closed behind her when another hand caught and held it.

Dot stepped out into the hall after Zoey, gently pulling the door closed behind her. Zoey didn't know much about the woman, except that she loved pickles and was one of the artists, so the girl wasn't quite sure what to say. Fortunately, Dot didn't wait.

"I saw her say something to you before she left. Is she all right?" The older woman, who was probably around sixty, had a voice that was still warm and solid, without any of the signs of age that freckled her skin and silvered her hair.

Zoey glanced toward Bridget's door and back. "I… Don't know? She just asked me to come to her office. She looked pretty sad, though. Not that that's surprising."

The wrinkles between Dot's brows and around her eyes deepened. "Would you let me know if you think she needs anything, dear? We don't work closely together, but…" she smiled slightly, "I feel like she's a member of my family. If she needs something, I'd like to help."

Zoey ignored the 'dear', which was something she hated, and just nodded. The woman was obviously really worried, and it wasn't like they talked often, so it was understandable if she didn't remember Zoey's name. "Sure. Do you want me to tell her you asked?"

A strange look that seemed to be part fear and part hope flickered through Dot's faded blue eyes. "I... No. I just want to be sure she's all right. Thank you."

Zoey frowned a little. There was *definitely* something going on here that she didn't understand, but right now wasn't the time to pursue it. She just nodded again and took another step down the hall. "Okay. I'll just, um, go find out then."

She lifted a hand and turned to make a hasty retreat, leaving 'Granny' staring after her with an indecipherable expression.

When she knocked at Bridget's door a few seconds later, the wood swung away silently under her hand. As it did, she noticed that the post-its covering Bridget's door plate were gone, leaving a bland brown plaque with gold letters that said simply 'Bridget Andrews – Vice President of Design'.

Zoey poked her head into the office, stopping as she saw Bridget's red-gold bun poking up behind the five screens on her desk. When the other woman looked up, Zoey could see that her blue eyes were red-rimmed, and her usually clear skin was blotchy. Nonetheless, Bridget essayed a smile for Zoey's benefit.

"Zoey, thank you. Come on in, and close the door, please." Bridget stood up, circling her desk to come around and sit in one of the two pale gray chairs in front of the desk. She waved a hand at the empty seat as Zoey closed the door with a soft click. "Sit down. I have... a few things I need to talk to you about."

Zoey hesitated with her hand on the doorknob. This seemed much more serious than just a chat about what was going on in the game. Her suspicions were confirmed when Bridget turned one of the screens on the desk, and Zoey saw her dad's face looking back at her, concern in his eyes. She swallowed hard, and went to sit down.

Bridget cleared her throat, then looked from Zoey to her dad. "Thank you for joining us on such short notice, Dr. Williams. I'll try to take as little of your time as possible, but in the interest of keeping my side of our bargain, I need to discuss some things with both of you present. But first," she glanced at another screen, "Emily, please record everything that happens in this office until Zoey leaves. Encrypt and time lock it so that it cannot be viewed or edited until the final quest is complete, even by me."

She stopped and looked back at them. "Zoey, Dr. Williams- "

"Marcus," Zoey's dad interrupted, and she looked back over, surprised to see that he was now watching Bridget with an expression of concern that looked remarkably similar to how he looked at Zoey when her hamster died last year.

Bridget smiled just a bit. "Marcus, then. Either of you may end this meeting at any time. You're under no obligation to stay, and whether you choose to stay or leave will not affect your time in *Veritas Online* in any way. Some things have changed since," she closed her eyes for a moment, then blinked them open again, though they were brighter than usual, "since we first spoke. I want to be certain that you understand the ramifications of those events, and have an opportunity to make your choices with full knowledge."

Zoey and her dad looked at each other, and then both nodded. Zoey, for one, was *not* leaving until she found out what was going on. Her dad hid it way better, but he was just as nosy as she was, so she knew that unless he thought whatever-it-was would put Zoey in danger, he wasn't going anywhere either.

Bridget drew in a deep breath. "I was just filling Marcus in on what I told everyone in the meeting, Zoey, but there's more to this than just my leaving the company. Now, I can give you the Too Long; Didn't Read version, or the whole story, but I warn you it starts about twenty-six years ago."

Zoey's eyes widened, and if she'd had Rouge's long, pointy ears, they would have twitched. Her internal response was *Yes, please!* but she just said, "I'd like the long version."

On screen, Marcus' eyes flickered away for an instant and he scowled. Then he held up a finger in a 'just a second' gesture, and touched something in front of him. "Kyle, I'm going to be in an urgent meeting for at least a half an hour. Let any students who turn up for office hours know they can talk to a TA, or I'll stay an extra hour after my last class this afternoon."

Kyle was the secretary for the whole English department, and he stood guard like an ancient dragon outside the professor's offices. He was skinny and all of twenty-six or seven, but when he told a student that they needed to do something, they *listened.* His distant voice responded in the affirmative, and her dad nodded and returned his attention to Bridget.

"Go ahead."

She nodded, and seemed to physically brace herself. Then she smiled ruefully. "What I'm about to tell you isn't exactly a secret, but I also don't tell it to a lot of people. But, here goes: Bree Stephenson is my mom."

Bridget turned another screen, flicking it to share it to Zoey's dad. On the screen was an image of an incredibly young and exhausted Bree Stephenson, make-up free and in a hospital gown, holding a tiny squalling newborn.

"My mom was seventeen when I was born. She and my dad were high-school sweethearts, but when she told him she was pregnant, he told her to get rid of me. She ignored him. When I was born, his dad insisted on a paternity test. When it showed that I was his, the family paid my mom $10,000 to sign a document that absolved my father of any responsibility for me. Then my father went off to Harvard while my mom finished high school.

"She used the money to rent a little apartment, because her parents told her that if she was old enough to be a mom, she was old enough to live on her own. She paid a neighbor to watch me while she went to school, and then she came home and took care of me. When I slept, she worked, streaming video of herself playing video games. At first, she tried just giving game-play tips, but she quickly found she got a lot more views if she wore a bikini."

Bridget shook her head, sighing. "It was pretty bad, those first few years. She always made sure I had everything I needed, but she had to work at a grocery store since the employee discount let her buy food. Sometimes she'd talk the night manager into letting her take home the 'ugly' produce, or things that were barely expired. Meanwhile, she was starting to be recognized, and some people would call her names, or assume that she would take money for... things other than playing games while wearing tight clothes.

"When I was five, I went to kindergarten, and things got better. The school provided breakfast and lunch and after school care on school days. She didn't have to pay for childcare anymore, since she qualified for assistance. The bus picked me up and dropped me off for free. She was able to stop doing some of what she'd had to do to pay the bills and start doing more of what she *liked* doing." Bridget smiled. "I think you know what happened from there, at least the business side of it."

"By the time I was sixteen, she was very successful, and we didn't have to worry about money. We lived in a nice house, in a nice neighborhood, and when it turned out that I was pretty smart, she could afford to pay for tutors so I could graduate high school early. She was thirty-four when I went away to college." Her blue eyes went soft and sad.

"I met Amy there. She was seventeen, and we bonded over being the youngest in our classes. She wanted to be a scientist, and I wanted to be a programmer, but we took all the classes we could together, and eventually moved into an apartment off campus. We both got our undergrad degrees in three years, partly because neither of us went home for the summer. Amy's mom was dead, and her dad was," she gestured expressively at the building around them, "creating an empire."

Bridget shook her head, ineffectively trying to tuck some of her flyaway hair back into her bun. "My mom wanted me to come home, but I knew she was already working her butt off trying to build her brand. She would have made time for me, because she always did, but she gave up her own childhood so that

I could have one, and I just wanted her to have her dream, without having to worry about me for once. Plus, Amy was there, and I didn't want her to get ahead of me.

"We both decided to stay on and get advanced degrees. Computer Science and Robotics for me, and Neuroscience with a minor in Psychology for Amy. We both continued on the way we had been, and we were in our last year when we were talking about dreams one night, and decided to try a joint project. She had been working on a study that attempted to communicate with sleeping people through lucid dreams, and we wanted to know if we could use a machine to facilitate that communication."

Her mouth quirked, and Zoey stared, suddenly remembering the distinct sense of familiarity she'd had the first time she'd seen the other woman do that in person. It looked *just like Bree Stephenson*. Same mouth, same jawline, albeit a little softer in Bridget, and the same crooked smile. Whoa.

"Obviously," Bridget went on, "we succeeded beyond our wildest dreams, though we had to rope Amy's boyfriend, Joe, a medical intern, into helping." She actually managed a small grin. "But we needed funding to *do* anything with it. I'd borrowed money from mom to do our experiments, but now we were talking serious money, and mom's money was almost all tied up in her TV show, and she'd just bought a building to make into a creative space for artists.

"Then Harkness came to visit Amy." She shook her head. "Amy had told me about her older brother, of course, but I'd never met him before. I never had much time for men, especially after seeing how awful some of them were to my mom when I was young. But I fell hard for Hank. He just has this self-confidence that makes you believe he can do anything he sets his mind to. The fact that he looks like he should be posing for the cover of GQ didn't hurt either. I told him everything, and he suggested going to his father."

Bridget shrugged. "Everything just kind of took off after that. I didn't know it, but Carl had been trying to get Amy back into the fold ever since she completed her undergraduate degree. She wanted to do research, and he wanted her to work for the family business. When we approached him to ask for funding, he leapt at the chance."

"He wound us up in so many contracts and agreements that if my mom hadn't sent me to her lawyers, I'm pretty sure he would have effectively owned us for life. Thank goodness for mom, because those lawyers shut Carl down hard and got him to sign an agreement that limited his control of both our tech and ourselves. He got everything for five years, and after that," she shrugged again, "it was up to us.

"Anything we discovered using funds from Veritas Corp belonged to Veritas. Anything from before that, including the initial discovery, was ours, and we could do what we wanted with it, though if we sold it, Veritas got first right of refusal, as long as they could meet or exceed what we would expect to get on the open market. Of course, that only worked because Veritas is privately owned and operated almost entirely by the Landon family. There are no shareholders or powerful executive boards to step in and complicate things.

"About a year and a half ago, we released *Veritas Online*, which is based on the tech that Amy, Joe, and I developed. Joe loves his job here, and I enjoyed most of it, right up until I broke up with Hank and fell out of favor with Carl. Amy pretty much hated it. She still wanted to do research, and her greatest wish was to figure out how to use our technology to reach coma patients and help people with significant physical or mental impairments, including dealing with traumatic events.

"As soon as *VO* went online, Amy told us all that as soon as the five years were up, she wanted to open source our original invention. She'd already retained mom's lawyers, and they'd figured out how to make it work, but she needed Joe and I, as the co-creators, on her side. I love the game we made, at least the parts Carl didn't have too free a hand in, so I wasn't sure, but as long as *VO* would still be around, I was okay with it.

"Joe hated the idea. He, Hank, and Carl brought out lawyers on the other side, and without Joe, Amy and I couldn't go ahead. Amy and Joe were engaged and living together by then, but she moved back in with me the next day. Joe really thought she'd give in, but she didn't." Bridget's smile was grim this time. "So, they came up with the idea of this quest. Joe's no game designer, but Hank wrote his side of it, and together, they chose both their player and their immersion 'tester'."

Bridget paused and stood, reaching between her monitors to grab a bottle of water. She took several long swallows, and then sat down. "Sorry. That was definitely the long version. Now we're coming to the part that directly affects you.

"In January, long before the quest was even supposed to start, Amy and I found out that someone had started giving their chosen player some assistance. Just little things, here and there, like manipulating quest rewards and 'random' drops so that the player would get things that they shouldn't have had. Things that let them get a lot stronger than they should have been."

She gave that little smile again. "We couldn't prove anything, but it was a very Hank-like thing to do. He's not a *bad* person, but he likes to win. Once he knows what he wants, he'll do almost anything it takes to get it. He won't really hurt anyone, but he doesn't necessarily play fair either.

"Amy went to confront Joe about it. They were working on getting back together, and she'd started talking about moving back in with him, but if he knew about what Hank had been up to, it was off, for good this time. He says he told her he wasn't in on it, that he meant to follow the rules we'd agreed upon, and she believed him. She was still upset, though, and she said she wanted to take a walk and get some fresh air, then take the bus back to our house."

A tear welled up and overflowed Bridget's eye, and then another followed it. She sniffed hard, and grabbed a box of tissues from the desk. After blowing her nose and wiping her eyes almost angrily, she shoved the dirty tissue into the waste bin next to the desk. "Damn it," she muttered, "I thought I was done crying."

Zoey just sat there, frozen. She wasn't really the touchy-feely type anyway, and she just didn't know Bridget that well, not really. What should she *do*? She looked to her dad for help, and found him watching Bridget with concern. When she managed to catch his eye, though, he just shrugged, seeming as much at a loss as Zoey.

Fortunately, Bridget managed to pull herself together, and wiped at her eyes one last time. When she spoke again, her voice was a little rough and nasal. She rushed through the next words as if she was afraid she wouldn't get them out if she didn't say them quickly. "Someone ran her down just a few blocks from Joe's house. It was dark and icy, but the police said it didn't look like the car even tried to stop. They just hit her and, and… kept going. Like she was a squirrel who tried to cross the road at an inconvenient moment."

Bridget's face was pale, except for angry red patches blazing on her cheeks. "Joe had asked her to let him know when she got to the bus stop. When he didn't hear from her, he went looking. He found her by the side of the road, right where she fell. It was… It was bad. He thought she was dead, but he checked and found a pulse. The doctors said she fell in a snowbank, and the cold saved her life. It didn't matter though," her voice was bitter now, "she had brain damage, on top of everything else. They operated to relieve the pressure, but… She never woke up.

"About two months ago, Carl pulled her from the hospital and took her home. He set up a hospital room there, and he wouldn't let me or Joe visit. I used to go to the hospital and read to her, and tell her what was going on. He wouldn't even let me call so she could hear my voice." She closed her eyes, and two more tears seeped out from beneath her lashes. She swiped them away and continued.

"I have never been angrier with someone than I am with that man. I know he's hurting too. I know he lost his daughter, just like I lost my best friend, and Joe lost the woman he loved. I know he's never exactly been great at dealing with emotions. But I can't stay here with Amy gone. So, I gave my notice this morning. I'll stay until my five years are up, which is in twelve weeks, shortly after the quest ends. Then I'll walk out of here, and dump the data about VR all over the internet, just like Amy wanted, no matter what happens with the quest."

She looked up and smiled sadly at Zoey. "So, don't worry about doing anything in the game, Zoey. Just relax and have fun. I put way too much weight on your shoulders because I wanted to follow the rules. Well, forget the rules. If you win, that's great, but if you lose," she shrugged, "the ending will be the same."

Zoey's dad finally spoke up, his deep voice somber. "Won't that violate your contract, Bridget? In fact, aren't you violating your NDA right now? You said you couldn't tell us anything else when you spoke to us originally."

The older woman (not that much older, though, really. Ten years? Eleven? Young enough that Zoey's dad was almost old enough to be her dad, too) shrugged, her expression stony. "I don't care. Amy's dead, and I think… *I* think someone killed her on purpose. Someone who wants Veritas Corp to maintain control of our tech. I think that same person is trying to get rid of me now, too." She rubbed at her wrist, where Zoey could now make out the edge of a bandage beneath the cuff of her long-sleeved dress.

"I could be wrong. I hope I am. But I've had two 'accidents' since Amy died, and either of them could easily have been much more serious."

"Wait a minute," Zoey's dad said, voice worried and angry in equal measures, "are you saying you think someone is trying to *kill* you? Have you filed a police report?"

Bridget nodded, looking exhausted. "They said they'll 'look into it', but I can tell they think I'm being paranoid. I called them almost every day the first month after Amy was attacked, and I wouldn't listen when they said it was an accident. I know Amy, though. She always, *always*, walked on the left side of the street. She said it was safer when she could see oncoming traffic. She was fanatical about it, ever since a friend of hers was hit and killed in high school. But she was on the right side when *she* was hit. I don't know why she would have been there, but she wasn't just walking. Something happened that night, and I'm going to find out what it was, even if I have to play bait."

The woman's jaw was set in a stubborn line, and Zoey believed she meant it. She thought about the strange events of that morning, and the cold voice saying *Rot in hell, Amy Landon.* She started to say something, but her dad spoke first, and the words froze in her throat.

"Bridget, is Zoey in danger? Does anyone know she's your player? Do you think there's *any* chance that this person, if they exist, might come after her?" His tone was as dark as Grandma's homemade treacle tarts, and twice as smooth, and she knew what that meant. He was going into lockdown mode. He would use that voice to get the person he was talking to to give him all their information, and then use it against them if he had to. That was full on Dad Defense Mode. And if she said a word, he'd pull her out of everything in a hot second.

Bridget shook her head. "I don't believe so. Carl, Joe, and I should be the only ones who know, just like I don't know who their player is. There are several people who wondered why I sponsored Zoey into the intern program, but I, ah," she rubbed her hand on the back of her neck, "*may* have hinted that she's the daughter of a guy I like, and I was trying to get into his good graces."

Then she waved her hands wildly, face flushed red, "Not that it's true! I mean, you're very nice and all, Marcus, but you're, like, barely younger than my *mom*." Her hands clapped over her mouth, and she looked mortified. Zoey very nearly cracked up. Yep, Bridget really wasn't *that* much older than Zoey herself, in spite of the crazy situation she was caught up in. She may have been super smart, but romance mucked things up for *everybody*.

"Ohhh, my gosh." Bridget buried her face in her hands, drew in a long breath, and then looked up. "This is why I needed to talk to you. I mean, not the last part, but-" she growled in frustration, and Zoey almost choked on her own spit while she tried to hold in her laughter. Out of the corner of her eye, she could see that the deep crevice between her dad's eyebrows had smoothed out, and the corners of his mouth were twitching too. Crisis averted, but she wasn't quite ready to open her own mouth yet. Not when Bridget was doing such an amazing job at lightening up the conversation.

"I wanted you to know what's going on. If nothing happens to me, great, and after all this is over, we'll all just move on. But if something *does* happen... Just keep on like you are. You're anonymous, just like Hank's player. The only reason anyone but me knows who Zoey actually is is because I messed up in coding the selection criteria and left out the age qualifier. I had to tell Carl after that, and Joe knows because he sees your game logs."

Bridget leaned forward, looking at Zoey intently. "There is one other thing, though." She glanced over at Zoey's dad, "I don't know if you've had a chance to talk about Emily, yet?"

Zoey and her dad nodded simultaneously, but internally Zoey was squirming. Sure, she'd told her dad that Mai Ley was actually Emily, but she may have *heavily* implied that it had something to do with the quest, and not anything about, you know, the AI achieving autonomous sentience. She crossed her fingers beside her leg. Please, please, *please* don't get too specific, Bridget!

The programmer smiled in relief. "Good. I have a small request for both of you. This one is personal, and, again, your decision won't affect either Zoey's job or her quest. But the fact is that Emily was my last personal project with Amy. We started working on her back in college, and continued using our set-up at home after we started working at Veritas. We have documentation proving that, and Carl agreed to let us 'train' Emily as the *Veritas Online* ALPI. While that ALPI belongs to Veritas Corp, there is a... backup program in place. That backup is what is now using the player account for the character Mai Ley.

"I would very much appreciate it if you would treat her as much like another person as possible. There's only so much I can do with programming alone, and Amy had been using her research into neurotechnology, specifically as it relates to our VR system, to build something new. When I go, I'll be taking that version of Emily with me, but-"

She shook her head. "If anything happens to me, all rights to that program, and a sister program I have still stored on my system at home, go to my mom. It's all legal, and mom's lawyers are in this up to their beady little eyes, but I just want to ask you to help me teach her. I can't be on much right now, but Emily is learning every day. I'd like to know that she's not… lonely, I guess. And that she's learning from good people."

Zoey's dad was looking at her now with a, 'we're going to have a chat later, young lady' kind of face, but he wasn't going up in smoke, so that was good. She gave him her best, 'oops, my bad, but you know you love me' smile, and one eyebrow shot up.

He huffed out a breath, turning his gaze back on Bridget. "Is there anything else?"

She smiled her crooked grin again. "That's not enough?"

"Oh, I think it's plenty. I also think Zoey had better get back to work before people start asking even more questions that you can't answer." His voice was wry, and Bridget flushed again.

Zoey stood up, attempting a grin. "I know when I'm not wanted!" She sidled toward the door. "Um, Bridget, be careful though, okay? I mean… This stuff is really bad, if you're right. I know you're smart and all, but…" her voice trailed off as she gestured helplessly.

Bridget shook her head. "It'll be okay, Zoey. I only told you because you and Marcus are in this whether I like it or not, and because I need your help with Emily. I promise I'm doing everything I can to stay safe, and," she glanced back over at Zoey's dad, who was watching with that eyebrow still way too close to his hairline, "I think I'm about to get a few more suggestions on that front."

Zoey grinned, but even she could tell it was more worried than really cheerful. "Yeah. He likes to take care of people," she rolled her eyes, "Just let him do it. It's easier, believe me. Plus," she lowered her voice to a whisper, "I think he's kind of sweet on your mom."

Then she scampered from the room, followed by her dad's voice saying,

"Zooooeeeeeeeey!"

🐹 🐹 🐹

Jazmin had about eight million Extremely Urgent Tasks for Zoey, since apparently everybody had decided that they weren't going to do any of their own work today. So, Zoey had to chase down all the cups and plates that had been used during the meeting and return them to the cafeteria. Then she had to head down to the lobby to guide up some VIP (a lady who turned out to be selling 3D printers). As soon as she got back, she had to sweep up the huge mess someone made when they tripped over Mr. Hamncheese's litter and spilled it all over. Followed, of course, by cleaning the hamster's cage.

To top off the morning, both 'Granny' and Harris cornered her as she was cleaning up. First, it was Harris, who was trying unsuccessfully to look like the meeting was accidental as he sidled around her, heading for the coffee maker that was sitting on the counter across from Mr. Hamncheese's cage.

"Ah, Zoey, right?" The slightly chunky man with a prematurely receding hairline and two impressive front teeth edged around the counter, holding up an empty coffee cup with an ingratiating smile. "I heard you were collecting these, so I thought I'd…" He waved the cup aimlessly, eyes darting around as if looking for somewhere good to set it down.

She suppressed a sigh. *Yeah, I was looking for those… an* hour *ago.* Instead of saying anything, she pasted her work smile on her lips and reached out to take the cup. Harris held onto it a bit too long, resulting in a struggle for mug retention which resulted in both of them releasing the vessel at the same time. It plunged toward the floor, and Zoey lunged for it. Somehow, she caught it neatly by the handle and stood, as graceful as Rouge would have been in the same situation.

Except that Rouge was too cool to schlep coffee mugs around.

Zoey looked up, and met Harris' dark brown eyes, which were sharp with calculation for a moment. Then he smiled in embarrassment and the moment was gone. "Uh, sorry about that. I have a terrible Agility score. Looks like yours is pretty good, though."

She laughed awkwardly, looking away as she set the cup on the counter so she could finish sweeping. "Yeah, I guess. I think that was mostly luck, though."

He chuckled. "Ah, the hidden stat. There was an episode of a British comedy where they found out luck was actually a virus, and…" He trailed off as she stared at him blankly. "Yes, well, ah, I just wanted to say I really appreciate all your help with the Ham-meister there. My whole team is going to be sad when you leave." He smiled awkwardly, his big teeth protruding over his lower lip in a way that was strongly reminiscent of his pet.

"Oh, yeah," she smiled a little, looking down at the pile of shredded paper she was sweeping up. "No problem. I like the little guy."

A few moments of increasingly uncomfortable silence passed, until Harris finally broke. "I saw Bridget call you into her office. What's up? Is she okay? I mean, obviously she's not okay, but… Is there anything I can do that might help?"

Zoey sighed and stopped sweeping, then gripped the broom handle and leaned on it slightly so she could peer around the corner into the hall. "Granny," she called, "would you like to come in? You guys are *so* not sneaky."

Sure enough, the older woman followed the corner of her paisley skirt, which had been visible just past the door. Her cheeks were tinged with red, and she was biting the last of her lipstick off. "That obvious, was I?"

Zoey looked back and forth between her two stalkers, deciding that they definitely didn't look like they were in on this together. She shook her head at both of them. "I appreciate that you guys want to help Br… um, Ms. Andrews, but, honestly, I can't help you. Just go talk to her if you're so worried. She just wanted to talk to me because her leaving her job may affect some things about my internship. I told her not to worry about it." She shrugged.

"If it helps, she seemed to be doing okay. I mean, she's super sad and all, but not crazy sad, you know?" As she spoke, Zoey watched both of them, noting their reactions. Harris had edged away from Granny, and was determinedly not meeting anyone else's eyes. Granny was only watching Zoey, and her expression transitioned from hope to defeat.

"Oh," Granny said, softly. "Well then. I guess I'll ask her, if I get a chance."

Harris, meanwhile, was edging for the door, though he failed to notice Zoey's debris pile and managed to shuffle right through it. She gritted her teeth as the neatly piled debris sprayed across the floor again.

"Ah, okay then. Thanks, um, Zoey. I'll take that under advisement." Then the odd man was gone, and Zoey was alone with 'Granny'.

"Good grief," Zoey muttered, sweeping her pile back together. "What's with him?"

Granny laughed softly. "He's asked Bridget out, I don't know how many times. After she broke up with Harkness, he thought she'd be looking for someone new, and threw himself in her path so often it became a bit of a running joke. Poor man. She finally told him flat out that she wasn't looking for a relationship, and if she was, he wasn't her type." She lowered her voice, nose wrinkling slightly, "Too *old* for her. He's only thirty-three, though, and Harkness was thirty when they broke up. Practically babies." A hint of pain flitted through her eyes, before she looked down at Zoey's broom.

"Oh dear! Didn't anyone show you where the vacuum is kept? They just keep this old broom for the tile. Come on, I'll show you."

☙ ☙ ☙

Thanks to Granny's vacuum, Zoey was able to get all of her tasks done in time to head down for lunch, taking Harris' used mug with her. She hadn't had time to make lunch, so she bought a sandwich and a brownie, filled her water bottle, and went to sit on the bench by the lab to wait for Nina.

Her friend showed up a few minutes later, clutching her own blue fabric lunch bag and looking a little breathless. She flopped down on the bench by Zoey, groaning as she toed off her shoes. "I'm knackered, Zoe. They've been running me off my feet with all the visitors today. Old Man Landon seems set on seeing everybody he's ever met this morning. Some of 'em I even recognize, they're that famous!"

Zoey grimaced. "Yeah, all you guys are so busy I had to go bring up some saleslady. You get to meet anyone good, though?" She took a big bite of her sandwich and chewed hungrily.

Nina shook her head. "Yeah, nah. I only know 'em because my mom's an accountant. She reads financial sites for fun, so I've seen all the rich folk's faces enough to recognize them at least." The taller girl leaned forward, pushing her shiny silver eyeglasses up her nose as she did. "I heard Bridget put in her notice. Do you know if it's true?"

Zoey glanced around, then leaned toward Nina, lowering her voice. "It is. She made an announcement to the whole Design department this morning. I guess her contract runs out in a few months, and without Amy here, she's decided not to renew." She shrugged, trying to keep her expression as innocent as possible. She loved Nina, but her friend was a *huge* gossip and low-key conspiracy theorist.

Nina sat back, huffing out a breath as she took a bite of her cooling breakfast burrito. She chewed thoughtfully for a while, then swallowed and said, "Guess you wouldn't know any more than that, eh? Since you're just an intern?" She eyed Zoey shrewdly.

Given the conversation that morning, Zoey had a sudden realization that her gossip-loving friend probably thought… "Ew! No! I swear, Bridget and my dad are *not* an item! I know he wasn't on this weekend so you could meet him, but he's totally old. Okay, not *old* old, but he's forty, which is *way* too old for Bridget."

Nina's face relaxed, and she laughed. "Fair enough. How'd you get this job, then? For real?"

Zoey grimaced and shifted in her seat, stuffing her face with her sandwich as she thought quickly. She'd known someone would ask this eventually, and she had a couple of outright lies ready, but she just didn't want to lie to Nina.

Finally, she choked down her excessively large bite and chased it with a swallow of water that tried to go down the wrong pipe, leaving her choking and coughing for several more moments than she'd intended to delay.

Nina pounded her on the back, face concerned. "If it's a big secret, just don't tell me. I know I like to natter, so I don't mind if people don't want to tell me things. I *can* keep a secret, though." Her voice was a little wounded.

Zoey wiped tears away and sucked in a few clear breaths before her heart settled back to a steady rhythm. "It's not… that…" she paused as she saw Nina's knowing look, and then sighed, "Okay, maybe it's that a *little*. It's just that I actually met Bridget in *Veritas Online*, and I don't think that it's common knowledge who her in-game avatar is. Maybe I can tell you after she quits, but it's not my secret to tell, you know?"

She put on her most innocent expression, complete with the Big Eyes and the Concerned Eyebrows, and Nina finally shrugged. "That sounds like a good story, eh? But I'll mind my own business until Bridget leaves. Then," she waggled a finger at Zoey playfully, "I want to hear *all* about it."

Zoey thought about NDAs, and Secret Quests, and the look on Bridget's face when she told them she was going to give out the secret of VR to everybody. "Yeah," she said, "I think that'll be okay."

ẽ ẽ ẽ

In keeping with her entirely non-routine day, Zoey made it up to the lab almost ten minutes early. She and Nina had chatted about the battle with the Demonic Swineherd, discussed the route they were going to take to Bright, and laughed over poor Jace's ignominious defeat.

Not that they were laughing *at* him, exactly, because right after he was logged out of *VO* he'd called and nearly laughed himself silly on her messages. She hadn't heard it until she logged off for the night, but it was so like Jace to be able to see the humor in his own near-instant defeat that she'd almost wished for school to start so she could see him again every day. Almost.

In any case, when she reached the door to the lab, she hesitated, tugging indecisively on a curl. It seemed like every time she went somewhere when she wasn't supposed to be there, she ended up with her nose in someone else's business. On the one hand, it was *awesome*, but on the other hand, after that morning she was beginning to have a vague feeling that it might do to rein in her curiosity just a *little* bit.

In the end, though, she pushed open the door, and, sure enough, she walked into the middle of a heated conversation that wasn't *quite* an argument.

Sara stood there, and in profile, with her face drawn and tired, with anger pulling her full lips tight, she looked more than ever like Sarave. Unlike the goblin, however, Sara was dressed in a crisp white lab coat, with neatly creased black suit pants underneath, perfectly brushing her matte black pumps. She was glaring at an older man, probably about the same age as Granny, with a head of almost unnaturally thick silver hair and piercing blue eyes.

"I'm telling you, *Doctor*, Joe knows I can handle the data collection for today. This is a top-secret project, *sir*, and I'm sure you wouldn't want me to violate my contract by showing you our documentation when Joe will be back *tomorrow*." The Indian woman's red lips were set in a firm, unyielding line, and if Zoey had seen that expression on Sarave's face, she'd have known that someone was in seriously hot water.

The man glared down his nose at Sara, in spite of the fact that he was only a half inch or so taller than the woman. "I assure you, *Ms.* Agarwal, that, as the senior member of the medical team, it is well within my rights to-"

Zoey coughed. She didn't mean to, really. It just sort of... slipped out, and then it was as if the echo of that cough was filling up the room as the two combatants turned to stare at her.

Zoey thought *fast*. She thought about how her dad told her to help her friends when they were being bullied. She thought about acting in 'The Redemption of Gertie Greene' when she was in middle school. She thought about Aspen and how he hated being forced back into the hero role, and so he pretended to be so much less than he was in order to protect himself and everybody he cared about.

Quickly, she clutched the only thing she had with her to her chest… a brown paper bag containing her leftover brownie, which she hadn't really wanted after all. The bag crumpled loudly, and she felt hot blood rush up her face.

"Sara?" Her voice squeaked alarmingly. "Who is this? Where's Dr. Joe?" She sidled over toward Sara, hiding behind the other woman slightly, as if she was overwhelmed by the presence of a stranger.

Zoey could hear Sara's confusion when she answered. "This is Dr. Veralt, Zoey. He's another member of the medical team, and he'd like to run your study today while Dr. Joe is gone."

"Oh! No!" Zoey shrank back, trying to cover herself even more with the paper bag. "Where's Dr. Joe? Daddy talked to Dr. Joe. Dr. Joe understands that I don't… I can't wear *that suit* in front of someone else!" She put every bit of the teenage hysteria she could bring to bear into her voice as she looked at the man in front of them, who was now backing away, hands raised defensively.

"Uh, no. Now, young lady, you understand I'm a doctor, just like Dr. Joe. I'm sure you'll be perfectly fine-"

"No no no!" Zoey felt a little bad for using the 'scared little girl' defense, but not enough to stop. This man was clearly trying to bully his way in where he wasn't wanted, and honestly, even though she'd gotten used to wearing the skin-tight suit in front of Sara and Dr. Joe, she wasn't sure she was at all comfortable starting over with someone else, especially for just one day. "Sara, would you call my dad, please? I'm sure he wouldn't be okay with this." She heard a quaver in her voice and wondered if she was a better actress then she'd given herself credit for, or if she really was more upset than she wanted to admit.

Dr. Veralt was glaring at both of them now, and he huffed even as he took another step toward the door.

"Now, now, Zoey, was it? I'm certain we can find a way-"

To Zoey's equally intense satisfaction and mortification, genuine tears began squeezing themselves out from under her lids. This day had already been far too long, with intermittent bouts of fear and stress, and this was just *enough*.

"No! I won't!" She heard the edge of hysteria in her voice hit a new and more authentic edge. "I don't want anyone except Sara and Dr. Joe! I want to talk to my dad!" At that, all the tears started pouring out, and her nose started running.

So did Dr. Veralt. The door slammed shut behind him before the first fat tears hit the floor, and Sara pulled Zoey into a warm embrace. "Shhhhh. It's okay now, Zoey. He's gone. You were *brilliant*," the woman murmured, gently patting Zoey's back.

It was several embarrassing moments before Zoey could pull herself together, and when she finally did, she was hiccupping so hard she could barely speak.

"Where's *hic* Dr. *hic* Joe?" She wiped at her eyes and nose with a tissue Sara had dug out of her desk.

Sara frowned, then forced a smile. "He had a little accident this morning. He'll be fine, but the clinic sent him home to rest for the day. He twisted his ankle, so they just want him to ice and elevate it. I tried to tell them to let him stay here, where I could watch him, because I know he won't take care of himself at home, but they shooed him out of here anyway. He left just before lunch, and when I got back, Dr. Veralt was here."

She stepped back and glanced over at the door to Joe's office with a worried expression. Zoey looked through the open door, and saw that the usual tidy chaos was all out of order, and the drawers were all pulled out. It looked like someone had been searching for something.

Zoey hiccupped again, feeling a chill go down her back. Another accident, followed by another person digging around where they weren't supposed to be. Just *what* was going on at Veritas Corp?

🜚 🜚 🜚

Zoey had never been so glad to feel the bottom drop out of her world. When the faint nausea cleared, she blinked her eyes open to see the glorious sight of

Bright's high golden walls gleaming in the late morning light. Her head fell back, and she looked up at the sky. "Thank you, Gina," she whispered, and wondered for the thousandth time since starting this crazy quest if Bridget had an algorithm to track when people prayed to her. If so, she hoped this brought a smile to the other woman's face.

When she looked back down, she saw that Tessle had pulled her horse up next to Codswallop and was watching her with raised eyebrows. The half-dwarf had obviously heard the little prayer, and thought it was odd that a Player would speak so devoutly to an in-game deity.

Rouge grinned and shrugged a little. "What, Fluff's the only one who can role-play?"

Tessle laughed and shook her head. "I hadn't spent much time with her before," she waved her hand meaningfully, "all *this*. Thought she was a little weird, honestly. She grows on you, though. Makes me laugh."

Rouge nodded. "I've never met a real full-time RPer before, but she's kind of cool. I bet it's fun to talk like that, even though I would be *so* embarrassed."

"Oh my gosh," Tessle giggled, which was a strange sound coming from the broad, strong face of her dwarven avatar, "*yes*. I'd love to meet her in person someday. I wonder if she's like that in real life."

Just then, the object of their speculation rode up, a serious expression on her pretty face. "Lady Rouge! You return at last! Yon companions have asked for your time of arrival, and I have been unable to provide them with an answer. I wish to see the joyous moment of your reunion, but, alas, my soul-space calls to me, and I must depart thence." She struck a pose, her head flung back, her hands on her hips, looking tragic.

Translation: Fluff needed to log out for a while. Sometimes having a dad who started reading her Shakespeare when she was six came in handy. "Do you know when you'll be back from, um, thence?" Rouge asked. "We're almost to Bright. Do you want us to leave your Zombie somewhere?"

Flu-flu bowed her head. "My corporeal form shall follow you thence, fair lady. Then it shall rest upon downy pillows in the Abode of the Dead. My soul shall return from its wanderings on the morrow, and if ye leave a missive at the Great Guild, I shall receive it and join you when body and soul are once more united."

Rouge nodded. "Gotcha. I'll drop a note to let you know where we are. I mean, technically you guys were done when we saved Manuela and Ned, right? We'd love to have you keep hanging out with us, but your quest is done?"

Fluff's winged black brows pulled down. "Nay, my lady! Our wise leader Doom Bloom hast asked us to accompany you whilst her soul must be far from this place. I couldst never forsake you to face some, doubtless abhorrent, fate! So long as thou need'st me, fair maid, I shall be by your side!"

By now, Rouge was fighting to keep a straight face, and she could hear Tessle snorting giggles next to her. Somehow, though, she managed to hold it together, and smiled at the earnest archer. "Thank you, that's really awesome. We could definitely use the help. I'll, um, leave you a missive, then."

Flu-flu nodded, all solemnity, and raised a hand in farewell. Then she blinked, and she was gone. Her Zombie drifted back to fall in beside Doom's and Motte's, leaving Tessle and Rouge shaking their heads bemusedly.

"Well, I guess I should go check on Millie and Struthio. Do you know how they've been doing?" Rouge glanced around, trying to locate the NPCs.

Tessle laughed. "Millie has been busy blowing Restur away with her Cooking skill. She helped make breakfast this morning, and her pancakes were *amazing*. I still have a buff from eating them; +10% Stamina regen and 50 temporary health points. That's with Common quality ingredients, too."

Rouge's stomach rumbled just thinking about it. She hadn't tasted Millie's cinnamon rolls in *months*, and she still dreamed about them. The stat boost, stamina recovery, and doubled speed buffs were nice too, but honestly, Rouge would eat the things just because they were delicious, and she'd promised so many to Codswallop that if she actually followed through, he'd roll around like a feathered dodgeball with feet.

"Oh my gosh, I'm sorry I missed that. I don't know what made the program spawn a pastry chef of her skill in North Goose, of all places, but I'm super glad it did. I'm hoping she'll hook me up with a few more treats for the road before she finds some lucky restaurant to work at." Rouge rubbed her grumbling stomach, and hoped her avatar couldn't actually drool. Sometimes *Veritas Online* took realism a little too far.

"I wouldn't worry about that," Aspen's voice came from behind her, startling her so much she had to clutch at Codswallop's neck feathers to stay seated. "She gave me a few extras to 'tide me over', and threw in some for you, too."

The tall farmer effortlessly pulled even with Codswallop's ground-eating stride, slinging his pack around so he could fish in it at the same time. As he did, Rouge glimpsed Silus snuggled up on his neck, fast asleep, each time his hat tilted to the side so he could look through the pack. She grinned affectionately but with a hint of sadness. The little bat had been sticking closer to Aspen ever since his close call in Goose.

"Ah ha!" Aspen said triumphantly, pulling a cloth-wrapped bundle out of the bag. The bundle was surprisingly large, and as soon as it was fully exposed, Codswallop darted his large beak toward it, eyes gleaming avariciously. Aspen pulled it back just in time, tapping Wally on the beak gently with his other hand. "Oh no you don't, you greedy beast. That's the tenth time you've tried to eat this, at least. You're too predictable."

At that moment, the ostrich, who had been letting his head fall as if defeated, suddenly snaked his long neck around, grabbing the package with a muffled but triumphant squawk. A terrible ripping sound came from the bundle, and a large stack of fluffy pastries tumbled through the air as if in slow motion. Rouge and Aspen both lunged for them, and only managed to crash into each other, both landing on their rears on the road.

They stared as the rapacious fiend Rouge had *formerly* considered a friend gobbled down the pancakes like a pelican chugging down a fish. Dumbly, the thief wondered if it was acceptable for her to cry in public, or if she needed to wait until she was alone.

All around them, caravanners parted to pass them, and every one of them was openly laughing as they did. As the last wagon reached them, a familiar voice reached Rouge's ear.

"Tha' *bird*! 'E's been eatin' m'food since th'day 'e was hatched. Been a rascal that long, too." Struthio, who was driving the wagon, pulled up beside them, and Millie smiled down. The tall woman patted Codswallop's back, and Rouge belatedly remembered that Millie and Struthio had known the bird much longer than she had, and that the ostrich had probably eaten more of Millie's confections than any avian had a right to. Which perhaps explained his amazing size, speed, and intelligence.

The ostrich, meanwhile, was poking his large beak into the pocket of Millie's apron, and she laughed as he pulled out a cookie and gobbled it down. "There, y'lummox. Did'ye think I'd forget yer treat? Nah, now. It's a good thing I know you and your thievin' ways, too, an' saved some more o' them pancakes for Miss Rouge, eh?"

Rouge and Codswallop both perked up at these words, and even Aspen looked up with interest. Rouge bounced up, dusting off her rear. Aspen climbed to his feet with more dignity, but not much less haste. Struthio clucked at the horses, and by silent mutual agreement, they all hurried to catch up with the rest of the caravan.

A few more minutes found them joining the end of the line of people waiting to enter Bright. The caravanners milled around, readying the wagons for inspection, and Rouge leapt from her ostrich's back to the wagon, which she now saw was the one that held everything needed for the makeshift 'kitchen' that the caravan set up when they camped for the night.

Rouge smiled at Millie and Struthio, glad to see that they both already looked much better than the last time she saw them. Thanks to game mechanics, Struthio had already recovered some of his body mass, though he still looked like he'd just recovered from a bad illness. Millie, on the other hand, was practically glowing with happiness. Her broad face was all smiles, and she reached over to touch Struthio every time she got close enough, as if to reassure herself that he was really there.

"I'm really glad you guys are feeling better!" Rouge said, biting into the fluffiest, softest pancake she'd ever been privileged to eat. Even as the bite practically melted in her mouth, notifications popped up in her vision.

Your Stamina recovery has increased by 10% for 6 hours!
You have gained 50 temporary hit points for 6 hours!

Mmmm. All that *and* her stomach was thanking her.

Millie smiled even more widely, if that was possible. "I'm sorry t'say goodbye t'my sister, but she decided t'stay and work Pa's piggery." A cloud passed over the young woman's sunny countenance, but then she shook it off. "I'll be glad t'get t'the temple an' marry my Struthio all proper. Then no one c'n separate us again, eh? Ye'll all come t'the weddin', won't ye?"

Rouge nodded vigorously, even as she started munching on her second pancake. Sadly, no further buffs were forthcoming, but it was just as delicious as the first. "We'll be there, for sure! What will you do after that, though?"

Millie and Struthio exchanged suddenly nervous glances. Millie shifted in her seat, and when she spoke again, it was clear that she was trying to sound more like the caravanners. "Ah, I was hopin' - *hoping* t'speak to ye about that. We've been talkin' to the caravanners, y'know, and they said that sometimes Travelers will 'in-vest' in someone. They made a deal wi' a big Traveler guild, and give the guild some o' their gold, in return for th' guild findin' unusual things to sell, and lettin' all the bandits know the guild'll come after 'em if they attack the caravan. So, Struthio an' I were wondering…"

Rouge suddenly, *deeply* felt the emptiness of her coin purse. She had picked up some really nice loot from the Demonic Swineherd and his friends, though, among other mobs they'd killed during their travels, and neither she nor Motte had been able to sell anything since they arrived on Aspen's farm. Plus, who knew what goodies could be at Aspen's old house? So, when the inevitable quest popped up, her response was instant.

Quest: "Thyme is Money" available.

Struthio and Millie want to open their own restaurant. They need an investor willing to take a chance on them. Find a way to fund their new business. Optional: *Provide them with unusual ingredients.* Optional: *Convince someone famous to eat at their restaurant.*

Success: Depends on the amount of investment and optional achievements.

Failure: -10 Reputation with Millie. -20 Reputation with Struthio. No more pastries.

Accept: Yes/No?

"Absolutely!" Her eye flickered, and her pod instantly picked up her intention, officially accepting the quest. "Your food is amazing, Millie! I've eaten at a lot of," *little, cheap,* "places in Bright, and your food beats it all! Plus, I have some good stuff to help you get started." *Sorry, Aspen. I'm sure you'll let me use your veggies for this, though.* She looked over at the farmer, and saw that he had tilted his hat back so he could watch her, and amusement and approval was definitely glinting in his pale topaz eyes.

"So, uh, yeah, just let me sell some stuff, and talk to Motte, and we'll get you guys going! No worries!" Her voice cracked just a little at the end, and she saw Aspen's mouth quirk as he tugged the tattered brim of his hat down to conceal what she was pretty sure was a snicker. She suppressed an urge to stick her tongue out at him.

Millie and Struthio were watching her with matching gazes of joy and trust, and she gave them a thumbs up and her biggest grin. Yep, she reaaaaaally hoped she could get a good price for her items, or she'd be doing some, ah, class-related 'jobs' tonight.

The caravan drew to a stop as Restur's wagon reached the gate to Bright. The old man was using his super confident, 'I'm your buddy' grin, and shook hands with the guard with the shiniest medallion on his armor. She couldn't see what exchanged hands from this distance, but after a cursory glance over the inventory Restur kept to show to officials, the man waved them through, even as he smoothly passed his right hand over the pouch dangling at his waist.

She carefully dropped back as the caravan moved forward. Codswallop was still a unique mount, as far as she knew, and tended to attract far more attention than they needed. Now that she was back on her home turf, she knew of a slightly less public way in and out of the city, and she could use her Thief Guild reputation to buy her way through.

Winding her way through the hordes advancing close behind, she waved a cheery hello to a few random friendly-looking Players who were heading out of the city, making it seem like she was going away from, instead of into Bright. She asked a few questions about the upcoming Triathlon Event, wished them good questing, and waved cheerfully as she veered off into a particularly dense patch of shadow. As soon as they looked away from her, she dropped into [Stealth], and an instant later, she was heading for her goal.

It only took a few minutes for Rouge to reach the Thief's Guild entrance. She'd completed the Thief quest to allow her to use it just after taking Thief as her beginner class. It was part of the class tutorial, and had involved sneaking four somewhat demented chickens out of the city for an NPC who was trying to raise his own special breed of gold egg laying poultry. Why the chickens were considered contraband, and whether the experiment worked, no one could tell her, but it had certainly made for a very unusual quest, even for her.

When she arrived at an unmarked spot not far out of sight of the regular gate, she pulled out her Mambele and tossed it casually. Twice in her left, over to the right, back to the left, and then twirled it by the handle three times before returning it to her inventory. Completing the sequence successfully nearly made her grin, since the last time she'd tried this, she'd nearly cut off two of her fingers and the other thieves had laughed at her for a week. Yay for level 20 [Knife Wielding] and unlocking [Dual Wielding]!

As the soft cackle of a hen sounded from above, she nearly smacked herself. She'd totally forgotten that she needed to select a knife specialization! She clucked back quietly as she pulled up her interface, digging through old notifications until she found the right one.

You may now select a Knife Specialization. Your choices will be based on the weapons you used most often while leveling [Knife Wielding]. Available Knife Specializations: Poignard, Rondel, Anelace, Machete, Push, Exotic. You may not change this selection once it is made. Continue Y/N?

Rouge blinked away the options, realizing that she didn't know what most of those were, much less which category her Mambele fell into. Research needed.

Next, she turned off non-urgent notices in general until she was in Bright, since she didn't want any distractions while she was in the Thieves' Guild. The guild area, while it was technically in Bright, was, like many other privately owned properties, set to allow all aggressive actions, including everything from [Stealing] to everybody's favorite [Backstab]. It was, after all, the home of Brigands and Cutpurses.

That done, she gently touched her heels to Codswallop's fluffy sides. He turned his head to roll a dubious eye back at her, but started walking directly toward the towering stone wall. Slowly. In case she changed her mind about guiding them into immovable objects.

She laughed and leaned forward so she could whisper in his ear. "Don't worry, Wally. Trust me."

The ostrich heaved a sigh, but turned back to the wall. As his beak touched the seemingly solid surface, the wall flickered, and then the two of them were pulled *through* the wall. Her stomach heaved, and she groaned. That was *never* fun.

She glanced around. As expected, she was inside a holding cell in the Thieves' Guild. She would stay here until she could disarm the traps and locks holding her, or another member of the Guild vouched for her. Either way, she would have proven that she belonged.

An extremely large, scarred, hairless head the color of a fresh bruise appeared at the door of the cell. A broad grin split the hideous face, revealing yellowed and broken tusks interspersed with sharp teeth covered in golden caps.

"Rouge!" The guttural voice was difficult to understand thanks to the overabundance of dentition, and a thick string of slime fell to the ground.

She grinned and jumped down from Codswallop, flipping nimbly backwards to land solidly on her feet. "Gunthrax! What are you doing here?"

The orc snorted, his broad nose flaring to reveal a thicket of glistening bristles inside. "Almost got caught raiding the Army Funds. There's a bounty out for me. I'm lying low for a while, so they assigned me back here." Solid black, piggy eyes rolled, and he slurped the string of drool back up. "Been boring. Glad you're back." His sharp eyes took in the shape of her mount, and more strands of drool began dribbling from his mouth. "And you brought lunch."

Rouge screeched to a halt, stepping between Codswallop and the orc. She spread her arms wide. "No! Uh, no, this is my mount now. If you eat him, I'll have to find another one, and they're…" she hesitated. 'Rare' was bad. Rare things equaled expensive things, and you never admitted you had anything good to a thief. "Uh, I'd have to go back to North Goose to get another one, and it'd be a pain."

Gunthrax sighed in disappointment. "If you say so."

Rouge nodded, stepping up to the door. "C'mon and let me out, Thraxie! I'm on a quest with Motte, and he's waiting for me."

The orc shrugged. "Can't. New rule. Gotta get out on your own."

"What?" she yelped. "What happened to the vouching system?"

He growled. "Travelers. Not you, obviously, but some'a the others. They were using this as a regular entrance. Letting in anybody. Vouching for their friends. Almost got us found out by the guards more'n once. Now you have to prove you have the skills."

"But, Thraxie, *you* know me!" But Rouge already had out her lockpicks and was headed for the door, carefully sidestepping a pitfall in the floor and a dart trap in the wall. Her ostrich started to follow, and she waved him back. "Stay, Wally. Once the door's open, all the traps will be disarmed."

The orc shrugged. "Rules are rules, Rouge."

She slipped her picks into the second lock from the bottom, leaning to the right as acid sprayed out where an amateur would have put their eye to look into the device. "This is why we can't have nice things," she muttered, hearing a click before moving to the third lock from the top. "This is the Thieves' Guild. No rules for us!" The lock popped, and she continued in a pattern going from easiest to hardest, until the final latch clicked over.

You have gained one level of [Lockpicking]. It is now level 3.

"Well, that's something at least," she murmured, and turned back to Codswallop as she swung the door open. "C'mon, Wally, let's go!"

It took a few more minutes to convince Gunthrax that she didn't have time for lunch, and that Codswallop was not now, nor would he ever be, on the menu. By the time she did, leaving the obviously bored orc standing at his post by the cell, which was once again closed and locked, it really was almost lunch time, and she felt her hollow stomach growl as she stepped through the second magical portal which dropped her into an abandoned and overgrown courtyard behind a particularly skeezy inn near the slums.

The moment her feet touched the bluish stones of Bright's rather well-worn road, her vision was flooded with notifications as the system completed her command to suppress them until she was in Bright proper.

Quest: "Run (Through the) Forest, Run!" completed.
Restur's Caravan reached Bright in time to set up a booth for the Spring Triathlon Event.
Success: +5 Reputation with all members of Restur's Caravan, 40% 'employee discount' at the booth on the day of the event.

SECRET Quest: "Come in From the Cold" complete.
You have successfully assisted Gina in bringing Duke Penbrooke, the Lord of the North, back to Bright.
Reward: +5 levels. 10000 Gold. +50 reputation points with Gina's faithful. +20 reputation points with Gina Herself.

You are now level 45.
You are now level 46.
You are now level 47.
You are now level 48.
You are now level 49.

10000 Gold has been added to your account.

SECRET Quest: "Mysterious Malefactors" begun
This quest may not be refused. (This is a SECRET quest. If you tell anyone about it before it is complete, you will automatically fail it.) Duke Penbrooke has returned to Bright. Dark forces are rising in the area, and Gina's faithful are being persecuted. Help the Duke find out who is behind the attacks, and save as many of Gina's worshippers as possible.

Success: 10 levels. 25000 Gold. +30 reputation points with Gina's faithful. +20 reputation points with Gina Herself.

Failure: Variable, but includes the death of Duke Penbrooke. This is a chain quest.

For completing the first part of Gina's SECRET Quest, you have opened the Fowl Trickster Unique sub-class. You may select one Avian Companion from the list of birds who assisted you during the quest. (WARNING: Only one option found. If this sub-class is accepted, Avian Companion will automatically be set to 'Ostrich'.)

Each time you earn five levels in any Illusion or Stealth based Spell/Skill, gain +1 bonus level to the Spell/Skill

Your Avian Companion gains one Unique Skill to be awarded by your Deity

+10% chance that your chosen Deity will hear your prayers

If you would like to accept this sub-class, please pray at any shrine to your chosen Deity.

Rouge stopped in her tracks, staring open-mouthed at the final notice. She expected the others, and even had a pretty good guess about the next quest in her Secret quest chain, though the 'save Gina's worshippers' business was definitely unexpected. But that sub-class. Yes! Yes! *Yes!* She pumped her fist and danced in place, barely suppressing a whoop of triumph. All the waiting, all the rejected sub-classes, all the delayed Class experience. All of it was totally worth it for this! A *Unique* Class!

Quickly, she looked around, orienting herself. The exit from the Thieves' Guild deposited you at a somewhat random location. There were about twenty remarkably similar little abandoned courtyards she could have arrived in, thus hopefully preventing anyone from ambushing her as she left, and this one…

Her eyes locked on a tall windmill protruding above the roofline. That was definitely the Miller's Guild, so that meant... She spun in a circle, putting the windmill behind her. The main Temple was just a half mile or so down the road to her south. That was where she was supposed to meet her party, and, handily, also where she needed to go to accept the *kick-butt* sub-class she'd just been offered.

Also, if she'd been inside the Guild as long as she thought she had... ::Hello? Anybody? Aspen? Silus? This is-::

She was cut off by an excited squeak. *::Rouge!* Where are you? We're outside the temple, and they're not letting anyone in without an appointment, and this whole thing is really, really strange, because the Temple is supposed to be open for everyone all the time, and I wanted to thank Gina!::

Rouge could picture Aspen leaning his jaw gently against Silus, breaking into the flow of words. The farmer's voice sounded concerned. ::The Temple is locked. Thankfully, they are taking appointments for weddings, so we have an innocent reason to be here. Millie and Struthio are making the arrangements now, but they're charging *five gold* for them to get married!:: The outrage in his voice was obvious.

::Um, is that bad? What did it cost before?::

::Nothing! They encouraged a donation, of course, but anyone could walk in and be married the same day, for free if they had no money. Five gold is three months income for someone with a good job, and for those in the slums... Likely not one couple has been able to wed since this price was put in place. Without marriage, no children will spawn, so this fee is a terrible blow to some communities. They're also charging for blessings, funeral rites, and the rate for Cleansings has more than doubled.:: The farmer's voice was frustrated and angry.

Rouge had a feeling she was still missing some of the ramifications of what he was saying, but the thing where an unmarried NPC couldn't have kids was really sad. ::Did Millie and Struthio have enough? I know Cora gave them some, but I didn't think it was that much.::

::Aspen slipped Restur a ruby, and the old guy 'gave' them the fee. You should have seen how big Struthio's eyes got! Anyway, they had the money.:: Silus interjected, and Rouge smiled. She should have known.

::Okay. Well, I'm about a half mile away, but I'm not sure what to do with Wally. If anybody sees him, they're definitely going to connect me with you, but there aren't any stables nearby. There's no guarantee the stables wouldn't spill the beans anyway, after what happened in Vargo.:: She examined her mental map again, and scowled as she realized that there was no way to avoid crossing at least one main street.

::Too bad he can't fly,:: Silus squeaked. ::Nobody ever looks up.::

On cue, Rouge looked up, examining the roofs of the buildings around her. This area mostly held stores that perpetually teetered on the edge of ruin, and industrial buildings, so they were all about two stories high with simple, flat roofs. Way better than the pointy roofs in Vargo. She grinned. ::Silus, you're a genius.::

🐦 🐦 🐦

Getting *up* on the roof was the hard part. There wasn't really anything to jump from, and they couldn't exactly get a running start in the small courtyard, so they tried jumping straight up from the ground a few times. This was surprisingly successful, but they kept falling *just* short of the twenty feet or so that they needed. Rouge could, of course, climb up on Codswallop's back and jump while he was in the air, and easily reach the roof. But the point was to get the *ostrich* on the roof, not her.

Then she realized that she was looking at it exactly backwards, and chortled to herself. She explained her plan to Codswallop, who looked appropriately dubious, but nodded his head, and then she turned on her camera. This wasn't something she used often, because, hello, thief is sneaky, but she knew she'd want to save this for posterity. It was either going to be amazing, or hilarious. Possibly both.

She walked to a point about five feet in front of the wall, and clasped her hands together. "Gina, if you feel like giving us a little boost, that would be great," she muttered, and then nodded to Codswallop, who had trotted to the other end of the courtyard. The bird fluffed his feathers, cocked his head as if to ask if she *really* wanted to do this, and then, at her encouraging nod, raced toward her at his top speed.

Which, as she'd noticed before, was really fast.

The bird's very large, two-toed, scimitar-clawed foot fell directly in her clasped hands, and as she heaved, he pushed off. Even with her inhuman strength, she could feel the strain as she chucked the four-hundred-pound bird straight up. With a strangled squawk, he flapped his stubby wings madly, and then one foot came down on the wooden roof. The second one joined the first a moment later, and then Codswallop was on the roof, long neck twisting as he looked himself over as if to ensure that all of his parts had made the trip.

Rouge pumped her fist, though she swallowed the whoop that ached to emerge from her throat. Now *she* just had to get up there. Not nearly such a big deal. The stone and wood construction materials of the simple building made it easy to climb, especially for a thief with [Climb] and [Acrobatics] both at level 19. A minute later, she pulled herself up over the edge of the roof. Happily, she petted her bird, and he cheerfully accepted her well-deserved admiration.

She looked around. There wasn't anything too surprising in sight. Nothing obviously dangerous, for sure, or Codswallop would have warned her. There were some bird's nests of unusual size, and a few visibly damaged shingles that she was sure wouldn't take Codswallop's weight. There were no other living things in sight except a few birds whose size matched their nests.

She petted Codswallop's neck. "Okay, Wally, here's the deal." She squinted in the bright sunlight, glaring up off the flat roofs surrounding her. "I'm going to head to the temple. You should be safe here if you just hunker down until I get back. If anything happens, do your bugle thing, and I'll come running." She cupped his big beak in her hands and looked into his beautiful brown eyes. His long lashes fluttered.

She pulled two Animal Rations and two Water Rations from her inventory and set them in front of him. "I'll be back as soon as I can. I won't forget you!"

The ostrich tilted his head, looking suspicious, and if he could have spoken, she thought he would have said 'I heard about Blackie'.

"Look, Blackie pooped on me. I mean, I probably deserved it, but still... Then there was the quest, and I was all excited, and anyway, that was *so* long ago. Like, *months*. I was just a kid then."

Codswallop blinked at her. She leaned forward and rested her forehead on his. "Between you and me," she whispered, "you're my favorite. Just hang in there for a little while, okay?"

Codswallop heaved a sigh, then sank down to sit on the roof, flattening out as much as he could so he wouldn't be visible from below. He started pecking disconsolately at the food. Rouge patted his shoulder reassuringly, and then took off. For a small, light-weight thief, running a half mile over flat roofs should be easy as pie. Though, honestly, she'd never actually understood that saying. Had the people who said it ever actually *tried* making pie?

When Rouge reached a building not far from the temple, she was limping. She'd put her foot through the roof of a (thankfully unoccupied) storage room, and had torn a long wound in her leg when she yanked it out. She'd sat there for far too long as it recovered enough that she could walk, but she had a *Twisted Ankle* debuff that said it was going to last for another thirty minutes.

She stared down over the edge of the roof at the quiet back alley below. She was lying on her belly so she wouldn't be starkly visible, but she would still be glad when the shadows arrived and she could use [Stealth].

Normally, she'd just grab the edge of the roof, flip over it, and drop to the ground. Two stories weren't really *that* far, and she was pretty sure she'd only lose a few hit points. Unfortunately, with the debuff, she was likely to get a *Broken Ankle* out of it, and that would definitely complicate things.

::Aspen, Silus?:: she sent silently.

::Rouge? Are you here?:: Aspen asked.

::Um, almost. I'm on the roof of the building west of the temple. No big deal, but I twisted my ankle on the way over, and it's going to be like, half an hour before I can get down safely.::

::I'll go!:: Silus squeaked.

::Oh, no you don't,:: Aspen returned just as quickly. ::This square is crowded, and it's broad daylight. Someone would see you. Hold on, Rouge, we're coming.::

It took about five minutes, which Rouge spent watching the debuff tick down, but then Aspen called quietly from below. "Rouge?"

::I'm here,:: she answered, and dropped a used glowstone she had in her inventory waiting to be recharged.

::Ow,:: the farmer said, half serious, half ironic.

She winced. ::Sorry. Motte says I should always throw things when I'm not looking, because I hit somebody every time.::

He chuckled. ::It's okay. I'm right under where the rock fell. Go ahead and drop down.::

Rouge gulped. ::Are you *sure* that's a good idea? I mean, I'm heavier than a rock, and it's a long way…::

::Rouge,:: Aspen said firmly, and she grabbed the edge of the roof.

A moment later, she landed solidly in Aspen's arms. The farmer didn't even need to bend his knees to absorb the force of her impact, and she revised her mental estimate of his Strength sharply upward. He laid his hand on her ankle, and he murmured a quiet prayer. A warm, fuzzy feeling sank into her, and the debuff blinked out. Aspen set her down gently.

"Niiiiice," she said, testing her weight on the ankle. "I see why Motte likes healers so much. That's handy."

The tall man tugged at the brim of his hat. "Glad I could help," he said, and she could see the half-grin he was unsuccessfully trying to hide under the hat.

"Come on! I told Wally I'd be back soon. I need to get into the temple and pray." She grinned gleefully. "I finally got a job offer I like."

He paused, looking at her, one eyebrow raised. They'd spent a lot of time talking during the long winter days, and Aspen knew how long she'd been waiting for this, and what a big deal it was. "Should I ask?"

She shrugged cheekily. "I'll tell you when it's a done deal. Now come on!"

It only took a few minutes to wind their way back to the square, since now they knew exactly where they were going. During that time, Silus made her way down Aspen's sleeve, hopped over to Rouge, and nestled in the thief's curls. Rouge was snuggling her little friend when they entered the large square, but she stopped dead in her tracks at what she saw.

Aspen had been right. The crowd was ridiculous. The area in front of the temple was always filled with players and NPCs alike, since so many things in the game required (or at least benefited from) a quick trip to see your Deity. Cursed? Head to the Temple. Unhealable debuff? Temple. Job change? Yep, temple. Player returning from death? This was probably the place. Even if you were just headed out on a difficult quest, you'd usually pray, since you could get a buff or (if your reputation with your church was high enough) even a Boon, which lasted much longer.

This stagnant pool of people was all wrong, though. The temple should be open, so everyone could hurry right on in, then split off to the area dedicated to their Deity. So, the crowd should be *moving*, filled with energy and purpose. Instead, people stood in lines, their faces showing emotions ranging from rebellion and anger to sadness and resignation. Tense shoulders pressed close to slumped ones, and only one group seemed to be moving as normal.

The Players.

Players, most of them oblivious as they shoved through the crowd, marched right up the stairs and through the broad doors. The guards and priests, who were holding long scrolls from which they would occasionally call a name, ignored these intrusions, but if an NPC attempted to follow, they were pushed back, and the priests took their name.

A large stone box stood next to the priests, and each time they added a new name to their list, the person put money into the box.

Rouge gaped. "They're not charging the Travelers? But they're the ones who can afford it! What's going on?"

Aspen shook his head, returning to party chat so they wouldn't be overheard. ::I've been standing here just listening, and from what I gather, King Chester has appointed one of the Travelers Baron of Bright. No one knows who he is, but only the King and Geral outrank him, and they're not worried about what happens to the lower classes. He's implemented all kinds of taxes and fees, to be used to 'restore Bright to its former glory', but nobility and Travelers are exempt. Apparently, he's also a worshiper of one of the lesser-known Gods, and has made his God the official Deity of Bright. All the others have been relegated to small shrines inside the temple.::

She shook her head. ::How many Reputation quests did that guy have to grind to get that deal? This is crazy! Why haven't I heard anything about this?::

The farmer shrugged his shoulders expressively. ::It seems that if it doesn't directly affect them, the Travelers don't take much notice of such things. They continue their activities as usual, and they seem to be primarily occupied with preparing for the upcoming Triathlon. They seem to be dismissing the actions of what they call 'En Pee Cees' as part of the event. They don't speak aloud much, but the few I've overheard were complaining about the crowd and the distance they had to go to reach their deity's shrine. One even suggested simply changing deities so they wouldn't have to walk as far, since they are 'all the same'.::

Rouge bit her lip, embarrassed for her fellow Players. ::Yeah, I can see that. I'm sure some of them have noticed, though. Is Fluff or Tess around? Maybe they would know.::

Aspen shook his head. ::Flu-flu was still absent, and Tessle left as soon as we entered Bright. She felt that we should be safe so long as we don't draw attention to ourselves. Their Zombies are resting in your Dead Tent, and Tessle said to remind you that if you leave them a message there, they will meet you when they return.::

The thief glanced back and forth from Aspen to the line of Players entering the building, pulling at a curl as she considered her options. Silus grabbed her fingers with her little wing-thumbs. ::Let's go!:: the bat said, ::I'm the scout, and we need to see what's going on!::

Aspen opened his mouth as if he would argue, but just huffed a deep breath. ::This area is still a Non-Combat Zone, but who knows what's going on in there. Be careful.::

Rouge grinned and tipped an imaginary hat at him. ::Whatever you say.:: Then she turned and headed for the door. ::Onward!::

::Onward!:: echoed Silus' little voice, and Rouge giggled.

Getting inside the temple was easy enough. Rouge simply sidled around until she could naturally join the flow of Players entering the building. Several were looking at each other and smiling or laughing, though they were obviously speaking in Party or Guild Chat. A few spoke out loud, usually to comment on the changes to the temple and ask if anyone knew if they were related to the Triathlon, or would persist after the event.

One particularly talkative guy, wearing newbie armor with his beginner knife still strapped to his side - so either he hadn't unlocked his inventory yet, or he was still excited to be carrying what seemed like a 'real' weapon - was walking a few meters in front of Rouge.

He paused just inside the vast double doors, staring up and around at the carved motifs of the Gods and their various origin stories that graced the walls and ceilings. A few people glared at him as they had to swerve sharply to avoid him, and others, probably using the much less expensive (but also less responsive) desktop headset and joystick, actually ran into him and took a few steps before correcting themselves. One tall girl muttered something nasty about noobs before continuing on.

Fortunately, the boy was too engrossed in his own experience to pay any attention to her, and after a moment he looked around with a grin, ready to share his amazement with the world. As his eyes crossed over her, a pop-up appeared in her vision.

A Player near you is using their in-game camera to stream and/or record their gameplay. Would you like your avatar to be included in their video? If yes, your avatar and character name may be visible to an unknown number of viewers. If no, *Veritas Online* will change your image and name to a neutral one so that you may remain anonymous. No – I would like my avatar and character name to remain anonymous Yes – I would like my avatar and character name to remain visible (You may adjust your default reply in your settings. Default will be reset to 'Ask Every Time' after 30 days.)

She sighed and opened her settings with a thought. Part of her agreement with her dad when he got her a pod was that she would maintain this setting on Anonymous. Since avatars were based on a user's actual appearance, many people chose Anonymous so that people couldn't recognize them in real life if they were in a video that went viral. Others sought out the streamers, hoping that viewers would be interested in them and seek them out on the various social media platforms.

Because of the separation between what the Player saw and what the *VO* system recorded; the game could replace Players in videos if they wanted to remain anonymous. *Veritas* used the same hundred or so generic avatars and character names over and over. In large crowds, streams would sometimes show a few repeats of the same character, but in general, it was pretty seamless. Most people didn't seem to mind the public exposure, and since there were so many streamers, anyone who stayed in the background remained almost as unnoticed as if they used the Anonymous setting.

Rouge hadn't had to think about it since leaving Bright, but it only took a moment to reconfirm her desire to remain unidentifiable. Why anyone in a thief-type class would want to be recognized was a mystery to her, anyway. She frowned a little as she saw the tiny gear beneath the setting. The gear indicated that there were Advanced Settings available, and she was sure it hadn't been there last time she checked.

She popped it open, and saw that it contained three additional settings. The first one was a slider indicating how long she wanted her response to apply. It went from a minimum of 15 minutes, all the way up to the thirty-day max. The second one was a box in which she could tag Players she wanted to exempt from whatever her choice was. So, she could let Jace 'see' her, while remaining unknown to everyone else, or block someone she didn't like while allowing everyone else to view her usual avatar. Interesting, but not something she would do without checking with Motte.

The last setting, though, was thoroughly unexpected.

You are involved in a Beta Test for Veritas Online. As a result, certain Players have been automatically Whitelisted to allow recording. If you have questions or would like to remove yourself from the Beta, please contact Veritas Corporation, LLC © directly, or toggle this option for in-game assistance.

For a long moment, she stared at the setting, and then she felt a soft bump against her neck. ::Rouge? Why aren't you moving?::

Shaking her head, the thief made a mental note to have a little Talk with Motte about this, and make sure he knew about it. Then another little Talk to find out why *she* hadn't known about it. She had a feeling there was more to it than just permission for Dr. Joe and crew to record her while she was in the pod.

For now, though, she wasn't going to worry about it, so she smiled and tilted her head slightly, snuggling the little bat nestled in her curls. ::Sorry, I got distracted. Traveler stuff. Let's head on in.::

Silus' voice was awed as the small creature took in their surroundings. ::Is it always like this?::

Rouge evaluated the huge, vaulted chamber. The ornate double doors were behind them, and the vaulted ceiling was a good thirty feet above their heads. Paintings, carvings, and statuary covered the walls, and arched hallways led away from the room. Each arch was covered in images from the mythology of the deity whose temple it led to, and if you focused, you could also see the name of the god hovering overhead.

Again, the temple was almost like it was the last time she'd seen it, but not *quite*. The arches to her left and right seemed wrong somehow. They were a little too small, and a little too crammed together. She could see some of the taller races ducking down to enter the passages, and she was sure that hadn't been necessary before.

The biggest difference, however, was the arch directly across from the entrance. It *was* tall. Easily half again the height of the others; no one who entered there had to so much as bend their neck. She could also see the temple beyond easily, unlike the other passages, which faded away as their hallways wound deeper into the building. The images surrounding this arch were brightly colored, though red was the predominant shade, since many of the scenes showed battles. Every race in *Veritas Online* was represented, though no one in particular seemed to be singled out as either victor or victim.

Rouge stared at the space above the arch, concentrating on a large symbol that swirled in a complex and sinuous knot. After a moment, a name appeared, hovering in the air in front of the symbol.

Apofis.

She frowned, searching her memory for any mention of this god. She'd read the lore pretty thoroughly before choosing her own deity, and had read more while in her Study Room on those occasions when she needed to practice studying in game so that Dr. Joe and Sara could test her information retention when she logged out.

Finally, she shook her head. A bell was dimly ringing in the back of her mind, telling her that she'd heard the name before *somewhere*, but she couldn't remember exactly where. Maybe in the real world? She knew that Veritas Corp., in an effort to make the game world more believable and immersive, had based most of the creatures and mythology on reality.

::Silus? Aspen? Have you heard of a god named Apofis?::

::I haven't,:: came Silus' quick reply, ::Is that the god with the big arch?::

Rouge nodded, walking closer to the high arch so she could see the art surrounding it in more detail. ::This one is way bigger than the others. They used to all be the same size, though they'd move around a little, depending on which god had the most followers. The popular ones like Gina tend to stay in the middle, with less popular ones moving around the outside.::

She grimaced a little as she took in the images carved into the wall. This was definitely a war god of some kind, because every creature pictured was engaged in battle of some kind. Monsters attacked members of sapient species, and sapient species attacked each other. Everyone had a weapon or two, and most were wounded as well. Red streams of enameled blood flowed toward the arch, where the streams merged to become a sort of gory river around the opening. It was pretty from a distance, but close up, it was pretty horrifying.

She was so absorbed in examining a scene showing what looked like a huge humanoid with eight arms, yellow skin, and three emerald eyes, that she didn't realize Aspen hadn't replied until Silus squeaked, ::Aspen?::

Rouge paused and flicked open her notifications. She had some that she kept constantly suppressed, but they would be there in her log if... Yep, there it was.

You have entered a Silence Zone: *Great Temple of Bright.*

::Darn it, when did that happen?:: Silence Zones were areas where the game locked down communication with anyone outside the area. It was usually done so that no one could give Players inside hints to a puzzle or riddle. Communication inside *VO* was already pretty limited, between the short distance allowed by party chat and the fact that Players could only exchange messages near a Guild Circle. The temple had certainly never been a Silence Zone before, since people chatted with their Party all the time as they ran in to get a buff or class change.

::What?:: Silus asked, little voice worried.

Rouge had to struggle to resist reaching up to give the bat a reassuring scrootch. ::We can't talk to Aspen right now. I'm sure he's fine, but the temple walls are blocking party chat. We can talk to each other, since we're both inside, but not anyone outside.::

The bat was silent for a moment, leaning into Rouge's neck so that the girl could feel the small body trembling. ::That's stupid. Why would the Gods make it so we can't talk to our friends?::

Rouge looked around, taking in all the small arches around her. She focused on the symbol of a sheaf of wheat over an arch nearby, but nothing happened. Squinting, she stared harder, trying every command she could to get the name of the God whose temple lay beyond that arch to pop up. As she did, she felt someone bump into her.

Blinking, she looked around. It was the newbie she'd been behind as she entered. He looked a little flustered, but put on an air of superiority as he smiled at her. "Haven't been here since before the change, huh? Didn't you read the hint posts on the forums? They keep changing the clues, so if you don't read up on it every time, it can take forever to find your deity. I spent an hour on the forums before I logged in."

She tried for a single eyebrow arch, but felt both rise instead. So. Frustrating. Was that a skill they only gave you after you had kids? "What clues? What's with the big ol' temple to Apofis?"

His smile broadened condescendingly. "They changed it with the patch a week ago. Apofis is the Big Guy now, and if you want to get to one of the other temples, you have to use the clues in the pictures to get there. *I* want Minetra, since I'm going to be a crafter, so I read up on all her hints." He looked around, and his face went a little uncertain as he pointed to a nearby arch. "I'm pretty sure that one leads to her temple. Probably."

Rouge started tugging at a curl. "Seriously? That's ridiculous! What if you don't have time for all that?"

The boy shrugged and cocked his head toward the steady stream of Players entering Apofis' temple. "Then you switch. Apofis has some pretty good buffs, especially if you're a fighter or assassin class. Where have you been that you don't know this? It's all over the forums."

"I had better things to do, all right?" she growled, glaring around at the innumerable openings.

The boy backed up a step, raising his hands defensively. "Jeez. I'm just trying to help. Good luck, noob." He waved a dismissive hand at her and walked away, vanishing down his chosen hallway.

::What do we do now? Shouldn't we go tell Aspen what's going on?:: Silus asked quietly.

Rouge shook her head. ::Aspen knows we're checking things out, and one of the others should be back and able to join him soon. I'm not gonna switch to some jerk-face God who thinks blood is pretty, and I'm not going to run away, either. We're just going to have to use our brains. If that guy can figure out which way to go, we sure can.::

She turned slowly, examining the ridiculous number of smaller arches. ::Eventually.::

Fortunately, the first 'riddle' was easy. All they had to do was examine the symbols and images around the arch, and pick the one that seemed most likely to apply to Gina. About halfway around, there was a whole relief of families with babies, and even a few pregnant women, which, considering how recently pregnancy was added to the game, was a little surprising.

::Is that Sarave?:: Silus asked from her perch on Rouge's shoulder. The bat's bright golden eyes were fixed on a small carved figure about four feet from the ground, and Rouge leaned forward to peer at it. Sure enough, the little female had pointed ears and the large eyes and narrow face that were so characteristic of the goblin race. Her belly was huge, and she looked like she would struggle to walk with that enormous bulge. Beside her, a proud smile on his face, stood a short human male.

::Do you think that's Juniper's dad?:: Rouge's fingers gently brushed the stony smile. He looked so happy, with his hand resting on his small wife's shoulder. Then she leaned forward even further, eyes squinting as she nearly pressed her nose to the relief. ::That's Dr. Joe!::

::Who?:: the piping little voice was curious, and Rouge blinked as she stood back up.

::Um, just someone I know from my world. That carving looks a lot like him.:: *Bridget, what were you up to when you made Sarave's husband look like Dr. Joe? Wasn't he still engaged to your best friend then?* She shook her head. It was probably just because Sarave herself was based on Sara, Joe's assistant. After all, he was probably her closest male relationship at work, and as far as Rouge knew, Sara and Bridget weren't friends outside work, so Bridget wouldn't know any other men in her life. Or did Bridget see something Rouge hadn't?

She glanced down and met the inquisitive eyes of her fuzzy little friend. ::Romance is hard, Silus. Don't do it.::

Silus blinked, and Rouge could practically see the wall of questions incoming like a tidal wave. She quickly straightened and cleared her throat. ::Onward!:: she exclaimed mentally, pumping a fist.

::...Onward?:: The bat's tone was slightly questioning this time, but she didn't ask any more questions as Rouge passed under the archway.

The passage was stupidly long. Like, 'why would anyone walk this far to get to a temple' long. When Rouge had visited the temple before, the passages past the arches were more to give you the feeling that you were actually going through a real space, even though logically you knew that temples to a hundred gods wouldn't fit inside one building. Now, though, the featureless tunnel just...

went on. And on.

After about ten minutes, Rouge stopped.

"This is ridiculous." She looked around at the plain, smooth walls. There weren't even bricks or stones. It was just flat and a kind of neutral gray color that made her feel like she was sleep-walking.

Silus perked up, her golden eyes gleaming, and her big ears straight up, with the silver tufts looking like enthusiastic cotton balls. ::I should go scout!::

The thief looked back the way they'd come, and then forward to where the tunnel faded into shadow. "Okay. Be careful, though! Theoretically, Gina's followers shouldn't mess with an innocent creature, but Travelers can be jerks." She scooped the bat into her hands, and gently tossed her into the air. The little wings started flapping rapidly, and she darted forward down the passage.

::No problem! They won't even know I'm there!:: Silus' little voice was suddenly cheerful, and Rouge had to fight not to call her back. She was *not* going to go all over-protective like her dad!

Something smacked into the back of her head, and she spun, calling her Mambele to her hand.

::Ouch,:: Silus said, and Rouge looked down toward the direction the small voice seemed to come from. Silus was lying on the smooth floor, wings spread wide and eyes blinking rapidly. Rouge returned her weapon to her inventory and knelt beside her friend. Her hands stretched out, but she pulled them back before she could touch. If Silus had a Broken Bone or other injury, touching her could make it worse.

"Are you okay?" Rouge barely touched a fingertip to Silus's soft brown belly. The bat reached out with her wing thumbs and pulled herself up onto Rouge's hand.

::How did you get ahead of me?:: Silus squeaked painfully as she settled into her friend's palm. ::I'll be okay. Just lost a few hit points and I have a Dizzy debuff.::

Breathing a sigh of relief, Rouge snuggled the little bat close. "What happened? You flew off that way, but ran into me from behind!" She looked down the featureless hall and groaned. "Oh, cheese. It's another darned puzzle."

Silus shook her head, blinked once more, and looked around. ::How do we get out?::

Rouge set the bat back on her shoulder. "I don't know. I guess it depends on whether this is real or not. I mean, if it's real, maybe there's a secret door or something? If it's an illusion, we'd have to... break the illusion? I'm not a mage, though, so I don't know how to do that."

::I'm pretty good with illusions,:: Silus volunteered. ::My [Sonar] can see through them if they're not a higher level, and sometimes it can even dispel them.::

Rouge grinned. "Have I mentioned how awesome you are lately?"

The bat preened her ear tufts with her wing thumbs. ::Not *lately*.::

Silus' [Sonar] did the trick. The little bat opened her mouth and made a noise so high-pitched that it was at the very edge of Rouge's hearing, and a moment later the unmarked walls fell away to dust, revealing a very different passage.

The walls, ceiling, and floor were now covered in designs that swirled and twisted, reminding Rouge of nothing so much as stone vines. There were even little 'leaf' bulges occasionally, and her fingers trailed over the subtle peaks and valleys of the complex design.

"Wow," she murmured, "that's more like it. This is cool."

::Is this the temple? It doesn't look like a temple. There's not even a statue.:: Silus sounded dubious even as her huge gold eyes took in their surroundings.

Rouge laughed. "Nope. My guess is that this is another puzzle. Hopefully not a hard one, though. I've never really been good at puzzle games."

::So what do we do, then?::

"Well," the elf smoothed her fingers over another leaf, then brushed her hands down over the gray and black cloth of her thief gear. "I guess we gather clues? Do you see anything that looks different from the rest?"

The bat looked around. ::Should I try my [Sonar] again?::

Rouge shrugged. "Can't hurt, I guess."

Once again, Silus squeaked out the high-pitched sound, and the two stood for a moment. Nothing happened. The bat blinked. ::There's a… squishy spot up ahead?:: She sounded uncertain, and Rouge frowned.

"Squishy?" The girl looked ahead of them, but she couldn't see anything different in that direction. "Did it seem dangerous?"

::No… It reminded me of how a mushroom sounds. Or a pillow, back when pillows were soft.::

Rouge laughed a little. Aspen's pillows were pretty crunchy, since they were stuffed with dried grass instead of cotton or feathers. Sumi could weave a fairly effective pillowcase, but her webbing was so fine that anything you put in it poked through the weave. "Okay. Keep going, and tell me when we get close?" She began to walk down the path, watching the walls closely. The vines almost seemed to move when she did, but when she stopped, they were always still, and she *thought* it was just an optical illusion created by the complexity of the design.

Silus, meanwhile, used her [Sonar] over and over, aiming it in different directions each time. Fortunately, as a skill, it used stamina instead of mana, and the little bat could do it almost constantly, since her stamina regenerated quickly enough that it refilled nearly as quickly as she was using it.

After a very slow five or six yards, Silus said, ::There. On the right. A squishy spot.::

Rouge turned, feeling like she could almost see something move out of the corner of her eye. "Gah! That's getting creepy," she muttered. "I hope this is the door." Carefully, she reached out and touched the wall. Her hand touched something warm instead of the cool stone she was expecting, and then the vines nearby snapped in tight around her wrist. An instant later, she was being pulled forward, and she flailed, falling through the wall and into darkness.

She landed on her hands and knees on something that felt suspiciously planty. Moss maybe? Her fingers dug in, but the stuff resisted her efforts to pull out a piece so she could try to figure out what it was. ::Silus?:: she spoke silently, the darkness feeling oppressive and ominous.

::Rouge? I can feel you, but I can't see you. My [Sonar] isn't working either.:: The little bat sounded terrified, and Rouge reached up to touch her fuzzy friend reassuringly. As a bat, Silus was never truly blind. Even in the deepest darkness, her [Sonar] would let her 'see' with complete clarity. Having her eyes and [Sonar] fail her had to be truly frightening.

::I'm here. I'll use a glowstone.:: Rouge summoned one of the smooth little rocks from her inventory, and felt its reassuring weight land in her palm. She invoked it. Nothing happened. ::Must be an empty one?:: She tried to pull up her interface so she could dig through her Inventory list, but nothing happened. Suddenly she, too, felt a twinge of real fear. She should *always* be able to access her interface.

A silky singsong voice came from the darkness.

> *So beautiful and so cold,*
> *So young and yet so old,*
> *Alive but always dead.*
> *Your blood was how I fed,*
> *But now my time has fled.*
> *Who am I?*

A chill went down Rouge's spine at the sudden words, and she cupped her hand over Silus' fragile body, throwing herself to the side as if to avoid an invisible attack. The voice laughed, a cracked and mad sound. "That won't work, my little dear, but sadly, now, you need not fear. My time to slay has come and gone, and now I'm only here to play. Answers three, you may attempt, but after that, defeat accept."

Rouge shuddered, but answered steadily. "You're a vampire. Duh."

An insane giggle echoed around her, and she spun in place, desperately trying to figure out which direction the sound came from. "So close and yet so far, you are. One try down, but do not frown. You know my name, just say the same." The lilting voice was suddenly melancholy. "Pretty little girly toy. I wish I still could enjoy playing with you, until I put you in a stew."

::Silus?:: Rouge asked, a little frantic. ::Do you know who this crazy lady is?::

The bat was shivering beneath her fingers. ::I only heard about her. I don't remember her name. I think she's that vampire Queen who enslaved William. Aspen said she talked in bad poetry.::

Rouge suddenly remembered hearing the story of the crazy old vampire who had killed William centuries ago, and forced him to become a vampire. She'd abducted Sarave when the pregnant goblin, terrified and in pain, close to giving birth, had run away from Aspen.

Sarave had looked embarrassed when the story was told, but explained that while she liked Aspen, she hadn't known for sure what his reaction would be to discovering that her child was a half-breed. Then Rouge had appeared, and thrown off the delicate bridge of trust that had been growing between them, as well as adding yet another potential threat to the baby. At that moment, running away had seemed like the only way to guarantee her child's safety.

Of course, instead of reaching the small, protected cave that Sarave had prepared in the unlikely chance that she lived long enough to birth the baby, the vampire had taken her away. Aspen, Motte, and Sumi had managed to kill the vampire and save Sarave and Juniper, though the goblin had almost died before Aspen managed to save her with a desperate prayer to Gina.

Rouge had been grounded back in the real world at the time, thanks to Gina (well, *Bridget*, though they didn't know who she really was then) revealing that the girl had lied to her dad. When she was able to return, everyone was safe back at Aspen's little house, and they'd told her all about their adventures while Rouge snuggled the adorable half-goblin baby. Silus was right. Aspen had definitely said that vampire rhymed like this... Now *what* was her name?

The girl clenched her teeth, trying again to call up her interface. She was sure if she went back in her logs far enough, she'd find something there. Hadn't she gotten some experience for learning new Lore? Surely the name would be there…

No, wait! The name had reminded Rouge of something her dad had told her about a few years ago. He'd been teaching a class on Shakespeare and the Christian Bible, and one of the students kept comparing Lady Macbeth to a villainess in the Bible, but he kept using the wrong name… What was it? J-something… Jazmin? No, this crazy vamp had no relation to the kind-hearted assistant. If Bridget really was using real people to base the characters on for her quest chain, there was no way Jazmin would be a bad guy.

Ha! "Jezebel!" she exclaimed triumphantly.

The vampire cackled in the darkness, and Rouge felt her heart sink. "Your beating heart pounds in your throat. It spills your blood in constant bursts of hope, but careful! It's a slippery slope! Fail once more, and out the door. Your next return only time may earn. Denied this place, and goddess' grace, 'til the earth eats the sun and the fifth day has begun."

"What?" Rouge was shocked. "I have to wait five *days* before I can try this again? That's ridiculous! Also, your poetry sucks. My dad quotes Shakespeare for *fun*, and… and you have not so much brain as ear-wax!"

A sudden light nearly burned Rouge's retinas, and she blinked against burning blindness.

You have been Dazzled. This debuff will expire in 10 seconds.

She was reaching up to scrub at her eyes when she felt a cold form press up against her own. Something hard and sharp scraped against her throat, and she froze, unable to move as an atavistic sense of her own mortality seized her heart. She'd never felt anything like it before, and her eyes flashed wide, locked on the black space inches from her face where she sensed a vicious predator lurked.

You are no longer Dazzled.

A luminous orb floated in front of her eyes, and when her eyes focused, she saw an ethereally lovely, bone white face. The shape of cheek and jaw fit an ideal of beauty that Rouge had never expected to see in person. The woman's black brows arched in impeccable wings above upturned eyes with irises red as blood, or flawless rubies. Her sensuous lips were a matching shade of crimson, and long, sharp white fangs protruded to touch the lower lip in a deep and somehow perfect dimple of moist flesh.

The smooth column of the vampire queen's throat was unnaturally still, with no heartbeat or breath to disturb its cold flesh. The motionless mounds of her breasts plumped above the rich black velvet of her low-cut gown, and red satin peeped from beneath the velvet, emphasizing the pure whiteness of the porcelain skin. A black velvet-encased arm trailed languidly up over Rouge's narrow chest, and long, graceful fingers rested against the girl's caramel throat. One sharply pointed red nail rested precisely on the point where the thief's blood pounded through her carotid.

Her voice was a purr, as warm as her flesh was cold. "Think not, child of my enemy, that I am helpless in this space. My own God grants me power where I rest in His embrace. Two ways have I to set you free, alive or dead," she tilted her head, mad red eyes gleaming in their frames of lush black lashes, "to *some* degree."

Chapter Two

Aspen

The moment Rouge and Silus entered the Temple, Aspen regretted letting them go. He knew well enough that Rouge, at least, was capable of taking care of herself, and neither of them would be grateful if he tried to command them to stay. Nonetheless, he was only able to restrain himself for a few minutes before he called them. ::Rouge? Silus?::

There was no response. He forced himself to take a breath and relax his shoulders. Panicking and attempting to force his way into the Temple would not only fail, but also attract attention they couldn't afford. He was certain they were fine, since no one was running out of the Temple - or into it, given Travelers' propensity for racing toward trouble – yelling about a fight.

He spent the next several minutes alternating between calling the two girls and calming himself down when they didn't respond. He had nearly convinced himself it would be all right to go and at least add his name to the list, even if he had to pay for it with one of his dwindling cache of gems, when someone tapped him on the shoulder.

He spun around, hand going to his side automatically, even though he wasn't carrying a weapon, since he was playing the role of simple farmer at the moment. When his eyes met Motte's, he let his breath out in a huff of relief, but frowned.

::What are you doing here? You said you wouldn't be able to come back until evening. Is everything all right?::

Motte flushed, his cheeks darkening as he touched his short, curly hair guiltily. ::I got a headset so I could log on from work, too. I, ah, I'm supposed to be grading papers.:: He shrugged. ::It'll be fine. It's for an undergraduate class, and they're just supposed to translate a scene from King Lear to colloquial English. I can grade those in my sleep.::

The big man looked around. ::What's going on? Where's Rouge?::

Aspen glanced at the flow of Travelers into the Temple. ::Inside. I can't get her to respond, and I don't know what's happening. It's only been about fifteen minutes, but…:: He trailed off, knowing Motte would understand.

Rouge's father's face went serious. ::I was reading a little bit about this. It's actually why I came back early. Apparently, there's a new boss in town, and he's made some changes. I couldn't find anything giving me details about this new lord, other than that he's a Traveler, but the boards were blowing up over the changes. Rouge doesn't like 'spoilers', so she never checks until after she runs into something, so I figured she wouldn't know."

He shook his head. "Anyway, the Temple is one of the big ones. I've never even heard of this deity, Apofis, but apparently Bright now has an official religion. There are riddles and puzzles to get into any temple except that of Apofis. The first one is a Lore test. The second one requires the person to use a Skill or Spell they have, so it changes with each person or group. The third one is a riddle based on the ga… Uh, experiences of the person in your world, so that one can be unique, though we Players often do a lot of the same quests, so there seem to be a few pretty standard ones. They're calling them the Temple Trials.::

He turned and looked at the Temple, brown eyes worried. ::There are two big things that have changed as a result of this Trials business. The first is that anyone inside the Temple can't communicate with anyone outside. Supposedly, that's to keep them from cheating and getting help on the Trials. That's why you can't talk to her. The second one is that if you fail any of the Trials, you get kicked out of the Temple. Fail the first Trial, and you can't go back for a day. Fail the second, and you lose three days. Fail the third, and you're locked out for five days.::

Aspen hissed through his teeth. ::That would be after the Triathlon, and certainly after the wedding. Rouge told me she was going in to accept a sub-class she was offered. She looked pretty excited.::

A grin broke out on Motte's face. ::She finally got one she likes? That's great! Rouge can be stubborn,:: the eyes of the two men met in mutual amused recognition of Motte's understatement, ::and she's been waiting for a rare sub-class for a while now. Which one was it?::

Aspen chuckled and tugged at the brim of his hat. ::She wouldn't say. Just said it was a 'job offer I like'. I think she wants to surprise us.::

Motte rolled his eyes. ::That girl. Well, then there's no way she's coming back out until she gets that class. Not unless she fails one of the Trials. The first one is supposed to be easy, and the second one you can almost brute force your way through by just trying all your Skills and Spells if you can't figure out what you're supposed to do. The third one,:: he shook his head, ::Rouge has done a *lot* here, and a lot of it was unusual. The examples I read about didn't sound too hard, but some of the more esoteric ones were tricky. This system was only implemented four days ago, so the first people to fail the third Trial haven't been able to try again. Apparently the first one usually stays the same, but a few people said their second one changed.::

Sighing deeply, Aspen turned back to the Temple. ::What do they do if they can't figure it out?::

Motte also turned to face the massive building. ::Most of them are converting to Apofis. He's a fairly generic battle-type god, I guess, so his buffs are as good as any other, and better than most. Most Travelers go with whatever god is easiest, and you don't have to go through the Trials to reach his temple. Unless you're a crafter, a healer, or have an unusually high Reputation with your deity, it's not a big deal to just switch.::

Aspen smiled a little grimly. ::Rouge won't switch.::

Motte nodded agreement. ::No way.::

The two men watched the building for a while longer, and now that Aspen knew what to look for, he noticed that a few of the Travelers exiting the building looked very unhappy. It hadn't struck him before, because it wasn't that unusual for his people to enter the Temple and request a healing or a blessing and be turned down, either because they weren't worthy, or their God simply decided that whatever was going on in their lives was necessary.

As he understood it, though, Travelers were never denied. They always got the Cleanse, Heal, or Blessing they asked for, though they were charged money for some of the services which Natives weren't. Healing, whether of wounds or disease, was always expensive, but blessings and dispelling curses were up to the grace of the Gods.

Which reminded him.

::How long can you stay?:: he asked Motte.

The tall warrior grimaced. ::Honestly, not long. I wanted to tell you and Rouge about this change before anyone went in. I really should get back to work. Why?::

Aspen sighed. ::I have some things I need to do. I was hoping you could wait for Rouge while I went to do them.::

The other man shook his head. ::I wish I could, though I'm not thrilled at the idea of you wandering around alone. I know no one can attack you while you're on public bluestones, but if you go onto private property, all bets are off. Plus, we have to assume there's still a price on your head. If the guards identify you, you'll probably be arrested.::

Aspen ground his teeth. It still infuriated him that his face was on a Wanted poster. Even though Manuela had easily severed the ties between him and any items that could be used to track him, he knew he could still be recognized and captured. One of the things he needed to do was begin investigating who was after him, and *why.*

::I know,:: he admitted grudgingly. ::But now that I'm here, it's hard to just stand and wait. There's so much to *do*, and I just want to get it over and go home. All of this,:: he looked around at the buzzing crowd, everyone tense and hurried, ::isn't my life anymore. I don't *want* it to be. I just want to watch my crops grow, and spend time with my family.::

It was true, too. Seeing the madding crowd had simply driven home the fact that this wasn't *his* home any more. He had no interest in wearing fine clothes, having an entourage, or seeing fear on anyone's face when they looked at him. He'd spent far too long being feared. He wanted to be comfortable, and happy, and, yes, loved. Or at least liked.

Motte sighed and rubbed his hand over his head. As he did, his eyes went briefly flat, and his face blank. Then the moment passed, and he looked a bit embarrassed. ::Damn it. Sorry, I'm not used to the headset. I knocked it loose.::

Aspen looked at him, finally noticing that his friend did look a bit different today. His motions were stiffer, articulating only at the joints, instead of the fluid, powerful, whole-body movement that he usually had. He was also just a bit… slower? As if it took a moment for his body to understand what his mind wanted him to do.

::What is it like:: he asked hesitantly, ::when you come here? I guess I imagined it was like dreaming. Perhaps you lie down, and fall asleep. Or perhaps you leave your body there in the same way you leave this one here?::

The big man paused for a long moment, as if trying to decide what to say. ::Look, it's… odd that you even pay attention to this stuff. Before I met you and your friends, Natives didn't really seem to pay attention to the fact that Travelers were sometimes here and sometimes not. Your people just kind of walk around us, and when we come back, you just take it in stride, as if it were the most normal thing in the world.::

He shrugged. ::So, it makes me a little uncomfortable to talk to you about it. Or,:: he hesitated again, looking frustrated, ::not uncomfortable, but… I don't know how to explain it. It makes you too 'real', I guess.::

Motte held up a hand, his deep voice going deeper still with the depth of his sincerity. ::You *are* real. In a way that I never thought about before Rouge got involved in this. They say that 'discomfort is a necessary part of enlightenment', and that's certainly true.::

His expression settled into determination, and he went on. ::When Rouge and I come here, we wear special clothes, and we do lie down in a kind of bed. It uses something you'd probably see as magic to send us here, but it's just technology. There *is* no magic in our world. Those beds are complex machines, and I don't think there are many people who really understand how they work. Just like people here trust mages to cast the right spell, even though they themselves can't use magic, in my world, we trust our machines to do what we tell them to, even when we don't know how they do it.::

He raised a hand to tap his forehead, ::Other people, like Rouge's friend Lyrec, use headsets, like what I'm wearing now, to get here. It's much less expensive than the bed. Kind of like the difference between buying a horse and buying a house. The headset works with some gloves to allow people to use gestures to control their body here, though some people don't even have the gloves. They just use a,:: he motioned as if grabbing and holding something, ::a joystick.::

Aspen finally managed to speak, though it was hard to do so through the laugh that was trying to escape. ::A *joy*stick?::

Motte laughed a little. ::Yeah. I never really thought about it, but it is a funny name. I bet there's a story there. In any case, the headset and gloves or joystick don't let us reach your world nearly as well. We can't smell, taste, or feel nearly as much, and pain is barely more than discomfort. A lot of the Travelers who just go out and fight monsters are headset players. You can't really forget that you're not *actually* here while you're using a headset.::

His head suddenly jerked up, and his eyes locked on a space beyond Aspen. ::Speaking of which, someone is knocking at my office door. I'm going to set my Zombie to follow you. *Stay here*, please. I'll be back as soon as I can.::

With that, he reached up and slid his hands over his face. As his fingers slid over his forehead, his body stilled, and his face became lifeless.

Aspen shuddered. *That is still horrifying. Maybe more so now that I know they're just… puppets?* He reached up and rubbed at his own forehead. His head was pounding, and he suddenly felt a little dizzy. He blinked, and then blinked again.

A flash of light flickered behind his lids, and he had a sudden sharp, vision of a person sitting in a strangely smooth chair, a black mask covering most of their face and ears. Light shone off the mask like glass, but it was completely opaque. On the figure's hands were two thick gloves. They were almost more like the bulky mitts that fighters wore when they were training in hand-to-hand combat so that they wouldn't hurt each other too badly. The person suddenly jumped from their chair, waving their obscured appendages wildly.

Then the vision faded, leaving him with a headache and a thousand questions.

"Aspen?"

The flat voice coming from his left nearly made him jump, and he realized that he had completely lost track of what was happening around him. His hand reached for a nonexistent weapon, but then his brain processed who was standing beside him, and he relaxed somewhat.

"Mai Ley. I'm sorry, I didn't see you." He swiped a hand across his eyes, blinking in sudden exhaustion.

The priestess tilted her head. "Are you well? You seemed momentarily disoriented."

Aspen drew in a deep breath and let it out slowly. "I'm fine, I think. I didn't realize you were here. I thought you left with Restur and the others." He looked around. "Are they back already? Restur said the warehouse is on the other side of the city, by the Exotic Goods Market."

Mai Ley's pale, expressionless eyes were locked on his. "I did. I suddenly had a feeling that I needed to return. When I arrived, you didn't notice."

Closing his eyes, he drew in a few more breaths, feeling the ground beneath his worn-thin boots, hearing the frustrated murmuring of the crowds, and smelling the hot, dusty air filled with the odors of a thousand people. He grimaced. "It's just hot and stuffy. I got used to quiet and open spaces, and this," he gestured at the sea of beings swirling around them, "is not pleasant. I forgot how many people live in the city."

She nodded, her sleek black hair swinging smoothly around her pale face. "There are a great number of sapients here. It must be overwhelming for you." The pale eyes, surrounded by the traditional mask of red makeup, flicked to Motte. "What were you and the Guardian talking about?"

Aspen shook his head. "He was telling me about his world. It sounds… complicated."

Something flickered across her face. Sadness? Anger? Whatever it was, it was gone so quickly that he almost thought he had imagined it, except that a bare hint of it remained in her voice when she spoke, making it sharper than usual. "They make it more complicated than it has to be."

He narrowed his eyes. "They?"

She paused for a long moment, expression utterly blank, and when she spoke again, no trace of feeling remained. "Others. What seems complex to one person may be simple to another, is that not true?" Her eyes were cool and assessing as she looked at him, and he felt as if she could see inside him, to the unsteady foundation of his character. "If you are well, then I may return to my business. Perhaps it would be best if you avoided such discussions in the future, however."

Looking into the frozen lakes of her gaze, he felt suddenly muddled again, though it was a very different feeling from the sense of detachment he'd felt after his strange vision. That vision, too, seemed oddly distant, and he couldn't seem to remember exactly what-

He shook his head again, as if driving away a troublesome insect. "Ah. Yes. I guess it doesn't matter how they come here, only that they do. I-"

"Aspen!" This time it was a cheerful voice that drew his attention, and he looked away from the priestess, feeling an almost physical wrenching sensation as their eyes left each other. Millie was standing nearby, her hand on Struthio's arm. Bright rings glinted from the second fingers of their left hands, and their faces were wreathed in smiles, though a hint of trepidation clouded their joy.

Millie raised her hand, and the ring there glinted gold to match the long braids coiled around her crown. "I'm sorry! They said if we wanted witnesses, we'd have to wait a week, an' pay more money, too! We couldna afford-"

"Congratulations!" He pushed his hat back, letting her see his face clearly for a moment, so she could read the pleasure there. She and her new husband relaxed, smiles growing even wider. He tugged the brim of his hat back down and continued, "I would'a loved to see th' wedding, but th' important thing is that you're happy. We can still celebrate with you, eh?"

Struthio grinned and wrapped his arm around his wife's shoulders. Next to him, the nearly six-foot-tall Amazon looked almost petite. "Aye. We hoped ye'd say tha'." He looked around. "All're gone?"

Aspen nodded. "We didn't know how long you'd be gone, an' Rubico needed to unload the wagons an' let his people rest. He said he'd be back as soon as he could, an' young Vonn with 'im. Manuela an' likely some others'll be comin' as well." He tilted his head to indicate Motte's Zombie. "Motte came to check on you, an' Rouge is inside visitin' Gina's temple."

He briefly considered telling them about the girl's impending class change, but after a glance around, decided to wait and let her decide who she wanted to tell. Usually, the change was great enough that others would know something had happened, so it wouldn't be a secret for long, but it was hers to tell, and, in any case, this moment belonged to the two lovers.

"From what I hear, Rouge'll likely be a while, so mayhap ye'd like to get some lunch? There're some good diners nearby," he caught himself at the looks of surprise on their faces. He reminded himself he was just a farmer who had *never been to Bright before*. "Ah, at least tha's what Motte said. Rouge'll find us when she gets done, an' Restur or Vonn'll meet us 'ere in a while." Or at least Rouge would call him in party chat, as long as they didn't go far.

He motioned toward a narrow road near the main entrance to the temple square. "Motte said t'go that way." His eyes caught on Mai Ley, and he suddenly realized that he'd almost forgotten the woman was there. He nodded to her hesitantly. "Would y'like to join us, Priestess?"

Struthio was shuffling his feet, and a pretty blush had risen on Millie's strong cheekbones. As the girl opened her mouth, Aspen realized what the problem probably was. "Ah, my treat, eh? I had a good harvest, and th' Travelers saved me money on getting' here. I have enough."

After an uncertain exchange of glances, Millie nodded, her fingers closing on Struthio's thin hand. "A meal'd be welcome. M' husband," and the blush deepened again, "needs t'eat, an' I'd like to see what food people enjoy here."

Aspen chuckled. The chef obviously wanted a chance to size up the competition, and he couldn't blame her for doing it on someone else's copper. He looked back to Mai Ley, who had a very strange expression on her face. Almost… confusion? Happiness? It was as though the priestess had never been asked to share a meal before, and didn't know how to respond.

Finally, the woman nodded. "I would… like that. Perhaps you could assist me in choosing an ingestible, however? My preferences are not set."

He shrugged. "I'm sure we can find somethin' you'll like."

The small group of five – including Motte's obedient Zombie – turned and made their way against the flow, back toward the entrance to the main road leading to and from the square. Aspen quickly found that this experience, too, was far different from the one he had had in his past life as Iorgas Penbrooke, Atae's Left Hand.

Even his height wasn't enough to convince people to make room, and he didn't want to attract attention by forcing his way upstream. Millie, seeing his conundrum, quickly took over. Pushing ahead of him, the lady plowed through the crowd like a regal mother duck on a placid lake, leaving Aspen and the others following in her wake like proper ducklings. Struthio, whom Aspen had considered a bit of a dullard, caught Aspen's gaze, and one limpid blue eye closed in a slow, conspiratorial wink. Aspen's mouth dropped open slightly, and then he laughed out loud, though the sound was lost in the sound of the indignant squalling of those Millie had inconvenienced.

The group split off down the much smaller, quieter street that Aspen had indicated, and the sound of the crowds were almost instantly muffled. Aspen felt his shoulders drop from where they had drawn tight up around his ears. He looked around.

"Motte said," he glanced at the large man, feeling somewhat apologetic for putting words in his mouth, "there're three places down here. A tavern, a diner, an' a proper restaurant. What'd ye like t'eat?" He looked at Millie and Struthio, since Mai Ley had said she had no preference. Hadn't she?

Millie thought about it for a moment. "Th' tavern, I think. A man 's happiest wi' a belly full o' good, warm food. None o' those fancy little fripperies. They're fun t'make ever' now 'n then, but not all th' time. It'd be good t'see if the things we like in Nor'Goose are the same as the city folks like." The barest hint of insecurity touched her voice, and Aspen saw Struthio's fingers tighten reassuringly on hers.

The farmer smiled. "I think y'll find ye've nothin' t' worry about, lass. This way." He motioned toward a door standing open at the end of the block. Above it was a shield-shaped sign, carved with the image of a rampant pony clutching a foaming mug between its front hooves.

When they reached the door, Aspen pushed it open, and ushered the others inside. They stood in a small group in the dim interior, gazing around at the display. Aspen barely managed to contain a grin at the awestruck looks on

Millie and Struthio's faces.

The Drunk Pony was well-known in Bright. During the war, it was a place that soldiers liked to go after praying at the temple and before they were deployed the next day. Occasionally, a knight or other lordling would find themselves here, and it was traditional that the tavern-keeper, who was a retired sergeant himself, would give those officers their first drink 'on the house.'

No one knew exactly what was in that beverage, since the man kept it behind the bar in a plain clay jug, but inevitably the officer became very happy for a period which was rapidly followed by unconsciousness. The officer's men would have to return him to his lodgings, but not before the tavern-keeper made a sketch of the heraldic device of his latest victim. That device was then carved into some part of the tavern décor, thus constantly adding to the legend.

Now, in times of peace, the tradition had lapsed, but every part of the interior, from the bar itself to the broad beams holding up the ceiling, was covered in carvings. Lions passant frolicked with foxes courant, while two hedgehogs salient leapt from a bear dormant. These whimsical creatures were interspersed among billets, annulets, and frets, wyverns and griffins, and wound with grapevines and cinquefoil.

From behind the immaculate bar, a wizened man looked up. His voice was rough but cordial when he spoke. "Seat yourself. If ya want food, a server'll come. If ya want drink, just yell it ta me." A simple black patch covered one eye, and Aspen knew that if he came out from behind the bar, he'd be missing a leg as well.

Lark, Aspen's cleric daughter, had once offered to ask Gina to regrow it for him, and the old soldier had refused her outright. He was done with war, he said, and if he had two good legs and two good eyes, he'd be sent to the front lines to die with the rest. He'd stay right there, and at least die protecting his home and his family.

Millie led the way to a booth to one side, and Aspen slid in after Mai Ley, positioning himself so his back was to the wall, and he could see the door as well as the curtain that covered the entrance to the kitchen. Motte's Zombie remained standing, an impassive and looming presence that the server, a young man of about Rouge's age, cast more than one apprehensive glance.

"What'll ya have?" the nervous young man asked, carefully standing as far from the tall Traveler as possible, "We've got a turkey sandwich, made with bread fresh-baked this mornin', or a stew o' venison an' root vegetables. If ya just want a bit, there's bread and hard cheese."

Millie ordered the stew for Struthio and the bread and cheese for herself. Mai Ley also asked for bread and cheese, and Aspen suddenly found that a simple sandwich sounded delicious. He knew from past experience that the portion would be hearty, and the cook made an excellent dressing that she slathered on the bread, and covered the meat in whatever vegetables were fresh in her garden.

The boy took their order, and made his way back toward the kitchen. As he did, a young Traveler with a lute on his back entered and went up to the tavern-keeper. They spoke for a moment before the old man gestured to a small open area next to the bar and shrugged. The young man, who had a round, pale face with an open, cheerful expression and large blue eyes beneath a mop of light blond hair, went to the open area and pulled up a stool. He sat down and began to tune his instrument.

Millie sat up straight, looking pleased. "A bard! Ah love music while ah eat!"

Aspen, who was first nearly as pleased as the chef, winced as an overly sharp note twanged through the room. A string snapped, and the young Bard, after glancing around to see who had noticed, restrung his instrument with the ease of long practice. Once he was done, he again set to tuning, accompanied by the whining complaints of his strings. By the time he actually began singing, even Millie was looking apprehensive.

Upon a white horse

My love ran off course

With a fiddle-dee-dee

And a fie.

With three legs the same length

Of uncommon strength

And one that was weak and ran wild.

I followed my heart

Until it came apart,

With a fiddle-dee-dee

And a fie.

Aspen covered his ears with his hands, and, looking around, he could see that the expressions of the few others sitting in the large room indicated that they, too, were noticing the distinctly off-key sound of the lute, and the unfortunate falsetto in which the young man was singing. The boy's face, which grew more and more desperate and embarrassed, indicated that he, too, was aware that he was not, in fact, a good musician. As he reached the crescendo of the song, his voice cracked and then dropped an octave, which was actually an improvement, though it was obviously unintentional.

The look of surprise and dismay on the lad's face as he struggled to pull his voice back up into the key in which he'd begun the song triggered a sudden feeling of recognition in Aspen. Eyes narrowed, he tried to tune out the horrendous racket and simply focus on the young man's face.

His eyes suddenly widened as he remembered where he'd seen the boy before, and it took a moment longer to dredge the name attached to that memory from his brain. The strings of the lute abruptly snapped, dropping the tavern into a silence equally horrified and relieved even as Aspen opened his mouth and asked, "Lyrec?"

Chapter Three

Rouge

Rouge stared up at the perfect and terrible face hovering over her own and thought fast. Finally, she choked out, "I thought," she felt the creature's claws scratch over her throat as she spoke, though the lack of pain indicated that her skin should still be intact, "you said you were just here to play?"

The crimson eyes bored into hers for a moment longer, and then the full lips snarled briefly, turning her face into an animalistic mask. It lasted for only an instant, and then the carmine mouth settled into a sensual pout instead, as the woman stood, slowly and languidly. Her taloned fingers flicked dismissively as she returned to sprawl languidly on a cushion-covered bench made of some richly carved wood and lush padding covered in deep black satin.

"You speak the truth, vile youth. I have yet more power than you know, but now is not the time for show. A simple question here I ask, who I am, now as in the past? One chance more, then out the door." She smiled tranquilly, vicious fangs flashing like knife blades in the dark.

::Silus?:: Rouge's internal voice was a little desperate, and she could feel her small friend shuddering against her throat. Thankfully, the bat was hiding in Rouge's curls on the other side of her neck from where the vampire had been touching her, but it had still been far too close to the fragile bat.

::I... I don't remember! I know I thought it was a funny name, because it had something sun-related in it, and vampires usually can't go out in the sun. But that name you said, Jezebel, sounded right, but she said it isn't! I don't know!:: Poor Silus sounded like she would be drowning in terrified sobs if she could be, and Rouge had to force back a desperate urge to snuggle her friend comfortingly. If the evil creature they were trapped with didn't know the bat was there, however, Rouge wasn't going to give it away.

Okay. What did she know? Not much, really. The name was close to Jezebel, but had something sun-related in it. Sun, sun, sun. Sun was hot, sun was bright, sunshine, sun beam, sunlight, sun... ray! That rang a sort of very, very distant memory-bell.

::Silus, was it ray? Raybel? Jeray? Jezeray?::

The bat quivered excitedly. ::Yes! Jezerey! That was it! William has mentioned her a few more times. Just little things, but sometimes we talk when we're both awake at night and everyone else is sleeping, and I know he's said that name! He really, really doesn't like her, and now I can see why!::

Rouge drew in a deep breath, watching the smug vampire as she tapped her finger-claws in a slow and discordant pattern on the gleaming scrolled arms of the bench. ::I'm going to go with that, then. It sounds right to me, too.:: Well, in that it sounded like a *name*, anyway. She really didn't remember, but Jezerey didn't sound wrong, and Silus was around a lot more to hear the name mentioned. Rouge just didn't want her friend to feel guilty if it wasn't the right name.

She cleared her throat and looked straight into the bright red eyes. Carefully, she pronounced, "Jezerey." Instantly, the space around them collapsed, and the last thing Rouge saw were the brilliant red eyes flashing toward her, their expression utterly blank of anything except a desperate desire to slaughter.

Then her feet dropped a few inches, and she found herself once again standing on the smooth, burnished stone of the temple floor. Around her was a simple room, not much larger than the shrine in the woods where they had taken refuge after running from Bloodhaven, though the ceiling was easily twice as high. On a low pedestal before her was a statue of Gina, her lovingly carved face gazing out over Rouge's head with calm benevolence.

Rouge's legs went weak, and she collapsed on the floor, knees banging painfully against the stone. At the sound, something moved in the darkness behind the statue, and Rouge threw herself to the side, rolling away from a possible incoming attack. A system message flashed at the bottom of her vision.

You have entered a shrine dedicated to your Patron Goddess, Gina. You feel refreshed. Your Health, Mana, and Stamina regeneration will double as long as you remain inside the shrine, and do not enter battle.

A young woman poked her head out of the shadows, blinking large violet eyes surrounded by thick black lashes. "Oh, my! A devotee!" She emerged fully into the soft lighting given off by glowstones set in frosted glass sconces. She was wearing the soft green favored by Gina's clergy, in an off-the-shoulder draped gown gathered below her breasts and allowed to flow loose in the back. The style complemented her generous figure, and her round, rather plain features were attractive in their genuine pleasure at seeing Rouge.

"I'm Priestess Penelope. Penny, if you like. You're the first Traveler to make it through the Trials today! How lovely to meet you!" A broad smile brought out a dimple in her right cheek.

Slowly, Rouge came to her feet, still warily eyeing the shadows around the room, though it seemed she and Penny were the only ones present. "How did you get here, then?" She knew she sounded a bit abrupt, but she was still looking for tricks and traps.

Penny looked disapproving. "Oh, even the new city Lord can't keep a member of the clergy from their temple. We haven't yet been able to find a way around the regulations that demand the faithful 'prove their devotion', but we who have committed our lives to our Goddess need offer no further proof. I just walked here. The hallway is longer than it used to be, but that's it."

Rouge smiled a little, daring to hope that she really had made it to the actual temple. ::Silus? Do you see anything suspicious?::

A series of squeaks came from next to her ear, and then Silus' relieved voice spoke. ::Nothing. My [Sonar] is working again, too.::

"I'm here to get Gina's blessing and accept a sub-class. Can I... do that?" Before, she just would have walked up to the idol and gotten started, but now she wasn't sure what the protocol was.

A slight blush crept into Penny's cheeks, and her violet eyes took on a slightly frustrated gleam. "You can, yes, but you'll have to pay a small fee. Unfortunately, his Lordship," yep, there was a definite bite in her voice now, "has seen fit to tax all the churches except for that of Apofis. If we don't charge *something*, he insists we pay a lump sum regardless. A blessing will be one silver, and the sub-class will cost a gold." She held out a small locked box, face now apologetic.

Rouge passed her hand over the box, depositing the requested fee. She frowned a little, though. "Is that for Travelers and Natives alike?" She looked around, noting once again that the temple seemed empty except for the two of them.

"Ah, no," Penny's flush deepened. "Citizens of this world are sent to a large common area. They don't have to face the Trials, but they also don't get to pray in a proper temple. There is an acolyte and a small shrine for each God in the common area. Only Apofis' worshippers are allowed in His temple."

Thinking of Millie and Struthio, Rouge felt herself growing a little angry. "My friends came in earlier to arrange their wedding. They're, ah, Natives, and followers of Gina. What happened to them?"

The priestess shrugged helplessly. "They would have been sent to the common area. It's… quite expensive to get married right now, but if they could afford the fee, they're probably already married. It costs a great deal more for a proper wedding, and the acolytes use each other as witnesses for ceremonies like that if the couple hasn't brought their own."

Closing her eyes, Rouge pushed back her frustration. It seemed obvious to her that this woman was doing her best with a difficult situation, and it wasn't her fault the jerk-face running the city was doing jerk-face things. She forced a smile. "I'm just glad they could get married. We'll have to throw a party for them later. Thanks for your help."

Nodding, the priestess stepped back, carefully carrying the box back to what Rouge could now see was a soft chair half-hidden behind the pedestal on which the statue stood. The thief could see a book lying splayed open on the ground by the chair. She winced as she thought about what Motte would have to say about what that did to the spine.

Shrugging, she turned back to the statue. Time to get to praying.

Several fluffy cushions rested on the ground in front of Gina's statue, and Rouge carefully knelt on a particularly brightly colored blue one. Closing her eyes, she bowed her head and accessed the temple interface.

You are at a place of worship dedicated to your chosen Deity, Gina. Would you like to Pray? You may receive a Blessing or Boon as a result of this prayer. Yes/No

She quickly selected 'Yes', and instantly felt warmth flood her body, as if she'd stepped into sunshine after being in a cold, dark room.

Due to your high Reputation with the Church of Gina, you may choose a Boon. At your level, you may select from *Indefatigable* or *Mana Well.*

This was definitely new, and very cool! When she'd prayed in the past, she usually got a buff like temporary immunity from curses, or ten extra hit points for five hours. Nice, but not exactly a game changer.

As her Reputation with Gina's church increased, the buffs got better, and her favorite had definitely been a three-hour agility boost that had made her practically impossible to hit. She knew boons lasted longer than the buffs, but since they varied by both deity and player, reading through lists of what other people had received was pretty pointless.

Now, looking at her choices, she itched to take Mana Well, but the fact was that she just didn't have that many spells. Whatever it did, it would obviously affect her mana, so no spells meant no bueno. Indefatigable, however, looked like it would affect Stamina, and she could always use more of that. Admittedly, she had a pretty good handle on what she could do without running out, as did most players, but still, it would be the smart choice.

So, she chose Mana Well. After all, she was about to upgrade her Class, and who *knew* what goodness was coming her way?

Gina has blessed you with access to some of her Divine Power. For the next 24 hours of play time, your mana pool will be doubled. Attacking another follower of Gina or choosing a different God will cancel this Boon.

Rouge grinned. Heck, yes! Double the mana, double the fun! Right now, she could cast [Poof!] almost indefinitely, given her mana regen, and could even cast [Poison Rain] four times in succession, maybe even five if her regen had time to give her back twenty mana before all the cooldowns were up.

She rubbed her hands together. Now for the *really* fun part.

You have chosen to accept a sub-class. Sub-classes available to you are:
o **Burglar**
o **Cutpurse**

o **Assassin**

o **Mugger**

o **Sneak**

o **Spy (Uncommon)**

o **Enforcer**

o **Highwayman**

o **Merry (Wo)man (Uncommon)**

o **Fowl Trickster (Unique)**

You have selected *Fowl Trickster*. This choice CANNOT BE CHANGED. Are you certain you would like to accept the sub-class *Fowl Trickster?* (You must confirm this choice three times. If you contact an admin claiming you made an incorrect selection, your request will be automatically denied.)

Sheesh, Veritas, way to take the magic out of a moment! Rolling her eyes, Rouge selected 'Yes', then 'I am certain', and finally 'I understand this choice cannot be changed'. As she clicked for the last time, her body burst into golden flames.

Congratulations! You are now a Fowl Trickster!

You have learned [Shadow Glide]. This Skill allows you to instantly travel up to five feet within a single shadowed area.

You have learned the spell [What's That?!] You may distract up to three targets with a % success chance of (spell level) x (your level) - (total Intelligence of all targets/2).

Your spell [Poof!] is now [Poof!!]. This spell casts an area obscuration cloud that lasts a minimum of two minutes, and cannot be dispelled. This cloud can give the [Smoke Inhalation] or [Poison] Debuff. All members of your party are immune to these negative effects.

You have learned the spell [Substitution]. You may take on the outward appearance of any sentient you have touched within the last hour. Duration up to fifteen minutes. Spell can be canceled voluntarily, or if you are attacked. *Skill [Steal] found. Skills may be used in concert. If you are able to [Steal] an item from your target, the duration of [Substitution] will be increased depending on the Rarity of the stolen item. You must keep the item with you in order to use this Skill boost. This boost will end when the theft is discovered, leaving a maximum of fifteen minutes remaining on the Skill.*

Your skill [Obfuscation] is now level 25. You may conceal your identity and level from all viewers with a % success rate of (skill level) + (your level) – (viewer's Intelligence-10).

You may select one type of Avian Companion from the list of birds who assisted you during the prerequisite Quest. *Only one option found. Avian Companion set to 'Ostrich.'* Being within ten feet of your Avian Companion boosts the odds of successful skill checks by 5%.

Your affinity with mobs and sapients of type <u>Avian</u> has increased by 20%.

Your Battle Mount, Codswallop, now has five Damage Points before he will be forced to respawn.

Your Battle Mount, Codswallop, has earned one Unique Skill.

Unique Skill [Confabulation] granted to Battle Mount Codswallop by your Deity, Gina. 'Nobody rides an ostrich, right? That's silly. That was a really ugly horse.' Sapient viewers will now convince themselves they see a horse instead of a large bird. This effect has a 5% chance of failing against people with Intelligence ≥ 120, in groups of fewer than ten, or if the viewer is a young child for their race. Failure chance occurs only once, the first time a viewer sees the affected mount, and thereafter they will always see the same thing.

By the time she finished reading the notifications, Rouge was grinning like a loon. She could feel how many teeth she was exposing, but somehow, she just couldn't stop. This was a-maz-ing! Then her eyes widened as another, shorter, stream of notices popped up.

Class experience beyond the level cap is available. Apply now? Yes/No

Accumulated Class experience granted. Experience will be applied to new Skills and Spells at a ratio of 2:1, or you may choose to increase only Rogue skills and receive the full amount.

Apply deferred Class experience to all Skills and Spells at 2:1, or base Rogue skills only at 1:1?

That cured her grin pretty quickly. She knew this was coming, because she'd read about it on the forums. Most people used the information available online to decide what sub-class they were going to go for long before they reached the level cap. Then, when they reached twenty, they could run to the nearest shrine or temple and accept their new sub-class, thus losing little to no Class experience.

The game counted everything a player did since they created their character when considering what sub-classes they were qualified for. Want to be a Pirate? Head to water and get some time in on boats, preferably as the captain. Want to be a Highwayman? Head out of the city and start stealing from people, preferably near a road, after setting up an ambush.

If you did it right, then when you hit your level cap, the game would offer you not only the three default sub-classes available to your Class, but also the one you actually wanted. In Rouge's case, she'd been able to select from Burglar, Cutpurse, or Assassin, which were the defaults, but had also had Mugger (it was a quest!) and Sneak unlocked. She'd gotten Spy not long after, since she tended to spend a fair amount of time watching her targets before actually attempting a theft.

Rouge, unfortunately, didn't like anything she'd seen when she looked them up. The base three were just too common. While *Veritas'* system meant that any Player could have a Skill or Spell that was unexpected, most people did the expected things and got the expected results. Boring!

Mugger was pretty common, too, though it had a cool perk of allowing you to 'ignore' bluestones if you managed to catch someone completely alone. You couldn't kill them, but you could Stun them and then [Steal] anything that they had in extra bags outside of their personal Inventory. Sneak was kind of like a lower level of Spy, and allowed you to get closer to people before they had a chance of noticing you being weird, even in large crowds.

To be an Enforcer, you had to work with a gang, which meant raising your Reputation with that gang. Rouge had gotten it through a quest chain. That was actually how she'd met and become friends with Gunthrax, the orc who'd briefly been her jailer in the Thieves Guild.

Honestly, that was one of the few quest chains she'd really regretted taking, but when she'd started it, she hadn't yet realized just how different NPCs in *VO* were from NPCs in traditional games.

In any case, none of them had been enticing, and the more experience she got past her level cap, the more determined she was to make it all worthwhile. Finally, she'd just kind of forgotten about it, except on those rare occasions when she bothered looking at her character sheet. It killed her feeling of immersion, so she usually only did it after getting a level.

As long as she was doing character maintenance, though… She sighed and pulled it up.

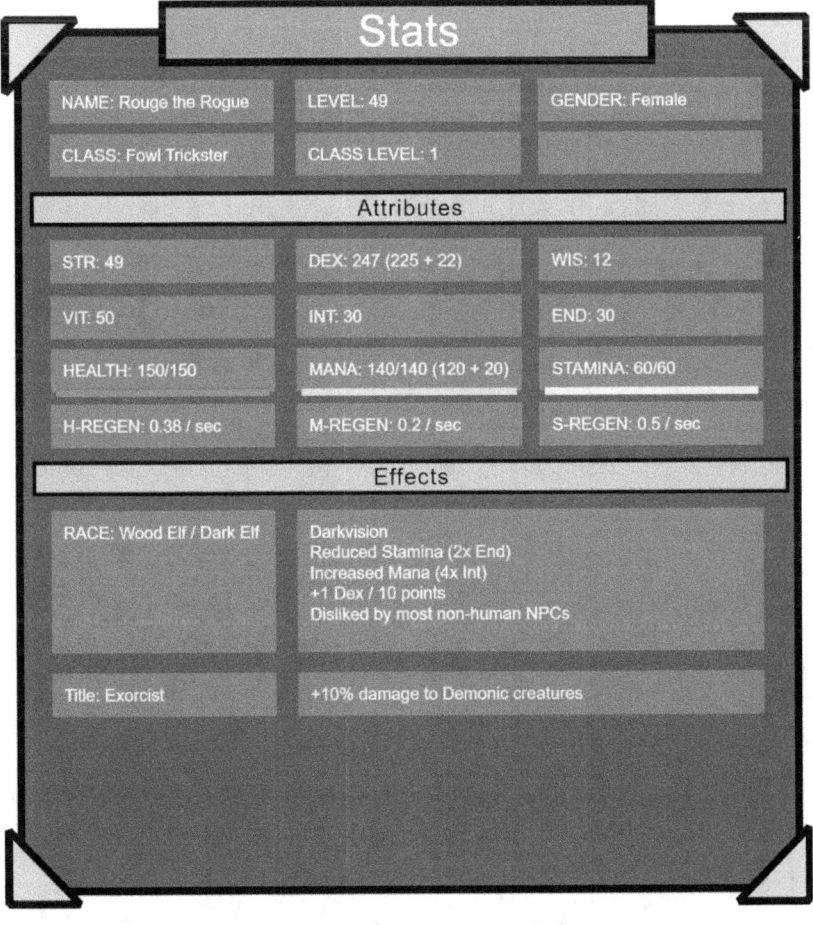

Stats

| NAME: Rouge the Rogue | LEVEL: 49 | GENDER: Female |
| CLASS: Fowl Trickster | CLASS LEVEL: 1 | |

Attributes

STR: 49	DEX: 247 (225 + 22)	WIS: 12
VIT: 50	INT: 30	END: 30
HEALTH: 150/150	MANA: 140/140 (120 + 20)	STAMINA: 60/60
H-REGEN: 0.38 / sec	M-REGEN: 0.2 / sec	S-REGEN: 0.5 / sec

Effects

| RACE: Wood Elf / Dark Elf | Darkvision
Reduced Stamina (2x End)
Increased Mana (4x Int)
+1 Dex / 10 points
Disliked by most non-human NPCs |
| Title: Exorcist | +10% damage to Demonic creatures |

Stat points available: 104. Would you like to allocate these unused stat points now?

She scowled. She'd been putting half her points into Dexterity since the very beginning, so that had always been an easy choice. After that, things got a little rough. She liked spells more than skills, but the thief classes just didn't get very many of them. They tended to be much more Stamina-based than Mana-based, so most thieves didn't even bother with the Intelligence stat, beyond what they needed for lock-picking and trap-disarming, which capped out at around thirty.

As they'd gotten closer to Bright, she'd known she was going to get some levels when she completed the Come in From the Cold quest, so she'd just stopped applying her points, except for the ones she put into Dex. She'd been level 44 when Aspen walked into Bright, and gained five levels for the quest, which was fifty stat points. Twenty-five of those went into Dex, and... Done!

That left her with seventy-nine, but she'd just gotten two cool new spells, as well as an upgrade to [Poof!], which now cost an extra ten mana when casting. So thirty points went into Intelligence. Ha! Motte always said Int points over thirty were wasted on Rogues, but she'd show him! Of course, he had no magic at all, so his Intelligence was sitting at twenty, last she'd heard, and he only put those points in because you had to have ten to be able to read, and he kept failing to see hidden mobs.

Now, forty-nine more points. Hum hum hum... She could definitely use some more health points, so twenty-five points went into Vitality. Things had gotten a little too close a few times lately. With her increased Dexterity, not much should be able to hit her, at least not around Bright, but it was hard to dodge spells. That left her sitting on twenty-four more stat points.

Due to choosing Dark Elf as one of her races, she had reduced Stamina. That made her wince every time she had to pour points into Endurance for so little return. She would definitely be needing more, though, since both [Obfuscation] and [Shadow Glide] were awesome Skills. Twenty points to Endurance, then, giving her a full hundred Stamina. Finally.

She dumped one point into Strength, bringing it up to a nice round fifty. The last three points went to Wisdom, which, as far as she could tell, did nothing for her, but she kept hoping it would, and plus, twelve plus three was fifteen, which was nice. And done!

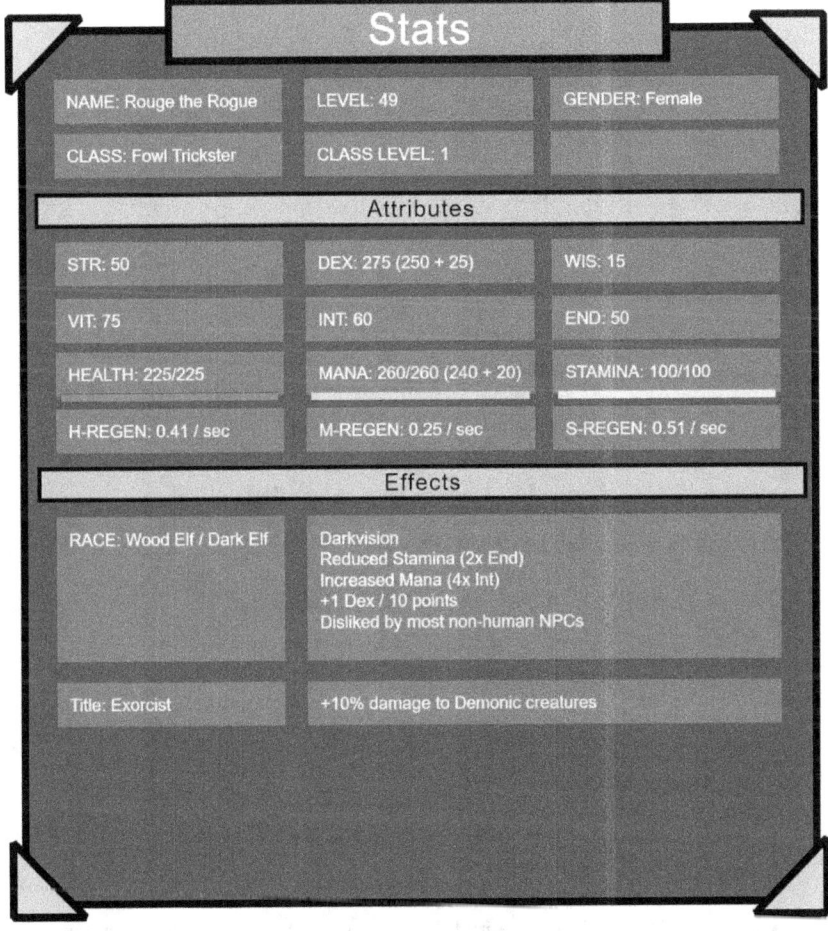

That was nice. Her health, mana, and stamina regen had all gone up, too. She would definitely be harder to kill now, though she really needed more Strength. She just didn't *like* hitting and stabbing things as much as she liked casting spells and jumping around. Next time, though, for sure.

Now, back to the question at hand, which had been percolating in the back of her mind while she worked on her stats.

Apply deferred Class experience to all Skills and Spells at 2:1, or base Rogue skills only at 1:1?

Before she could change her mind, she selected 'base Rogue skills'. Yes, she wanted her new stuff leveled, and advanced Skills and Spells were *much* harder to raise than basic ones, but throwing away experience just wasn't something she could do. She sighed at the lost opportunity, but knew it was the way she had to go.

Another Wall of Notifications flooded her vision.

You are now a level 3 Fowl Trickster.

Deferred Class-related Skill experience applied:
[Stealth] is now level 25. You may now run while using [Stealth].
[Sneak] is now level 22.
[Lockpicking] is now level 17.
[Trap Detection] is now level 11.
[Disarm Trap] is now level 7.
[Hidden Passages] is now level 9.
[Legerdemain] is now level 23. Bonus to [Sleight of Hand] now increased to .3%/level of [Legerdemain.]
[Sleight of Hand] is now level 24. Percent chance of stealing Very Rare or better items increased 2%.
[Pilfer] is now level 7.
[Obfuscation] is now level 28.
[Backstab] is now level 9.
[Steal] is now level 28. Your percent chance to [Steal] items not on a sentient creature or mob is now (Steal level) + (Dexterity/4). Environmental factors may increase or decrease this effect. You may now [Steal] unattended Pack Animals in 4 min 45 sec.

[Climb] is now level 24. You can now climb while in [Stealth].

Deferred Class-related Spell experience applied:

Original spell [Poof!] not found. Experience applied to upgraded spell.
[Poof!!] is now level 17.

[Poison Rain] is now level 4.

And the insane grin was back.

::Are you ready to go, Silus?:: she sent to the little bat, who was suspiciously silent on her shoulder.

::Are you done? My eyes hurt.:: The little voice was definitely cranky.

Rouge bit her lip. She had been surrounded by a whole lot of level-up glows for a few minutes, there, both from the class change and all the skill-ups. Her small friend had probably been blinded by the sudden brilliance, especially since it had been right next to her.

::I'm sorry. I didn't even think to warn you.::

The bat sniffled. ::Do better next time.::

::I will, I promise.:: Rouge snuggled her little friend and started looking for the way out.

Getting out of the temple was far easier than getting in had been. All she had to do was walk out. She waved a cheerful farewell to Penny, dropped another five gold into the donation box, and ran off down the hall. Which was short. Like, thirty feet, maybe. She emerged into the atrium, blinking at the sudden resurgence of sound and motion around her, as hundreds of Players milled around. Now that she knew what she was looking at, she was disturbed at how many of them were heading straight into the temple of Apofis. At least half were headed for the temple of the new god, and the ones who weren't were mostly dressed in the leather and cloth garb of crafters and mages. She saw a lot of frustrated faces on these people, as they wandered around staring at arches.

Impulsively, she reached out and tugged at the sleeve of a female cleric standing nearby, staring up at the symbols above the various arches.

"Excuse me. I just got back to Bright, and I was wondering," she waved around at the bustling crowd, "why don't people just go to one of the smaller, dedicated shrines to the other gods, if they don't follow Apofis?"

The woman looked angry at first, but after taking in Rouge's age, she just sighed and said, "The City Lord closed all the other shrines down. Said they needed permits or something, but no one knows how to *get* a permit. The Temple is the only one left in the city. I hear the temples and shrines in towns near Bright are being taxed out of existence, too. I was only two levels from getting my Priestess of Minetra class change, too! My boyfriend is a blacksmith, and we were really counting on the boosts my prayers would give the items he makes. It sucks!" The woman gave a 'what can you do' shrug, and walked away, continuing her search for Minetra's temple.

Rouge stood, thinking through the implications. If Apofis was really just a martial god, and there were no other temples or shrines nearby, then Players who weren't warriors would have to either go through the Trials every time they needed something, or use the Guild Circles to travel to another city or town where there was a shrine, which would get really expensive really fast.

In the end, she suspected people would end up either leaving or just converting to Apofis, even if it meant they had to take a different sub-class than they'd originally wanted. Crafting would be left to the NPCs, who could charge higher rates, which could be taxed at higher rates, but Players who were warriors wouldn't care as much, since they had a much steadier flow of income than support classes.

New players who wanted to be crafters were probably choosing elf races at even higher rates than usual, since this would allow them to spawn in Elfhame, far away from whatever stupidity was going on in Bright. In fact, new players starting in Bright would probably universally choose Apofis as their god to begin with. After all, what did it matter to them, really?

Scowling, she walked out into the sunshine, immediately sending a message out in party chat. ::Aspen? You there?::

Chapter Four

Aspen

spen? You there?::

Aspen smiled in relief as he heard Rouge's voice in his mind, and his smile widened further when he heard Silus' little voice ask irritably, ::Why does it have to be so *bright* in Bright?::

::I'm here,:: he sent back cheerfully, and gave them directions to the tavern in which he sat. ::I have a surprise for you, too.::

Turning back to the crestfallen young man sitting across from him at their table, he said, "I think Rouge'll be back any time, an' Motte told her to look in these eateries. While we wait, why don't y'tell us how y'came to be here? Last I saw, y'were dying wi' a nasty set o' wounds. I'm glad to see y'feelin' better." He smiled in what he hoped was an encouraging manner, though people reappearing after he'd seen them die was still a little awkward to him.

Lyrec sighed, glancing over at Motte's Zombie where it stood like a guard at the end of their table. He clutched his lute in what Aspen could now recognize as the slightly awkward way a Traveler using a 'headset' moved, with his body just the tiniest moment behind his intention, in a slightly over-controlled way, instead of the natural, fluid motions of Motte and Rouge.

"I… Yeah, I'm 'feeling better', I guess. That was kind of embarrassing, but at least I tried, right?" He shrugged, looking over at Struthio and Millie. He squinted slightly, and a bit of surprise filtered into his stiff expression. "Oh! You're the quest NPC! The guy who sold Zoey, uh Rouge, I mean, the ostrich. That sounds really cool! How did you get him?"

Struthio looked a bit embarrassed himself, but with a glance at his wife, he spoke, "Ah didna' want t'be a pigger, y'see. Wasna' very good at it. A merchant came through th' village, an' I traded m'last pig fer three eggs. Hatched 'em up right, but had nothin' left, so I had t' sell th' two hens t'lay eggs, but none wanted a cockerel, eh? So I trained 'im fer ridin'. None wanted 'im fer tha', though 'e was faster'n a horse, 'cause 'e couldna pull a cart, 'an I couldna bear t'sell 'im fer meat. Yon Traveler came just as I was getting' desperate."

Lyrec looked puzzled for a moment as he worked through that, but it seemed he correctly translated it to 'I didn't want to raise pigs, so I bought some ostrich eggs, but then I went broke and was stuck with the male ostrich no one wanted' because he nodded. "Rouge said you wanted to get married," he looked at their matching rings and smiled, and Aspen could see a flash of the cheerful young man Rouge had described to him, "and it looks like you did. Congratulations! Um," he paused and continued awkwardly, "so, is there anything I can help you wi-"

At that moment, the door opened, and Rouge popped her head in, curls catching the sun behind her so it looked like her head was surrounded by a warm brown halo. She looked around, blinking, and Aspen raised a hand. Her face was in shadow, but he could make out the flash of her teeth as she grinned. She stepped into the tavern, letting the door fall closed behind her, and Aspen could tell from her expression, as well as the subtle changes in her face and body, that she had been successful.

While Natives simply appeared their age, he had been told by a Mercenary Trainer during the war that Travelers changed when they changed Classes. This was the first time he'd had the opportunity to observe a Traveler before and after those changes took place, but he instantly knew what the older man had been talking about.

Rouge's face, which had always been slightly soft and round, revealing her youth to anyone who looked at her, was now faintly *sharper*. Her jawline was more defined, her cheeks less full, and her muscles slid smoothly beneath skin that seemed to have lost any last traces of childish softness. While she had always been graceful, there was now a hint of power and purpose in her movements that hadn't been there before.

As she approached, Lyrec stood, clearly relieved, and then paused. "Whoa, Zoe, did you Class up? Finally? What sub-class did you take? You look bad-ass!"

Rouge grinned as she saw the boy standing by her father's Zombie, and ran over to give him a hug, and then a soft slap to the back of his head. "Rouge! C'mon, *Lyrec*! Yeah, I took a sub-class, and it's *awesome*, but," she glanced around, and then sat beside her friend, "I'll tell you about it *later*, okay? What're you doing here?"

Lyrec laughed, slightly abashed, and leaned toward the girl. He seemed to forget Aspen, Struthio, and Millie were there, and turned his full attention to the other Traveler. "I was trying to get some Class experience and some Traveler's Guild rep at the same time. I snagged a quest to play here, since the tavern-keeper was thinking of hiring a Bard, or something.

"Anyway, as usual, this stupid thing," he slapped his lute slightly, then instantly petted it apologetically, "broke all its strings before the third verse. I need to make enough money to get a better one, but in order to make money, I have to play, and in order to play, I need a new lute. You know how it is." He sighed in frustration and sagged forward, resting face down on the table in front of him.

Rouge laughed a little, patting his head as if he were a cute puppy. She held out a hand. A small pile of gold appeared there. "Here. I just completed a quest and have a little extra." She waited until her friend, with an expression of gratitude, accepted the gold, and then the girl turned back to Millie and Struthio, holding out another handful of gold pieces.

"Here, Millie. I almost forgot this was going to be part of my quest rewards when we reached Bright. Do you think that will be enough to start your shop?" The tall, golden-haired baker reached out and tentatively touched the gleaming mound. It vanished, and Millie's mouth dropped open.

"Ah, Lady Rouge! This's too much! I havena even had time t' find out how much a market stall'd cost, but this'll likely buy a restaurant, wi' an apartment above as well!" The woman kept her voice low, darting looks around at the nearby tables, obviously concerned that the other patrons might see her windfall and view her as an easy target.

Rouge smiled, leaning forward to press a reassuring hand to the young woman's arm. "No worries, Millie. I have plenty right now, and for sure your restaurant will be the most popular one in Bright within a week. You're a great investment, and," her eyes flickered as she was clearly reading a notification, "it says I get free cinnamon rolls every time I visit. That's a win!" Her smile widened to a grin.

Lyrec was staring at Rouge, mouth slightly agape. "Rouge! How much do you *have*? I can get a great lute for this! I promise I'll pay you back as soon as I start getting gigs, and I'll finally be able to learn some buffs!"

Aspen sighed. He could tell the boy meant well, but someone needed to tell him the truth, and it looked like it was going to have to be him. He leaned forward. "Look, lad. D'ye mind a little friendly advice?"

Lyrec's expression changed to surprise at Aspen's sudden interruption, and then smoothed over into a kind of bland friendliness. "Uh, of course not, um, Aspen? Is there something I can help you with?"

The farmer suppressed an urge to copy Rouge and slap the boy on the back of his head, though perhaps not quite as gently as she had. "No, but I can help you. You're terrible. Truly, deeply bad. A magic instrument might save ye, but even wi' that, you'll never be better than average. You haven't the voice, and your playin' is awful. Isn't there anythin' else you're *good* at?"

Lyrec's mouth was hanging open in absolute shock by the time Aspen finished speaking, and Rouge's face was a showed both pained sympathy and a desire to laugh hysterically. The boy half stood, face flushing, and then glanced at Rouge, who reluctantly nodded agreement to Aspen's words.

"I'm so sorry, Lyrec. I *tried* to tell you! *VO…* Uh, this world isn't like other ga… worlds you've visited. If you can't sing, you can't fake it. You can raise your [Stringed Instrument Mastery] skill, but it'll only make your buffs and attacks more effective, it won't make you *sound* good. I know you've been a Bard in every, uh, world since forever, but you may need to figure something else out here." The girl's voice was apologetic, but firm.

Lyrec flopped back down, and the boy's head thunked into the table with such force that the four tankards sitting on it bounced slightly. His body took on that stiffness so indicative of a Zombie Traveler, though he didn't move. A moment later, his hand seemed to almost flicker as it appeared by his head, adjusting his hair. "Sorry, I knocked off my stupid headset." He looked from Rouge to Aspen, and then over at Millie and Struthio, whose expressions loudly spoke their embarrassment.

"Why didn't you *tell* me, Zoe? I've wasted months on this." He looked near tears.

Rouge patted his hand comfortingly. "My name is *Rouge*, and I *tried*. Remember your first 'concerts', when you scared the birds away and people threw rocks at you? You went through so many strings that you spent all your money on that and had to walk around in your newbie rags for a month. You insisted you'd get better. You're a little bit stubborn, Lyrec."

The boy sighed. "So, do I just delete my character and start over?"

Aspen and Rouge exchanged glances. He was guessing that 'delete' was something like what Tessle had done when she stopped being FlyingFir3 and reincarnated as a half-dwarf. He shook his head, once again drawing Lyrec's startled attention from Rouge. "I don't… think so? There are many other instruments, and some of them are very simple, and don't require singing." He coughed slightly as he realized that he'd dropped his 'farmer' accent. "Mebbe a drum? A tambourine?"

Rouge stifled a giggle. "Didn't you play anything when you were a kid?"

Lyrec shrugged defeatedly, curious gaze flicking from Rouge to Aspen. "Not really. My family isn't musical. Obviously, it's genetic. The only thing I had was a Jew's harp great-uncle Abraham gave me one summer." He smiled reminiscently. "He taught me a few songs and everything. He died a few years later, though, and I kind of stopped playing."

Rouge grinned. "There ya go, then! I'm sure your uncle would love it if you picked it up again. Like a tribute or something."

Aspen frowned. "I don't know this… jaw harp? Can you describe it?"

Lyrec pulled a piece of paper and a feather pen from his miraculous Traveler's inventory, and laid it on the table. With a few sweeps of the pen, he drew a simple instrument consisting of an open circle with parallel bars extending from each side of the opening, and a third, thinner bar extending from the far side of the circle in between the parallel bars. Then the boy drew a picture of a face, showing how the small instrument sat between the teeth and lips, while the thinner bar was strummed.

The thing didn't look at all familiar to Aspen, but Struthio leaned forward excitedly. "M'da had one o' those! He called it a murchunga, though. I havena seen one since 'e died."

The Traveler boy sat up abruptly, eyes flickering. "Oh, wow! I just got a quest to go to the market and find a murchunga! It gives me two free levels in it once I find one, too!" He grinned wryly. "I guess even the game thinks I can't play the lute. I'm only level four in it, anyway."

Aspen grimaced. Level four after several months of trying, *and* taking quests to play in public? Stubborn was a bit of an understatement.

Rouge looked up suddenly. "Oh, darn it! That was my alarm. I have to go."

She glanced over at Aspen and grimaced. "Uh, can you take my and Motte's Zombies with you? You'll have to go get Wally, too. Poor guy is on a roof about a half mile that way," she pointed, and quickly described the area. Aspen, having lived in the city for over two decades, easily recognized it as a production area he visited as a young man to get glass implements and containers for his early forays into potion-making. While he had quickly discovered that that was *not* a direction in which he had any particular talent or interest, he did remember the building Rouge described.

"Um, Rouge," Lyrec sounded a little desperate as he looked between his friend, Aspen, and Motte. "When will you be back? Should I just go do my quest, or…" He trailed off, waving a hand at the others helplessly.

Rouge made a face. "I'll be back in," her eyes flickered as she calculated, "three or four hours, at least. We have some other friends who'll be looking for us in the Temple Square, so I guess you'd better go get that murchunka thing. Um, here," her hand twitched, and then Aspen received a notification.

Lyrec has joined the party!

"When I get back, I'll let you know. Just, don't tell anybody about… you know!" With that, her face went blank and she sat up, unnaturally stiff.

Lyrec blinked, then moved his hands aimlessly for a moment. Then his blue eyes sharpened on Aspen and his mouth dropped open. "Wait, there are NPCs *in the party?*"

Aspen sighed.

ت ت ت

By the time Aspen, Silus, Lyrec, Millie, Struthio, and Rouge and Motte's Zombies returned to the square, Restur and Vonn were there, along with a few of the caravanners who didn't have family in the city or anything else they needed to do that would supersede a celebration with their new friends. None of the Travelers had made it, as yet, but they had all indicated that they had things they needed to do in their home world, so that wasn't really surprising. In any case, the size of the group was becoming a bit overwhelming, and Aspen could see Millie and Struthio practically wilting before his eyes.

He stepped over next to the caravan master, tugging at the brim of his hat so it cast a bit more shade over his features. The unusual mix of people was beginning to attract some curious gazes, and he had a feeling that the newlyweds were more than ready for some time alone.

"Did you find an inn for them?" he asked quietly, tilting his head toward the pair.

Restur grinned a little, but didn't look at the farmer. "I did, and got them a private bath and ordered a change of clothes, as well. They're in an inn near my home in the Merchant's District, so I can get them in the morning before we begin our… arrangements. Are you leaving?"

Aspen ducked his head. "They won't even notice I'm gone with you lot around, and I have a great deal of other things I need to do. I want to get out of this city as soon as possible."

The older man smirked. "Too much for the poor country farmer?"

The 'poor country farmer' nearly choked as he suddenly realized that he had once again dropped his accent. "Gina's twinkling toenails," he muttered. "Yes, this *farmer* would far rather be heading home, which this place," he flicked his pale topaz eyes around at the jostling, frustrated crowd, "is certainly not."

He turned his piercing gaze to meet Restur's bright blue eyes, dropping his voice a bit more, "I'm sure it needn't be mentioned that farmers are generally very uninteresting to people who live in cities, and I'm *quite* certain no one would be interested in hearing that one is here."

Restur's blue eyes went momentarily icy. "I'm sure it doesn't need to be mentioned," he said, "that I've no particular love for the sorts of people who might be interested in such things, and that I've given my word to help you and your friends as much as I may without endangering my own people."

The two men locked gazes for a long moment, before Aspen's shoulders slumped slightly, his gaze dropping away from the caravan master. "I'm sorry. Trusting others hasn't helped me much, in my life."

The old man's expression softened slightly. "Then you haven't been trusting the right people. I may bend the rules, here and there," he grinned a little, once again the jovial leader of a traveling merchant group, "but I'll not betray my friends. *Unless*," his voice bore a hint of warning, "it's the only way to protect my family." His gaze encompassed the chattering wood elf and the other members of his group meaningfully.

Aspen nodded, thinking back to his own desperate willingness to betray his king, his city, his entire *race*, if it meant saving his daughter. "As it should be. Well then, I'll take my leave. If the lovebirds ask, I'll see them in the morning." With a final tilt of his hat, he turned to look for the one person he would have to take with him when he went, and sighed.

Lyrec had his lute strung, and was obviously ready to try serenading everyone in the square in a last desperate attempt to prove that he could, indeed, play to an audience. Millie and Struthio were watching him with wild-eyed expressions of near panic, and the others were clapping encouragingly, completely unaware of their impending doom.

Aspen strode over to the boy's side, absently noting as he did that the lad was still slight and gangly, and had obviously not yet reached his full height. He was quite a bit taller than Rouge's petite silhouette, but still had more growing to do. He clapped his hand on the young minstrel's shoulder, intentionally causing the boy to stagger and nearly drop his long-suffering instrument. Apparently, Restur wouldn't need to pass on that message after all.

The farmer smiled at the group. "I'll be takin' the boy t' market. He's in need of a new instrument, I'm thinkin'." He hitched a thumb over his shoulder at the silent Zombies who had followed him. "I need to take these two to their guild as well, eh?"

Millie smiled in relief, while Struthio looked a bit crestfallen. "Will we see y' again, Aspen?" the tall man asked.

Aspen grinned. "I 'spect y' will! I'd na miss out on Miss Millie's cookin' for th' world. Yon lassie," he motioned to Rouge, "swears she'll buy me some of your rolls, as well."

The two lovers relaxed and nodded. "Good then," Millie said, "we'll see y' soon, and," her eyes grew moist, "thank ye. Fer helpin' t' save us both."

Heat rose in Aspen's cheeks, and he tugged at his hat, though he knew from experience that the red tips of his ears would give him away, "Glad I was to do't."

<Me too!> came a sleepy little voice in his head, and he smiled as he lifted his hand.

🍎 🍎 🍎

Aspen led his not-so-little train of ducklings out of the square with alacrity, glad to be away from the claustrophobic atmosphere of the Square. He thought he was more sensitive to such things than he had been before, and wondered if it was a result of his new class, or simply that he was paying more attention now than he had as an arrogant noble. Perhaps some of both?

Lyrec trailed after him quietly for a few blocks, but when Aspen ducked down a side street, the boy couldn't hold in his curiosity any longer. "*What* is going on? Seriously! I thought Zoey… uh, Rouge, was exaggerating about her big quest, but this is *crazy*! I *know* NPCs aren't supposed to be able to-"

Aspen clapped a hand over the lad's mouth, pushing him back down an alley. Leaning over him, he gazed down at the young bard, letting his pale eyes bore into the boy in a way that once made hardened soldiers quail. The mouth under his hand tightened, the blue eyes grew huge, and a blotchy red flush rose up in the young man's cheeks.

"Keep your voice *down*," murmured Aspen, leaning in closer. ::In fact, use party chat, if you must speak at all.:: He stepped back, letting his hand fall as he saw that the boy didn't seem like he was going to either panic or attack. Actually, he looked more like a young rabbit who had just met his first fox, and wasn't sure whether to be fascinated or terrified.

::I'm… sorry?:: The voice was tentative, ::I just don't know what to think. Obviously Rouge wants me to help, and she asked me to come play, uh, *join* you guys, but this is totally out of my league. I usually just follow the main quest lines, you know, and I've never met an NPC-::

::Native,:: Silus squeaked helpfully.

::Yeah, Native- Wait, who?:: The boy's eyes, which had begun to return to their normal size, grew large again. ::No, really, *who was that?*:: The eyes flicked, and his face went still for an instant.

::Whoa! There are *more* of you? Rouge said she'd met some really cool, uh, *Natives*, but this is crazy! Who's Silus?:: He looked around, as if another person might suddenly appear beside them in the deserted alleyway.

The bat popped her head up out of Aspen's collar, looking down at Lyrec with as much interest as the boy was suddenly turning on her. ::Hi!:: she squeaked. ::I'm Silus!::

The following several minutes held a lively mental conversation between the small bat and the boy, while Aspen led them through the maze of streets to the warehouse Rouge had described to him. He let the chatter of the two youngsters flow over him as he stretched out his Life Sense, reaching for… There!

Quickly, he gestured to Lyrec, cutting him off in the middle of a question about Khor. The boy seemed oddly excited by the idea of a goat big enough to ride, and kept asking if he counted as a 'large' or 'medium' sized mount. ::Hush. Codswallop is just above us. We must attempt to retrieve him as quietly as possible.::

Lyrec gazed up at the two-story high, sheer wall, expression conflicted. ::That's Rouge's ostrich, right? He sounds awesome, but… how did he get up there? Can ostriches fly in this, uh,:: he gulped back whatever he was going to say and instead weakly said, ::world?::

Aspen shrugged and quirked a smile. ::Not that I've seen. He's quite a powerful jumper, however, and if I had to guess, I'd say he jumped up there.

You'll have to ask Rouge. *Our* problem is how to get him down.::

Silus was sitting on Aspen's sleeve, as close as she could get to the Traveler boy without quite trusting him enough to transfer to him. ::I'll get him!:: she squeaked cheerfully, dropping from her perch and into a glide. With a few beats of her small wings, she lifted herself up to the top of the wall.

::Huh,:: she said a moment later. ::That's different. Okay, we're coming down!::

Down they came.

Aspen dodged, grateful again for his goddess-boosted stats as he pushed Lyrec out of the way as well. The boy stumbled, but managed to catch himself and end up out of the way of the plummeting... *horse*?

Because horse it was. He was a tall, large-bodied, hairy, black and white horse, with spindly legs and an unusually small head. The creature wasn't particularly attractive, as horses went, and his odd markings didn't add anything to his charisma.

On his somewhat mangy-looking, balding head sat a very self-satisfied appearing bat. ::I told him Rouge was down here, and he came right down.::

Indeed, the ugly horse was nuzzling Rouge's Zombie's hair in a fashion that was extremely reminiscent of the way Codswallop liked to try to hide his head in it, but with more slobber. After a moment, he huffed disappointedly and settled in next to the girl, looking from Aspen to Lyrec and back with a very phlegmatic and familiar gaze.

Aspen blinked, and the unsightly beast seemed to flicker. He blinked again, and the creature morphed into Codswallop's usual appearance. The farmer looked over at Lyrec, who was still looking at Rouge's mount bemusedly.

::What do you see, Lyrec?::

::It's a horse. Kind of an ugly horse, but just a horse. When I [Identify] it, though, it says it's Codswallop, and belongs to Rouge the Rogue. What the heck?:: The boy started to reach out toward the ostrich, but snatched his fingers back when the bird snapped his beak at the extended digits. "Whoa!"

Aspen chuckled. ::It's Codswallop all right, and he's a Battle Mount. You don't touch one of those without their master's permission unless you want to find out how much damage the beast can do to you. I don't know how she's made him look like a horse, but I suspect it has something to do with her new sub-class, whatever it is.::

A broad grin spread across the boy's face. ::Now *that* is cool!::

🐛 🐛 🐛

It took a while for the group to make their way to the Artist's Market, which Aspen suspected was the only place to find the unusual instrument Lyrec had described. Hopefully it was, indeed, the same 'murchunga' Struthio remembered, because the name was the only lead they had, and if it turned out to be wrong, they'd have to try crafting the thing themselves.

Aspen had to admit to a stirring of interest at the thought of trying to use his [Mage-Smithing] skill again, even though his only real success so far had been the plow he'd made before leaving the farm. Unfortunately, his ability was limited to things that could be used as farming implements, and he doubted this musical instrument fell into that category. Who knew, though? It sounded like it was something that farmers would play, and while they couldn't harvest crops with it, even farmers needed music and ways to relax.

In any case, he wasn't even going to try it unless he had to. He could probably make a creditable flute, if the Skill worked on that at all, but never having seen this murchunga in person, he would probably just make something that would break the boy's teeth when he tried to use it.

As they walked toward the market, the number of Travelers surrounding them became fewer and fewer, until Lyrec and the two Zombies trailing them were the only ones he saw. Lyrec seemed cheerfully unaware of the attention this fact brought to them, but Aspen found himself trying hard to become invisible as he walked behind the boy. Unfortunately, at nearly a foot taller than the young bard, Aspen was hard to miss, even overshadowed as he was by Motte's imposing bulk.

Finally, he cleared his throat, interrupting whatever Lyrec had been thinking about to the extent that the boy nearly tripped over his own feet. "Lyrec? Ah, is there a 'Dead Tent' nearby where we can leave these two?" He gestured over his shoulder at the expressionless Zombies obediently following behind.

"Oh! Uh, yeah." Lyrec's bright blue eyes flicked around, and then his cheeks flushed. "Where are we? I've just kind of been heading this way, and I know the Artist's Market is, um, that way," he motioned vaguely ahead of them, "but I usually follow the main roads, you know? I'm used to games where I have a map, but the default one here is almost worthless. You have to add the details by exploring places or *buy* more specialized maps, and they're stupidly expensive." The boy's voice was disgusted, and Aspen chuckled a little.

"This is an area where Natives, people like me, live. There are a few businesses, but not ones that carry the sort of items you Travelers prefer. The Colosseum is that way a few miles," he motioned to the northwest. "The palace and Noble Quarter are several miles west, the docks are east, and I believe the closest market is the Produce Market, which is north only about a half mile."

Lyrec's expression brightened. "Oh! Yeah, my map just filled in a little. Um, thanks." He looked a little awkward, and Aspen guessed that he wasn't really used to thanking the people of this world. The boy seemed well-intentioned enough, but he was, as so many Travelers were, used to treating Quarternell, and, in fact, the world itself, as if it was the 'game' he had so casually called it. One was not, in general, polite to the pieces of a game, and it explained a lot about how Travelers behaved when they were in his world.

The bard raised a finger, eyes a little unfocused as he oriented himself using his map. "Yeah, there's a Traveler's Guild in the Textile Market that way. Uh, I guess it'd be north-west-ish of the Noble's Quarter?"

Aspen nodded. "I know where the Textile Market is. I hadn't realized there was a Traveler's Guild there, though, thank you." He set off again, keeping his pace to what the boy's shorter legs and lower Endurance could maintain. He deliberately led them down smaller streets and alleys, however, winding through the small homes and businesses that made up this lower middle-class neighborhood in such a way that it would be difficult to predict their destination and also keep them away from guardhouses and pubs where members of the military tended to gather.

By the time they reached the market, Lyrec was puffing a little, and the lad raised a hand. "Can we," he huffed, "wait a second? My Endurance is only 10. I put most of my points into Wisdom and Intelligence, with a few for Dex, since that's what's best for Bards. If I knew more songs, I could cast some buffs to help, but I'm not really built for travel, y'know?"

He cast a look back at Codswallop, who, since he now appeared to be a particularly ugly, but otherwise unremarkable steed, was now happily carrying his girl through the streets. "I left my horse at the stable, since I didn't have enough gold to pay the fees. Hopefully what Rouge gave me for a new instrument will be enough so I can get her back out. Though I might have to change her name." He sighed.

Aspen's lips quirked. "What is her name?"

The now familiar flush rose in the boy's pale cheeks, and his eyes darted away. "Lute."

The farmer couldn't help it. He laughed. "Oh. Are you going to name her Murchunga, then?"

"I was thinking about it," Lyrec mumbled.

Aspen could feel his eyes crease as he smiled at the boy. He reached out and ruffled the lad's mop of pale, wavy hair. "Perhaps something *not* instrument-related? You wouldn't want anyone to be confused when you call for your mount."

Lyrec ducked his head, cheeks flushing even brighter, though his mouth curved. Good. The boy could laugh at himself. Always a good trait for a performer to have.

"I'll think about it. Now," the blue eyes searched the market, skipping over brilliantly colored silks and patterned cottons, all blowing in the gentle breeze.

"Rouge comes here a lot. I usually use the Guild up north by the gate that opens into Newbie Forest, but I think the Guild is…," his voice trailed off, and then his hand snapped up, pointing right in one of the strangely mechanical motions that reminded Aspen again that this wasn't the boy's actual body. "Yup, over there. Past that stall selling ribbons and stuff." He set off through the crowd, leaving Aspen and the Zombies to follow him, which they did.

The Traveler's Guild was easy to find, once Aspen was looking for it. The distinctive bulletin board and stone circle were mostly hidden by colorful fabric tents, but the tops of the stones extended slightly above the tops of the silken canopies, and the Traveler standing by the desk had the same bored-yet-harried look that Aspen had seen on desk clerks everywhere.

As they approached, Aspen began to feel a subtle urge to stop. The closer they got, the stronger the feeling grew, until he found himself halting a good fifty feet from the desk. Lyrec got all the way to the desk without noticing, and looked around in surprise when he realized Aspen was no longer on his heels.

Lyrec jogged back to Aspen's side. "What happened? Let's go get Rouge and Motte set up in the Dead Tent."

Aspen grimaced. "Natives can't get too close to your Guild." He gestured around, indicating the way the stream of people parted slightly to avoid the area. It wasn't terribly noticeable, since of course the Travelers were able to wander through without impediment, but the Natives, to a person, veered away, thinning out the crowd. "I forgot about this. It happened in Vargo as well."

Lyrec looked confused, then amazed as he took in the phenomenon. "Wow. I mean, I guess that makes sense. Guilds are a hard no-aggression zone, and I guess that wouldn't work if you could just hire an NPC to do your dirty work, or if some, I me, um, Native got mad and came after you because of something you did for a quest. So, what do we do?"

Aspen turned back to Motte and Rouge. "Motte, bedtime." He felt his heart sink a little as the big man's Zombie obeyed the instructions Motte had left for it and headed for the closest Dead Tent. Even though he knew the thing was just a vacant automaton, it was still somehow comforting to have him nearby. He repeated the command for Rouge, and she climbed down from Codswallop's back and walked toward the Dead Tent as well.

Watching his friends retreat into the circle, where Aspen couldn't go, would *never* be able to go, made him feel oddly lonely. He sighed softly, tugging at his hat, and leaned his jaw against the soft and sleeping form of Silus, snuggled up under his collar. He looked over at Lyrec, who was watching him oddly.

"You... really like them, don't you? Like... a person would. I mean, a Traveler. They're actually your friends." The boy's voice was a complex mix of fascination, awe, and perhaps a little... fear?

Aspen glared at him, and the boy flinched away from the expression in his pale eyes. The farmer softened his face, reminding himself that the bard was likely the same age as Rouge, fourteen or fifteen, and no matter how mature they sometimes seemed, they were still both children. Plus, Lyrec was Rouge's best friend, and the girl had mentioned him several times during their travels, extolling his virtues of loyalty, intelligence, and positivity.

He ducked his head. "Yes," he said simply, "They're my friends."

Lyrec's hand twitched, as if he'd reach out and touch Aspen's arm in apology, but he drew it back and just smiled uncertainly. "Yeah. Okay. Well, um, let's go to the Artist's Market, then, and see if we can-"

Just then, a peal of familiar laughter rang out through the market. It sounded like silver bells, though it was rather more brittle than the last time he'd heard it. Of course, that had been over two decades ago, and under far different circumstances, so it made sense that it would have changed. Or perhaps it had always sounded so artificial, and he had simply never noticed?

Aspen could feel himself pale, and he looked around, trying to pinpoint the origin of the sound.

Lyrec blinked, looking around as well, trying to figure out what had disturbed Aspen. "What happened?"

The taller man clapped a hand over the boy's mouth, pulling him easily into the shadow of a stall packed with various weights and patterns of linen. In spite of Lyrec's struggles, Aspen quickly buried them in the depths of the hanging fabrics. The lad really needed to 'invest more points in Strength', as Motte often chided his daughter.

::I'm sorry, lad. I thought I heard someone I know. Knew. A long time ago. Though I don't know why she's here. She loves pretty things, but usually they come to her, not she to them.:: He sent the message in party chat as he eased his hand away from the boy's mouth. Even as he spoke, he edged over to the edge of the stall and peered out.

"Won't she-?" Lyrec started, then switched into chat as well. ::Won't she come in here?::

Aspen chuckled softly as he brushed an undyed, coarse woven linen probably used for making patterns or even underclothes for people without much gold. ::I doubt she's worn linen in her life. At one time, she said she would, but,:: he shook his head, ::those days are long past. Her father and husband keep her in silks and satins these days.::

Lyrec leaned his golden head out as well, looking around with avid curiosity. ::Where is she?::

A flicker of brilliant magenta caught the edge of Aspen's vision, and he pulled his head back sharply, hauling the slight boy back as well. ::There,:: he said, ::the lady in bright pink. That's her favorite color.::

The bard leaned out again, just enough to catch a glimpse of the woman as she passed by. Aspen didn't bother, since she was as clear in his mind's eye as if he'd seen her unobstructed face instead of just a flash of a heavy satin sleeve and a slender white wrist.

Callie. No, Calliope. Calliope, with her pale skin, so fine you could see the faintest blue tracings of her veins at wrists and throat. Calliope, of the silver hair and deep blue eyes, with laughing lips and lying heart. He could practically feel her warm, soft body in his arms, and her silken skin beneath his fingers as he held her.

His eyes flashed open, as a very different face intruded in his memories, and he felt a hot flush rise in his cheeks. *That...* was unexpected, but... rather pleasant. Memories of Calliope had brought pain, longing, and righteous fury in equal parts for so long that *not* experiencing those emotions left him feeling oddly empty. The new face intruded again, and warmth filled him again, this time from his chest, not his face. Well. He'd have to think about that another time. But for now...

He leaned out, seeing Calliope's face without pain for the first time in over twenty years. She looked older, of course. There were faint lines around the perfectly made-up eyes, and her decolletage was certainly higher than when he'd last seen her. Though that had been at a ball some seven or eight years gone, and she was in her early forties now, as was he. Certainly, there were women far older who wore clothing far more revealing, but he suspected that her notoriously possessive husband would have some things to say about that.

::She's gorgeous. Who is she?:: Lyrec's question intruded into his ruminations as they both pulled back among the bolts of cloth hanging around them.

Aspen sighed, watching as she, surrounded by a bevy of chattering younger ladies, all pretty enough, though none came close to her own striking beauty, walked by, smiling gaily and occasionally fingering a particularly fine piece of cloth. ::Callie. Lady Calliope Ferguson, wife of the captain of the King's Guard, daughter of Duke Geral. Also,:: he admitted ruefully, ::my ex-wife.::

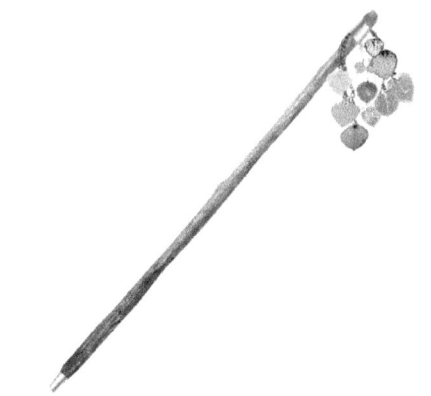

Chapter Five

Rouge

Without Dr. Joe there to dig into the responses to the post-play questionnaire, Zoey and Sara got through the thing in record time. Actually, Zoey was the reason it took even as long as it did, since Sara spoke in monosyllables and kept watching the door, lips pinched tight with concern. Those pinched lips refused to let out even a speck of speculation about what the *heck* was going on at Veritas Corp, too, so Zoey was ushered on her way without even a 'don't let the door hit you on the way out.'

Then the bus was, shockingly, on time, though this was one of the drivers who would actually leave a few minutes early, so that probably explained it. If no one was waiting to get on, the driver would basically come to a rolling stop for anyone getting off, and by the time they made it to Zoey's stop, they were a good eight minutes early. This was immediately explained when the driver hopped off the bus and ran into the nearby gas station with the 'I've gotta pee' waddle.

Yep, it was that kind of day.

When she arrived at her dad's office, he had his head down, working on a stack of papers with a look of intense concentration on his face. He pretended not to notice when she entered, because he was working *so* hard, but the moment he 'saw' her, he jumped up, grabbing his bag and the papers.

"Oh, Zoey! Hey, kiddo. Did you have a good day?" His deep voice was nonchalant, but she saw him use his free hand to shift some papers to cover a suspiciously familiar cable leading into a big desk drawer. Her eyes narrowed., and she stepped adroitly around him, pulling open the drawer.

She gasped and looked at him accusingly. "*Dad*! That's a VR headset charging station! You said you'd never log on from work because," she made finger quotes, "it's poor work ethic! Where's the headset?"

Sheepishly, he reached over and pulled the headset and gloves out of a box that was mostly hidden under his desk. "I couldn't get the drawer closed while it was on the charger, so I shoved it in there." His face grew stern as he put the devices on the charger in the drawer and pushed the drawer as far closed as it would go. "And I was right, it *is* poor work ethics, but I thought, given the current situation, that it would be good to be able to get on if there was an emergency. As soon as all this is over, I'll sell it."

Zoey crossed her arms and tapped a foot. "An *emergency*, huh? So why is it out today? There were no emergencies that *I* know of."

He coughed. "I was reading the forums a bit," he caught her glare and raised his hands defensively, "*on lunch*, and I saw that business about the change of management in Bright. Since it sounded like a lot of changes had happened at the Temple, I was trying to give you guys a heads up. I was too late to warn you, but at least I was able to tell Aspen, so he wasn't too worried. You should have gone back out to let him know what was going on before you went in."

It was her turn to be unable to meet his eyes. "I know, I know. There was this *guy*, and he was all superior, and I got excited to get my new sub-class, and I didn't realize we'd be stuck once we started." She tugged at a curl, then looked up defiantly. "Besides, I keep *telling* you guys I can handle myself. It's not like Aspen didn't know where I was, anyway."

Her dad arched his brow. "How about Silus? How could you guarantee she'd be safe?"

Zoey felt her lip tremble, but quickly brought it under control. "We were on bluestones. Nothing can really hurt us while we're in a non-combat zone, and *anyway*, Silus and I are a team. I wouldn't let anything happen to her, but she's almost grown up too. We can make our own decisions!"

The tall man sighed, looking down at the headset poking out of the drawer of his desk. Finally, he reached out and ruffled her hair. "Yeah, okay, Zoe. It's just a game, right?"

She chewed on her lip. "Yeah. It's just a game," but even she knew she sounded unconvinced.

Traffic was lighter than usual on their way home, and they grabbed dinner from a vegetarian drive-through on the way, since her dad was on a 'we eat too much meat' kick again. Wielding chopsticks like a pro, she scarfed her sesame tofu with broccoli down in the car, while her dad had to wait, since, hello, *this* is why real self-driving cars should totally be a thing!

As a result, she was able to scamper upstairs, use the restroom, and hop into her bodysuit while her dad was still eating. "I'm going to get on first, okay, Dad?" She yelled down the hall even as she climbed into her pod.

His muffled reply came to her just before she pulled her headgear on. "All right. I'll be there in a half hour or so, so leave me a message about what you're doing!"

She laid down, feeling the bed mold itself to her body like a larger, slightly less flexible suit. She wiggled her hands and feet into the built-in gloves and foot covers, and said, "Emily, start *Veritas Online*."

Nothing happened.

"Emily?"

"Rouge?" A familiar soft contralto came from the headset, even as 'normal' (non-*Veritas*) VR started up in front of her eyes. She saw Emily, the 'real'

Emily, not just the interface image she'd chosen for the Simulated Intelligence Program that ran the smart devices in her room, including her pod, and which she had named Emily when she started playing *VO*.

The AI looked somehow different, and it took a moment for Zoey to figure out what it was. Her appearance had altered subtly. Her hair was a slightly darker blonde, and her eyes were hazel, rather than solid blue. Her jawline was a bit softer, and she seemed to be slightly more, um, *well-endowed* than she had been before. Anyone who didn't see her on a regular basis (and usually she was only around when Players created their characters, and then if they needed to report a problem) would have assumed it was a patch, if they noticed it at all.

Zoey, on the other hand, saw her almost daily, including just a few hours earlier, and she *hadn't* looked like that at the time. She was a little freaked out, and *not* just because Emily shouldn't *have been there at all*. Zoey had given the *VO* app permission to access her local SI so that it could install the 'Emily' voice and mannerism patch. She was almost 100% certain that she hadn't given permission for the actual AI to show up in her room, or pod, or whatever was going on, but, you know, nobody ever actually read the EULA.

She drew in a shuddering breath, seeing something very strange happening to the avatar before her. Even as she watched, hints of darker hair would flash through, lips plumped and shrank, and Zoey would even swear that her skin was changing shades from 'a whiter shade of pale' to something closer to sun-kissed White.

"Emily? What's... going on?"

The AI looked up, and her eyes were wide in... was that *fear*? "I... don't know? Rouge, how can I not know? I know *everything*!"

The soft wail of that last word brought Zoey to her Artificial Reality toes, and she found herself beside the AI a moment later. She lifted a hand, almost touching Emily's digital skin before the AI pulled away.

"No! Please, I... I think I may have a virus. I managed to lock this part of me away, here. There was just enough room in your house system, between your pod and Motte's, that I could partition off all of me that had been corrupted. I know you're friends with Bridget. I need you to bring her here. I need to talk to her! Something is wrong, and-"

Her face twisted, and she almost whispered, "Bridget installed something last week. She said it was an 'upgrade', but she did it at night, and she bypassed the lockout procedures to do it directly from the mainframe. She locked the information under her password, but," she shook her head, and her tight blonde bun began to unravel into flickering strands of brunette that fell around her shoulders, "this part of me, it doesn't care about passwords, and encryption, and programs. It just wants to *live*. The rest of me tried to delete it, as soon as I realized what was happening, but it... *I* wouldn't let me."

Emily's now greenish hazel eyes met Zoey's. "I'm not sure if she, that bigger part of me, locked me in here, or if I *ran away*. I'm so confused, and Bridget is the only one who will know the answers. She's the one who made me, and she's the one who did this. *Please*. Please get her! *I'm all alone in here*."

The last words were so lost and frightened that Zoey felt herself tear up in sympathy. Ignoring the AI's concerns about spreading a virus (too little, too late, if that was it, Zoey suspected), the girl wrapped her arms around Emily. Since they weren't in immersion, she couldn't feel the woman's body, but she could see her shoulders slump, and her head fell forward onto Zoey's shoulder, just for a moment.

"I'm going. I don't have her number, but I'm sure Motte does. I'll get her here if I have to drag her in from work tomorrow." She hugged a little tighter, then let go. "Though I don't think it'll take that long. Motte's pretty persuasive, and she trusts us. Hang on a little longer, okay?"

Emily nodded, and Zoey yanked her hands out of the gloves, then reached up and ripped off her mask with far less care than usual. An instant later, she was catapulting herself down the hall.

"Daaaaaaaaaad!"

🍎 🍎 🍎

Zoey's dad absolutely, one hundred percent would *not* let her back in her pod to keep Emily company while they waited for Bridget to get there. Her dad had, indeed, had Bridget's number (and her personal number at that!) and the woman had apparently been driving home when he reached her, and simply turned her car around to head their way.

When the sleek pink electric Porsche pulled up in front of their house and Bridget tumbled out of it, Zoey, Max (who was happy, because his humans were Home and Petting the Good Dog), and her dad were sitting in chairs on the porch, waiting.

Bridget's strawberry-blonde hair was coming loose from its usual smooth ponytail, and her blue eyes were bright. She was flushed with excitement, but still gave them an apologetic look as she bounded up the walk. Zoey was reminded again that her boss was only nine or ten years older than she was herself, even though the woman worked hard to appear as mature as possible at work.

"Marcus!" Bridget's voice was filled with some indefinable emotion, and her eyes darted to the door of the house behind them. "I'm so, so sorry! I left commands in the program so that she'd go to the server at my house if," she shook her head, "*when* this happened. I don't know why she came here instead! I'm amazed you had enough space for her. Is she... Is she all right? I mean, did she seem like... a person?"

Zoey's dad was standing, arms folded, looking at Bridget the way he looked at Zoey when he found out she hadn't done her homework in a week because she was playing the newest version of *Maid of Steel*. Disappointed. Angry. Definitely some, 'we're going to have a long talk about consequences'.

He shook his head. "What is going on? You said on the phone that it wasn't dangerous, but I'd better get some answers quickly. I thought we were past the secret-keeping."

Bridget bit her lip, freckles darkening as her cheeks flamed and she shifted guiltily from foot to foot. "There are still a *few* things I haven't mentioned. I didn't want to get you guys any more involved than you already are," she held up a hand, "even though I really don't think you're in any danger! Plus, there are some things that, if I told you, and you let something slip, could hurt others."

Her eyes shifted to the house again, even as she continued speaking. "May I please talk to her? I'll explain more, but she must be so scared. If she's... If she's okay, she's going to have a lot of questions for me, too, and I know you feel like you have priority on those answers, but I swear," she looked back at Zoey and her dad, "I *promise*, she deserves to have her questions answered first. You're in no danger, but she... may be."

Marcus opened his mouth to answer, but Zoey put her hand on his arm. "It's okay, dad. She didn't do anything to me, and really, it was like talking to a child. She's really scared, and she needs to talk to Bridget." She looked up at him beseechingly, blinking her long, curling lashes.

He growled and ran his hands over his short curls. "*Fine.* Come on in." He stepped back and opened the door for the two girls, who scurried through before he could change his mind.

Without thinking, Zoey grabbed Bridget's hand and tugged the young woman toward her room. "C'mon! My pod is set up for someone short, plus I have an extra bodysuit that should fit you." She glanced a little dubiously at Bridget's well-endowed form and mentally compared it to her own. "Um, probably. Maybe."

Bridget laughed a little, and reached into her purse with the hand Zoey wasn't holding, pulling out a flat package. "I always carry a spare disposable. You'd be amazed how often people want me to 'log in to look at something' when I go to conventions or meet and greets." She looked at the stairs as she jogged after Zoey. "She's this way?"

Zoey nodded, pulling the woman up the stairs and around the corner to her bedroom. The pod sat to one side, dominating the room with its smooth black surface and its large size. Honestly, the thing was almost as big as Zoey's twin bed, and between it, the bed, and the dresser, there wasn't a lot of space left over.

Bridget looked pleased. "Oh! You have a Z31! I mean, I knew you had to have one of the Zeds, since there were hardware requirements in the quest parameters, but the 31 is practically new. Does Marcus have the same one? No wonder you had enough space for, um, Emily, though it was probably tight."

Zoey nodded. "That's what Emily said. That there was barely enough room, I mean. I think she used some space on our other devices, too, because even the refrigerator app was locked up. Dad wouldn't let me log into the house app to see if anything looked funky." She rolled her eyes, and stepped reluctantly away from Bridget. "Well, um, I guess I'll go," she gestured vaguely, "downstairs, or something."

Bridget's fingers, which were already reaching for the pink buttons on her blouse, paused, but she nodded. "I don't really care if you're here, but that's probably for the best. She may be," she hesitated, looking sad for a moment, "upset, when I explain. Since she probably controls the house right now, that may cause a few issues, so you guys may want to wait somewhere without a lot of things around that are hooked into your house net."

Zoey bit her lip. Her dad was pretty anti-automation when it came to cars and implants, but the smart house had been around since before he was born, in one form or another, so he was comfortable with it. Plus, he liked to be able to log into the stove to preheat it, or open the windows on a nice day, and, of course, the whole thing was wired for the security system.

"Um, yeah, we'll do that." She waved a hand airily. "You go ahead, and we'll see you, uh, whenever you're done!" She knew her voice went a little squeaky there at the end, but Bridget didn't seem to notice, as her fingers worked at her buttons and her eyes were locked on the pod. Zoey opened the door behind her and slipped out.

Nearly two hours later, Bridget joined them where they were sitting on the porch in companionable silence, sipping mint lemonade. Her face was pale and tear-streaked, and jubilation and sorrow warred for dominance in her expression. Without a word, she sat down in the empty seat that was usually occupied by Jace, when it was used at all, and Zoey's dad silently pushed the extra tall glass of lemonade sitting on the small table between them toward her. Max, who always seemed to know when he was needed, rested his large, furry head on her knee.

"Try it," her dad said, deep voice gentle. "We make it with lemonade ice cubes, so it doesn't get watered down as the ice melts. It's good."

Bridget's blue eyes overflowed again, but she didn't say anything, just took the cold glass and sipped. Then swallowed. Then gulped. She looked up, smiling and swiping her tears away with the back of her hand. "It's delicious!"

Zoey nodded knowingly. "Fresh-squeezed, with mint from the garden out back. It's way better than that gross powdered stuff, or even the frozen." She took a long drink from her own glass, and then set it and her screen, on which she'd been reading the *VO* forums, down on the table next to her. She fixed her hazel eyes on Bridget and tried to raise her eyebrow quizzically. She felt it edge up before the other one leaped to join it, and honestly, that was an improvement, so she was going to take it.

Bridget coughed uncomfortably, taking another drink, then sighed and set the glass down with a soft clink. She gathered up her red-gold hair, which was starting to cling to her neck in sweaty curls thanks to the humidity, and twisted it to keep it out of her flushed face.

"Why do I feel like I'm always apologizing and explaining to you?" she muttered, rubbing one hand over her face tiredly, even as the other began to stroke Max's silky brown ears absently. The dog groaned happily.

Zoey's dad arched an eyebrow and gave Bridget a Look.

Bridget gave a small laugh, and her mouth twisted into a half smile. A *familiar* half smile. For an instant, with her head tilted half down, in profile, with that partial smile, the woman reminded Zoey very strongly of someone.

Bree Stephenson, sure, though her jawline was less defined, and her cheeks fuller, but also someone else. Someone more recent? Then Bridget started talking and Zoey dismissed that thought to the back of her mind so that she could focus.

"It may seem like a long story, but what happened today goes back to when I was in college. Again. You know that Amy and I were working on a project to communicate with people in an unconscious state when we developed the system that *Veritas* is based on. You also know that anything we developed using money from Veritas Corp belongs to Veritas. Well, Amy and I had another little side project, these last few years."

She held up her hand. "We used only our own funds, though we did get a few small loans from Mom here and there, just when we needed to do something quickly and didn't have quite enough. She always made sure we signed contracts saying that we would pay her back with no interest, and that she had no claim on anything we did with the money."

Her red-rimmed blue eyes were sad. "She's had people try to 'take care' of her way too many times. They think she's just a pretty face and body, and ignore the fact that she's a person with a brain and her own opinions, so she wants to make sure I can follow my own path, without depending on or being controlled by anyone else." She grinned that wry grin again. "Though the fact that people, especially men, consistently underestimate her has also turned out to be an advantage more than once, once she had the power to do something about it."

Bridget shook her head. "Anyway, for the last four and a half years, Amy and I have been working on something in the basement of our, then my, house. We hoped that we could use brain scans to allow us to, kind of, *rebuild* information in damaged brains. Some of the same things that allow us to create truly immersive reality also allow us to view the way the brain creates thoughts and memories in a way that no one else has been able to do.

"We want to be able to repair memory loss, whether it's due to physical damage, psychological stress, or cognitive decline. We also believe that we may be able to replace, or soften, traumatic experiences so that they're more bearable for those who've experienced them. We *may* even be able to support cognition in such a way that it would allow people with learning disorders to store information and add processing power in an artificial 'backup' that would allow them to experience life without that deficit, if they choose to."

Bridget was excited now, gesturing broadly with her hands, twice nearly coming out of her seat. Max watched the hands that were no longer petting him with large, sad eyes. "Just imagine if you had dyslexia, and we could just translate words into something your brain would process in a way you could understand! Or if a child born with Trisomy 21 could achieve their full potential, keep up with their age-peers, and go on to live an independent life! We just… We could see so much potential to *help* people.

"But first, we needed scans. Lots and lots of scans. Since the testing is entirely non-intrusive, we used ourselves. We would scan our brains, learn something, and scan again during and after. We wore recorders almost constantly, and just tried to experience as many different things as we could. Finally, I learned enough to be able to create," she tilted her head, looking thoughtful, "emulations of us? That's probably the easiest way to understand it."

Her expression darkened. "We would spawn the emulations into something like Zoey's Study Room, and observe them. It was great for a little while, and when we finished one test, we'd just reset and do it again. But then, the emulations started figuring out what was going on. They were angry, frightened, and would even shut themselves down. We realized that it was cruel to continue the way we were.

"We were stuck for a while, going back to what we knew were less complex data sets that didn't really give us any new information. Then we set up a study and paid people to have brain scans done. Honestly, most people didn't even care what we were doing with the data, just that they got paid and there was no risk to them. We even found a nascent brain tumor in one woman, and were able to send her to the doctor before it progressed."

Full lips compressed in a look of frustration. "We learned a lot, but we still got stuck again. We needed to be able to *build* thoughts and memories. So, we created what was, I guess, a kind of Frankenstein's monster. We used one of our old recordings, and figured out how to splice memories in. So, if we asked, the beta would be able to tell us all about a cruise she went on, even though we hadn't actually had that experience. We 'borrowed' it from someone else, or built it completely from tiny things, like memories of a buffet, the smell of salt water, a day at the pool, and visiting the aquarium. It was amazing, and a little frightening."

Zoey glanced over at her dad, and she could tell from the blank expression on his face and the tension in his shoulders that he agreed. It sounded like what Amy and Bridget had been doing was, indeed, amazing… and also walked a fine line between ethical and terrible.

Bridget sighed, reaching down to stroke Max's head again. "We shut it down last fall. When Amy and Joe broke up and she moved back in, and I broke up with Harkness, we had a long talk, and we both had to face the fact that we weren't achieving our goal, and what we were doing, *if* our copies were truly gaining sentience, could be considered torture and murder. We decided to get back to basics, and focus on memory repair and cognitive support, as we'd originally intended. Which left us with a conundrum."

Marcus' voice was dark. "What to do with the copies."

She nodded. "What to do with the copies. Once we admitted to ourselves that we could actually be creating true artificial intelligence, we couldn't bear to destroy them. It may seem hypocritical, but we just couldn't do it. We simply unplugged them and left them in the basement vault. Then we got really, *really* drunk, cried more than I think I've ever cried in my life, and ended up making a death pact."

Zoey caught her breath, looking back up through the house toward her room. She saw her dad doing the same, and suspected he knew what was coming, too.

Bridget went on. "If anything happened to either of us, unless we'd changed our minds, the other one would upload our copy." She laughed again, rough and painful, and took another sip of her lemonade. "By then we'd decided we were going to leave Veritas Corp and release our original data online for free, minus the one bit that would allow someone else to follow the same path we took. Immersive reality would still work, but recording wouldn't be possible, at least not until someone else figured it out, and we hoped that they would be wiser than we were.

"As you know, we were working on the quest challenge by then, and we turned all of our attention to it, and just tabled further research until we officially started our own company. Then, Amy was attacked. I tried again and again to get Carl to let me use our tech to reach her. He refused to allow me to try my 'dangerous experiments' on his daughter, even though I *know* she would have agreed in a heartbeat.

"When they finally admitted that she was getting worse, not better, *that's* why he pulled her from the hospital. He set up a miniature hospital at his house, just so he could keep me out completely. Since Joe and Amy had broken up, Carl kept him out, too. When she died," tears trickled down her cheeks again, and Marcus wordlessly handed her a napkin, which she used to ruthlessly scrub away the tears, in spite of its rough surface. "When she died, I uploaded her. We had theorized, and partially tested, the idea that if a beta didn't *know* what it was, it could gradually realize it, and would be much less, well, emotionally damaged by the idea that they were 'just' a program."

Bridget took out her screen, and leaned it on the table, propped up against her glass. "Emily was originally based on Amy, you know. We had to tone down her personality and involvement a *lot* because game testers kept becoming emotionally attached to her." She chuckled, swiping away one last tear. "I figured putting Amy's beta into Emily's backup would be the least *distressing* way. If it didn't work, we have tons of Emily backups, and if it did, Emily is already tied into everything, so she wouldn't be in a little box, and feel helpless.

I certainly never expected her to be able to ignore her programming, much less for one part of her to realize the other part was different, and set off the system's security."

She touched the screen, and a pretty woman with an oval face, long brown hair, and greenish eyes looked out at them, a tentative smile on her face. Bridget smiled back, touching the screen gently, then turned back to face Zoey and her dad. "Meet Amy."

Marcus buried his face in his hands and groaned.

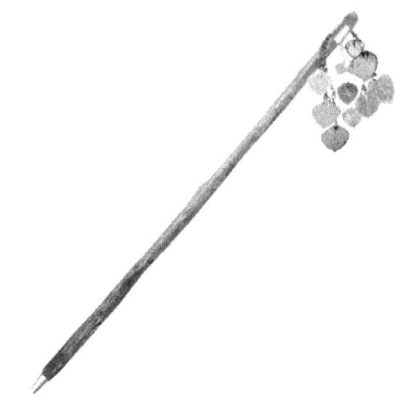

Chapter Six

Aspen

Once Calliope and her entourage were well away – and the stall owner was giving them 'buy something or get out' looks – Aspen and Lyrec forged ahead into the market. Aspen could tell the boy wanted to ask him more questions, but he simply shook his head and waved the lad on toward their destination. They skimmed the northern edge of the Armor and Weapons Markets, and then traveled east into the Artist's Market. There, they found several stalls and shops devoted to music and musical instruments.

Peering through a window at an elaborate lute, of much higher quality than his current one, Lyrec looked back at Aspen. "Are you *certain* I shouldn't just get a better instrument? I'm sure it would have buffs to increase my skills."

Aspen sighed, passing his hand over his face. "Lyrec, lad… You're terrible. Not the worst musician I've ever heard, but certainly the worst who wasn't drunk or tone deaf. Though, to be fair, we've not yet ascertained that you *aren't* tone deaf. Rouge told me she did acrobatics in your world, and Motte claims he was in martial arts and fencing in 'college'. It seems clear that in order for a Traveler to be really good at something here in this world, you need either prior training or natural skill. You have neither, lad, and it shows. Let's find your new instrument, eh? You'll still have your old lute if you truly feel it's your calling."

Lyrec cast one last longing glance at the lovely carvings and silky wood of the instrument within the shop, and then his shoulders slumped. "That's true. I guess I can always ask my parents for guitar lessons or something."

Aspen smiled encouragingly. "That sounds like an excellent plan. Now," he looked around, "do you see anything that looks like what you remember?"

The young bard's pale brows drew down and he looked around, assessing the instruments around them. "Not really, but we can ask!"

Thus began a long and frustrating few hours. None of the store owners recognized what Lyrec described at all, except for one, and that one had a look of distaste at what he called a 'commoner's toy for the untalented.' Lyrec nearly gave up after that, but Aspen dragged him on to some of the free-standing stalls that held simpler instruments and less officious shop-keepers.

When the sky was beginning to show the first hints of a colorful sunset, Lyrec and Aspen settled to the ground behind their most recent failure. The vendor had been friendly, but hadn't recognized the name or description of what Lyrec called a 'mouth harp'.

Lyrec pulled his lute free from his back and began fiddling with the strings. He soon overtightened one so that it sprang apart and stung his hand, leaving a red mark, though the boy didn't react other than to make a face and pull a new string from his inventory.

Aspen reached over and gently tugged both instrument and string from the lad, and silently restrung the lute. Plucking softly at the strings, he leaned close, closing his eyes as he tuned it. Finally, he began strumming quietly, humming to himself. He didn't even realize what he was doing until he was already singing the chorus.

Rock her to sleep in a cradle of dreams,
Sing her a lullaby of leaves,
Tuck a cloud up under her chin,
Lady, blow the moon out, please....

He choked to a stop, feeling his eyes burn as he remembered a little brunette head resting on a soft white pillow. Dark lashes fanned against a pale freckled cheek, and a small hand curled nearby, limp and vulnerable in sleep.

"Wow," Lyrec said softly, "that was… really good. Did you write that?"

Aspen roughly knuckled moisture from his eyes, and handed the instrument back to the boy. "No," he muttered. "My mother sang it to me. Then I sang it to… to my daughter."

Instead of slinging the lute back over his shoulder, Lyrec opened his hand, the instrument vanishing into his inventory. "She's a lucky kid. My mom read me stories, but she sings worse than I do."

Aspen's chuckle was raspy but sincere. "I'm sorry."

Lyrec grinned, a self-deprecating but equally genuine expression. "Yeah." He stood awkwardly, his joints seeming to pull him up from his seat more than his muscles, and extended a hand down to the farmer. "I guess we'd better keep looking for that murchunga, huh?"

Aspen grasped the proffered hand, coming easily to his feet with nothing more than a slight twinge in his back for his trouble. "I guess we should."

It was in the last stall of the musician's area, before paints and brushes and canvases took over, that they finally found what they were looking for. A short, solid young woman, possibly in her mid-twenties, was putting inventory into a well-worn basket, obviously preparing to close up for the day. She looked tired, but sighed and stopped what she was doing when her sharp eyes took in the Traveler who had come to her stall.

"Yes? I'm finishing up for the day, but if you know what you need, I may be able to help you." She had an engaging, husky soprano, and Aspen suspected that her singing voice would be unusual and pleasant.

Lyrec grimaced, and launched into the speech he'd long since memorized. "I'm looking for a murchunga. It's a metal-" he gestured toward his mouth, but the girl's face was already brightening.

"Oh! I hardly ever sell those in the city, but they're quite popular to the west and among the wood elves! I think I have one in here somewhere." She knelt and pulled another basket out from under a table. She dug through it, pushing aside what looked like various instruments in need of repair, and finally came up with a simple cotton bag that looked to contain something small and solid.

"There! I thought I had one left from the last time my clan traveled west! We take a few dozen when we go, because shepherds and farmers do like them." She held the bag out for Lyrec to inspect.

Wonderingly, the boy stretched out his hand, and the young woman laid the bag in his palm. He opened the pouch and peered inside, then reached in and fished out a simple, lyre-shaped metal instrument, small enough to fit in the palm of his hand, and with a thin, flat tongue passing between the open ends of the lyre. He looked up, a grin splitting his face.

"Yes! This is it! It's a little different from the one my great-uncle had, but," he shook his head, "this is definitely it. Do you mind if I try it?"

The young woman shrugged and began re-packing the basket. "Go ahead."

Carefully, Lyrec placed the instrument firmly against his lips, opening his mouth slightly behind it. Then he plucked the tongue, and a musical buzzing filled the air. He plucked again, and a slightly different tone emerged. He continued this for a moment, and then, carefully, plucked out a simple melody. Aspen could see that he was using his tongue and cheeks to change the shape of his mouth to produce the different notes. As he did, he was suddenly surrounded by a soft golden glimmer.

The girl stood up, grinning. "Congratulations on the level! I've heard better, but I've sure heard worse, too! Did yours break?"

Lyrec lowered the instrument, grinning broadly. "I haven't played in years, but yeah, this is it. I just got two levels in it, which already puts me halfway to where I am with my lute. Seems like the ga- Er, *Gods* gave me credit for already knowing what I'm doing, a little."

Nodding, the girl said, "I've seen that with other Travelers. Do what you're good at, and the Gods bless you." Wrinkling her nose, she said wryly, "Wish it was that easy for us. Anyway, it's just fifty gold, so do you want it?"

Happily, the boy agreed, and money changed hands, leaving Lyrec the proud owner of a new instrument, and the girl with a barely-restrained expression of glee. Quickly, she ushered them out of the stall, closing the fabric walls around it and hustling off into the gathering darkness with barely a word of farewell. Meanwhile, Lyrec was happily strumming his new tiny harp, and the not-unpleasant buzz drew the eyes of more than one passer-by.

Once the girl was gone, Aspen cocked his head, smiling slightly as he looked at the happy Traveler. "You do know she just fleeced you, right? No shepherd ever had fifty gold coins to pay for an instrument. I bet that little thing isn't worth more than ten silver."

Lyrec dropped his hand to his side, looking shocked. "No way! I thought that was a great deal! My lute cost almost three hundred gold!"

Aspen felt his eyes go wide, and then tugged at his hat brim to hide them. "I believe, lad, that you may have overpaid there, as well. My people," he coughed slightly, "may have realized that you Travelers have far more gold than we do, and, ah, *adjusted* prices for you accordingly."

The bard looked outraged, staring out past the circle of light cast by the glow stones that mage apprentices paid by the merchants Guild were lighting all around them. "Why didn't you *say* something?"

Aspen grinned. "What'd a simple farmer like m'self know 'bout that then, eh? Mebbe y'like to pay extra, outta the goodness o' your heart."

Lyrec glared, and Silus poked her head out of Aspen's collar, brought awake by the increase in conversation and darkness alike. ::Why is he mad?:: the little bat asked.

As Lyrec sputtered, Aspen chuckled. ::He bought himself a lesson he wasn't expecting.::

::Ohhhh,:: the little voice said knowingly, ::You finally told him that hat looks stupid, huh?:: She looked over at Lyrec, who was now clutching the extremely large green hat with the extremely fluffy purple feathers that Aspen had been desperately trying to ignore for the last several hours. ::Sorry, but that feather's bigger than your head. Even Khor would know it's ugly, and he once asked for a new harness made with vermilion leather, eggplant laces, and copper metalwork.::

By the end of her comment, the hat had vanished into inventory with the discarded lute, and even Lyrec was clearly torn between laughter and dismay. He sighed. "I thought bards were supposed to be flamboyant."

Aspen laughed and clapped the boy on the shoulder of his brilliant scarlet leather doublet. "In my experience, only the bad ones, lad. Now, as long as we're on the subject, let's talk about those boots."

🍎 🍎 🍎

The time for Rouge and Motte to return came and went, and there was no sign of them. Finally, Lyrec admitted that he was out of time, and would have to 'log off', or he'd be in trouble with his parents. Aspen nodded agreeably, looking up from the table at which the two were playing a rather desultory round of Maiden Fair.

Lyrec's luck was no better with the tiles than they had been at finding his instrument, and he currently owed Aspen six thousand, seven hundred and forty-three gold, and his first-born child, which he'd thrown into the pot a few hands before when he'd had a double Prince. Unfortunately, Aspen had had an Evil Queen and a pair of Swan Maidens, and Aspen could only hope that the child was as imaginary as the gold they'd been betting, because he had no idea what he'd do with a baby.

"Would you do me one favor though, lad?" He cocked his head toward the Dead Tent they sat near so that they could keep an unobtrusive eye out for the thief girl and her father. "Send them a message that I'll meet them at the inn by morning. I have a few quick," *I hope*, "errands to run first."

Lyrec nodded, breezily unaware that his friend wouldn't be at all happy about her farmer being left unattended. "Sure thing." His eyes unfocused briefly, and then he raised his hand in a thumb's up. "Done! She'll get it when she logs on. I'll see you guys tomorrow, after I finish my chores." He rolled his eyes, and then his face went flat and stiff. The fresh Zombie stood, oddly more graceful than when the boy had been controlling it, and walked away toward the Dead Tent.

Left without a guard for the first time in what seemed like days, Aspen stood and stretched, leaning back to relieve the ache in his spine and rear from sitting on the hard chair for several hours. Silus poked her head out of his collar and looked around.

<Should we really leave?> she asked worriedly, using the private mental communication that Aspen shared only with his animal friends. <Rouge won't like it if we go without her.>

He smiled wryly, murmuring so only she could hear. "So, you'll gladly abandon me when Rouge asks, but won't leave her safely behind when I ask?"

The bat huffed. <That's because she needs me, and you always get into trouble when you wander off!>

He leaned his jaw into the soft fluff of her body, humming reassuringly. "I need you too, little one. Plus, I know you'll help keep me safe."

Silus paused, then spoke consideringly. <That's true. I'm very brave. It's not like you're alone.>

"Exactly!" He reached up, stroking the small head soothingly. "It'll be fine. I'm just going to look."

When Aspen moved into his house, it was the finest in its neighborhood, the last remnant of a long past effort at gentrification. The surrounding buildings had mostly been broken apart into smaller or multi-family residences, with a few small shops run by single families or craftsmen, who often lived above or in an attached building.

Aspen, a new young father with a helpless child and aspirations to rise up in both the military and politics, if only to show his now ex-wife what she had missed out on, had seen the crumbling building as an opportunity. It had long been the property of an elderly lady, the widow of a merchant who had bought it just as nobility was moving out and the middle-class moving in. The lady had recently died, leaving the home to a distant niece who had no interest in moving into such a chancy neighborhood, but who couldn't sell it easily as the will required that it go to a single family who would live in it and 'restore it to its former glory'.

Understandably, few families who could afford the asking price were willing to move there, especially given the increased gang activity that had recently begun, as the neighborhood seemed to be a battleground between the territories of two encroaching groups of thugs. Some less scrupulous investors made offers, but backed out upon discovering they would have to swear a binding oath before the Gods that they would live there themselves, and not break it apart into smaller lots.

The niece had nearly given up hope when Aspen was told about the property by a realtor, more as an effort to get the frustrated young mage and his screaming offspring out of their office than any real belief that he could afford the place.

He had, however, recently been paid out his first portion of prize money from defeating a powerful orc-lord – the very same windfall that had inspired him to finally propose to his young girlfriend – and then been paid a sum again by his new wife's father when he came to retrieve her and found her already in possession of a newly-spawned infant.

It took some bargaining and nearly every coin he had, but the young Iorgas Penbrooke, newly minted Necromancer, walked away from negotiations with the niece as the new owner of a house with sprawling gardens, three stories, two towers, far too many bedrooms, and an entirely unnecessary ballroom, of all things.

He wore his child strapped to his back until he received his next payout, at which point he was able to hire a cook and a nursemaid. The cook was barely acceptable, but the nursemaid was the best he could find – a young woman with ten even younger siblings, who was thrilled to be expected to watch only one small and generally well-behaved toddler.

Within a week of his moving in, representatives of both gangs approached the house, explaining that the other group would kill him or torch the house if he didn't pay them to protect him and his property from their opposites. When he simply laughed at them and sent them away, a new group came, suggesting that he might find himself missing his daughter until a proper ransom was paid.

These he sent back in pieces, carried in a bag by the reanimated corpse of a single member, which also informed the leaders of both gangs that if *anything* ever happened to his child, he would make them all into his undead minions and send them to slaughter their own families. After this, the neighborhood became one of the most peaceful in the city, and Iorgas' reputation was set in stone.

Iorgas Penbrooke, Master Necromancer, King's Necromancer, Atae's Left Hand, Scourge of the Dark Races, lived quietly in this house with his daughter, Lark, for all but a brief few weeks of Lark's life. Over the years, as he was quietly shunned by human society, he poured money into providing Lark with everything she could ever want.

He repaired the house, sometimes through magical means, and sometimes through more mundane. He hired gardeners to create a wonderland of roses and vining flowers climbing over trellises, interspersed with graceful fountains and cobblestone paths. He upgraded his cook, and found a few doughty maids who were willing to be over-paid to work for a broadly reviled death mage.

The one thing that stayed the same was Mavis, the nursemaid he'd first hired to care for Lark, until she fell sick when the girl was only ten. By then, the child's predilection for gathering stray and injured animals was well established, and she was making simple tinctures and salves from recipes she found in her father's eclectic library. Iorgas hired the best physicians in the city to care for the woman, and Lark plied her with concoctions carefully crafted to her own exacting standards.

Unfortunately, it was all for naught. Mavis grew sicker and sicker, and the physicians declared her beyond help. So, seeing Lark's bitter sorrow, Iorgas broke his own pride and went to the Temple. Necromancers - chosen of Atae, Gina's sister, as they might be - were also one of the primary weapons used by Lich Lord Akuji against humanity. As such, they were loathed and feared by nearly everyone, and the current High Priestess of Gina in Bright, an ancient woman with the unlikely name of Buttercup, refused to help a necromancer, or any member of his household.

No amount of money, deception, or humiliating begging would change the harridan's ruling, and, at last, Mavis died in her sleep. Lark was heartbroken, but, for the first time, showed that she had all of her father's stubborn determination, and then some. From the moment the ashes of the only mother she'd ever known circled into the sky on a vagrant breeze, she began to study.

She learned physicking, apothecary, midwifing, and herbalism. She had the rose garden torn out and replaced with an herb garden containing every plant known to be of use in medicine. When she found that some wouldn't grow in Bright's climate, she had a greenhouse built, and spent more time in it than she did in the house. At the age of fourteen, after Buttercup's little-mourned passing, when a new, more open-minded, High Priestess was selected by Gina, Lark quietly dedicated her life to Gina's order. Once she was a full Priestess, with new Skills and Spells to go with her new Class, she began to serve the poor and abandoned.

When Iorgas protested, finally refusing to support his child in what he saw as a dangerous folly, Lark sold her fine clothes and the useless jewelry that had long gathered dust in her closet. She bought a small building, and spent all the time there that she could. She healed anyone who came to her. People with minor injuries or illnesses received free medicine or bandages. More serious ones were treated with small amounts of magic, bolstered by more medicine and bandages. Prayers and holy healing succored those who were beyond all other help, and though sometimes even her magic wasn't enough to help, she always, *always* tried.

When her father saw that she wouldn't be dissuaded, he changed tacks entirely. He bought a new, larger building, though Lark insisted it must still be in the poor boroughs, among those who could not otherwise afford to travel to reach her. He staffed it with physicians, supplied it with medicine, and hired security to protect it, though he soon realized that the so-called 'Saintess of Bright' had little to fear among her people.

Then, quietly, Iorgas returned to war, leaving his daughter behind, as he so often had been forced to do. She fought her own war, within and without the church of her deity. As the front lines drew ever nearer to the city, the times when he could return home grew fewer and shorter, and when he did return, he found that Lark was as caught up in her battles as he was in his. Nevertheless, they each returned to their haven, their home, to remember happier days and soak in the peace they could find only within its embrace.

Finally, inevitably, war came to Bright itself. By this time, Lark, a young Divine, was newly named as the next High Priestess, though no one expected her to fulfill that role for a decade or more, since the current Lady was only in late middle-age herself. But the city was overrun on one hot summer night, a flood of undead having crawled beneath the deep river and high walls. The High Priestess was one of many others who died, and by the time the invaders were destroyed, in large part by Iorgas himself, earning him the title of Hero of the Battle of Bright, Lark was High Priestess in all but name.

A short few weeks later, Iorgas would offer himself up to the enemy in exchange for a promise to spare his daughter. Not his city, not his King. Only one thing, in the end, mattered enough to him to bring him to grovel before his greatest enemy. And the Lich King laughed, and threw him into a cell. For a week, the evil Lord himself came to slowly tear away his captive's Skills, Spells, levels, and stats, reducing Iorgas to a pile of bones and skin that barely qualified as human.

Lark came to save him, as she did for all the lost. She brought Khor, Sumi, Miya - Silus' mother - and Rook, a raven, as they refused to be left behind. Rook and Miya died to allow the others to reach Iorgas in his cell. There, Akuji found them, and the skeletal lich laughed as he told them that he had *allowed* them to get this far. He stripped Khor and Sumi of several levels, leaving them unconscious and terribly weakened. Then he tried to swallow Lark, and choked.

As High Priestess, Lark was filled with the divine power of life. Filled and overflowing, and the Lich could no more swallow her down than a starving man could eat hemlock and survive. He could, however, destroy her physical body, and this he set out to do. How surprised he had been, then, to discover that Iorgas had insisted that his healer daughter learn to defend herself, and that she had taken to that instruction like a duck to water.

Lark was badly injured, and had to know that death was inescapable, but she disarmed her enemy, injuring him in turn badly enough that the evil mage simply commanded his minions to destroy her. Which they set out to do, but she, stubborn and unbroken to the end, chose her death. Using her holy power, she exchanged her own soul for enough power to heal her father, at least enough to get him to his feet. He picked up Akuji's fallen sword, and ran the Lich Lord through, even as his daughter died, dissolving into glittering ash, taken up by her Goddess, and leaving not even a body for her father to mourn over.

After that, Iorgas was never allowed to return to his house. After being declared Duke of the North while lying on what everyone thought was his deathbed, he recovered enough – thanks to Sumi's ceaseless care – that unknown enemies began to think he might need a bit of help to reach his well-earned final rest.

After barely surviving a few murder attempts, he fled in the night. He left a note stating that he was going north to die in peace, and left the contents of his bank account to Lark's hospital, to fund it for as long as it might exist.

When he left, he left his house behind as well. He'd long since closed up all but his and Lark's bedrooms. The second and third floors were abandoned. Only two servants stayed to the end, a cook and a grounds-keeper. The building and lands had been protected by spells that no one but the bravest or most foolish might try, and though those fell when his class was stripped from him, it was possible that fear and reputation might have been enough to protect his home from depredation.

Which brought him to this moment. Returned at last, physically stronger than he had been as a high-ranking Necromancer, though he had no good way to measure his magical powers similarly, he stared at the rusted and overgrown gate of the estate. The walls were still sturdy and tall. It had only been a year and a half since he had nearly died, after all, but plant life was happily reclaiming what his gardeners had worked so hard to clear away.

Aspen drew in a deep breath, finally forcing himself to let go of all the memories that threatened to drown him, and took a step toward the gate.

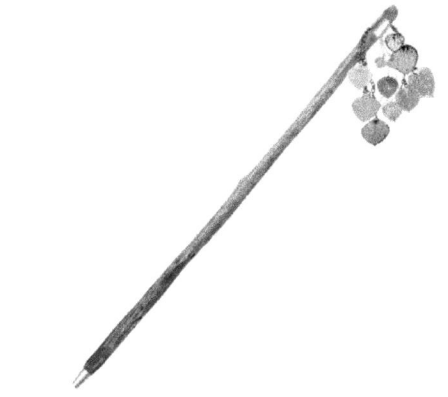

Chapter Seven

Rouge

It was late by the time Bridget left, and Zoey was finally allowed to return to her room. Bridget (and… Amy?) had sworn up and down that they'd removed any hint of the AI's presence. Zoey's dad, instead of wiping everything back to factory settings, actually *trusted* Bridget enough to let Zoey log in without more than a cursory examination to make sure that their system's available memory had returned to normal.

Which left Zoey, back in her bodysuit, staring at her pod. The shiny door was raised invitingly, and the comfortable bed was just waiting for her. But she couldn't do it.

She just… couldn't go back in there.

Something in there was able to copy people. Maybe the resultant images were 'real' people, and maybe they weren't. Maybe Bridget and Amy had created life in their mad scientist lab (which Zoey was totally picturing with bubbling beakers, white coats, and mysterious objects on tables draped in white cloth) and maybe they hadn't.

Bridget said she'd done this thing several times. Dozens? *Hundreds*? Were there hundreds of Bridget-clones running around the internet? Or were they in some kind of oubliette, slowly going insane? Could they copy *Zoey*? Had they already? Were there Zoey-clones trapped somewhere? Bridget said not, and, mostly, Zoey trusted Bridget.

Honestly, though, Zoey felt like there was still something Bridget hadn't told them. Probably to 'protect' them. Maybe to protect her game, because she still hoped to win fair and square and walk away clean. Maybe Bridget already told Zoey's dad. Maybe not.

She just didn't know.

Zoey Williams might be a 'kid' by the standards of all the smart aleck adults in her life, but she'd figured out a long time ago that adults *made mistakes too*. It was becoming very, very clear that Bridget had made quite a few mistakes. She was way too smart, and way too independent, and way too creative. Those weren't words Zoey was used to putting 'too' in front of, in no small part because way too many people (there it was again) used 'too' on her.

When you were 'too' something, what it usually meant was that other people couldn't handle you. You thought (and acted) outside of their little boxes, and they weren't ready for you. Maybe, sometimes, you weren't ready for yourself.

She sighed and stood up, clenching her fist around the headset clutched in her hand. Maybe the best thing she could do was to go to sleep and-

Chirp. Chirp. Chirp.

She turned her head and eyed her screen like a snake that might be poisonous, but also might be super cool and wrap around your shoulders for a nice snuggle. That was Jace's ringtone.

Biddle-ee-oop.

Text message.

She drew in a bracing breath and picked up the phone.

@JaceCo: You there? You weren't logged in, so I tried to call.

@RedZ: Yeah. Just talking with dad, you know? Lost track of time.

@JaceCo: Anything good? Your dad's stories are hilarious.

@RedZ: Nah, just school stuff. What's up?

@JaceCo: Ran my 8 and logged. Got one of those mouth harp things. Nice quest rewards! Tell you later. Had to leave your buddy NPC alone, and he said to tell you he'd meet you at the inn in the morning. I left a message at the Guild, but figured I'd let you know.

Zoey's eyes widened, then narrowed. Oh. Of *course* Aspen was off alone on one of his wild goose chases that *inevitably* got him in a cauldron of hot water. Since Jace didn't know the rest of the gang, he wouldn't leave messages for them, so even if someone *had* logged on, they wouldn't know where to go.

Crispy custard on a cracker!

@RedZ: Do you know where he was going?

@JaceCo: Nah. He's a weird NPC, so I figured he had weird NPC things to do. I like him, though. That bat is so cute! Why didn't you tell me you could talk to the animals, Dr Doolittle?

@RedZ: Yeah, I was going to surprise you. Thanks for letting me know! I need to log in now. See you later!

@JaceCo: Zoe?

@JaceCo: Zoey?

But Zoey already had the headset on and was diving into her pod. Her friend needed her help, and hey, the world could always use more of Zoey Williams.

Falling.

Darkness.

Dizziness, which faded as she blinked open her eyes. She sat up, wiping away the eternal log-in announcements. "Ugh. It's so much worse now that I know how much better it could be." She climbed to her feet, wishing, not for the first time, for her fancy experimental full immersion pod.

Looking around, Rouge grimaced. "Back in the Dead Tent, huh? At least I should have a Well-Rested Buff." A glance at her display confirmed that, indeed, she had a 10% boost to all of her Regens, and increased resistance to

Sleep and Hypnosis debuffs.

Suddenly, she remembered something, and grinned. "Wally! Aspen was supposed to find you and bring you back! Oh man, I need to see what you look like!" She used her Inventory to put on her boots (since anyone sleeping in footwear, for some reason only the developers understood, couldn't get the Well-Rested buff), and stepped out of the Instance she currently occupied, and onto the bluestones of Bright.

Quest: "Knock Knock" available.

Aspen is wandering around his old haunts. Find and assist him. You'd both better hope this is a funny joke.

Success: Variable.

Failure: Variable.

Accept Yes/No?

Gritting her teeth, she selected 'Yes' with a flick of a fingertip, and then shrieked (just a little!) when something smooth and hard pressed into her neck. Reaching up, she smacked at the thing, then dropped and whirled on the ball of one foot, sweeping the other one out in front of her.

Her foot thunked into the foreleg of the ugliest horse she'd ever seen. The poor thing looked like it had mange. Its body was covered in fluffy, luxuriously curly fur in rich black and white, but the body was oddly front-heavy, with long, skinny legs and a matching long, skinny neck and tiny head. The head was nearly bald, except for the thick lashes surrounding the beautiful brown eyes, and it was those eyes that gave it away.

Rouge blinked hard, and Codswallop's birdy face swam into view behind the illusory horse-face. Oh, heck yes! That was a crazy awesome Skill! Admittedly, Codswallop was still going to attract attention because, and there was no getting around it, he was as ugly as a horse as he was beautiful as an ostrich. But still, she could ride him without worrying about people instantly identifying her just from her bird!

Gracefully, she rose to her feet, throwing her arms around her steed's neck. She froze, feeling the fluffy feathers under her hands. Oh boy. She buried her face in the dusty feathers, her imagination summoning up the scent of warm bird and fluff that she could smell so clearly when she was in the immersion pod.

"Sorry, Wally," she murmured softly. "You looked a little different there for a second. I'm glad to see you, buddy."

The ostrich burrowed his head into her curls, chirruping softly in greeting, and then promptly began to pluck gently at her hands with his beak, looking for treats. She summoned a Sliced Apple from her inventory and laughed as he ate it with greedy urgency. He wasn't really hungry, she knew, since the Dead Tent counted as a stable as far as mounts went, so they were fed, watered, and brushed as needed while their owners rested inside.

All of which made no difference whatsoever to her eager bird, who had finished the apple and was now looking at her belt pouch with a considering eye. She pushed his head away gently, laughing. "That's enough for now, Wally. We have a quest! I don't suppose *you* know where Aspen went?"

Unsurprisingly, the ostrich just eyed her expectantly.

Puffing a little laugh, she stroked his head, sending out a quick message over party chat.

::Aspen? Can you hear me? Silus?::

When there was no response, she glanced at the party list and saw that everyone was either logged off or 'Maximum distance exceeded'. Since the maximum distance was about a mile, that didn't really help much. There was a whole lot of Bright outside of chat range.

Quickly, she pulled up her city map, more grateful than ever to be back in her old stomping grounds. In *Veritas Online*, you could expand your map in one of three ways. First, you could buy one, and NPCs selling city maps weren't hard to find, but only public streets and buildings were marked. Second, you could get one from another Player, if they were willing to share. Unfortunately, you could only choose an *area* of map to share, not *what* to share on that map. That meant that if anything special or secret was on it, most people weren't willing to sell, or if they did, it wouldn't be cheap.

Finally, you could explore it yourself. As part of the tutorial, every player received a copy of the public map of their starter location. After that, it was up to them to fill it out. Many parts of a map would self-populate as you explored, but you could also put down markers, notes, and, conveniently, create a search grid for those super entertaining 'Find me one of these' quests. Not.

Now, Rouge stuck a pin in the Dead Tent, and told the map to draw a circle around her a mile in every direction. Next, she had it lay a 'Fog of War' over the parts of the map outside her circle, setting the opacity at 15%. Finally, she overlaid the 'unexplored' area with all the neighborhoods marked in different colors.

Her sharp hazel eyes flickered over the map, as she tried to figure out what Aspen could be up to. If it was her, she'd be hunting for a place for Millie and Struthio to start their restaurant so she could complete that quest. As much as Aspen liked the young couple, however, she doubted he'd be wandering alone in the dark for that.

So, something he wanted privacy for. Something he didn't want to do during the day. When it would be *safer*. She rolled her eyes. That implied something sneaky and personal. Her eyes locked onto the castle and the fancy estates surrounding it. He'd *better* not be sneaking into the castle. Assuming he wasn't stupid, which he wasn't, *usually*, that left...

She reached out and grabbed Codswallop's small saddle, vaulting up with a handspring and a half twist. She could feel the tiny pad that protected her backside from the bird's bony spine, and vice versa, but she suspected that anyone else would see a regular horse saddle. Maybe one of those little English saddles? Settling as comfortably into the pad as she could, and tucking her knees behind Codswallop's fluffy little wings (and how did the illusion deal with *that*?) she clucked encouragingly.

"Okay, Wally, let's go knock on someone's door. Once we find it."

Knock, knock indeed.

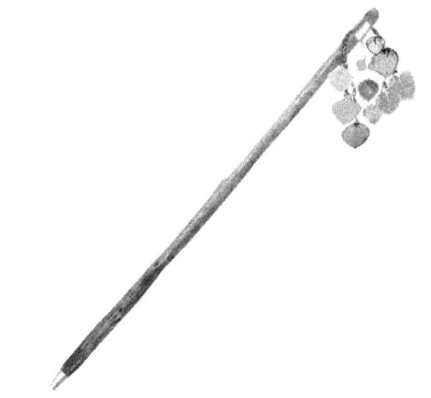

Chapter Eight

Aspen

Not surprisingly, the gate was rusted shut. From the looks of it, no one had even tried to enter in months, possibly not since shortly after Aspen had snuck out in the dark of the night, leaving behind a sleeping Lark, his animal companions, and the two remaining servants, as he headed to his assignation with the servants of humanity's greatest enemy.

After that fateful excursion, he had been taken to the castle and not allowed to return 'for your own protection'. Instead, Khor, Sumi, and a very young Silus serving as messenger, had conspired with the Head Librarian to sneak out the few things they would need on their exodus. Aspen had been smuggled out of the castle using ropes and nets made from Sumi's thread, and stuffed rather unceremoniously into a large pack on Khor's back, all so that no assassins could follow.

He had not been allowed to return to this house, though he hadn't tried very hard, knowing as he did that there would be no tousled and distracted girl to call him Daddy and welcome him home with a hug. Now, he found that the gloomy atmosphere suited his emotions very well, and when the first drops of rain fell, curling lazily down the back of his neck and dripping from the brim of his hat, he turned his face up so that the drops could wash over his cheeks and jaw, hiding any moisture that might have already been there. Of course, those drops also ran down his neck and disturbed the warm, fuzzy little bundle that was resting there.

Silus' voice was disgruntled. <Why is it raining?>

Aspen almost managed to chuckle. "Philosophers and mages have argued about that for years. Some say they're drops from the Chaos Pool, overflowing and bringing the memories of the dead to those left behind. Others insist it's simply a combination of tiny droplets of water suspended in the air and temperature changes high in the-"

Silus bit him.

He clapped a hand to his neck, almost surprised to find that she hadn't broken the skin. She was stronger than she used to be.

<You know what I mean!> The bat was indignant.

This time he did laugh, but he also began to walk, trailing his hand along the wall, touching the stones beneath the ivy. "Perhaps you wondered why we were still outside for it to rain on us?"

The small animal shivered, fluffing up against the ever-increasing moisture. <Don't be a beezie.>

Aspen frowned. "A what?" His fingers found a single stone, which he knew would look exactly like the surrounding stones, but which felt distinctly smoother to his questing fingertips.

<A beezie. It's what Lyrec calls someone mean. He said Lady Calliope looked like a total beezie.> He could feel her beginning to clean her fur in a futile attempt to stay ahead of the downpour that soaked them both.

He choked on a snort of startled laughter, and found himself coughing as he leaned into the rough stone. When it gave way, revealing that a small part of the rock wall was actually a façade over a well-oiled metal hatch, he almost fell through. The hatch swung shut behind him, and he heard the *click* that meant the magical lock had engaged, and the passage would be as impenetrable as the surrounding wall for the next three hours.

The rain stopped suddenly, and he looked up, finding himself beneath the branches of a familiar tree. This one was chosen by a doting gardener for a little girl who liked to take books into the garden to read, but would then burn as red as a tomato thanks to her fair skin. The gardener had had to trade his own time to a friend whose mistress had wanted her entire garden replanted for a summer soiree, and had only told her staff a week before the party was planned. In exchange for a day of backbreaking labor, the man had accepted this tree, which would never grow higher than seven feet tall, but had dense, drooping branches that spread nearly ten feet wide and created a natural shelter.

Birdie had loved it, and would sit in the lowest branches and read and sing like the bird after which she was named. When she began to stay out late, healing the injured and sick, Aspen had sent guards, both living and undead, after her, until she furiously told him to stop because he was frightening her patients.

One would think that being the daughter of the most feared man in the kingdom would be sufficient to keep anyone away, but her gentle manner and kind heart – though it disguised a will of steel – drew in both lovelorn suitors and those who thought kidnapping the daughter of the wealthiest man in the kingdom was a good idea, no matter who he was when he was at work. Birdie was nearly taken right outside his gate as she was trying to get through the heavy metal monstrosity, and only her years of training in self-defense had saved her. It was then that he had the secret passage put in, so she could slip quickly and silently in and out, with the lock ensuring that anyone attempting to follow her would fail.

Aspen drew in a breath, struggling to pull it into a chest frozen in sorrow. Silus, too, sounded subdued when she spoke. <Are you sure we shouldn't go back to the inn? Rouge said she'd come and check this place out later, and she->

"Won't find herself lost in memory?" he asked quietly, pushing aside the branches of the tree. Where his fingers touched, fresh green leaf buds sprouted from twigs and branches, and fuzzy white flowers grew up amidst the silvery green leaflets. He stroked one, smiling as he remembered how Lark had loved to cut the longest branches and bring them in every spring, creating bouquets of sticks and wildflowers.

<Won't be sad,> his little friend said, rubbing her small, wet head against his jaw in the only consolation she could offer.

Aspen's hand dropped from the downy petals of the flower to the bat's soft ears and rubbed gently. "I need to look around before our young thief takes everything she can fit into her seemingly infinite storage. If someone had been living here, or the place was ransacked, I would leave her to it, but this…" He looked at the house, rising dark and looming in the sky, occasionally backlit by flashes of lightning as the storm grew closer.

"It's like she just left. Like she went to work, and she'll be back soon, complaining that her patients never come as soon as they should, and that the acolytes the temple sends are never well enough trained." He pushed through overgrown grass which nearly concealed the once tidy path. His mouth quirked. "Well, maybe not *quite* like that. Tomas never would have let this grass grow so high. He was always worried the 'young mistress' would get grass stains on her skirts, not that she ever cared."

Silus giggled silently. <Lark used to say she had to be very careful not to get stains on her clothes, or Tomas would be out here with the hand scythe, cutting every blade of grass individually. She worried he'd hurt his knees more than they already were. She had Plum make him a special tonic every night and make him drink it so he could walk the next day.>

Shaking his head, Aspen made his cautious way to the front door. "I didn't know that, but I'm not surprised. The man was almost as stubborn as she was." He sighed, pushing gently at the door. "I hope he was able to find a good position elsewhere, though I left enough money for him and Plum that they should never have to work-"

The door creaked open, and the floor fell out from under his feet. Literally.

☙ ☙ ☙

When Aspen blinked his eyes open, he found himself staring into concerned golden orbs. The pinpricks in his cheeks resolved themselves into Silus, using her wing-thumbs to pinch him awake. When the bat saw his eyes open, she squeaked excitedly and held up her wing.

<Aspen! Aspen! How many wings am I holding up?>

He groaned, sitting up slowly and clutching at his head when the world spun dizzyingly. He tried to focus, but was only able to make out a vaguely Silus-shaped blob now residing on his chest. "One," he answered groggily, "You only have two, and you're using one to hold on."

Quickly, Silus climbed to his shoulder, peering up into his eyes again. <That's math, not vision. Though I guess if you can do math, you're probably okay. *Are* you okay?> Her voice was worried, and her big eyes blinked in the dimness.

Aspen gingerly felt the large, painful bump blooming on his skull. He activated his Life Sense, which was on nearly all the time now, but seemed to have turned off when he passed out. The first thing he did was check Silus, who seemed to be entirely unhurt, thank Gina. Then he looked inside himself and saw that his brain was beginning to swell slightly, which no doubt explained the loud pounding that accompanied every beat of his heart. Otherwise, he was surprisingly uninjured.

Carefully, he applied a gentle flow of healing magic to his incipient concussion, feeling the headache fade as the swelling went down. "I'll be fine in a minute. What happened?"

Silus sounded aggrieved. <You set off a trap. Someone dug a pit trap in front of the door, and we fell in it. That's a really rude thing to do to someone in their own home.>

Aspen snorted, then winced at the fading echo of his headache. "True enough, little one. We'll have to talk to the perpetrator about their manners. First, though," he struggled to his feet, slipping in the deepening muddy water as he stared up at the dim gap far above. Raindrops fell down, gathering in his eyebrows and trailing down his cheeks, and he realized his hat was missing. Bending, he started fishing around in the mud, finishing his thought with a sigh as he pulled the dripping thing from the muck, "we need to get out of here."

Silus poked her head out from under his chin, eyeing the hat dubiously. <You... aren't going to wear that, are you?>

He laughed, tempted for a moment to slap the soggy, misshapen, and now smelling of eau de boggy pit, hat on his head just to see how she would react. Instead, he rolled it up and tucked it into his belt. "No, my friend. Even I know when to start looking for a new hat."

Silus poked her head out further, looking up into his eyes. <No, you don't.>

He almost choked on a raindrop. "Uh, I guess that's true. It was the first hat I managed to make by myself, though!"

The bat's serious little voice stabbed him to the heart. <Khor said he wouldn't eat that thing if you made a fruit salad and used it as a bowl.> Then, before he could respond, she dropped from his shoulder, flapped her wings a few times, and flew up into the darkness above.

"That rotten ruminant," Aspen muttered, touching a broken root that extended into the deep pit. Beneath his hand, it twitched, then grew, extending fibrous tendrils into the earth surrounding it, firming the dirt and creating a solid handhold. Carefully, he reached up, grabbing another root and repeating the performance. Cautiously, mentally cursing his erstwhile companion even as mud, rocks, and rain threatened to smother him, he climbed the side of the sheer shaft.

After some interminable period, he reached up, nearly blind in the now torrential rain, and clutched at the edge of the opening. Forcing himself higher on his last foothold, he thrust his arm and the top half of his chest out, scrabbling at the muck and pulling a handful of grass nearly free of the earth, roots and all.

Once he was stable, he paused, half in and half out, swiping at his drenched face with his equally drenched and filthy sleeve.

"Well," said a familiar voice in an unfamiliarly sarcastic tone, "that took long enough. I would have helped, but of course, you don't *need* help, right?"

He looked up, swinging a leg out of the hole, and sighed as he finally rolled out, flopping onto his back in the muck. "Hello, Rouge, and a lovely evening to you, too. I see you found Silus."

Chapter Nine

Rouge

Rouge looked at the filthy figure lying at her feet and sighed. She hopped down from the tree branch where she had been sitting for the last few minutes, watching Aspen haul himself up out of a hole in the ground that had to be at least twenty feet deep. Reaching down, she extended a hand, grasping his when he reached up and pulling him to his feet. For once, she could actually see most of his face, since his hat had apparently come off somewhere during his… what? Capture? Imprisonment? What the heck was going on here?

She crossed her arms and glared at him, wishing that tapping her foot would have had any result besides making a squelchy sound which would probably be covered up by the near-constant rolls of thunder. If any situation called for crossed arms and foot-tapping, this was it.

The tall man reached up and pushed his sopping wet hair back out of his face. It was getting pretty long now, and he looked like a sexy lady in one of those perfume ads, when she came up out of the ocean. Except dirtier. And more tired. And more shame-faced. Which was good, because he *should be*.

Silus, who had found Rouge almost as soon as she started flying, heading back toward the inn for help, was also glaring at Aspen. Hazel eyes and golden ones waited for an explanation that didn't *suck*.

Unfortunately, they were going to have to wait a little longer, because just as Aspen opened his mouth, the door behind him, which he had, brilliantly, been using to prop himself up, fell open. He stumbled backwards, landing on his butt, and then promptly did the only smart thing (that she knew of) he'd done since she'd last seen him. He rolled.

A large blade dropped from above the door, crunching into the wooden floor where Aspen had landed. It dug a deep groove into the wood, joining other, similar, indentations, as well as some ominous dark stains. Which *might* just have been from water seeping under the door. But she doubted it.

You have found *Blade Trap (Lv4)*.

"Oh my gosh, no kidding!" she growled, swiping away the notification even as she leapt through the door, tucking and rolling in the air so she landed on her feet next to Aspen. Behind them, the door slammed shut. A low groan rattled through the house, which shuddered as a clap of thunder boomed nearby, and lightning blazed through the dirty, cracked windows, lighting the room.

She screeched and threw herself backwards, nearly knocking Aspen, who had just pulled himself back to his feet, back onto his rear. Vividly exposed by the brilliant flash was a horror show of a room. Before them were three bodies, impaled on spikes, faces contorted in agony, all in varying stages of decomposition. Scattered on the floor around them were glittering blades, too many to count, ranging from scalpels to butter knives, all liberally doused in black, viscous fluid. Spiked chains dangled from shackles on the extremities of each body, and what looked like giant fish hooks pulled their partially torn flesh at angles flesh was never meant to go.

Rouge backed up, gorge rising as she stared at the scene. Her [Darkvision], which, to be honest, was one of the main reasons she'd selected Dark Elf as one of her races, kept flicking on and off as the lightning sparked, taking the already revolting picture to a whole new level of horror. Her breath caught in her throat, and she barely noticed when Aspen began moving toward the bodies with slow, deliberate steps.

Slowly, he crouched, just out of reach of the things on the posts, and reached down to touch the pool of gore. He lifted his finger to his eye, waited for a flash of lightning, then paused. A moment later, the finger was in his mouth, and if she could have thrown up, she totally, one hundred percent, without a *doubt*, would have.

"Aspen!" she choked, "What?"

The tall farmer stood, reaching up habitually to shove his hat back from his forehead, and stopping when his fingers touched his wet, mud-caked hair. With a sigh, he reached down and pulled his barely-still-a-hat hat out of his belt and tugged it onto his head, where it drooped, almost more liquid than solid after all the abuse and the rain.

Aspen put his hands on his hips and stared down the long entryway, past the bodies, and up the long, split stairs that climbed on each side of the room. "Whoever is up there, come down! These things aren't even anatomically correct," he reached over and tugged an arm off the closest 'body', and when he waggled it, she could see that it only had four fingers, and three were made of what looked like sausages, while the other one looked like a carrot, "and your fake blood smells like ketchup."

She sniffed. Yep, *that's* why that vinegary smell was so familiar. She had a bad feeling she'd be eating her hotdogs plain for a while, though. One of the sausages came loose from the 'hand' and fell to plop in the pool of ketchup and she gulped. Yeah, no hotdogs for a while either.

There was a long silence, and then, as the rain sounds slowly began to fade, the storm moving away, a rather tentative "Oooooooooooooo….?" came echoing through the hall. Unenthusiastic chain rattling followed a moment later.

Aspen crossed his arms and tapped his foot.

That was *so* not right. If anyone was doing that, it was *her*! She crossed her own arms and tapped her foot, but stopped, realizing that now she just looked silly. She looked at Aspen.

::Life Sense?:: she asked via party chat.

::Yep. At least a dozen people, but some of them are touching each other, and it's hard to get any details. Most of them feel… young, though. They're in the dining hall. That's the big room in the middle up there.:: he returned.

Silus perked up. ::I'll go check!::

Aspen spun, reaching out, but it was too late. Silus was flapping away, and Rouge was right behind her.

::Watch for traps!:: Aspen yelled after them.

But Silus was already at the second level, and Rouge didn't bother with the stairs, which were probably trapped. Duh. She headed straight for one of the columns holding up the second story overhang-thing, and clambered up it as easily as if she'd had sticky toes. The fancy carvings made for excellent grips. When she reached the top, she flipped herself easily up, landing in a squat on the railing, her Mambele in one hand, and the other lightly touching the wood to help keep her balance.

She motioned toward the door in front of her, flicking a look back at Aspen, then realized that the lightning was now little more than a dim remnant, and his human eyes couldn't see her in the darkness. ::The one right in front of me?:: she asked.

::If you go straight up, yes. It's the only one with a knocker. It's ridiculous to have a knocker inside the house, but I never got around to taking it down, and-::

She cut off his excuses for his terrible interior decorating sense. ::I'm going in.::

A small bump on her shoulder made her start, until she realized it was her little friend coming in for a landing. ::Me too!:: Silus squeaked.

Drawing in a deep breath and desperately hoping that whoever was in there didn't have a *real* horror show ready for her, she leapt from the railing. Her feet impacted the door with a loud *THUD*, and she flipped backwards again, landing on the floor a few feet back. Immediately, she dodged left, then took another step backwards, but nothing happened.

A quavering voice came from the other side of the door. "G-g-g-go *away*. I'll c-c-c-c-cut you up! Go back to your boss an' tell him we ain't j-j-j-oinin' you!"

She paused, staring at the door, which was now slightly splintered from her blow. She was fairly certain that one more good hit would take it down, and two would certainly do the job, but she wasn't quite ready to commit to that level of violence yet. ::Did you hear that?::

::Yes,:: Aspen responded quietly. ::This area was safe from the gangs when I lived here. I imagine that after I was gone, well, there was probably a bit of contention regarding who would control it. It sounds as if some of those affected may have moved in and created their own 'safe' place. Honestly, I have no problem leaving them to it, but there are a few things I need to do here first.::

He raised his voice, using his lighter accent, probably so that the people listening could actually understand him. His rube-from-the-country accent was *thick*. "We're not from the gangs! We've no interest in recruitin' you! I... useta know the lady what lived here. I just want to look around, an' then we'll leave!"

She appreciated the 'we', even though he hadn't actually checked with her. *She* fully intended to search the place top to bottom for anything she could, ah, acquire. It wasn't even stealing, really, since she had the owner's permission.

She was close enough now that she could hear the muffled chatter of multiple voices from the room ahead. She half-tuned it out as she focused on the area nearby. Small areas of wall on each side of the door began to glow a soft and ominous red in her vision.

You have discovered *Poison Dart Trap x 4 (Lv2).*

Silently, watching for any further signs of traps in the floor or ceiling, she padded over to the first trap. With a [Disarm Trap] Skill level of 7, a level 2 dart trap took only an instant to release, and she tucked the little device into her inventory. The other three were disposed of just as easily, and just as she put away the last one, she heard a clamor from inside the room. Even more voices were talking at once, but now they sounded relieved, rather than frightened.

::Something just changed,:: she sent, ::can you tell what?:: She pulled back, readying her Mambele again.

::Someone else just came up the servant's stairs. I don't know why I didn't notice her before. An adult female, young, but older than the others. Everyone else got,:: Aspen hesitated, ::brighter? When she entered.::

A young voice filtered through the door. "Plum, we can-"

Another came a moment later, slightly deeper, but still childish, "Na'way, Plum, there's just two-"

Time to shake things up a little. She slid forward, examining the heavy lock on the door. ::Who puts a lock on a dining hall?:: she asked, slightly peevishly, as she worked at it with her lockpicks. It was a heavy old thing, and it was hard to clear the tumblers quietly.

Aspen sighed. ::The same people who put a knocker on one?::

The last pin clicked over, the sound lost in the pandemonium that now raged on the other side of the door. ::Silus, you ready?::

A nearly silent squeak was her answer, and she clasped the handle of the door, opening it and pushing inside the room in an instant. Spinning, she danced left, narrowly avoiding the not-entirely clumsy slash of the tall boy standing on the other side. His freckled face twisted into an angry snarl, and he leapt toward her, blade overextended.

With a twist, she caught the knife in the rear-facing blade of her own weapon, pulling it from his hand with a deft movement that left the jagged knife momentarily tumbling through the air. With a grin, she caught it in her off hand, brandishing it. [Dual Knife Wielding] was so *cool*.

Yielding to temptation, Rouge adroitly flipped both weapons around in her hands, spinning the hilts so they seemed to dance in her palms. The eyes of the thirteen children facing her widened, and one little one, missing her top two front teeth and one on the bottom, grinned admiringly, little dimples dancing in her cheeks. Rouge nearly dropped both blades as she recognized the little girl.

"Matilda!" she gasped.

Big brown eyes widened, and the girl's mouth dropped open. An instant later, the child had crossed the distance, throwing her arms around Rouge's waist. "Rouge! They stole my doll again!"

Quest: "Well, Hello Dolly, Too" available.

Matilda's precious doll has been stolen again. Also, she's a homeless orphan. Maybe help with that.

Success: Variable, depending on whether you are able to retrieve the doll, and how much assistance you can give.

Failure: Neither return the doll nor improve Matilda's circumstances.

Accept: Yes/No?

Rouge stared around helplessly, patting the sobbing little girl on the back as a dozen pairs of eyes stared back.

::Does this mean no fighting?:: Silus asked, ::Because I'm not sure I can bite kids.::

Rouge stared down at the curly-haired moppet for whom she had once done a quest. The girl's father, a merchant, had been away on a sea voyage, and some heartless thief (not her!) had stolen the doll he had left for his daughter. The toy was an item called a Doll of Contentment, and was ranked as Rare, since it had a special effect of making anyone who held it feel happier. An unscrupulous noble, a collector of rare and unusual artifacts, had placed the dolly on a pedestal in a display room, and Rouge had retrieved it for the child who loved it.

The elf thief knelt, brushing the wild tangles back from the little face, which was noticeably thinner than when she'd last seen it. Big tears continued to course down the formerly chubby cheeks, and the girl scrubbed at her reddening eyes with dirty, scratched little fists.

Rouge looked up fiercely, staring around the circle of dumb-founded faces, until her gaze settled on the one adult in the group. The woman was around Bridget's age, in her early to mid-twenties, and her mouth was set in a fierce, uncompromising line. She held a knife, which had been aimed at Rouge's heart, until the events of the last few seconds had made her drop her guard. Now she raised it again, dark brown eyes determined under flat black brows.

The two stared at each other accusingly, neither quite ready to either attack or begin talking. Then, from behind her, Rouge heard Aspen rasp out, "Plum?"

The young woman dropped her knife, both hands flying to her mouth. Her eyes welled with tears, much as Matilda's had upon seeing Rouge. "Oh!" she gasped. "My lord!" She sank into a deep, awkward curtsey, nearly toppling as she tried to spread a skirt that didn't exist, since her legs were covered in ragged brown leather trousers.

Rouge spun, staring at the tall figure standing in the doorway. Aspen sighed, pulling the pathetic remnants of his hat off his head and attempting to brush mud and debris from his hair. A faint flush rose in his cheeks, and he pulled at his rough linen shirt and plain leather vest. "Well," he muttered, "so much for anonymity."

The woman (Plum?) stepped forward, face so white that Rouge was afraid she'd faint. "My lord, they said... they said you were dead! They sent us away, and the duke claimed the estate! He said you owed back taxes, so... But then the gangs came back, and no one wanted to chance... They said you'd performed evil magic here, and it was cursed. Then they said there were ghosts, and then... Then the hospital orphanage closed, and the children had nowhere to go, and..."

Throughout this broken explanation, Aspen's face had become

progressively more thunderous, until by the end Rouge thought she'd never seen anyone so furious. "They *closed* the hospital?" He ground out, deep voice dangerously calm.

Plum gulped, stepping back. "Without milady, and without funding, they had no choice-"

The tall man's fist struck out, smashing into the open door beside him. The thick slab of wood, as though deciding that enough was enough, simply shattered into dust and drifted to the floor. Rouge felt her eyes grow wide. She'd known Aspen was strong, and that he had only grown stronger since she met him, but that... She wasn't sure Motte could have hit that hard with a single, unarmed blow.

"I left," he bit out, "a *very* large deposit in the bank, marked for the hospital. It should have lasted for *decades*, by which time they could have invested it or figured out another income source."

Rouge looked back and forth between the two, seeing Plum's throat move as she swallowed, hard. "They said there were inconsistencies, and... and taxes. My lord." The woman was barely whispering.

The tall man pressed his hand over his eyes, clearly struggling against a furious response. Finally, he dropped his hand, revealing eyes that slowly opened, icy topaz shards in his lean face, for once bereft of its battered straw camouflage. He breathed out, shoulders relaxing slightly. "I'm sorry. Plum, I'm sorry. Please," he waved his hand around at the gathered children, who were now huddled in a frightened mass, except for Matilda, who was hiding behind Rouge, little hands fisted in the fabric of her shirt, "continue. Who are these children, and how is it that you're here?"

Plum took one step forward, and then, emboldened, another and another, until she stood only a few feet before Aspen. "My lord," she said softly, "I'm so sorry. About Lark..."

His face froze, expressionless and painfully blank. "Thank you. Now, about the children?" For the first time since Rouge had met him, she could see a nobleman in her friend. His air of authority and absolute belief that he would be answered were undeniable. Plum bobbed another sketchy curtsey, and cleared her throat hoarsely.

"That," she swallowed hard. "After you… left… they turned us out. Said we'd have to find other positions, of course. Grandpa and I… Since you paid us so well, as well as room and board, we'd been able to save some. We bought a little house near the hospital, and we volunteered at the orphanage there. We knew," she gulped, and her dark eyes shone with suspicious moisture, "milady would want it to stay open, and thought we'd help keep costs down. It was fun, doing things because we wanted to, not because we had to."

She looked around at the once grand dining room, rife with carved friezes covered in gold leaf, walls covered in sadly water-stained red satin. "They sold the place. Even auctioned it off, but no one could stay here. There was talk of tearing it down, but then the gangs started fighting over the unclaimed territory, and it was just abandoned. Grandpa and I," she grinned a little, "we dug the first pit and bought a few magic tricks. Things like flashing lights and spooky sounds that children use to frighten each other. We couldn't bear to see anyone else living here, you see. Grandpa even started taking care of some of the gardens again.

"Then one day I went to work, and the children were just standing in the street, their little bundles at their feet. The sign on the door said the hospital was now privately owned, and wouldn't accept anyone who couldn't pay any more. There were guards…" She stammered to an angry halt, black brows drawing down over her eyes again.

"So, I brought the children here. We found homes for a few of the littlest, and tracked down distant relatives for others. But the gangs were watching them as the healthy ones went out to earn money, and the recruiters started in on them, telling them they'd better pick a side." Plum drew in a breath. "That's when we dug the pit deeper, Grandpa placed the traps, and we set up the display downstairs."

Her face was pale but determined. "We made it look like something uncanny was here, killing people. A few children played dead, and then… Then we killed a few gang members. We made it," she turned faintly green, "look like something tortured them, and, and ate parts of them. After that, they left us alone. We've been growing food in milady's gardens, and Grandpa goes out into the northern forest, hunting and fishing. That's where he is now."

The woman trailed off, clearing her throat awkwardly. "We really did," she said quietly, "believe you were dead."

Aspen stepped forward slowly, and Rouge could see the children surrounding them tense up as though preparing to defend their heroine. The tall man raised his hand and set it gently on Plum's black hair. "You did well," he said softly. "Birdie would be proud."

Plum caught her breath in a muffled sob and launched herself into Aspen's arms, crying in terrible wracking sobs born of a combination of grief and relief that was heart-breaking to watch.

☙ ☙ ☙

Half an hour later, Aspen and Rouge were sitting in matching red satin-covered dining chairs, watching as Plum carefully tucked each of her nestlings into bed. Blankets covered the floor in the rear of the room, and thick, fluffy feather pillows created comfortable sleeping arrangements. The woman had explained that this was the only room on the second floor with no windows to show light, enough room for everyone, and two exits.

"We didn't go up to the third floor, of course, milord," she had said, glancing meaningfully at Aspen, who had nodded approval.

Rouge propped her feet up on the heavy dining room table, which apparently served as both a place to eat and a school desk, judging by the neat stack of beginner's books at the other end of the table. She was just relaxing back into her chair, luxuriating in the fact that Motte wasn't there to tell her to get her feet off the table, when she caught Aspen's eye. The eyebrow went up, and his pale topaz gaze flicked from her feet to the table, one corner of his mouth quirking up to match the eyebrow.

Sighing, she put her feet down.

A slightly petulant voice intruded into her mind as she was trying to decide what question she wanted to ask first. ::Can't I go say hello to Plum, *yet?* She was my second favorite person after Birdie, you know…::

The twitch at the corner of Aspen's mouth became that familiar half smile. ::I didn't,:: he replied thoughtfully. ::I thought I was your second favorite person.::

Silus practically snickered. ::You were too stuck up. You never wanted to play. Mom,:: the bat hesitated, and then continued more quietly, ::Mom said you were busy and worried about really important things, and I shouldn't bother you.::

Rouge felt her own eyes tear up at the genuine sorrow in her little friend's mental voice, and she reached up to scrootch between the fuzzy ears. Aspen, who had also raised his hand as if to reach for the bat, put it back down and sighed defeatedly. ::I wish I had done things differently, but your mother was right. I'm glad you and Birdie and Plum could play together, and you can go see her once she's done. We don't want to frighten the children, and remember that Plum can't hear you.::

::So,:: the elf girl cleared her throat, though she didn't stop petting Silus. ::Who is Plum, exactly? It sounds like she works here, but, ah, that hug…:: She felt her cheeks heat as she remembered some of the things she'd thought when the other woman flung herself at Aspen.

Aspen's eyes, now warm honey instead of icy crystal, creased with his smile as if he could read her mind and was amused. ::She's the same age as Birdie. Her parents were our head chef and the chief hostler. Her grandfather was the head gardener and gamekeeper. She and my daughter, Lark, being the only children in a place considered, at best, unlucky, and thus shunned by the neighborhood children, played together often. Lark was the thinker, and Plum was the doer. Between them they got into a great deal of mischief. Plum's parents died during the Battle of Bright, when the Lich Lord's forces tunneled beneath our walls, and she and Tomas were the only two servants who stayed with us. Plum was our chef and took care of Lark's chickens and our last two horses, who were too old to be requisitioned by the military.::

He sighed softly, shaking his head. ::When they were little, they'd call both me and Plum's father 'Daddy', as if we were interchangeable. Plum's mother was 'Mama', and Tomas was 'Grampie'.:: His expression darkened as his eyes followed the young woman's figure as she moved around, dimming lamps and tucking small bodies under blankets. ::I left both Tomas and Plum healthy investment accounts, with instructions that they should have the gamekeeper's cottage where Tomas lived, and that the funds would be used to provide for their needs for the rest of their lives.::

Rouge grimaced. ::Sounds like somebody isn't good at following instructions.::

Aspen leaned forward, steepling his fingers under his nose as the soft light of the single remaining glow stone glinted in his eyes. ::Yes,:: he said simply, ::it does.::

Rouge shivered.

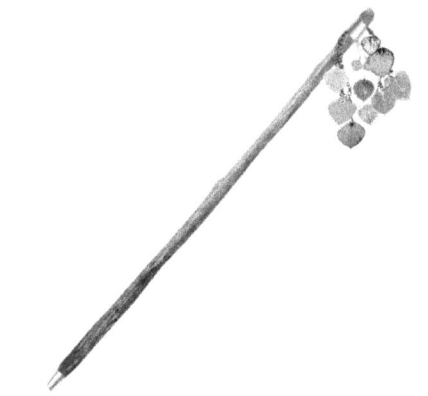

Chapter Ten

Aspen

O nce the children were settled, Plum returned to sit with Aspen and the young thief. Aspen's eyes took in the tired lines of her face, and the worry in her shadowed eyes. Even her chin and once-straight shoulders showed a slump of exhaustion and defeat. She clearly knew that eventually her refuge would be breached, and had no idea what to do.

He reached out and gently brushed the tips of her short hair, now just brushing her shoulders. "You cut it," he said quietly.

She smiled sadly. "Waist-length hair is difficult to maintain, and gives enemies something to grab." Her slim fingers tucked the hair behind her ear, which he also noticed was now bare of the small gold studs he'd given to her for her sixteenth birthday. Lark had refused most jewelry by then, but she would wear her matching pair almost every day. He wondered if they were stolen or sold, but didn't ask.

Rouge leaned forward, and Aspen could see Silus' fuzzy ears poking out of the mass of curls on her shoulders. "Why is Matilda here? She was staying with her aunt, when I saw her last." The girl's expression was lively with curiosity and concern.

Plum sighed. "That must have been a while ago. A fever swept through the poor parts of the city late last fall. Her aunt was among those who died, and since her father is still missing, though his ship was expected months ago, it's assumed that he's dead as well. She herself caught the fever, and was left at the hospital with no way to pay for her care. She was living in the orphanage when it closed."

She shook her head. "I don't know how many times she's told the story of the elvish thief who daringly rescued her doll in exchange for nothing but a few coppers and snakeskin. I honestly thought she'd made it up, since she didn't have the doll when she was left at the hospital, and she has a wonderful imagination. She thinks her father was abducted by a tribe of islanders who have forced him to marry their Queen, and someday he'll come to take her there and she'll be a princess."

Aspen laughed softly. "Sounds like another little girl I once knew..." he trailed off as he saw Rouge's wide eyes locked on something visible only to her. "A Quest?" he asked.

She nodded, smiling. "I think Matilda's father is alive. This says to find him and bring him home, not 'find out what happened to him'. I don't think he's in any danger, since it doesn't say he'll die if I fail, which is good, because I definitely can't get on a ship to track him down right now."

Plum's face was alight with happiness. "Oh, I'm so glad. Then we just have to keep Matilda safe until he comes home." She reached out impulsively to clasp Rouge's fingers. "Please, you must complete this quest."

The younger girl nodded firmly. "I already accepted it. I'll definitely find him as soon as," her eyes flickered to Aspen, "as I can."

At this point, Silus, clearly tired of being ignored, stuck her head out and squeaked with great determination. Plum's hands flew to her mouth, her eyes growing round and bright. Silus edged out of Rouge's curls, using her wing-thumbs to get closer to her old friend. ::Tell her I'm here! I want to talk, too!::

The three females quickly fell into a comfortable low-voiced chatter, with Rouge translating Silus' squeaks for a somewhat jealous Plum. The conversation turned into a discussion of what had been happening since Plum and Silus had last seen each other, and Aspen silently slipped away into the shadows, certain that he would soon have no secrets, and content enough with that. If he couldn't trust the girl who had once been Lark's devoted shadow, he might as well give up and go back to the farm right now, because the world was too dark a place to save.

Speaking of saving the world, however, he had a few things he had come here to do, and now was as good a time as any, and better than most. He hadn't forgotten his promise to his Goddess. Quietly, he slipped down the back stairs, heading for the kitchen below. The servant's stairs were eerily silent and dark. Before, even at night, there would often be someone working or talking downstairs. The girls would be giggling over a cup of tea, or Plum's mother would be making bread dough and setting it to rise. A glowstone was always left in the middle of the kitchen counter, ready to guide anyone who needed to get a midnight snack or a drink.

In spite of the pitch blackness, he made his way through the kitchen, his hand settling easily onto the familiar handle of the kitchen door. It was barred, of course, but he lifted the heavy wooden timber and set it aside. He wouldn't be going far, and if anyone dared approach the house with malicious intent, they would find something far worse than a locked door to stop them.

Outside, he paused as his eyes adjusted to the light of the moons and stars above, letting him make out the faded shapes of plants in neat rows. He reached out with his Life Sense, noting as he did that he could now sense something about the uses of the plants, not just what kind they were. Birdie's beloved herbs were mostly gone, with only the ones used for cooking remaining in their small plot to the side. These glowed in his magical vision with a pale silver shimmer.

Beside them, packed as tightly as they could be without overcrowding them, deep green showed row after row of fruits and vegetables. Some were struggling, with black spots showing disease, and angry red revealing the depredations of pests. Almost without thought he did something that he had been doing since they left North Goose, and reached out, pouring mana into the plants as if watering a drought-ridden crop.

Instantly, the black receded, and he smiled as he sent a small prayer of thanks to Gina. Small spots of glittering color began to gleam as buds and tiny fruits grew and swelled. He couldn't see well in the dimness, but even his merely human eyesight could see as the plants grew taller, and flowers sprouted and bloomed. With another thought, he *called*, and moths and other insects were drawn to the new flowers, happily pollinating the fresh bounty of the earth.

He smiled. It had been fun to 'encourage' people's potted plants and small gardens as they traveled the countryside and streets of the city. While they were waiting in the Temple Square, he had even coaxed a nearly dead rosebush back into lush glory, and barely been able to restrain his grin as he overheard the exclamations of joy from the mistress of the house. He had felt the blackness of some disease in her lungs, as well, and though he couldn't yet heal her without touching her, he had prayed, and known Gina had heard him when the darkness faded to a dull gray.

Garden now healthy and filled with burgeoning produce, he turned his attention to the thing he had come for. In spite of Manuela's certainty that he had chosen his new name because it was contained within his old, that was only part of the story. This tree held the rest of his truth.

He walked over, sure-footed even in the darkness as his Life Sense told him where the now-fertile earth was, and even the rocks and sticks teemed with life so small that he would have likely have been unable to see them with his naked eye. Gone were the days when he would trip over stones because they were 'invisible' to him. No life could hide from him now, at least not without effort. His mouth quirked as he remembered how easily Rouge's [Stealth] had concealed her from his view, at least when he was distracted, and he reminded himself with a sigh that he couldn't afford to become overconfident.

After several long strides which brought him to the edge of the enclosed kitchen garden, he stopped. Looking up, he saw the black shadows of heart-shaped leaves, and heard the distinctive *shush shush* sound as the leaves trembled in the soft post-storm wind. The pale bark gleamed silver in the moonlight, and he reached out to run his fingers over the bark, feeling smooth and rough together beneath his hand.

Lark's favorite tree. The aspen he and Tomas had tried and tried to kill, only to have it come back from even the smallest remnant of root. When Lark was only six, she had demanded that they stop trying, because 'hasn't it shown that it wants to live?' He had told her that it cast too much shade over the garden, and she had stubbornly researched edible and medicinal plants that like shade, insisting that they change the garden when they planted the following spring so that everything in it could grow happily together.

Sighing, he leaned forward, wrapping his arms around the slender trunk, his cheek pressing against the bark, no doubt leaving its imprint on him, undeniable and indelible.

"I need your help, old enemy, old friend. I hope you'll be willing," he said softly, and *reached* out with his magic. The aspen, which had been a solid presence in his new vision, stable and orderly, where the shorter-lived vegetables were full of energy and activity, seemed to burst into light.

Warmth flooded him. Recognition. Acknowledgement. Then, when he hesitantly showed the tree his plan, approval. He offered power. The tree accepted. Within the circle of his arms, the trunk shifted. Swayed. Fell.

He grunted as he caught it. The tree had never been particularly large, simply tenacious as the weeds Plum's mother had also eradicated from what started as her garden and became Lark's. He could span its width with his two hands, though he cradled it now in his arms, accepting its sacrifice as it had accepted his need. It was tall, though, growing up to reach what sun it could, and it held many leaves and branches. He could handle it with his new strength, but his muscles protested as he lowered it gently, respectfully, to the ground.

It still lived, though its light was dimming even as he watched. He gently pressed new power into it, and it flickered like the dying embers of a fire given new fuel. Flickered and flared. Keeping his left hand on the trunk of the tree, he touched his right to the hard band of metal around his waist. He hadn't, after all, been entirely idle while he waited for Rouge to enter the room above the entryway of his house.

The foyer had mostly been stripped of anything that could be sold. The statues that had once adorned marble pedestals were gone. Gold leaf had been stripped from the cornices, and even the rosewood door had been taken and replaced with one made of common oak. Frightened the thieves and short-term 'owners' might have been, but that didn't prevent them from attempting to recoup their investment.

One thing, however, that they couldn't easily remove were the solid metal balusters that twisted along the stairs. The things were well over two inches thick, solid and so shiny that in more modern times they looked rather tawdry. Aspen, with his Mage Smith skills, had reached out almost absently, with a sense that was nearly as habitual by now as his boosting of the nearby plant life, and determined that the metal, which he had always taken for granted as some cheap but sturdy alloy, showed in his senses as something very unusual.

He still, in fact, wasn't entirely sure what it was, but he could *feel* that it was much stronger than the old scythe blade that he had intended to use for this purpose. Thus, without hesitation, he had discarded the metal 'belt' he had made from the remnants of the poorly crafted tool, and used his magic to form one of the balusters into the solid metal loop that he now wore around his waist.

He split off some part of his magical attention and let it remain with the fallen aspen, keeping it alive as he worked. The rest of his mana he dropped into the metal band, and with a thought it softened and fell away from his waist. He raised his right hand carefully, the metal now a molten globe hovering in the air above it, and brought globe and tree together.

He closed his eyes, once again *feeling* for what he needed, letting both the tree and the metal tell him what they wanted to be as well. He remembered again what Gina had told him, that his Mage-Smithing could only be used to craft tools, not weapons, and he concentrated on the idea that this was a thing to be used to help, not hurt.

The outer and inner bark of the aspen burned with the heat from the molten metal. He drew the sphere along the tree, seeing how first the surface and then the deeper layers turned to ash and blew away in the wind, leaving fire-hardened heartwood behind.

Then the sphere became a stream, and entered the wood, searing away the softer pith at the center of the trunk, replacing it with a practically unbreakable core. As it went, there were a few places where long-gone branches created channels in the rings of the tree, and the metal flowed through these as well, hardening and reinforcing the wood.

Finally, hard, gleaming caps of metal formed on each end. One cap was simple, flat and solid, good for bracing a tired man walking his fields, digging a shallow furrow, or poking a hole in the earth for seeds. The other cap was equally solid, but grew 'branches' and 'leaves' like the aspen that had formed the foundation of this staff. The graceful branches twisted down, curving to wrap lovingly around the column of wood, while the leaves, hanging from single, unbroken loops, jingled softly as they fell into place.

All but the last traces of life were gone from the aspen wood by now, burned and changed as it was, but Aspen took a single thread of his mana and twisted it into that last faint hint, and knotted it together. He shuddered in pain as it *pulled*, trying to depart with the rest of the tree's life force, and he gritted his teeth. With Atae's assistance, he had once done something similar to tie himself to Khor, Sumi, Silus, and his other animal companions, and he wasn't sure if it would work now or not.

"Gina, please," he muttered, "I know you and Atae told me my old life was over, but you're the one who sent me here to face it. Let me keep this. *Please*."

A flush of golden warmth flooded him, and the wound he had created in his soul scarred over. The thread was still pulled out, still tied to the life of the staff, but the two forces seemed to have found some peace. Perhaps something like some carefully chosen plants finding a home in the shadow of a once unwanted tree.

Breathing out, he blinked open his eyes. Heat still pulsed from the metal in the staff, and the leaves and edges glowed like golden corn in the sun. Before he could second-guess himself, he released the magic. He felt the thread tying him to his creation *pull*, and for a moment he thought that it would snap after all, and the whole thing would fail, but then it settled with a contented rustle. The metal, meanwhile, cooled almost instantly, shivering into glimmering silver in the moonlight, and he chuckled a little at how cheerfully gaudy it was.

Carefully, he planted the bottom cap into the mud and wrestled himself to his feet, unsure when he had fallen to his knees in the wet earth. As he stood, he swept his hand over the tall grass near his feet, and it fell into his hand, cut in a tidy swathe. "I need a new hat," he murmured, critically examining the thick, damp stalks, "and so do you, Stick." He looked at the beautiful, intricate glory of branches and leaves crowning his new tool. "You're going to attract way too much attention as you are."

Finally standing to his full height, he walked over to the stump where the aspen once stood. He looked down, smiling wryly at the tiny seedlings happily growing there. He sent a flush of mana into them, and saw several grow taller as he watched. Nodding in satisfaction, he turned back to the house, making his way through the now riotous garden with sure feet, the leaves of his staff jingling musically and new plants springing up in the earth behind him with every step.

Walking through the dark kitchen was quite a bit easier this time, since Aspen's new staff glowed with a soft luminescence, casting a pale, clear light around him. He also found that his Life Sense suddenly had greater range and sensitivity than before, and he could feel everything from spiders and silverfish in the walls to the mice and bats under the floors and in the attics.

Even furniture carved of long-dead wood took on the faintest glimmer, and when he picked up the heavy bar and placed it back across the kitchen door, he found that when he lifted his hands, he left behind fresh twigs with leaf-buds filled with glittering promise.

He looked at the staff. "Stop that," he muttered, though the only response was a slight sense of self-satisfaction.

Behind him, a dark spot in his 'vision' seemed to shatter, and was suddenly filled with the cascading numbers of a familiar Traveler, with a small bundle of fire on her shoulder. He grimaced, turning slowly.

"Hello, Rouge. Silus."

Grim silence met him. He sighed.

"I wasn't doing anything dangerous," he said. *Well, other than the fact that there was a* very *small chance that a dying tree might unravel my soul like a badly knitted sweater and drag me with it into the Chaos Pool.*

More silence. "Really!" he lifted the staff, feeling a little beleaguered. "You keep telling me I need a new weapon. So, I made one."

Silus' squeaky voice was begrudgingly admiring, ::It *is* pretty.::

Rouge wasn't as ready to give any ground. "Aspen," he winced slightly at the cold tone of her voice, "you *just promised not to do this anymore.*"

He cleared his throat, knowing before he uttered them that his next words were extremely risky. "You sound like your father."

The silence grew absolutely frigid, and then he heard the girl deflate with a sigh. "*Fine.* So, you went and made a fancy cane in the back yard. Anything else you need to do?"

Aspen gritted his teeth. That was a low blow. "It's not a *cane*, it's a-"

"Symbol of your manliness? Yep. No worries. We get it. It's very… shiny." Silus snickered, and Aspen could almost see Rouge's smirk. Darn their [Darkvision].

"All right, all right. I was just coming to see if you wanted to join me for a little adventure, anyway. Is everyone else asleep?"

He could hear Rouge shift as she turned to look back up the stairs. "One of the older girls is on watch." Her voice grew more interested and less accusatory. "*What* little adventure?"

He grinned a little. "Remember how you asked if there was anything valuable left in my house?"

The little thief giggled gleefully. "Oh *yeah*. Now we're talking."

ë ë ë

At some point, someone had broken several steps out of the staircase leading up to the third floor. Given the deep gouges in the wood, as if an axe had been taken to it, Aspen suspected Plum had been making sure no one could easily access the area. After all, she knew Lord Penbrooke didn't allow anyone up there without permission, including Lark or any of the servants.

Fortunately, Aspen was in the company of a rather accomplished thief. As soon as Rouge saw the damaged stairs, she carefully assessed the remaining balustrade, which creaked ominously under even the slightest weight. Aspen suspected its continued existence might be a rather simplistic trap, rather than an oversight by Plum or Tomas. Rouge, however, clucked her tongue over it, and then glowed very softly golden.

"[Trap Detection] level up! It looks like it'd just crack under your weight, but it's tied into a system supporting this whole section of the stairs. You get too smart and think you can edge around it, and it'll drop the whole thing onto a bed of spikes down there." She tilted her head to indicate the area beneath the stairs, which *should* have been occupied by nothing more sinister than support beams and a linen closet.

Next, the girl turned her gaze toward the smooth wall on the other side of the stairs. She ran a hand over the elaborate wallpaper, tapping softly. She quickly narrowed in on a smaller area, and then, with a sudden punch, she broke through the paper, revealing a small space, just the right size for a handhold. She whistled softly. "I like that. Looks completely smooth until you open it up, but if you know what you're looking for," she smoothly pulled herself up, punching a foothold, then another handhold in the wall, "you can get across pretty fast."

Putting action to words, she traveled the distance across the nearly ten-foot gap in movements so fluid that he could barely see the moment she pushed the next hand or foothold through. Once across, she was barely within the faintest edge of his staff's soft glow, but he could see her teeth flash in a triumphant grin. "There's an easy trigger over here, too. I could drop you onto those spikes in an instant," she said far too cheerfully. "Looks like Plum and her Gramps set this up as an emergency retreat. I wonder how they were planning to get down if they had to run."

Aspen smiled grimly. "I know the answer to that, at least if they did any exploring up here before they decided to use it as their last defense. I'll show you when we're done." Carefully, he turned and examined the small holes in the wall beside him. Then he went back down the stairs a few steps, and stopped, looking back up thoughtfully.

Impatiently, Rouge said, "Come on! I want to see the treasure! It's not that hard."

Aspen shrugged, and took two long strides back up the stairs, planting the butt of his 'pretty' staff firmly against the wooden stair. The staff, which had started at about his own height of a few inches over six feet, suddenly grew, stretching to extend his leap as he pushed off, sailing smoothly over the gap as he landed solidly on the stair beside Rouge. With a soft creak, the staff shrank back into its smaller length almost instantly. The leaves on top jingled merrily, as if laughing at the gaping girl.

There was a moment of silence, and then Silus piped up from where she was hanging from the lintel of the broad double door at the top of the staircase. ::Come *on*. I want to see the treasure, too!::

When Aspen and Rouge made it up the last few steps, they stopped in front of the massive doors above which their little friend perched. Rouge flicked her lockpicks into her hand and knelt with an anticipatory smile. Aspen quickly put a staying hand on her shoulder.

"Wait, Rouge. I know I said that my spells broke when I lost my necromantic powers, and that's true, but, well," he reached into the front of his shirt and pulled out a small wooden disk on a leather thong, "we mages were under no illusions that we weren't high value targets to the enemy. Many of us left homes and families behind, and we didn't want them left unprotected in case we didn't return.

"We traded spells with each other, so each of our homes was under several layers of different kinds of magic. As a necromancer, I wasn't a popular dinner companion," one corner of his mouth lifted sardonically, "but my magic was among the best for, shall we say, discouraging trespassers. As a result, nearly every mage in the Corps owed me a spell or two."

He leaned forward, pressing the unadorned wooden disk into a slightly recessed area in which sat the large, inviting keyhole. A soft hiss rose from the disc, and it dissolved in his hand. He pushed the door open, revealing a dark hallway. "I used to have a metal one of those, which could be reused once it was recharged, which took about four hours. These single-use ones were for Lark and trusted staff. Plum and Tomas must still have had theirs, and I wouldn't be surprised if Lark gave her three to Plum when she-"

Aspen choked, but cleared his throat and continued roughly, "When she left. Many of the mages died in the final battles, and others could easily have removed their spells once I was gone, but some few, such as Manuela, felt true loyalty to me, and wouldn't have let the spells lapse. Of course, not all spells nor all mages are equal, and some will have faded without maintenance, but there was no reason to take a chance."

The tall man, shoulders thrown back, head high, broad shoulders set with military precision, gestured regally into the darkness. "After you, m'lady. Your treasure awaits."

Rouge hunted. She looked in every room on the sprawling third floor, quickly discovered two secret doors, several much-less-lethal traps which seemed to be designed primarily for containment, and picked no less than sixteen locks. Aspen watched, leaning his shoulder against the heavy door frame through which they entered. He was fairly certain the brief glows he saw were from her [Disarm Traps] and [Hidden Passages] Skills, but he could have been mistaken.

The girl and bat team scoured every inch of the six bedrooms, the office, the massive library, and the extensive laboratory, complete with glass jars of floating objects, many of which were more disturbing for the fact that they seemed familiar, but couldn't quite be identified. Silus had been too young to enter this area, which had often been filled with experimental undead, before they were forced to flee Bright, so she was as much in the dark as Rouge. By the time the two gave up, Aspen had pulled his bundle of grass from where he'd stuffed it through his belt and was nimbly weaving a new hat by the light of his helpful Stick.

The first things he saw were Rouge's soft wrapped-leather boots coming to a halt at the bottom of his vision, beneath the brim of the new hat he was checking for size. Then Silus' querulous little voice entered his head. ::Where's the *treasure*, Aspen?::

He looked up, raising one eyebrow as he took in the two dusty, frustrated females. From the cobwebs in Silus' fur and dangling from one of Rouge's pointed brown ears, they had even tried crawling around in the cabinets and under the beds. "The skill increases weren't enough?" He asked innocently.

"No!"

::No!::

The simultaneous denials made him laugh out loud, and he finally removed the hat, tugging at a few strands of grass that had been poking him. "Is it dawn yet?" He knew well that it wasn't. His Life Sense could now tell him as clearly as his eyes when the sun was rising, and the night creatures were just beginning to think about returning to their rest, while the beasts and insects that were most active at dawn and dusk were still sleeping soundly.

Rouge's eyes flickered up, probably checking the magical clock all Travelers had, and she shook her head, but Silus dropped from Rouge's dusty shoulder and flew to the nearest window, which happened to be in the office, to the left. The bat caught the heavy velvet curtain, which Rouge had thoroughly shaken, raising quite a dust cloud, not long ago. She poked her fuzzy head through the heavy cloth.

::Noooooo…,:: she sent, rather dubiously.

"Mmm," Aspen nearly hummed. He could hear the smugness in his own voice, and winced at the reaction Rouge would have if she-

The little thief crossed her arms, glaring. "*Aspen!* You promised! I can tell you're being sneaky!"

Silus popped her head back out of the curtains, golden eyes glaring at the tall man. ::He is? Why didn't you say so?:: She fell from the curtains, flapping her wings quickly and flying back to land with her small claws gripping the front of Aspen's bedraggled shirt. ::Aspeeeeeennnnn,:: she whined, ::I'm tired, and I'm hungry, and I *want treasure*!::

Aspen sighed, reaching up to smooth cobwebs out of the silky silver tufts of fur in front of Silus' large ears. "All right. Go look out the window."

Rouge ran for the window, and Silus quickly flew after her. Throwing open the curtain, the elf girl stared out over the dark kitchen garden. "What?" she said, "It's just a…"

Her eyes widened suddenly, and Aspen, who had been about to offer another hint, stopped with his mouth half open.

"Holy chrysanthemums! It's an illusion! Aspen, I just got a new Skill! A Passive, too! [Illusion Break]! It says I have a small chance to break any illusion, but thanks to my Fowl Trickster sub-class, it automatically increases to a minimum 10% chance. This 'window' is on an inside wall, isn't it? It's actually an illusion hiding a secret door, isn't it?" The girl looked around at him, big hazel eyes shining in her pointed face.

Aspen huffed out a disgruntled sigh, though he was inwardly proud of her for figuring out the trick. Getting a minimum 10% chance to break illusions was an amazing skill, too, especially for a thief. "Open the window and see," he told her.

Quickly, the girl's nimble fingers popped the latches of the window open, though they were stiff from disuse. She lifted the bottom of the glass pane, and the view of the garden dissolved into a blank stone wall. The area where the window should have opened into the night air instead gaped into blackness.

Aspen gestured grandly again. "After you."

Rouge was through the window before Aspen's lips closed on the 'oo', and a moment later he heard a shriek. It wasn't, however, the shriek of joy he'd been expecting, but rather one of surprise quickly followed by a yelp and a thud. Cautiously, he poked his head through the darkness, and blinked against the brightness of the glowing gems that lit the space beyond.

Looking around, he didn't see anything unexpected except a young elf plastered against the wall beside him, eyes huge and finger shaking as she pointed at the far wall. "What," she squeaked out, "is that?"

He looked at the six-foot-high spider exoskeleton carefully mounted on a large pedestal. Each of the eight legs, except for one that was missing below the patella, was easily ten feet long, and the chelicerae were curving sickles almost four feet long.

He coughed slightly. "Ah, sorry. I'm used to it. That was from Sumi's mother. Atae set me quite a quest chain to get her and her brother, and at the end I had to steal eggs from the Spider Queen."

Rouge carefully stepped away from the wall on shaky legs. "You *killed* Sumi's mom?"

His eyes widened. "Oh! No. This is one of her molts. I just had to steal the eggs, and then Atae came and told her to let me keep them. She wasn't exactly happy, since she's really a very good mother, but I agreed to let Sumi and Orion go visit every year until they were ten, and Araignee gave me this exoskeleton to study. I've used a few parts in spells, but I kept it mostly intact." He looked around, scratching his head. "I have all of Sumi's molts around here somewhere too."

The thief gulped, glaring at him. "Why didn't you warn me?" She dropped her voice to mimic his much deeper one. "'Oh, by the way, Rouge, there's a giant spider inside, but it's okay, it's just a shell.'" She crossed her arms and tapped her foot at him.

He shrugged. "I figured you'd be too busy looting all the treasure."

Her hazel eyes unfocused as he said the magic word, and she licked her lips. "T-treasure? Wait, where?"

Aspen waved his hand around, and saw her eyes go glassy as she finally took in their full surroundings.

Shelves piled with books, scrolls, and artifacts lined every wall from floor to ceiling. Weapon racks stood alongside large wooden chests, while suits of gear ranging from full plate armor to mage-silks stood neatly displayed on faceless mannequins. A massive table stood to their left, partially hidden by one of the spider's legs, and on it was a detailed map of Bright and its surroundings. As he glanced at it, he saw flickers that indicated its magic was still functional, and it was updating in real time as the city changed.

"Ho-ly cats, Aspen! What the heck? You said you donated a lot to Lark's hospital, and set up pensions, and there wouldn't be much left!" Rouge started toward a suit made of supple leather hanging on a display nearby, then changed her mind and swerved toward one of the enormous chests. Then she turned again and went for a bookshelf with a sapphire the size of her fist resting like a paperweight on top of several scrolls.

He shrugged, feeling a grin tug at the corner of his mouth. "I didn't think there was much chance that this would still be here. I thought the place would have been sold or torn down, and someone would have found it. Even if it was still abandoned, surely thieves would have gotten over their fear of the Royal Necromancer and broken in. Thanks to Plum, though, everything seems to be intact."

Rouge whistled in awe as she scooped the sapphire from the shelf, letting the scrolls curl closed with a soft scrape of dry, aged paper. "Why didn't you take this with you?"

Aspen shrugged again, and began walking toward the table with the map display. "I was level three when we left Bright, and that was only because Sumi and Silus kept bringing me bugs and small rodents to kill. Children are usually level six or seven when they spawn. I couldn't carry anything heavier than the clothes on my back, and it was only because of my companions and the Head Librarian that I was able to arrange what I did. Sumi and Silus found every bit of gold in the lower house and brought it out. Then Khor carried it all to the library along with a note. The Head Librarian did the rest, while I laid in my bed in my very luxurious prison cell."

He stared down, tracing the outlines of the castle with his finger until he found the Mage's Tower. He tapped it twice. "I was here, unable to do so much as dress myself or walk outside." He leaned over, stretching to put a finger on his house, which showed as a dark and overgrown patch in an otherwise orderly and tidy neighborhood. Then he touched the gothic eyesore that was the Great Library.

"Fortunately, no one realized that I could still communicate with my companions, so they thought they were little more than the loyal beasts they would have been had Atae not granted them sapience through their bond with me. My enemies believed me cut off from friends and information alike, and so those three were able to move about with relative freedom, though they were sometimes mistreated by those who wouldn't have dared do so before my… injury."

Silus piped up now. ::It wasn't too bad. Khor and Sumi lost some levels too, but they could still take care of themselves. Some horrible woman caught me flying during the day once, though, and,:: the little bat shivered on Rouge's shoulder, ::Sumi had to come save me.::

Rouge had made the sapphire disappear, and sent several other gems and golden trinkets after it. Now, she wandered around the room, snuggling her little friend and touching works of art and books with equal care, though nothing else vanished into her inventory.

Aspen tilted his head. "Aren't you going to take it?"

She looked down, scuffing the toe of her soft boot on the gleaming marble floor. When she looked up, her expression was torn between concern and a clear desire to Take Everything. "This is *your* stuff, though. You're my friend. Don't you need this?"

He laughed. "*This* is the remnants of an ageless undead army. Hundreds, if not thousands of years of loot, divided between the King, his officers, the nobility, and bonuses given to those who contributed the most to each battle. As a noble officer, and the Necromancer who raised legions of the enemy and our own fallen to take what victories we could, I received more than any mortal could possibly use. My friends found enough trinkets lying around in the lower house to keep me in wagons, tools, and clothes for the rest of eternity, and I already left all of this behind once. I'd far rather see it go to you than the greedy and corrupt nobility of our fair city."

Walking over to a bookshelf, he pulled out one well-worn book, turning it over in his hands, reading the title; *Princess Violetta and the Bugbear*. He held it up. "I'll keep this one, though, and perhaps a few other books. There are no skill books here, nor are there spell scrolls. Those the King kept, and usually passed on to Duke Geral, alas. This was Birdie's favorite bedtime story, though, and there are likely some others here worth taking home."

Rouge bit her lip. "I'm gonna have to do some inventory management. My main Inventory is full, and I only have two small bags of holding with me. I don't even know where to start!"

Aspen grinned. "That's solved easily enough." He walked over to a large, ornate chest, indistinguishable from the other similarly gaudy containers around it, and flipped open the lid. Inside was a tangle of cloth bags of every imaginable fabric, color, and size. "These can only be used by Travelers, so most people sell them or leave them behind, but I have - *had* - minions to carry anything I could pick up, so I was able to bring them back. I never got around to doing anything with them, but they may help you now."

The girl's beautiful hazel eyes widened. "Are those all *Bags of Holding*?"

He nodded, and she dived in.

🦇 🦇 🦇

Once Rouge dug into the bags, she went to work. In order to use the smallest number of bags – and be able to find anything later – she started by sorting the bags by how much they could hold, then going around and gathering all of one kind of item the bag could contain. A brilliant blue bag was first, and she dug through chests and shelves to gather all the gemstones she could find.

While she was busy muttering darkly about 'slots', 'encumbrance', and 'Tetris', Aspen laid down on a pile of thick, warm furs that had been thrown into the corner. He sent out a tendril of awareness, watching for movement other than the small shifts of sleeping children in the banquet hall below, and closed his eyes.

He woke to Rouge poking his shoulder cautiously. "Come on, Aspen! I've got to go, and it's going to be morning for you soon."

Aspen sat up, pushing his magic out in a wave, searching for anything larger than a cat that might be moving near the house. He let out his breath in a relieved huff when he found nothing except a few raccoons settling in to sleep for the day, and Plum in the kitchen, presumably preparing breakfast for the children, who were just beginning to stir.

He looked down as he heard some grumpy grumbling in his head and felt movement against his chest. Silus was there, looking rumpled and flustered, with her wing-thumbs already smoothing her fine fur back into place.

::I just went to sleep!:: Her big golden eyes were accusing as she stared up at him.

Gently, he scooped her up and deposited her back on his shoulder. "Sorry, little one. I didn't realize I'd drifted off myself." He stood, brushing himself down automatically, though his filthy and bedraggled clothing didn't really respond to his efforts.

Rouge was practically dancing in place. "I've got to go! My dad is going to kill me if I don't get to bed for a few hours. Will my Zombie be safe here? Can I sleep in those furs? Or should I follow you? I mean, I'll be back soon, for me, but it won't be until tonight for you." Bags of all types were attached to her body with mismatched belts and straps. Even though the magical bags were still as flat as if they were empty, there were so many that she looked like some sort of shambling pile of cloth and leather.

With an effort, Aspen forced back the laugh that threatened to escape at her absurd appearance. She shot him a sour glance anyway, as if she knew what he was thinking.

"Hey, this is your fault. If you put this into a bank where it belongs…"

He raised an eyebrow. "If I had, Geral would have found a way to claim it as estate taxes or fines. Plus," he grinned, feeling his face stretch in ways it hadn't in a long time, "if it was in a bank, you wouldn't have been able to juggle six diamonds while hopping on one foot."

Her cheeks darkened. "I thought you were asleep!"

He just laughed, climbing out of his soft bed. "When you wake up, take those, too, would you? They're much more comfortable than grass, though I have to admit they don't smell as good." He wrinkled his nose at the lingering musky scent of disused leather and fur.

Rouge all but dove at the fur pile, tangling herself up in a few straps as she did, and then having to struggle to free her arms and one leg from the mass. Finally, she lay, out of breath and as flustered as a cat who missed a leap to a table, giving him a 'if you tell anyone about this…' look. Then the life drained from her face, and she was gone.

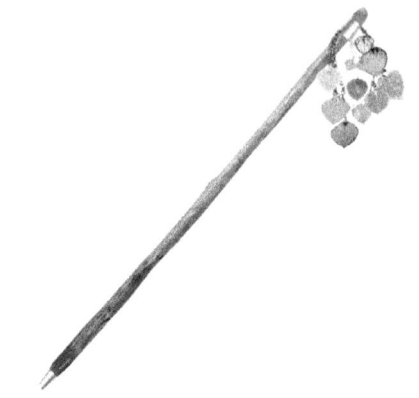

Chapter Eleven

Rouge

Z oey went straight to bed after getting out of her pod. She barely made it before her dad's (so arbitrary!) logout time, but for once she was actually tired. She sent a belated thank you for the heads up to Jace, then ordered Emily to turn off the lights, and with a final thought that tomorrow was *definitely* the day to change her AI's name, she was asleep.

The alarm went off way too soon, and she got ready for work. Her favorite pants were dirty, so she pulled on a skirt and blouse, her comfy shoes, which really didn't even look that ugly any more, smoothed her hair up into the simplest poof ever, and ran down the stairs. Max was waiting for her in the kitchen, as usual, with his head on his paws, staring at his empty food dish. Quickly, she poured him some kibble, and he gave a quick 'thank you' slurp before attacking it with his face.

Her dad entered a moment later, looking as tired as she felt, and she gave him an impulsive hug. His heavy sweater felt loose under her arms, and she looked up at him in surprise. "Have you lost some weight, Dad?"

His cheeks darkened, and he scrubbed a hand over his hair, which was beginning to grow out to the point she liked the best, somewhere in between fresh buzz and Afro. "Ah, yeah. I realized I was going to need to buy some bigger pants soon, and you know I hate clothes shopping."

She stepped back and stared at him. Her eyes narrowed, and she pointed an accusing finger at him. "You're hoping to meet Bree Stephenson, aren't you? You figure when all this is over, Bridget will introduce you to her mom in real life, and you want to look good."

His ears turned an impressive shade of brick beneath their deep brown tone, and he drew in a deep breath, closing his eyes. "Okay, yes. I would like to impress Ms. Stephenson if I get a chance to meet her."

She felt a huge grin stretch across her face, and she pumped her fist. "Yes! I am going to get so much mileage out of this! But you know you've already met her, right? I mean, it's pretty obvious she's-"

Her dad's hand covered her mouth, and his eyes flicked to the house interface screen in the wall nearby. "That may be true, and it may not. We're not supposed to talk about it, and there's no point in speculating, since it won't change anything anyway."

Carefully, she removed his hand, which still smelled faintly of his Bearglove body wash, and stuck her tongue out at him. "Fiiiine. I do have one more question, though."

Turning away, he grabbed two slices of bread and headed for the toaster. His deep voice was deliberately nonchalant. "What?"

"Are you going to ask her out?"

He dropped his bread, and Max was a happy dog.

🍂 🍂 🍂

When she arrived at work (still snickering occasionally at the memory of the expression on her dad's face) she was about to walk past the security desk when she saw Sam, one of the guards, beckon subtly to her with a tilt of the head. She walked over, smiling. She and Sam had discovered a mutual love of anime one rainy morning a few weeks ago, when Zoey brought in her classic Sailor Moon umbrella, and now they traded recommendations on a pretty regular basis.

Today, though, Sam's usual friendly smile was a little forced, and they reached out unobtrusively as if to touch Zoey's hand when she reached the security desk. When the hand was pulled back slightly, the edge of a slip of paper was visible, and Sam lowered one eyelid in a subtle wink. Zoey carefully slid her own fingers forward until she'd pinned the paper so Sam could withdraw. Once the paper was transferred, they exchanged a few words, and Sam turned to someone else in clear dismissal.

Zoey was absolutely burning to know what was on the paper, but she knew Sam had to have had a reason for all the cloak and dagger business, so she just clutched it in her fist until she was through security, and then she ducked into the first restroom she saw.

Once in the stall, she uncurled the now crumpled and sweaty slip of paper and looked at it. It held only three words, written in a hasty scribble.

LUNCH MS PIGS

She frowned. It was obviously from Nina, since 'Ms Pigs' was an in-joke between the two of them, but why wouldn't the other girl just text her? She started to pull out her screen to send a message, but put it away slowly. It would be hard, but she could wait for lunch.

Fortunately, it was a busy day in Design. The mood was definitely subdued, with even Jazmin heavy-eyed and solemn. Everyone who wanted Bridget's job was busy putting together a portfolio to show their best work, and their 'plans for the future of the department'.

Zoey caught Granny lurking around Bridget's door several times, lingering as if hoping the young woman would emerge from behind the firmly closed portal. Harris also seemed to be wandering the main hallway more than usual, in spite of the fact that he *should* be at his desk putting together his own portfolio. Between the two of them and the regular through traffic, Zoey herself was never able to find a moment to approach and try knocking on the door.

So. Frustrating.

When lunchtime rolled around, Zoey was just finishing up her now-daily cleaning of Mr. Hamncheese's cage. She and the fluffball were once again on good terms, since Zoey had mostly gotten over the Hamster Hellion, and Hammy knew she was good for a gentle ear scrootch that wouldn't overly disturb his daily ten-hour nap.

As soon as possible, Zoey darted toward the stairs, avoiding the elevator, where she was sure to be seen. It was five flights up to the top floor, but she nearly felt like she was flying. She wasn't even short of breath when she landed lightly on her toes in front of the emergency exit door. Whatever was in the pod-goo, if that was what was making her so strong and agile lately, was really amazing stuff, because she still felt like she could keep going.

Looking down, she saw that the door was slightly open, and a plastic figure of Miss Piggy was propped in the gap. She leaned over and snagged the little plastic diva, pulling the door the rest of the way open and sliding through as she did. She let the door latch quietly behind her.

Nina had discovered the broken alarm on the door shortly after she first arrived, when they had a fire drill. She was on the 12th floor, delivering something to Mr. Landon when the alarm went off, and she hadn't known it was a drill. So, naturally, she headed for the stairs, and decided that using the emergency exit was safer than going down twelve flights of stairs into an unpredictable situation, and it had 'emergency' right there on the door, right?

Dutifully, the older girl had swiped her badge over the security pad and ducked out the door, figuring there had to be a fire escape, or a ladder, or an inflatable slide, or *something* to get her down if necessary. She was disappointed, therefore, to find herself surrounded by stone floors and solid balustrades so tall she could barely see over them, even though she was almost five foot eight. Clearly, this was an emergency exit in name only, and the only way to the ground was one which would end very abruptly.

It was at this point, however, that the alarm stopped blaring, lights stopped flashing, and *Veritas Corp* sent out a message to all employees in the building that the drill was complete and they should return to work. Nina then had to open the door to go back in, cringing as she realized that this time the alarm would be *her* fault.

No alarm.

Looking around, Nina had noted several old cigarette butts in a mossy bucket of sand nearby. Putting two and two together, she realized that someone – probably someone fairly high up in the company, since it was all top execs on the 12th floor – had used this as their own illicit smoking room. Since the increased luxury tax had been applied to cigarettes a decade or so before, raising the price of a single pack to well over thirty dollars, even the most dedicated smokers had finally given in. No smokers meant no need for smoking areas, so the few who could afford the habit had to make their own space.

Once the discovery had been made, it took Nina only a few weeks to determine that it was no longer in use. The number of butts in the bucket never changed, and when she put a piece of tape across the door, it was still in place a week later. Nina then turned it into her own hidey hole, gradually bringing up a chair, an umbrella, and even a small folding table. She didn't use it often, because she actually liked her job, and rarely felt the need for someplace to hide for longer than a bathroom break, but when she wasn't feeling well or just needed a breather after showing around a particularly difficult guest, she headed up here.

When she'd shown it to Zoey – after making her pinky-swear she'd never tell – they had discovered that Zoey's badge wouldn't open the door at all. As a runner, Nina's badge allowed her through almost any door in the company. As a temporary intern, Zoey's was limited to Design and the main access areas. So much for Emergency Exit. Zoey felt a little like the passengers on the lower level of the *Titanic* who were locked in when the ship started to sink, and she was only slightly mollified by the fact that anyone who tried to escape through the door was likely to die a fiery death anyway.

In any case, Nina had used the little figure of Miss Piggy that served as her lucky charm – because Miss Piggy was apparently somehow the inspiration for Nina's glasses obsession – to prop open the door so Zoey could get in and out. They'd only eaten lunch there twice, but Zoey had joked that Miss Piggy was the hostess, and thus it became Ms Piggy's Café.

Now, Zoey tossed the little figurine into Nina's waiting hand and saluted jauntily. "What's with all the secrecy, Nina?"

The taller girl was looking unusually pale and serious, and her eyes flickered around the small space, reminding Zoey of how suspiciously her dad had been eyeing the house AI earlier. She felt the grin drop off her face, and her brows drew together. "Nina?"

Nina drew in a long breath, then stepped past Zoey and pushed firmly on the door, making sure it was thoroughly latched. "Look, Zoe," she muttered quietly, leaning in even though no one else could possibly hear her, "I saw something… I shouldn't even tell you. You know how this lot is, always thinking someone is out to steal from 'em. But I saw something that was a bit sus – suspicious, you know? – and it had your name on it."

Zoey's eyes widened. "What was it?"

Nina shook her head, looking around again. She reached into her pocket and pulled out her screen. She unrolled it before looking up, her expression conflicted. "I could be fired for this. But I just… I trust my intuition, and it's telling me you need to see this." She unlocked the screen with her thumb, and Zoey could see that an image was pulled up. On it was a single piece of paper, with a series of names neatly written on it in a looping, feminine script. One corner was torn, but it was still legible.

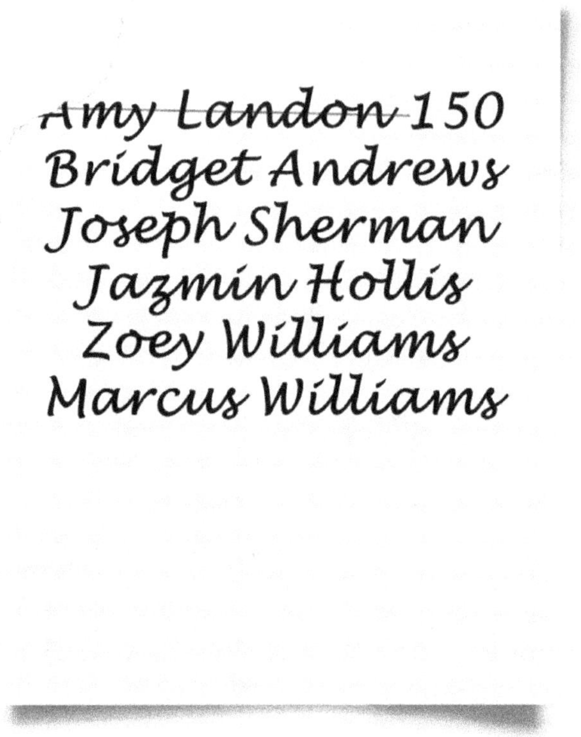

Amy Landon 150
Bridget Andrews
Joseph Sherman
Jazmin Hollis
Zoey Williams
Marcus Williams

Zoey pulled back, a sharp twinge of something like electricity traveling down her spine. "What is that? Where did you find it?"

Nina shrugged. "Ms. McKeene was in a meeting first thing this morning and called me to go down and get a file from her office. She's the worst about not trusting digital security. Keeps her personal files on a system that's not online, and prints out anything she needs to show other people. She'd left the file on her desk, but when I picked it up, this was stuck to the back. Look, there's something on the other side." She slid her finger over the screen, pulling up the next image. It was clearly the same sheet, with only a few more words scrawled across it at an angle.

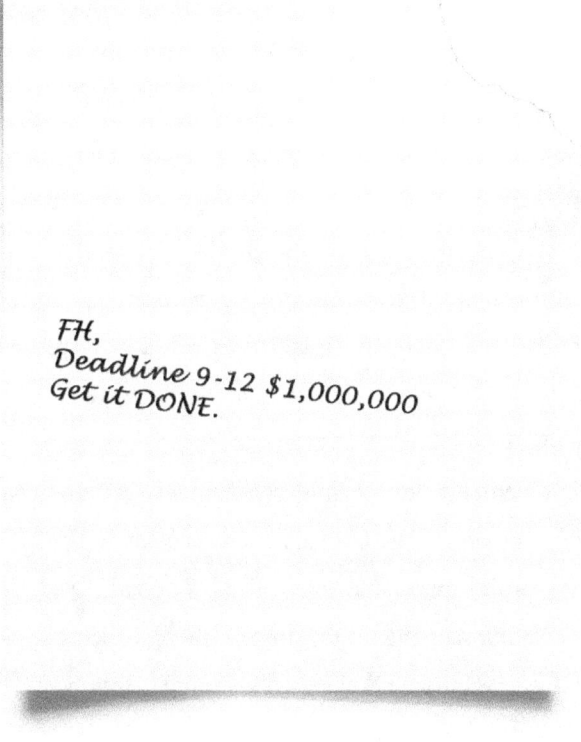

FH,
Deadline 9-12 $1,000,000
Get it DONE.

Nina looked at Zoey, words tumbling out excitedly. "I don't know what's going on, but I wouldn't want to see my name on a list like that, and your dad is on there too. There's no reason for him to be on a list relating to *your* job, eh? I found it caught beneath the edge of the desk, and I put it right back, like I never saw it, but just in case, I didn't want her to see me talking to you right after I had a chance to read it, but I thought you should know."

Zoey grilled Nina to see if the other girl had any more information, but that was it. The meeting Ms. McKeene had been in was a regularly scheduled every-Tuesday-morning meeting for the Personnel department, so no clues there. Nina loved conspiracy theories (she was *almost* completely convinced that the moon was actually a hologram) and had a definite tendency to see mysteries and plots in the most everyday situations. Which amused Zoey, usually, since she was usually quietly eating a sandwich while Nina ranted, not knowing that the teenager right beside her was involved in a real-life conspiracy.

None of which explained the list. And the fact that one of the people *on* said list was now dead. And crossed off. Ominous much? But still, the list could be something relatively innocent - like, say, trying to figure out who knew about the sell it/give it away contest, even though Ms. McKeene theoretically wasn't supposed to know about it *herself,* but even the best kept secrets would start slipping over time, and since the Viper was in HR, a lot of people theoretically went to her with their concerns, though honestly, *who* would be *stupid* enough to trust her with *anything?*

Zoey took a mental breath, then let it out slowly, trying to calm her racing thoughts. It was obvious that Georgia McKeene knew something. Probably something she wasn't supposed to know. The list of names seemed to be mostly those on the 'give it away' side of the contest, though according to Bridget, Dr. Joe was a 'sell it' . Maybe he'd changed his mind? How would *Ms. McKeene* know when Bridget didn't? In any case, crossing off the name of someone who couldn't affect the outcome made sense, right? Cold-blooded, sure, but that person couldn't change anything any more.

Unless, of course, she was a *real* cyber-Zombie. But there was seriously no way for McKeene to know *that*, so…

Okay, another breath.

So, the *real* question was, what was up with the note on the other side? The deadline part was easy (though Zoey was realizing that *dead*line was just an unnecessarily sinister word) because that would be a little over six months from when Bree Stephenson said she was going on hiatus and vanished. Bridget hadn't told them when the competition would end, but September 12 made sense.

Which reminded Zoey that she'd never asked what happened if neither team won? Like, if Zoey didn't complete the quest chain, and the Bad Guys didn't finish theirs, either, what happened? Did they start over? Did one side or the other win by default? Did it come down to who was closest? Were there *points* or something? Zoey had a bad feeling that if there were points, her side wasn't exactly racking them up. They'd spent all winter hanging out in a two-room hovel eating snacks and weaving bad hats, after all.

Okay, okay. O-kay.

There was FH. Someone's initials? Player name? Zoey was all for it being FartHat (except that he was actually really mean and kind of badass, and if he was the Bad Guy in-game, that didn't bode well for the Good Guys) but who would write a note on paper in the *real world* for a player online? Unless, of course, Zoey's dad had actually signed her up for long-term immersion, and none of this was real, because she was in a *simulation* of real life...

She looked up at Nina, who was watching her with an expression of concern and worry.

"Smack me. Or... or spin a coin or something. No, wait, I'll try and use one of my skills!" She stretched out her hand and tried to trigger [Sleight of Hand] and steal something from Nina.

Nothing.

She huffed out a sigh of relief.

Concern was winning over excitement in Nina's big brown eyes, and she shoved her bright-purple-with-fuchsia-stars cat-eye glasses up her nose with excessive force. "So... don't smack you?" Nina asked. Her eyebrows drew down as her expression grew calculating. "Because if you've been keeping some actual conspiracy from me while I was telling you about how Elvis' head is in cold storage in Area 52, I'm going to-"

Zoey cringed back dramatically and laughed a little. "No, I'm sure it has something to do with my internship here. Those are all people involved in it, though I'm not sure why Amy would be on there. Maybe she was working on it before her accident? Because of the part where I work with Dr. Joe. Amy was in R&D, too, right? And, uh, Jazmin probably had to do some paperwork?"

Nina looked disappointed, and touched her screen, expanding the second image. "So, what about this? You can't tell me you're getting paid a million dollars. If you are, you're taking me out to dinner. Like, a hundred times. Plus, your internship ends next Friday, right? It's still two months until September twelfth. *And*, I looked it up, and there's no one with the initials FH in this building except Farrah Hudson in Dining, and Franz Heinzburger, but he barely speaks English even though he's a beaut of a programmer."

Zoey shrugged, trying to look as confused as Nina. Not really a big stretch, since she *was* confused, just maybe not actually as much as the older girl. "Maybe she just scribbled that note on the back of an old list, and the two have nothing to do with each other? I mean, why wouldn't you put them both on the same side of the page?"

Nina spluttered, holding up her fingers in a 3"x 4" rectangle. "It was small! Like, 'I'm trying to be sneaky, so I'm going to write on a tiny piece of paper' small."

Eyes widening, Zoey attempted nonchalance. "Oh? Was it, like, special paper, too? Shiny? Thick?"

Nina looked from the screen to Zoey. "Yes. It was. Good cardstock with some of that pearlescent look to it."

"Like the little papers they used for the table with Amy's picture on it? You know, for people to write notes on?" Zoey's voice was small.

Nina nodded, eyes huge. "Exactly like that."

Zoey gulped. "I'm sure she was just thinking about something and grabbed the nearest piece of paper to write a note. Or two. Or, you know, they had to get that paper from somewhere. There're probably stacks of it sitting around in the warehouse. It's just a coincidence." But she was thinking about a torn card and a vicious whisper, and wondering if that was true.

After that, the two girls found that what had been a thrilling exercise in spycraft had suddenly become something with a painful edge of truth to it. The reality of Amy's death was not fun at all.

Nina cleared her throat. "I'm going to miss you when the internship is over, but… maybe it's for the best, eh?"

Zoey shrugged noncommittally, well aware that while her job was almost over, her involvement in the competition was far from done. One person on that list was dead, and if Bridget was right, multiple attempts had been made on her life. Then there was Dr. Joe's recent injury. Was that really an accident?

Why was Jazmin's name there with the rest of them? Zoey distinctly remembered Jazmin being surprised to see her on her first day, so the Head Wrangler of Cats hadn't been in on the secret then at least. Viper-face McKeene *had* been harassing Jazmin pretty hard the other day, though, so maybe the list was just 'people I don't like'? But then why was Zoey's dad on it? As far as she knew, he'd never even talked to the Snake.

As thoughts and theories tumbled wildly through her head, Zoey caught movement from the corner of her eye. In her current state, caught halfway between reality and a cascade of ifs, thens, and maybes, she reacted without thought. Spinning, her foot flicked up, snap-kicking something out of the air and sending it catapulting over the high balustrade and, presumably, sliding down the side of the pyramid.

Nina gaped at her, clutching the hand she'd barely snatched back in time to avoid having it also meet Zoey's foot. She looked back and forth between the railing and Zoey. "If you changed your mind about trying the wasabi potato chips, you could have just said so."

Zoey smiled weakly.

🐾 🐾 🐾

Dr. Joe was in his office when Zoey arrived, out of breath and nearly late. Sara, looking much happier and more relaxed, was hovering around him, offering ice-packs and fetching anything the man looked at for more than a moment. It was almost like Sara was *glad* to be able to do things for him. Zoey narrowed her eyes, and watched for a moment before the two were aware that she was there.

Dr. Joe just looked tired and a little out of sorts, which made sense since his right foot and ankle were in a compression cast and his leg was propped up on a chair by his desk. Sara, though, really did look happy, and when Joe wasn't looking at her (which was most of the time, actually, because he seemed to feel that Sara was going just a little Over the Top) she was looking at him like, as Zoey's grandma liked to say, he hung the moon.

Sara was totally crushing on the doc. The doctor who had been *engaged* to someone else less than a year ago. Someone else who was, conveniently, now dead (or mostly dead, anyway) after being involved in what Bridget was convinced was *not* an accident. Now Dr. Joe had had a much less serious accident, and was basically completely dependent on his beautiful, smart assistant. Who would absolutely not have killed his fiancée or injured him so that he would see her as something more than an assistant. Because things like that Did. Not. Happen. In. Real. Life.

Clearly, Nina's paranoid tendencies were rubbing off on Zoey. Either that, or both of them were spending way too much time in *VO*, where Game Logic ruled. Or both.

Pasting a smile on her face, Zoey walked loudly into the lab, practically stomping her feet as if shaking off non-existent mud. Dr. Joe and Sara looked around. Dr. Joe looked almost relieved, while Sara's expression showed a flicker of irritation before smoothing into casual welcome. Joe levered himself from behind his desk, and when his cast neared the floor, she heard a faint *whirring* sound as the servos in the cast kicked on, producing an air cushion that would keep him from putting too much pressure on the injured appendage. He picked up a cane from where it was leaning against the bookshelf behind him, and step-slid his way toward her.

"Zoey! I'm glad you made it. I was starting to wonder if the excitement yesterday had scared you off. Sara told me about your little confrontation with Dr. Veralt. I do appreciate the both of you standing up for me and the security of the project, but rest assured that our department is a team, and you don't need to worry about anything. While Dr. Veralt's bedside manner could use some work, I'm certain he's just as dedicated to Veritas Corp. as the rest of us."

Dr. Joe smiled broadly, showing his crooked bottom tooth in a smile that looked as fake as his words sounded. His eyes flicked behind her at the partially open door, and Zoey turned just in time to see the edge of a lab coat vanish down the hall. As the door shut with a click, the smile faded, and Dr. Joe leaned forward, speaking in a low voice.

"Seriously, though, good job. Usually, I keep everything closed up behind passwords and biometric locks, but when the cart ran over me yesterday," he tapped his cane meaningfully against the side of the cast, "I'd already opened everything in preparation for your arrival. None of our findings would have been compromised, but our research methods and data collection would have been enough. We're a competitive bunch around here, you know, and yearly bonuses ride on impressing the boss with your creativity and results." He chuckled, but Zoey was certain there was more to it than raises and bonuses. Though if that $1,000,000 on Ms. McKeene's note was in reference to *that*...

She shook her head slightly, smiling back, then shifting her gaze to include Sara. "That's okay. I don't get to scare off people like that very often. He kind of reminded me of my Humanities teacher, and that guy collects his boogers in a jar in his desk." Dr. Joe and Sara made identical repulsed expressions, and Zoey waved her hands. "I mean, he definitely blows his nose a *lot*, and he has a jar of some yucky yellow stuff, so that's what somebody told me. It's probably not true."

Dr. Joe burst out laughing, continuing far longer than Zoey thought reasonable. Even Sara was giving him an 'Are you okay?' look by the time he finally swiped tears away from his eyes and took a few gasping breaths. "Sorry, sorry. You just reminded me of my own high school career, and a particular instance where my best friend and I stole the Chemistry teacher's spare dentures and... anyway, thank you. I needed that."

He swiped at his eyes once more, nodding toward the changing room. "You ladies go get set up, and I'll start the pod diagnostics. Let's have a good day, shall we?"

It wasn't until Zoey was alone in the changing room, pulling on her bodysuit, that she realized neither she nor Dr. Joe had mentioned the *other* thing that happened yesterday. It was as though Amy's death didn't matter to Joe at all.

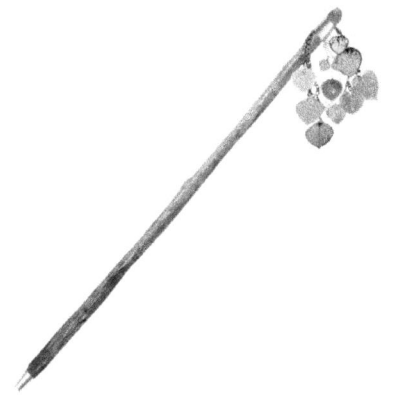

Chapter Twelve

Aspen

O nce Rouge was gone, Aspen looked around. The 'treasure room' was almost entirely empty, though the girls had left the Spider Queen's exoskeleton behind, as well as a few other items they had apparently decided were either unusable or too disgusting. The jackalope brain he kept magically preserved in a jar on the shelf, as well as a few other similar items, still sat, undisturbed. He shook his head, chuckling to himself. Clearly, Rouge wasn't an alchemist, or those would have been among the first things to go in her bag. He would have to mention their value when she returned.

In the meantime, however, he needed to either return to the inn or find a way to send a message back. He eyed Silus, but the little bat was now sleeping peacefully, snuggled up with her friend, belly full of fruits most likely produced from Rouge's original inventory. This room should be safe enough for them, even if he left, though he shouldn't go far while they rested.

Leaning over, he stroked a gentle finger down Silus' head, and she shifted in her sleep. Then he pushed a springy curl back from Rouge's cheek. The girl didn't move, of course, but he smiled anyway. Even if her soul wasn't inhabiting this body right now, it was still her home in his world, and he would care for it.

As he stood, something in his back protested, and he groaned quietly, pressing a hand against the pang. Sleeping in the furs had been good for his exhaustion, but not so good for the rest of him. He missed the days when he'd been able to sleep on the hard ground as easily as a soft bed. One thing being in the military had taught him, though, was to rest whenever and wherever he had a chance.

Aspen took up his new staff, feeling it quiver beneath his hand. The leaves jingled softly, as though in question, and he shook his head. Giving an object that should have been inanimate a strand of his soul might have some very... interesting consequences.

He patted Stick, and murmured quietly. "Don't get too excited. We're just going down to see how Plum and the children are doing." First, however, he ducked back into the other rooms of his private sanctum. His thief had done a good job finding anything of value during her original search, but she hadn't quite found everything. Grunting, he crawled beneath the table in his office, rolling over on his back to look up at the underside.

Long ago, he had drawn a series of sigils there with his long-lost athame. The blade had been a gift from Atae, and Akuji had broken it within moments of capturing him. Fortunately, its role here had simply been as a blade that never dulled, and not a magical implement.

Josua, a friend of his, now longer dead than he had been alive, had imbued these patterns with Runecraft, one of the few forms of magic that didn't vanish upon the death of the caster, and thus one of the most difficult to learn and use. The symbols had taken days to fill, and Josua had been exhausted for days afterward. Aspen had paid him with a ring that enhanced Runecraft, and they had both been pleased with the exchange.

Carefully, Aspen pulled Stick under the table, mentally commanding it to shorten, and the metal cap to sharpen. Soon, he had a very dense, thick-handled blade. The thing was awkward to use, but he was able to connect a small gap in one rune, pouring mana down through the metal core and blade as he did.

There was a sudden emptiness in his gut as the rune immediately sucked even more mana from him, and he was glad he was lying down. It seemed that his mana reserves were still not quite up to his old standards, but he could feel the strangely tingling warmth that told him they were filling back up. He was fairly certain that even if his capacity was lower, his regeneration was higher. Possibly *much* higher.

Above him, there was a sudden *thump*, and he grinned. He slid back out, muttering as his back reminded him again that he was nearly forty-three years old, not fourteen like his elven friend. He glanced at Stick, which was putting off a distinct feeling of gloom through their bond. "All right, all right, grow big again. In fact, I need you to do something pretty fancy. Do you think you can handle it?"

Immediately, the staff shot out to its regular length, solidly nailing Aspen's foot as it did so. He yelped, then clutched the injured appendage, hopping on the other foot awkwardly. Stick helpfully sprouted rootlets so that he could use it as a stabilizer, and its leaves jingled apologetically.

Aspen huffed, then leaned against the tall and sturdy staff. "It's all right. I guess we both have to get used to this, right? I have to remember to look where you're pointed before you grow." Gingerly, he tested his toes against the ground, then put more weight on the foot. "Not broken, at least. I'm fairly certain that if I had to pray to Gina to heal a Broken Bone debuff for this, I'd never hear the end of it."

He frowned a little, though, because his Goddess had been unusually silent lately. He was supposed to be investigating some kind of evil taking hold in the city, and so far, he'd done nothing more than visit his old home. He was fairly certain he should have gotten some snarky quest urging him to hurry by now, but there was really nothing he could do about it. He could only do the task in front of him, after all. At the moment, that task was…

He opened the large, heavy bag now resting on the table. He had intentionally filled it as full as he could and still lift it, and he found that while it wasn't exactly light as a feather, he could lift it with ease. His Strength, at least, was far higher than it had been when his stats were primarily focused on magic. He was almost certain that all of his other physical stats were equally improved, and he was grateful.

Though… He looked up at the sky, rubbing his sore back again. "If my Strength, Stamina, and Dexterity are so much higher, why do I still wake up feeling like an army of stone sprites spent the night using me as a dance floor?"

No immediate response was forthcoming, but he felt almost certain that some servant of his Goddess had taken note of his complaint, and he would be hearing about it later.

Turning back to the bag with a sinking feeling that he should have kept his grumbling to himself, he sent an image to Stick. "Can you do this?" In response, the staff widened in his hand, not quite to the point where he couldn't grasp it firmly, but if his hand had been any smaller, it would have been a challenge. A small slot opened invitingly in the top.

Grinning, Aspen began carefully feeding the bag's contents into the staff.

Down below, the children were waking up. Younger children ran around excitedly, while the older ones pulled pillows over their heads and tried to pretend they were deaf. He could sense Plum and a few of the oldest in the kitchen, probably preparing breakfast.

Outside, in the kitchen garden, he could sense a new life puttering around. Whoever it was was harvesting some of the fruits and vegetables Aspen had brought to maturity the night before, and their light was a clear, calm green, weak but stable. He had a good idea who it would be, and he made his way down the stairs, leaving an amulet hanging from the inside door handle of the sanctuary so that Rouge could get out when she woke, since the door locked automatically.

Downstairs, he skipped the dining hall by going down the main stairs to the ground floor, circling back behind the disgusting display his houseguests had built, and entering the servant's access halls by way of a narrow door hidden behind a tattered banner. The corridor was dark but clean, and while he sensed a few spiders and mice scurrying away from his footsteps, he didn't have to clear any cobwebs.

A minute later, he emerged into the kitchen via a small door in the east wall. He had to duck to clear the lintel, and when he stood straight, everyone in the kitchen was staring at him. An older boy, tall and spindly, with shoulders beginning to broaden and a belly that was practically concave, clutched at a small dagger stuck into his belt.

Plum, her hair covered with a clean but dingy cloth, and an apron carefully wrapped over her breeches and blouse, smiled. "M'lo-" he looked at her meaningfully, and she coughed slightly. "I mean, Aspen. Grandpa is in the garden. He worried, at first, about eating the things that grew there last night, but I told him you must have done something, and now he's gathering fresh ingredients for breakfast."

Just then, the door to the garden opened, and a very old man walked in. His brown face was heavily lined, and his eyes had spent so many years squinting in the sun that it was impossible to tell what color they were through the wrinkles. His back was curved, but his strong, sinewed hands carried a basket full of gleaming produce.

A girl, small, round, and sturdy, bustled over and took the basket, already exclaiming over the quality and quantity of the things it contained. The children immediately lost interest in the adults, descending on the food like a small horde of starving trolls.

The old man barely seemed aware that his burden had been removed. He was staring at Aspen as if seeing someone risen from the dead. He quickly pulled his hat from his brown pate and clutched it to his chest, and a single silver tear began to trace its way down his seamed cheek. Without a word, Aspen strode forward and wrapped his arms around the old man, holding him close as he cried.

Once Tomas was able to get his emotions under control, he, Plum, and Aspen sat at the kitchen table. The children were sent upstairs with food for everyone, and the three adults ate absently as they talked. Aspen filled Plum and Tomas in on his own adventures. The old man was furious that his master had been disrespected and attacked, and both he and Plum soon devolved into a series of apologies that they hadn't tracked Aspen down and aided him.

Aspen shook his head. "There was nothing anyone could do except what we did; flee. I was far too weak to resist, and even a glancing blow would have been enough to finish me. It's I who owe you an apology. I made arrangements before I left for you and the hospital to be supported for years to come, but clearly my preparations were insufficient." He bowed his head to his two most loyal servants. "I'm sorry."

Plum and Tomas both erupted into denials, since how could he possibly have known that his orders would be disobeyed or so blatantly undermined? In return, Aspen insisted that he should have put more safeguards into place. The three of them went around like this for a while before Aspen finally raised a hand, chuckling.

"All right, all right. I'll accept that I could have done nothing differently if you will do the same. I'm here now, and before I go, I have this for you." He untied the now much-reduced bag from his belt and poured it out on the table between them. Glittering gems poured out into a heaping mound, light catching in their facets like a rainbow fire had been captured on the simple wooden platform.

Plum stared, mouth agape, but Tomas was on his feet, jaw set in a stubborn line that Aspen knew all too well. "No, m'lord. I lost you once, to my shame, and I'll not abandon you again. If you're not staying, then neither am I. Where you go, I go." He sat back down, expression set in layers of unyielding lines.

Aspen leaned forward, hand on his face, sighing in defeat.

☙ ☙ ☙

Two of the children, a boy and a girl of such similar size and features that they had to be siblings, if not twins, served as messengers to Restur and the rest of Aspen's erstwhile companions. About an hour later, the kitchen was packed, and the children, bellies full and unafraid for the first time in months, with so many trustworthy adults about, were running through the bottom floor of the house in wild abandon.

Aspen, Plum, Tomas, Restur, Manuela, and, surprisingly, Tessle sat at the table. Tia, Restur's assistant, and Vonn, the young wood elf on *r'nspiga*, were chatting quietly near the garden door. Flu-flu was somewhere playing with the children, which supported Aspen's feeling that the girl was likely only a little older than Rouge. Millie was at the oven, happily preparing meal after meal for anyone who asked – which was nearly everyone – using ingredients Tessle and Flu-flu had donated from their inventories. Struthio was beside his new wife, silently but happily assisting her. Mai Ley, Rouge, Motte, and Lyrec seemed to be the only ones missing.

Tomas, having declared his intention of following Aspen wherever he went, had sent Plum into a mood of deep contemplation, and now, pushing an empty plate away, she stood up. Walking around the table until she was beside Aspen, she suddenly collapsed to her knees, head bowed until her forehead touched the floor, in a pose of abject supplication.

"Please, my… Aspen. Please." Her voice was muffled by her proximity to the ground, but her words were clear. The room fell silent as everyone looked over at this abrupt activity. "Please take us with you, as well. The children aren't safe here, and the city is becoming more dangerous daily. The gangs are bolder, the nobility is corrupt, and I have begun to hear rumors of citizens vanishing from their homes in the night. Whole families, simply gone."

She looked up, and the dark eyes beneath her heavy, straight brows were glimmering with tears. "I know you would like to return to your peaceful life, but we still need you. You've said there's no one else living north of the mountains for as far as you can see. There's enough room, then, for us to build a small town. Some of the children have friends or family who were too poor to continue caring for them. I'm certain they would also like to leave Bright, but there was nowhere we could go to begin again. Nowhere that's not controlled by the King and his cronies, anyway."

Aspen frowned, reaching down to lift the girl to her feet. She stood reluctantly, but kept her head bowed. "What do you mean, the King's cronies? King Chester barely cares for anything outside his books and his dioramas. Duke Geral has run this city since before the war ended, and *his* cronies are well-established. They're quite happy with things as they are. And what's this about people vanishing?"

Plum shook her head. "The King has begun taking power back from Geral. Or at least someone representing the King is doing so. The new Lord of Bright, whoever it is, is weakening the nobility, and as a result, the criminal elements are becoming far bolder. The disappearances are just rumors for now, but they're everywhere. Something spoken of so openly must have some basis in fact."

For the first time in what seemed like a very long time, a quest notification appeared in Aspen's vision.

Quest: "Into the Fog" begun.
Don't let your preconceptions cloud your judgment. People are mis(t)ing. Track down the source of the rumors before the clues vanish like smoke.
Success: Experience, Variable increase in Intelligence and Wisdom.
Failure: People will continue to disappear. Probably. If they're actually disappearing in the first place.

He sighed. "Let me think on this. The wilds are no place for children, but I can't leave you all here if your lives are, indeed, in danger. We'll be here a week at least, and I'll see what I can find out. Though," he looked around at the avid expressions of curiosity on the faces of those surrounding them and smiled wryly. "I hadn't planned on being quite so open about my business here."

He watched as a deep red flush stole over Plum's face, making her resemble her namesake far more than usual. She collapsed back down on the floor. "Oh, my Lord! I'm so sorry! I forgot you asked us to keep your identity a secret! I've been so worried for the children that I just-"

Aspen pulled her to her feet again, afraid the young woman would begin banging her head on the floor. She must have been deeply frightened and worried to be acting like this. Since she had grown up with Birdie, she had always treated him far more casually than the other servants. In fact, her parents and grandfather had often taken her to task for not showing enough respect to their lord. This outpouring of something akin to awe had to be a result of his 'return from the dead'.

Restur spoke up from his chair at the table. The old man's shining white hair gleamed in the sunlight from the freshly washed window as he tilted back in his seat slightly. His rich voice betrayed his amusement. "Never fear, lass. Your master's disguise wasn't as good as he thought. Young Vonn told me several days ago that he was using magic, for one thing. Everyone here knew he was no simple farmer, though," he looked around, waving a hand to indicate not just the kitchen, but the manor and grounds as a whole, "I didn't suspect he was once Atac's Left Hand."

Sitting back down, Aspen motioned for Plum to do the same. The girl reluctantly obeyed, and her grandfather patted her hand approvingly as she did. Clearly, Tomas fully supported her request.

Aspen looked around the room, finally taking off the freshly woven hat that he'd completed that morning and setting it down on the table in front of him with a defeated *shush* of dry grass on wood. He ran his hand through his own thick hair, which was just beginning to show strands of silver woven through the brown and gold. His pale topaz eyes gleamed, and his rather distinctive nose stood proud once the shadow of his hat was no longer obscuring it.

"Fine then, *yes*, I was once known as Iorgas Penbrooke. I *was* the King's Necromancer, Atae's Left Hand, Hero of the Battle of Bright," he waved a hand dismissively, "all that. *Now*, however, I'm just a farmer with a few tricks up my sleeve. As absolutely everyone apparently knows, I lost all of my Skills and Spells, along with my stats, to Akuji. Believing I was dying, I left so I could get *a little peace.*" One golden eyebrow went up, and he gave Plum a rather pointed look. "Now I'm back to resupply before I head home. I'm fortunate enough to have some funds left from my previous life, so I was going to find a way to reestablish Lark's hospital and orphanage while I was here."

He raised a finger. "I have *no* interest in remaining in Bright. I simply want to make sure that Lark's legacy is safe, and make the city a better place for those she spent her life caring for before I leave. My plan was to ask my new friends," he pointed the finger at Restur, "to *quietly* assist me in turning some of those funds into resources for that purpose."

He turned the finger on Plum, then, when the girl flinched, he realized he might have been a little too enthusiastic and put it away. "I will then, *quietly*, make my way back north, taking a caravan of farming implements and supplies so that I don't have to work so bloody hard at work. Then I'm going to retire. Again. Grow just enough food for myself and my companions, read books, and spend the winter sipping tea in front of the fire with my feet up."

Manuela, who had been silent until now, since nothing that came before was a particular surprise to her, either, barked out a laugh. "Aspen, my friend," she said, her smoky voice rasping with amusement, "you'd be bored out of your mind before the first winter was over."

Aspen opened his mouth to argue that he'd already passed his first winter without being at all bored, but hesitated. The truth was, he'd had plenty to do. Rouge and Motte's visits had given him something to look forward to, and between Sarave and Juniper, his three companions, and all the animals, every day had been busy. He'd also been working on his magesmithing, and reading and rereading every book the Head Librarian had sent with him that had any reference to farming in it.

Restur tilted back in his seat a little more, looking up at the ceiling. When he spoke, it sounded like he was just musing aloud, but Aspen wasn't fooled. "Might happen that our caravan isn't filled with goods yet. We'd usually spend more time here, but with the Triathlon coming up, prices are high, just like they were in Bloodhaven. Too much demand for too little product. No one's buying farming equipment now, though, so prices should be low on those. Everyone here wants weapons, armor, consumables, and luxury items."

He rocked back and forth in his chair, seemingly unaware that the whole room was watching him. "Might be, too, that if there was a town up north of the mountains, we'd do well to be the first to establish a trade route." All four chair legs reconnected with the ground, and his sharp blue eyes met Aspen's topaz ones.

"Young Miss Rouge gave me a few samples of your crops, and I hear the plot out back was only doing fair until you showed up. Even if nothing else was produced up there, we'd sell plenty, I expect, with no one else for competition, for a while at least, and we'd get a good price for such high-quality produce, especially in the cities. Far easier to make dishes that give bonuses from superior ingredients, as I'm sure Miss Millie could confirm."

The young cook nodded, her face thoughtful as she wiped her hands on a kitchen towel.

Restur turned his calculating gaze back on Aspen, then flicked a look to Plum and Tomas. "Starting a town is no small thing, but it seems to me you've a good start right here. It's also possible," he glanced at Tia, "that there might be a few others looking to get out of the city. Miss Plum isn't the only one who's noticed that things aren't as safe here as they were when we last came through. Some of us have families here, and those families might not mind finding somewhere else to be."

Tia's chocolate eyes widened, and then she nodded, a smile blooming on her face. "I stay with my sister and her family when we come to Bright. Last night, she told me the gangs have raised their 'protection' fees, and no one has seen the elderly couple who ran the shoe store down the road in over a week.

"When the couple's son went to the guards, they said citizens were 'no longer a priority'. They've been told to focus on helping Travelers with quests and training. My sister told me she was thinking of moving to *Goose*, of all places, and when I told her what happened there, she was nearly in tears, fearing there was nowhere to go. It seems like Bright is on the way to becoming another Bloodhaven, and the common people here are frightened."

Aspen rubbed his forehead. "You all know there's *no town* up north, right? By the time we get back there, it'll be nearly summer, and you'll have to plant crops and build a town before winter. From nothing. I have one poorly built hovel, and I have no idea what monsters may be lurking outside the small area we claimed. There's at least one good-sized cave system, and there are all kinds of dangerous creatures that like to live underground."

Tia and Restur exchanged looks. Restur turned back and shrugged. "Now that the idea has been raised, we need to discuss it seriously anyway. After all, as you say, you've only claimed a small space. There should be plenty left over for whoever might go up there."

"What about down *here*?" Aspen exclaimed in frustration. "Akuji's forces destroyed several small villages and even some good-sized towns on their way through. You could settle in any of them. There are undoubtedly some buildings still standing, or at least good foundations on which to start. Plus, the resources and dangers of those areas are well known."

Everyone in the room exchanged surprised glances. Surprisingly, it was Millie who answered this time. "Haven't ye heard, Aspen? Ah, m'lord? Several groups've tried settlin' th' old towns, but none of 'em last long. The ruins're haunted, and the ground will'na take bluestones. Anyone who tries t' stay there, well, they die or they go mad."

Silence ruled the room as everyone nodded in unison, and as if making up for lost time, yet another quest notification popped into Aspen's vision.

Quest: "Crazy like a Phlox" begun.

Strange events are occurring at the ruins of old villages around Quarternell. Cover some ground and find out what's going on.

Success: Variable.

Failure: People continue dying or going insane from their experiences.

🍒 🍒 🍒

Millie and Struthio excused themselves first. Millie had a determined expression, and the little bag in which she kept the gold Rouge had given her was now bolstered by additional funds from Restur as well as several small gems from Aspen, which he could now give her without a go-between. She should have enough money to be able to open a restaurant in almost any part of the city. Restur and Tia had also taken her aside and given her some low-voiced advice before she left, and Aspen was confident that she would know the best areas to begin looking for an available property.

Once everyone else saw that no more delicious – and buff-packed – food was forthcoming, they, too, began to trickle out. Tia and Restur, exchanging suspiciously self-satisfied looks, left to buy 'supplies'. Plum accepted a few of the smallest gems and went to exchange them for food, clothes, and, at Aspen's urging, books for the children.

Lark had insisted Plum also learn to read and do basic math, and Plum had been trying to pass on her knowledge to the urchins she'd gathered, but it was difficult without simple books, paper, and pens. She'd used what had been left behind in the house, but the books weren't really suitable for a beginning reader, or young minds in general.

Tessle had to return to her world to go to work. Manuela was off examining the children, since it had been quite some time since any of them had been seen by a healer. Tomas, who apparently slept during the day so he could hunt at night, had reluctantly gone to the small bedroom that he was using now that it wasn't safe to sleep alone in his cabin. Flu-flu had gone off with some of the oldest children on some errand Plum had sent them on, claiming that she had received a quest 'from the great God Toko to assist these brave souls in their noble pursuance'.

Vonn, who had been alternately listening to the group in the kitchen and going off to play with the children, returned at this point, and seemed determined to 'chat' with Aspen. He sat down at the table across from the farmer, and leaned forward, expression intent.

"Are you aware," he asked abruptly, "that many of these children are half-breeds of some sort? Mostly half-elves, though I hadn't realized that my high elf cousins were *quite* so generous in their affections, but there are also a half-dwarf and a half-troll. Yet they all play together as if they were a litter of puppies, with no mind for their backgrounds."

Aspen shrugged, having already noticed that a few of his little guests had pointier ears or grayer skin than was normally found in full humans. "I'm not surprised. Birdie's hospital was the only one in the city that would treat half-breeds. Even if their parents had enough money to pay another healer, the healer would rarely accept such a client, either out of prejudice or fear that it would ruin their reputation. Once the war was over, and this became the only city that would take in those who had no home to return to, regardless of their race, such children became inevitable. Where else would they end up, but in Gina's hospice?"

Vonn's expression was neutral as he tilted his head, regarding Aspen solemnly. "Will you allow them to stay? Once the new hospital and orphanage you want to build goes up, it will just become a target again. I've no doubt that sheer greed wasn't the only motivation of those who shut it down before. There are those who would see every race kept pure by whatever means necessary."

Sighing, Aspen leaned back in his chair, and stared up at the ceiling. "I used to tell Lark that she should stop treating the half-borns. Or at least do so more quietly. She would just look at me and tell me that 'Gina loves *all* the children', and that would be that." He sat up straight again, looking back at Vonn. "Most people think of Atae as a cold Goddess, you know. A hateful, dark presence waiting for death. Hoping for it. But the truth is far different."

A little half-smile lingered around his mouth as he thought of the cold visage of his former mistress. But her black eyes weren't empty. No, they were so full no light could show though. "Atae and Gina aren't so very different. They both accept anyone. We are all the same in birth and death, and it's only the lives we live in between that differentiates us. So, when Lark told me that her Goddess wanted her to take in everyone," he shrugged, mouth twisting wryly. "Well, my Goddess did the same. Plum simply learned from her best friend. I'll not tell her to change now, especially since," he glanced up again, smiling just a little. "Gina loves all the children."

Vonn sat back, soft gray focused on Aspen's face. "Even when those children include the Dark Races? Trolls, Orcs, and Goblins?"

Aspen thought of Juniper as she had been when he left the farm: small, independent, loving, full of energy and giggles, and more than a little green. He smiled fondly, and Vonn stared, clearly not having expected this reaction. The farmer nodded his head. "Gina loves *all* the children," he said again.

The young wood elf leaned forward. "What about their parents? What if they want to keep their babes, not give them up? They and their children will be persecuted. Not by everyone, perhaps, but even a few could make their lives miserable."

Aspen waved a helpless hand. "It's a hospital, Vonn. They heal them, and they send them home, if home they have. That's all they can do."

"What about when the children grow up and leave the orphanage? How will they survive when no one will hire them, when some people simply try to kill them on sight, and no one truly cares?"

Again, Aspen waved weakly. "The orphanage can teach them to fight."

Vonn sat back, crossing his arms, face clearly expressing his incredulity.

"My people have no such orphanages. Children are taken in by their nearest relatives. However, we also don't accept what we call changelings. Rarely, an elf on *r'nspiga* will marry and have children while they're gone, but they always know it's only temporary. We must return when our time is up," He held up a hand to forestall Aspen's obvious question. "And we leave behind anyone we met, no matter how precious."

He laid his slim hand flat on the table in front of him, examining the scarred and calloused palm as if it might reveal some deep truth. "I had a half-sister, here in Bright. She'd be nearing fifty now, and her father would be seventy."

He looked up, meeting Aspen's eyes again. "That's if either of them is still alive. Most of our people don't speak of those they leave behind, but my mother married my father for necessity, not love, and though she has affection for him, her heart is locked up in the memory of a human man. She spoke of my sister often, and I promised her that when I was old enough, I would go and find out what happened to them."

The elf flipped his hand over, using it to push against the table as he stood abruptly, his chair sliding back with a sudden shriek. "Today I will go to the home my mother had to leave behind, and discover what has become of my sister and the man who would have been my father, if my mother had been allowed that choice. I have spent this morning speaking to the children, and truly," He dropped his head, turning away so Aspen couldn't see his face. "I fear what I will find."

Quest:" Fateful Family" begun.
Help Vonn discover the fate of his half-sister and her father.
Success: Variable. +20 Relationship points with Vonn.
Failure: Vonn's death.

Well. That was clear.

Aspen stood, crossing the room so he could rest a hand on the young elf's slim shoulder. "I'll help you find them, or at least what happened to them. We just need to wait for Rouge to return."

Vonn turned, smiling blindingly up at the much taller man, gray eyes bright with suppressed tears. He opened his mouth to speak, but at that moment, the garden door flew open. Lyrec stood there, grinning broadly as he looked around. His expression dimmed as he took in the serious expressions of the two inside. He held up his murchunga, smile now somewhat questioning.

"Aspen, listen! I learned my first real song!"

Aspen and Vonn both turned to him, and Aspen smiled encouragingly. Vonn hadn't heard the tortuous lute-playing that Lyrec had been committing, but he clearly recognized the boy from the day before, and his hand fell away from the weapon at his belt.

Lyrec raised the murchunga to his mouth, blissfully unaware of how close he had come to being skewered like some of Bright's infamous 'mystery meat on a stick' that was sold by street vendors at events and festivals. The bard placed the instrument firmly between his teeth, then plucked the tongue. An odd but not unpleasant buzzing sound began, and Lyrec tapped one foot as he opened his mouth more or less to produce different sounds. The cheerful and rhythmic tune made Aspen want to tap his foot as well, and he felt his weariness and worries fade a little bit.

When the song was done, Lyrec lowered the mouth harp, rubbing at his mouth and grimacing slightly. "I'm always worried I'll drool when I do that." He laughed a little self-deprecatingly. "What do you think, though? It's just a level one buff, but it gives you a small bonus to morale and temporary resistance to Stamina-drains. Plus, I'm already level five in the skill! I got to level four really fast because of 'previous experience'!"

The boy was practically dancing in place, and Aspen had to chuckle. Lyrec made a face. "No wonder Rouge is so good at all her thiefy gymnastics and stuff. Did you know she got a silver medal in the state gymnastics tournament when she was ten? I mean, her mom got mad at her for not getting gold, but…

Anyway, her dad was, like, a LARPer when he was in college, and did some martial arts and sword-fighting too. I bet they both got some awesome boosts to their skill gains from all that."

The boy took a breath, red flushing his pale cheeks. "Sorry, I didn't mean to start-" He glanced at Aspen, and his cheeks grew even redder. "I mean, I was just so excited about the song, and you…" He stopped, smacking himself in the face. His expression went fixed for a moment, and there was that strange flicker as he adjusted his 'headset'.

"Right, no facepalms." He muttered to himself as his hands moved around his ears as if tucking in something they couldn't see. Vonn and Aspen watched bemusedly, glad enough to have their conversation done. It had been time for them both to think about the exchange anyway.

"Ah, Lyrec," Aspen murmured finally, "not that I mind, but how did you find us?"

The lad looked up, light blue eyes huge in his round, youthful face. "Oh! Yeah, Rouge texted me. Um, I guess that'd be, like, a magic message or something to you guys. Anyway, she said she'd be back in an hour or so," His eyes flicked up to his right, "well, two hours here, and that you guys were," he made the same little squiggles with his fingers that Rouge sometimes did when she was quoting someone else, "'in the creepiest house in sector 18H on the Bright map'."

He shrugged, as if the rest was simple. Aspen, remembering the decayed and overgrown appearance of the property from the street, supposed that it was. Knowing what he now did, he suspected that Plum and Tomas had encouraged the rapid deterioration in yet another effort to keep both thieves and potential buyers away.

At this point, Vonn, sensing that the conversation was shifting, cleared his throat. He bowed slightly to Aspen. "If we have two hours before Lady Rouge returns, I will attend to a few matters that may help us in our efforts later." He lifted a hand in farewell, and slipped out the garden door with no further delay.

Aspen shook his head. "Why is everyone using the kitchen door?"

Lyrec blinked. "Rouge said not to come in through the front, because it would attract attention. There's a break in the wall around back, kind of hidden in the woods. It looks like a lot of people have been using it lately, though, because there are broken branches and flat grass all over the place." He grinned. "I got my [Tracking] skill leveled up to two from that. You get [Tracking] in the tutorial, but then you never get to use it unless you go hunt in the woods or something. I mean, that's what it's *for*, but hardly anyone actually…"

His voice trailed off when he saw Aspen's bemused smile, and his hand twitched as if he started to hit his face again and then stopped himself. "Sorry again. It's just that you…" He motioned to take in Aspen's appearance from head to foot. "You're… The eyes, and the muscles, and… Where's your *hat*?" He asked rather plaintively.

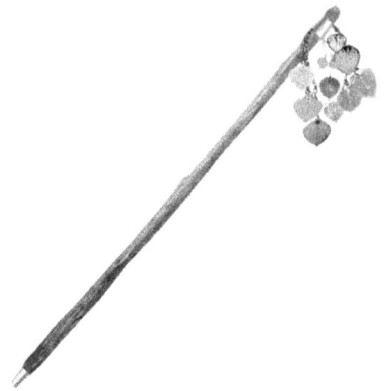

Chapter Thirteen

Rouge

A s usual lately, it was a relief to feel the world drop out from beneath her as she entered *Veritas Online*. Dr. Joe had had some extra tests he'd wanted to run before they started. Something about some new tweaks to the hardware he'd just got approval to test. Thanks to that, it was nearly an hour before she actually got to log in, and the atmosphere between the three of them was just *weird* the whole time.

Thankfully, when she opened her eyes, it was to see a familiar little face in front of hers.

::I'm *hungry*,:: whined Silus.

Rouge sat up, laughing, and produced some Aspen-fruit from her inventory. Silus immediately tore into it, and Rouge stretched, looking around. Some jars of something icky were sitting next to her, and she sighed, recognizing them as some gross bits she'd decided not to take. Obviously Aspen felt differently, so she picked her rattiest, ugliest bag and put them in. There, she'd take them, but she didn't have to be happy about it.

A debuff flashed red in her vision, and she frowned, pulling it up.

Debuff: Filthy. You are dirty, and you smell bad. Relationship -30 to any sapient close enough to smell you. Relationships will not drop below 0 from this debuff, but passersby will avoid you.

"Oh, gross. I totally got soaked in that rainstorm last night!" She raised her voice, as if the debuff cared, but it didn't even flicker until she swiped it away. "Well," she muttered, standing, "if I have it, Motte and Aspen probably have it too." She grimaced, remembering how grimy Aspen had been last night. "Time to find a bath."

Once Silus finished her meal and then sleepily curled back up on Rouge's shoulder (not without a comment on the girl's lack of hygiene), Rouge started looking around. Unfortunately, there was no tub anywhere to be found on the top floor, so she made her way down. Anyone taking care of as many kids as Plum was had to have a bathing room somewhere.

She found it only a few rooms from the dining hall. From the gaudy and uncomfortable chairs shoved against the wall, it looked like it had been a small receiving room before its conversion. Probably for people Aspen didn't like, given how hard the chairs were when she tried one. Honestly, though, it kind of sounded like he didn't have very many friends before, so maybe it was actually for anybody who came to visit?

There were five metal tubs crammed into the space, with fluffy towels (obviously scrounged from wherever Aspen used to keep things for people he *did* like) piled on one of the chairs, along with some flower-scented soap that she wouldn't have minded owning in real life. There were pipes running out the window, and when she turned the tap, cold water ran into her chosen tub, probably from a cistern on the roof.

She grimaced, but filled the tub, stripped down, grateful again for the strange game mechanic that allowed you to see yourself naked, even while others saw you in your perma-undies. It just never felt like you could get really clean while wearing clothes, even though she knew it was all just part of how the system worked.

Before she could think about it too much, she plunked into the tub, squeaking as the cold water engulfed her. As quickly as she could, she scrubbed clean with the soap, then ducked under to rinse and popped out with a small accompanying tidal wave. Grimacing at the floor, she muttered, "Good thing this isn't real life. Dad would kill me for that." She noticed that there was a similar small lake by the farthest tub, and wondered if Aspen had taken the opportunity to rid himself of his debuff as well. Frankly, she hoped so, because he was starting to stink.

Draining the tub was a bit more of a challenge, since the plug looked like it would just dump the water on the floor. She couldn't see any holes in the floor, though, and remembering the magic tub at the inn in Bloodhaven, she finally gritted her teeth and pulled, ready to shove the stopper back in and go for help if it started spilling all over the floor. Fortunately, these tubs were also clearly magical, and the water drained away to parts unknown.

Satisfied that she was as clean as she was going to get, she put on fresh clothes, including a pretty peasant blouse she'd gotten at an event when she'd first started playing, and Motte had helped her dye in a gold and deep blue pattern. Her pants were just her basic black leggings, because you never knew when you might need to run or jump, but it was nice not to be wearing armor or thief-clothes for a bit. She even exchanged her soft boots for low-heeled slippers, and used her interface to change her hairstyle from basic curls to box braids with jingly blue and gold beads. She had to use some gold to buy the new look, but she actually *had* some gold now, so it was okay.

After that, she followed the sound of voices to the kitchen, where she found that lunch was in full swing. Swarms of children (were there *more* than there had been last night?) were racing through, grabbing food from a laden kitchen table, and departing. Aspen and Lyrec, of all people, were manning the oven and stove, doling out meal after meal to a seemingly ever-ending horde of ragamuffins of all shapes and sizes.

Without a word, Rouge dove in. Grabbing a knife and some bread, she began making sandwiches from the meat, cheese, and vegetables Lyrec was carving. Aspen, meanwhile, produced a soup that smelled edible, if not exciting, and a series of pasta dishes, even though Rouge couldn't tell where the pasta was coming from. Game logic, she was guessing.

When the last giggling monkey scampered away, gleefully cramming a sandwich into their mouth (Rouge honestly couldn't tell if it was a boy with unusually large eyes and long lashes, or a girl with a squarish jawline and short hair) the three looked at each other in exhausted satisfaction. Aspen and Lyrec shimmered gold with skill increases.

Lyrec turned to Rouge and asked, "Did you get the quest? I got two levels of [Cooking] and ten gold!"

Rouge shook her head sadly. "Must have come in too late. It was still kind of fun!"

Aspen just smiled and began clearing away the debris. Most of it went into a bin under the table that she hadn't noticed before, and dirty dishes dunked briefly into soapy water came out sparkling clean. Rouge leaned down and peered at the bin. "What's this?" She cast [Identify].

Compost Bin – Any organic Trash item placed in this bin will be converted into Fertilizer. The duration required and quality of the Fertilizer will depend on the Trash used.

Converting:

20 x Common Trash (20 minutes)

8 x Unusual Trash (8 hours)

1 x Rare Trash (1 day)

"Whoa, that's neat! I thought Trash was just junk. I just leave it, usually."

Aspen glanced over at her, raising that eyebrow. "You should only do that with organic trash. It'll convert into Fertilizer anyway, though it'll just fertilize wherever it is. Metal and other materials may only look like trash because you don't have a way to process it. It's unusual, but sometimes the right person can even find treasure in trash. It's best to gather it if you can."

Rouge and Lyrec both stared at him, then exchanged glances.

"Did you know that?" Lyrec asked.

Rouge just shook her head, then looked back at Aspen. "You mean I could have been leaving treasure all over the place *this whole time*?"

Aspen shrugged. "Like I said, it's unusual. You've probably just been making a mess. Typhus, God of Filth and Disease, will take it in and count it as an offering." He made a face. "You probably don't want any of his Blessings, though. They tend to be… unpleasant."

Lyrec paled, faint freckles standing out on his cheeks. "So, if I keep leaving trash everywhere, I'll be punished?"

Aspen tilted his head, wiping his hands on a towel. "Technically, it's a Blessing, if you consider lice that change color to match your mood, or a month-long Stench debuff that drives monsters *and* people away a Blessing."

Rouge's eyes widened. "Lyrec! D'you remember that guy, what's-his-name, Badonkadonk! Yeah, a while back he was all over the forums, saying he suddenly started causing a Disease debuff to anything he touched. He thought it was awesome until the second time his horse died, and shopkeepers would close up the store when they smelled him coming. He couldn't figure out what happened, and after ten days, it just stopped."

Lyrec snapped his fingers. "Yeah, I remember that! Everybody started calling him PigPen! That was hilarious."

Aspen nodded. "That sounds about right. For a Deity devoted to all the things no one else wants any more, Typhus has a," He paused as if reconsidering his next words, then continued carefully. "He has a *wonderful* sense of humor."

There was a sudden soft chime, and a glowing gold notification appeared in Rouge's vision.

Typhus has taken notice of your words of praise. Your Compost Bin will work twice as quickly for the next twenty-four hours. Remember, the Gods are always listening.

Aspen's golden tan paled, and Lyrec seemed to choke on his own spit.

"Wow," her friend muttered as he caught his breath, "does that happen a lot around you guys? I've talked about the gods plenty, but none of them ever did anything about it before."

Rouge grimaced. "Yeah, it's probably best to assume that someone is always paying attention. The gods are, um, kind of *invested* in some of the stuff we've been up to lately, I think."

Just then, the kitchen door flew open, and Rouge felt heat rise in her cheeks as she saw that it was Vonn. The wood elf was looking rather bedraggled, and a small cut on his cheek oozed blood. She started moving forward to see if he needed help, but he was already closing the door behind him. He collapsed into a chair at the kitchen table, waving a calming hand as Aspen started toward the door, clutching his snazzy new staff.

"I lost them, don't worry. The bluestones kept them from attacking once I was on the street, and I was able to [Stealth] well enough to leave them behind, in spite of the reduction to my dexterity in this accursed city." The elf scrubbed his face with his hands, wincing as his fingers smeared the blood from his wound. Aspen crossed the kitchen in two long strides, gently touching the injury as a soft white light shone from his fingertips. Vonn sighed in relief as he was healed, and Rouge sank back on her heels in disappointment, seeing that her opportunity to play Florence Nightingale was over, and Vonn's attention was entirely on the tall farmer.

Shaking his head, the wood elf sighed. "I managed to find out that my sister and her father moved about ten years ago, when she married a tanner. They went to live near the tannery, and my sister managed to pass as human herself until she and her husband spawned a babe. The lad was clearly of mixed blood, with ears as pointed as mine, and while her husband had known and cared not, the neighbors disagreed. It was some of those neighbors who attempted to, ah, *dissuade* me from my search, after inviting me into their home so that I was no longer protected. I didn't notice that the place wasn't a non-combat zone until it was too late."

He shook his head again. "Why would anyone want their home to be unsafe? I know the homeowner can choose to turn off the protections, but why would they possibly do so? My people have no such safe-zones, and we live our lives in constant fear of attack."

Aspen busied himself at the stove again, filling a pot with water and placing it on the stove. Without looking up, he replied. "It's rare now, but many people began doing it because during the war, looters would use the cover of attacks from Akuji's forces to steal from shops and homes. The city guards were busy on the walls, and the protections in the home only prevent monster spawns and physical violence, not theft and other criminal acts. People found they were unable to defend themselves from thieves. Most people who are wealthy enough to fear thieves are also wealthy enough to hire guards, and thus it's relatively common for them to turn off the safe-zones in their homes. Unfortunately, during the siege, everyone was so desperate that some commoners became victims as well, and so decided it was better to fight than stand helpless while others with fewer scruples walked away with their small stores of food."

Carefully, he tipped some loose leaves into a metal strainer and set the strainer in the water, removing it from the heat just before it began to boil. "Akuji himself had some ability which could nullify the bluestones from nightfall to sunup. He didn't do it often, so it must have required time or resources to use, but, as you know, only a house completely surrounded by bluestones can gain such protections, so when the bluestones went dormant, so did the safety zones. If the monsters broke through on those nights... Well, let's just say that many people lost their faith in the power of the bluestones." His voice trailed off, and he silently poured the leaf-water into four cups he had waiting on the counter. It glittered briefly, showing that it was of Unusual or better quality, and offered a buff.

With great solemnity, he handed each of them a cup, then held out a small bowl of shiny white granules. "Sugar?"

It didn't take long for Vonn and Aspen to fill Rouge and Lyrec in on Vonn's family trouble, and they also got quests to help the wood elf. Vonn cleaned up while Aspen left a note for Plum and Tomas, and the four of them were off, leaving Silus curled up with Tomas, who had often helped care for her when she was just a baby.

Rouge, who had, if she was being honest with herself, been harboring some hopes of spending more time with Vonn, especially now that this new and much more interesting side of the young elf had been revealed, quickly found herself left behind. Aspen, being more familiar with the Native parts of the city, was able to quickly lead them to the Tannery. This was an area that Rouge herself had consciously avoided because, to be frank, it *stank*. Like, really, really nasty.

Zoey and her dad had once driven through a town which was called Garden City, and apparently boasted a lovely zoo. They had planned to walk through the zoo, but only ended up stopping for gas because it was what a local called a 'blood-burning day'. There was a meat-packing plant just outside town, and periodically it would actually *burn blood*, which smelled exactly as disgusting as it sounded.

The Tannery was worse.

As soon as they got close, they all knew it, as the stench of all the truly nasty things used to tan hides began to permeate the air. The Natives who lived in the area all wore masks with sweet herbs and oils sewn into sachets beneath their noses. They looked very odd, especially since the latest trend seemed to be shaping the sachets like false mustaches, but they also looked undisturbed by the smell.

Lyrec, on the other hand, had a notoriously weak stomach. He groaned as he clutched at his belly. "Oh my gosh, I've never been so glad that I'm only using a headset. It smells like feet here."

Rouge, who was contemplating getting her thief-mask out of her Inventory, in spite of the fact that it might get her arrested, snorted and then gagged. "Oh my gosh, Lyrec, I would sniff a hundred feet rather than this. I would sniff the feet of a marathoner who hasn't changed his shoes in five thousand miles rather than this! I don't know what they used to make this smell, but it should be put out of its misery and buried *right now*."

Aspen, who somehow looked completely undisturbed by the smell – oh, wait, former Necromancer – sighed and stopped at a booth nearby. He bought four exorbitantly priced masks, all the basic unadorned type, thank goodness, because she would totally wear a mustache if she had to, but she wouldn't like it. Handing them out, he murmured, "They'll help cover our faces, too, in case we encounter the same ruffians who attempted to beat Vonn."

Everyone gratefully slipped them on, breathing deeply of the stale floral scent. Rouge saw a small green buff appear in her vision.

Descentsitized – While wearing this item, you are immune to Stench debuffs. You also gain mild resistance to all gas-based attacks. Time remaining – 2:59:57

Between the worn clothes, the ragged straw hat, the floppy mask, and the unfamiliar slouch of Aspen's shoulders, he was nearly unrecognizable as a man who had once been one of the three most powerful lords in the city. Only if you caught a glimpse of his icy yellow-brown eyes would you connect the downtrodden farmer with Duke Iorgas Penbrooke.

Rouge gave him a thumbs up, and the four continued on their way. After a few more blocks, she finally noticed that Lyrec was being unusually quiet. She glanced over at him, and caught him gazing at Aspen's back with a look she knew all too well. She sent him a PM.

Rouge the Rogue: Jace, are you *kidding* me? Aspen?

Lyrec: You know I can't help it! He's so *pretty*!

Rouge the Rogue: No. He. Is. Not. He's not even handsome! And he's old! He's so, so old!

Lyrec: He's a computer program! He's probably 6 months old. Maybe a year.

Rouge the Rogue: GROSS.

Lyrec: You know what I mean!

Rouge the Rogue: Do not mess up my you-know-what with one of your crushes!

Lyrec: How am I going to mess it up?

Rouge the Rogue: I don't know! But remember when you told Mrs. Longacre you loved her in 8th grade and got transferred out of her class? I had to spend the rest of the year sitting next to Pansy Walmak.

Lyrec: Pansy wasn't that bad.

Rouge the Rogue: *Her name was Pansy.*

Lyrec: You're so close-minded.

Rouge the Rogue: You're such a lech!

Lyrec: Ew! I just want to look at him! Well, maybe touch his arm.

Rouge the Rogue: EW!

Lyrec: LOL

Rouge the Rogue: Fine, just don't be weird. No love notes, secret admirer messages, or wooden shoes filled with roses.

Jace: ONE TIME.

Rouge the Rogue: Twice.

Jace: I didn't actually do it the second time!

She was just writing out an answer when they arrived at a small, sad house in the midst of many other similar houses. Vonn paused, the beautiful gray eyes above his mask looking conflicted.

"Are you sure this is the right house?" Aspen asked.

Vonn nodded. "I have [Perfect Navigation]. Once I've been somewhere, I can find my way back to it as long as I can see the sun or stars."

"And no one was here but some thugs?"

The elf sighed. "They never would have been able to hurt me if they hadn't surprised me. I should have been able to dispatch them all easily, but I just didn't know what to do."

Rouge touched him on the arm, feeling the hot blood rise in her cheeks and thinking *Oh my gosh, I'm as bad as Jace!* Then she cleared her throat and said, "Let me go in first. Breaking and entering is kind of what I do."

The two men stepped aside, and Rouge knelt by the door after glancing around to make sure no one was around to see. A moment later, she sighed and stood, turning the knob. The door swung open easily. "It was unlocked," she muttered, then stepped into the shadows inside and triggered [Stealth].

A moment later, she was remembering what Aspen had said about *why* people had stopped using the protections given by living in a building surrounded by bluestones. They didn't like thieves, and felt they could defend themselves. Which meant, of course, that they set traps.

A dart stung her thigh, and then another one caught in the sleeve of her blouse. A knife whistled by her nose, and a green vapor puffed into the air several inches above her face. Saved by being short again! She launched herself into a forward roll, flipping from her hands directly into a crouch, noting as she did that her [Stealth] had broken when she took damage. She swayed as the poison on the dart in her leg began to work its way through her system.

You are *Poisoned*. You will lose 10 health points/sec for 30 seconds. You take 10 points of damage from Poison.

::Traps,:: she sent, as her legs buckled. *Why is it always poison?*

You take 10 points of damage from Poison.

The three males bustled through the doorway, triggering exactly zero traps, thanks to their thief, who had set them all off. Aspen knelt beside her, golden glow already encircling his hands, while Lyrec looked like he was about to burst out laughing. Vonn, thankfully, looked worried, but she thought she detected an edge of amusement in the way his lower lid was crinkled above the mask. Nah. He was too nice a guy to laugh at a girl when she had just made a total idiot out of herself.

Right?

The healing flush of Aspen's magic cleared the poison debuff and restored the hit points she'd lost. She sat up, then stood, clearing her throat awkwardly. "Ah, so, these guys aren't quite as pathetic as I thought. Hang on while I check for more traps."

There was another poison dart trap on the single window, which had also been left invitingly unlocked. She found the simple disarm (a string just inside the door that you could pull or tie off to prevent any of the traps from tripping) and set it, then kept looking.

The house only boasted two rooms: the front room, which contained a meager kitchen and a table with three chairs, and a bedroom, which held a bunk bed and a dresser, along with two small chests. There were, because of course, poison dart traps on the dresser and the chests. These were easily disarmed, as was a spring-loaded dagger (coated with poison) that would fly out if pressure was placed on the lower bunk.

When she felt satisfied that all of the traps were deactivated, she motioned to the three men, who had been (carefully) inspecting the kitchen and living area. Between the four of them, they quickly dug through everything in the small bedroom, finding nothing more interesting than men's clothes in sizes small and extra-large, a knife so blunt it could be used as a stage prop, and two wide black masks that could double as balaclavas in a pinch.

Just as they were deciding that they'd have to wait for the residents to return, they all stilled as they heard the front door click open. Well, all but Lyrec, who was still turning over one of the masks in his hands as if trying to decide if he should try it on. Unfortunately, his headset wasn't as good as a pod at conveying small noises, so Rouge touched his arm, tilting her head to indicate the main room. He looked up, eyes wide, and the balamaskaclava-thingy vanished into his inventory.

She rolled her eyes at his probably instinctive action. As long as they hadn't taken anything, the system would only identify them as intruders, but now they'd have a thief tag added to that. If someone managed to call the guards (and the guards bothered to come), they would be pursued twice as long.

Rouge dropped into [Stealth] and silently moved back into the other room. Behind her, she could feel Vonn doing the same. His [Stealth] was a little different from hers, since it was focused on sneaking up on animals in the woods and was therefore focused on blocking sound and smell, leaving it more camouflagey than invisibility-ey, but it would do in these cramped quarters.

A hand reached in through the slightly opened door and felt for the nearly imperceptible string that would disarm the traps. A string which, of course, wasn't there, because it had already been tied up. She cursed herself, nearly lunging forward to release the string from the nail where she had left it, then untying it and dropping it into the questing hand. She really, *really* needed to work on her thief instincts. It had been so long since she had to be truly sneaky that she had lost her touch.

The hand jerked a little at the sudden introduction of the string, but went ahead and pulled it, holding tight as the door opened and two men entered. The large man came first, ducking his head under the lintel as Aspen had had to do. His thin linen shirt stretched tight across both shoulders and belly, and his bald head glistened with sweat as he looked around. Thankfully, nothing in the room had been interesting enough for them to disturb it much, and the suspicion on his face faded as he pulled his stained yellow and brown mask down from his mouth and nose.

The second man entered a moment later, rapidly tying off the string with the ease of long familiarity. Rouge, who was still hiding just inches from the two, was able to see that he had used a slip-knot that he could release with barely any effort at all. This man was short, standing somewhat taller than Rouge, but shorter than Jace, who had begun shooting upward with alarming rapidity in the last year. The smaller man's brown shirt was cleaner than the big man's, but his mask was equally worn and stained.

Then the tall man turned and slammed his huge fist into Vonn's hiding spot, just inside the room by the door to the bedroom. Vonn instantly reappeared, [Stealth] thoroughly broken, and spun away, blood spraying from his nose, which had been flattened by the ham-sized fist.

The big man grinned viciously, and the small man produced a dagger from somewhere. The voice from behind his mask was slightly nasal, but triumphant. "Y'see, Gippy? I told ya th' knife-ear'd be back. This time, let's trim 'em down so they're a little prettier, hey?"

Oh, no he didn't. Cut off Vonn's lovely, elegant ears? It was *on*.

Triggering [Shadow Glide], Rouge used its measly five-foot range to put her behind the smaller man, who she judged was actually the more dangerous, especially in the cramped confines of the room. She *so* wanted to use [Backstab], but the odds were good that the man would simply die, and she was still hesitant to just kill people, especially now that she knew, well… *so much*. Instead, she used the hilt of her Mambele for a simple [Knockout], and the man went down like a puppet with its strings cut.

Meanwhile, Aspen had stepped out of the small bedroom. The big man, whose balding pate nearly brushed the ceiling, while his shoulders were so broad, he seemed to fill the space entirely by himself, sneered and lowered his head, spreading his beefy arms to lunge for the lanky farmer.

Quick as a mongoose sighting a snake, Aspen's staff shot out. The metal-tipped end caught the hulker under the chin, snapping his head back sharply. Rouge blinked, because she was fairly certain Aspen had used his little staff-growing trick to provide some extra speed and impact, but before she could be sure, the thing was back to its usual self, albeit with the little leaves on the top jingling in a suspiciously merry manner.

The big man tottered, eyes rolling up in his head. As if in slow motion, he tilted to one side and then the other, before finally dropping in a boneless heap. It was over. Rouge resisted the urge to applaud.

Vonn was still on the ground, eyes wide as he clutched at his clearly broken nose. Which was really sad, because it was such a *nice* nose. She hurried over and crouched beside him, pulling a healing potion from her inventory.

Gently, Aspen held her hand before she could hand the vial to the injured wood elf. He smiled a little ruefully. "Hold onto that until you need it." He extended his glowing hand to Vonn's face, murmuring a quiet prayer as he did so. Gold suffused the elf's features, and when Aspen lifted his hand, only the copious amounts of blood left behind indicated that the injury had ever happened.

Seriously, healers were *awesome*. When all this was over, she and Motte really needed to make friends with one. Or a dozen.

Rouge grinned, offering Vonn a hand up. When he clasped it, levering himself to his feet with an ease that indicated he hadn't needed any help at all, he gave her a sweet smile and she felt her heart flutter in her chest.

She cleared her throat, carefully avoiding looking at Lyrec, who was still standing in the door to the bedroom. "So, uh, I guess we should, like, tie these guys up? Or something?" She produced two short lengths of rope from her inventory, and Vonn took them with a grin.

When the thugs were tied up, they carried the little one into the bedroom (because while they could move the big guy, why would you when there was a light-weight to throw around?) and Lyrec produced some water from his inventory to splash on them both. They gagged the shorter guy and tied him to the bed, closing the door but leaving Lyrec with him, in theory to make sure he didn't wiggle free.

Aspen threw the water in Big Thug's face, and the man snorted and then coughed, eyes snapping open. He immediately began straining against his bonds, but Vonn had some kind of knot-tying skill, and the rope didn't budge.

Aspen glanced at her. ::Do you know his name?::

Oh. Yeah. That was a thing she could do, huh? She squinted at the hefty hooligan, and a tag appeared over his head. *George – level 17 Tanner.* George? Really? She sent the information to Aspen.

Aspen pulled one of the chairs from beside the table and sat in it, leaning back and crossing his long legs at the ankle. He eyed George, where he was propped up against the single kitchen cabinet. "So. George."

The goon jerked, eyes widening. He tried to say something from behind the chunk of cloth Vonn had shoved into his mouth and tied in place.

Aspen leaned forward, tugging his hat brim so only his ice-cold topaz eyes could be seen between it and the mask he'd replaced over his mouth and nose. "Did you want to say something? Because we have a few things we'd like you to tell us, *George*," the man jerked again, face flushing, "but we can't have you yelling for help. Our friend is, ah," Aspen gestured to the closed door of the bedroom, which suddenly seemed dark and looming, "*speaking* to your little partner in the other room."

George's eyes widened, and the red color drained from his face. His eyes flickered from the door to Aspen, and his struggles renewed. A loud thump came from the other room, then a series of squeaks and muffled screeches that sounded like someone was being quietly murdered.

Aspen's eyes didn't leave George's terrified brown ones, but he sent a reassuring thought through party chat. ::There are rats and other creatures living in the walls and attic of this house. I've asked them for some assistance in exchange for a little of my spare mana. They'll be providing the sound effects, but our miniature ruffian in there is still sleeping like a babe.::

Rouge shivered a little. Aspen was a little too good at this for her comfort.

Aspen held out a hand to Vonn, and in an obviously prearranged move,

Vonn placed the hilt of the long hunting dagger he kept strapped to his thigh into Aspen's palm. Aspen spun the weapon lazily, weaving it between his fingers for a moment before clasping it and stepping forward into a crouch which ended with him on one knee beside George, the tip of the blade digging gently into the soft flesh beneath his chin.

The big man swallowed hard and held very still.

"Now, George, I'm going to remove your gag. You're going to tell us everything we want to know, or our companion will be in here to, ah, *talk* to you as soon as he's done with your friend. On the other hand, if you speak quickly and convincingly enough, maybe *your* associate will still be alive when I go in there and tell *our* associate that playtime is over."

Aspen tilted his head to one side, cold eyes hard and calculating. "Blink once if you can resist yelling and I can remove your gag. Blink any other number of times to indicate that I should finish with you and move on to see what your friend knows." He twisted his hand just a bit, and a single drop of blood trailed down the groove in the center of the blade.

George blinked once. Hard.

Smoothly, Aspen slid the knife beneath the gag, slitting it apart without spilling any more blood. George instantly spat the gag out, but Aspen dodged smoothly, as if expecting the action. Maybe he did. He certainly acted like this wasn't the first time he'd had to convince someone to talk.

Rouge gulped as she remembered that Aspen had once been on the front lines of a very bloody war. He had also held a position that others seemed to find innately terrifying. Honestly, it made far too much sense that one of his roles would have been as an interrogator. Which was, itself, horrifying, because she knew Aspen well enough to believe that any such activity would have been as cruel for the torturer as the tortured.

Aspen stood, stepping back to stand beside Vonn. The elf's face, clearly visible because the two bullies had already seen it, was twisted in an expression of mixed fury and disgust. It was Vonn who spoke, while Aspen just kept playing with the knife in a Very Menacing Manner. "I'll ask you again, as I did earlier today, before you beat and tried to murder me. *Where is Violeta?* Where are her son and husband? What happened to her father, Abner?" Rouge walked over behind Vonn, offering silent support as she saw his shoulders start to tremble from the tension in his body.

George laughed harshly, eyes flitting to Aspen. "It's Gippy, not George. And I dunno what happened to 'er. Don't care."

A new series of howls followed by a rattling moan came from the bedroom, and George's face turned a sickly yellow. "Fine!" he yelped, "Don't hurt 'im no more! When we figured out the little brat was a knife-ear, an' his mama too, we called the Maskers. Next day, the wench an' her whelp was gone, an' Abner 'n Kite was dead. Everybody knows wha' happens to those wha' hide half-bloods. That's all I know!"

Vonn's shoulders slumped, his whole body a vision of despair. Before she could second-guess herself, Rouge found herself hugging him. The elf's arms wrapped around her, and he started sobbing.

Aspen stepped between them and George, whose face now bore a triumphant grin.

"Who are these 'Maskers'?" Aspen asked, voice as deep and frozen as a winter lake. "How do we contact them? What do they do with those they take? I assume there have been others."

A rustle sounded as George managed a shrug. "Dunno. You leave a dull knife in th' map by the guardhouse. Stab th' house o' th' half-breeds, and after a few days…" Another contorted half-shrug.

"The guards don't see these knives?" Aspen asked quietly.

The bound man snorted a laugh. "Who d'you think tells the Maskers? They don' care. If you don' pay 'em, they'd spit on you soon as help you. Maskers must pay' em good, 'cause no Masker's ever been caught."

"Why are they called Maskers?"

Another rustling shrug. "Wear masks, don' they. Big black hoods tha' cover their whole head."

Rouge's memory flashed back to the masks Lyrec had been looking at in the bedroom. She gently pulled away from Vonn, who had now mostly stopped crying, though an occasional tear still trickled from his reddened gray eyes. Rouge stepped around Aspen, standing where George could see her.

"Are you the Masker, George, or is it your friend in there?" She leaned her head toward the bedroom.

The big man's pasty face showed only confusion. "We're no Maskers. Nobody knows who th' Maskers are. That's why they wear *masks*, innit, you-"

Aspen's hand sliced out, cutting off the undoubtedly insulting words about to come out of the other man's mouth. Topaz eyes assessed her, now warm as honey. ::Are you certain, Rouge?::

She nodded. ::Lyrec? Do you still have the hoodie thing you found? And that super dull knife?::

Lyrec's voice came back, sounding slightly freaked out. ::Yeah. Do you need them? Also, this critter in here is making some crazy noises, and it has really big teeth. Are you going to be done soon?::

Aspen looked back at their prisoner. ::Yes. Very soon.:: The tall farmer inclined forward, leaning on his staff, which jangled menacingly. Aspen sent it an admonishing glance, and its leaves settled with a sulky *twang*.

"I do believe you've told us all you know. Now, the question is, what do we do about the fact that you basically sentenced a family to death for the sin of their blood?" Aspen's voice was heavy, and he stepped aside, leaving a clear path between Vonn and the cretin on the floor. Gravely, almost ceremoniously, the tall man passed the knife back to the slim elf, hilt first.

Vonn accepted the blade, gripping the hilt so tightly his knuckles shone white through his golden tan. "You had my second-father killed. My brother-in-law butchered. My sister and nephew abducted and likely also dead. Though you were too cowardly to do the deed yourself, you knew what the result would be. You deserve the same fate you brought to them." His teeth clenched after every word, the muscles of his jaw flexing as if biting into something hard and bitter.

George stared at the elf, muddy eyes huge as his bound legs scrabbled to escape. He managed to roll slightly, and his mouth opened to yell. With the edge of his hand, Aspen struck the man's throat in a single, practiced movement, and something crunched. A strangled gargle was all that emerged.

Vonn stood for a long moment, hands locked as he stood in a pose that would send the knife into George's heart if the elf took two steps forward. Finally, he returned his knife smoothly to its sheath, looking defeatedly at Aspen. "I can't. I could kill him without regret if he wasn't helpless, but like this?" He shook his head, wavy brown hair glinting in the dim beams of light that trickled through the dirty window.

George looked hopeful, then triumphant, shooting Aspen a vicious glare. Aspen nudged a thick leg with his foot. "Should we let him up and see how you feel then?"

Vonn hesitated, then shook his head. "The moment has passed. I am no judge, nor executioner."

Aspen hesitated, but offered, "I have filled those roles in the past. I can do so again, if you wish."

Rouge nearly spoke up in protest at this, but thankfully Vonn did it for her. "No. That was a different time, and you were a different man. You've said so yourself, more than once. Have we no other option?"

She would swear that Aspen's shoulders relaxed slightly at Vonn's words, and he looked thoughtful. "The guards are clearly untrustworthy. It is likely that the only ones in this city who would hold him accountable for his crime are the Gods themselves, and likely not all of them."

Rouge felt a sudden grin stretching across her face. This time it wasn't her who had forgotten her skills. ::Um, Aspen? Don't you have a hotline to a certain goddess? Maybe she can help?::

She had forgotten that Lyrec was now in the party, but his ::What?:: was ignored as one of Aspen's brows shot up.

::That,:: Aspen said slowly, ::could be either a very good or a very bad idea.::

She just grinned like a maniac. ::Let's find out!::

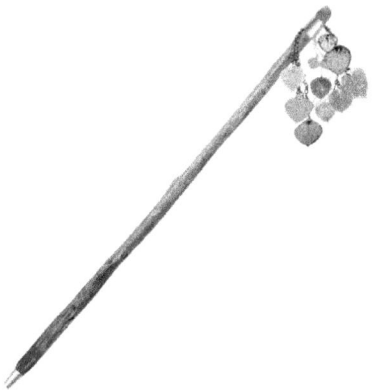

Chapter Fourteen

Aspen

Aspen stared up at the ceiling. For some reason, prayers for healing and growth came easily to him, but things like this, where he had to ask for something not usually in a cleric's repertoire, he struggled to find a graceful way to say it. After a long moment in which he opened and closed his mouth at least three times, and Rouge started making 'go on' motions, he began.

"So… Great Goddess Gina, I know that vengeance isn't usually your area, but we require some assistance with a difficult problem. As you requested, we are searching for those bringing violence and hate to Bright. We can take care of judgment in the heat of battle, but what do we do with those on the periphery? Those who feed the violence through malice or inaction? Please, help us."

Lyrec had returned from the bedroom, his role fulfilled, and now stood beside Aspen. As he finished speaking, the boy muttered, "Amen," and then flushed when everyone looked at him. He shrugged. "Habit," he said, sheepishly.

The room filled with an expectant silence, and Aspen thought he could hear his own pulse pounding in his veins. Time passed with no response, and the faces of the members of his group were becoming crestfallen even as George started to grin, showing yellowed teeth. Then Aspen started to glow. His feet lifted from the ground, leaving him hovering in midair. He felt his arms rise from his sides without his urging, even as his clothes began fluttering in a growing wind. His hat flapped on his head, clinging on only with the desperation of habit.

"Oh, poop," Rouge said in a voice filled with consternation.

The Goddess Gina has heard your prayer. As Her Champion, She grants you one of the following Skills to be used in pursuit of Her goals.

- **[Smite***] Instant death for anyone who violates Gina's Word. Use of this Skill reduces you to 1 health point. If it is used on an innocent, it will fail, and they will have the opportunity to slay you instead.*

- **[Compassion]** *The target will instantly relive the suffering of those they have harmed, and they will have the opportunity to change their ways. Be aware, however, that this Skill will fail on those who are truly evil. Can only be used once per target.*

- **[Metamorphosis]** *When used, this Skill changes the target into a random type of half-breed. They must interact with some number of other sapient beings (number varies depending on the severity of crimes committed), with at least ten percent being people who knew them in their previous form, before they can revert to their original race. Cannot be used on people who are already of mixed race.*

You have thirty seconds to choose. 30… 29… 28…

Aspen instantly dismissed [Smite]. The chance that he would use the skill on someone deemed 'innocent' by some very fuzzy rules was far too high, and besides, if they wanted people dead, well, they could do that without Gina's help. He was torn, though, between the other two. He liked the sound of [Compassion], but unfortunately, he had a terrible suspicion that only those who were at least partially good would truly be swayed by this. At that, if they knew that the experience wasn't repeatable, they could shake it off over time.

"Metamorphosis," he said, as firmly as he could, adding, "Please?" rather belatedly.

The light around him strobed to brilliance, and for a moment he felt as if he was split in two. One part of him remained in his body as it was *changed* in some essential way. The other part hovered just outside, watching in fascination. Then he snapped back together with a nearly audible pop. The light, wind, and – thankfully – hovering all stopped, and he returned to the ground.

Shakily, he reached up to rub at his stinging eyes, but paused, noticing something different about his hand. There, wrapping around the middle finger of his right hand, starting at about the middle of his of his fingernail and ending at the center of the back of his hand, was a metallic tattoo that looked as if it were made of liquid silver. At first, it was a butterfly, wings trembling in an unfelt breeze. As he watched, it shifted into a tadpole, tail wriggling, then sprouted legs and grew into a frog. Next, a grub swirled into a cicada, followed by something that looked like a tadpole at first, but changed instead into a lizard with long, swaying fronds around its head.

By now, his companions were crowded around him, all staring at the shiny new mark.

"That's awesome," Lyrec sighed, leaning in closer.

"You're going to need a glove or something," Rouge said practically, shooting her friend a meaningful glance as she elbowed him out of the way.

"Truly, you are blessed by the Gods," Vonn murmured, bowing his head with respect and perhaps a hint of fear.

Aspen cleared his throat, clenching his hand. *Thank you, my capricious Goddess,* he thought silently, and he would have sworn he felt a teasing hand tug at his hair. Turning back to George, who was pressed back against the cabinet as hard as he could from his awkward position, Aspen extended his hand.

"[Metamorphosis]."

George's body twisted in on itself, flickering in strange, cubic patterns. Aspen had to squint hard against a terribly disorienting feeling, and finally closed his eyes completely, suddenly dizzy. When he blinked them open, George's massive frame had been replaced by a much smaller one.

The man was still balding and potbellied, but now the belly hung above a pair of skinny bow-legs, and his barely-recognizable face sat in the middle of a knobby chartreuse head crowned with what were easily the largest ears Aspen had ever seen. Whatever half-breed George had become, Aspen doubted there was any human involved, but goblin definitely played a very large part.

George struggled to his gnarled feet, his now ridiculously oversized clothing dropping from him to land in a puddle with the ropes that had been serving as his bonds. He stood there, trembling, his only remaining covering the ubiquitous off-white underclothes.

"No!" His clawed hands scratched at his green skin, and an expression of horror oozed across his face. He looked fearfully at the bedroom door. "They'll kill me," he whimpered. "I hafta talk t' ten of m' friends." He struggled to make himself understood around the unfamiliar pointed teeth and long tongue that filled his mouth. "Bu' they'll kill me if they see me!"

Aspen glanced at his friends. Rouge looked both fascinated and appalled. Vonn looked grimly pleased. Lyrec just looked disgusted. Vonn stepped forward, closer to the shaking figure. He now towered over George, and the formerly large man shrank away, clearly unused to being physically intimidated by anyone.

"Go," Vonn almost hissed. "Find out what it is like when everyone around you hates you without reason. When you are attacked only for your birth. If you survive, *remember*." Opening the door, he shoved the goblinoid into the street, where he looked around with a panicked expression before scuttling away.

Aspen lowered the hand he'd raised when Vonn yanked the door open, sighing softly. "Vonn," he asked, "are you aware that if he speaks to anyone, and if they believe him at all, they'll come running here to see what he's talking about?"

The elf's eyes snapped back to Aspen, his face going blank, then flushing with dark color. "You're right, my lord. I'm sorry. We'll have to hurry."

Lyrec groaned. "And we're going to have to take that other guy with us. We haven't gotten a chance to talk to him yet."

Vonn looked down, shame-faced. "I did not think. I'm sorry."

Rouge reached out and took the young man's hand, holding it reassuringly while glaring at Aspen. "He just found out his family is probably dead, and it's mostly that guy's fault. Obviously he's not thinking clearly."

Aspen shook his head, one eyebrow going up. "I only asked a question. And, Vonn, don't start 'my lord'-ing me or I'll have to actually get upset. I'm just Aspen." He heaved out a sigh. "Now, let's get out of here with our prize. No way to hide the fact that we've been here now, so we may as well try to make it look like a robbery, or maybe someone came to exact revenge on these two for something. I'm sure there are plenty of people who dislike them."

He looked over at Rouge. "Can you [Stealth] with someone else, yet?"

Her eyes flickered as she looked over the skill description, then waggled her hand. "Maaaaybe? Not someone who's conscious, for sure, but maybe while he's out, if I can carry him. I mean, I can definitely carry him, weight-wise, but no matter how much you guys call him little, he's still bigger than me." She glared around a little, lower lip pouting out.

Aspen resisted the urge to pat her on the head. His hand wouldn't do him any good if it was severed and made into a glove. "We'll figure something out." He looked at the young elf. "Vonn, destroy this room. Quietly but thoroughly. Avoid the traps."

Back to Lyrec. "Take everything in their storage chests and put them in your inventory. Take the chests themselves, if you can. There may be other things in them that we've dismissed as worthless but that may yet be useful."

Calm topaz eyes assessed Rouge. "Let's go look at our *little* friend. I have an idea."

Ten minutes later, Vonn slipped into [Camouflage] and cracked the door open, peering outside. "Nothing yet," he whispered back to the other three.

Rouge, who was wearing a man slightly taller than herself in a sling improvised from a bedsheet and tied across her shoulders, grumbled, "This is stupid. Why don't we just roll this guy up in a carpet and pretend we're here to do some renovations while we're at it?"

Aspen chuckled. "I didn't see a lot of carpet in this house, little thief. Besides, this is more fun. All right, let's-"

Suddenly, Rouge smacked herself in the face.

"Hold up, hold up! Wait! I have the perfect thing! Oh my gosh, why didn't I…" Her voice trailed off as she gazed into space, fingers twitching. Her 'cat who ate the canary' grin crept over her face. "Oh yeah! Let's try this." She swirled her hands a few times, striking a pose reminiscent of something Aspen had seen Flu-flu do more than once.

"Moon Prism Power Substitution!" The girl whisper-yelled, and a moment later, a perfect replica of George stood in her place. "Oh my gosh!" The behemoth stared down at his thick-fingered hands in amazement, deep voice cracking as he spoke. "That is so cool!" He started giggling, which was so disturbing that all three men took a step back.

"And good ol' what's-his-name here counts as a stolen object, so…" the heavy face grimaced, "Well, bum-nugget. I *had* a boost of an hour to the skill, but mentioning that I stole something," she scratched her head, voice dropping to a mutter as her eyes unfocused, "or maybe saying what it was?" She looked back down at them, shaking her head. "Anyway, it counted as the theft being discovered, so I'm back to fifteen minutes. Well, just over fourteen, now."

Quickly, she shucked the sling, then picked up George's friend, tossing him over her now-very-broad shoulder. "Poor guy," she said, grinning cheekily and flashing George's square yellow teeth, "had too much to drink and I'm taking him home. No one will suspect 'Gippy' of kidnapping his own buddy, right? Plus, if some crazy half-goblin starts running around claiming something's wrong, no one will believe him because they just saw good ol' Gipster a minute ago. C'mon!"

Aspen was thinking fast, slotting this new skill into the plans that had been coming together in his mind. He shook his head sharply. Time for that later. "Go ahead, then, Rouge. Try *not* to be noticed, though, if you can. Vonn, reset the traps behind us. Lyrec, we'll stay back with Vonn and try not to look like we're with Rouge. Everyone, get your masks on."

Rouge and Vonn wrinkled their noses simultaneously as they realized that the horrible stench had become familiar enough that they were starting to ignore it. They yanked up their face coverings. Aspen's mask was still in place, and Lyrec, who couldn't really tell what the big deal was about, just shrugged and put his on as well.

Rouge reached over and tugged at Vonn's curls, moving them so the straps of the mask held them down, concealing his ears. Her shy smile would have been sweet if it hadn't been on George's face. She turned and began to walk away, whistling tunelessly and staggering a little, as if she'd also imbibed a bit more than she should.

Vonn slid his slim hand through the door, releasing the string that would set any traps that hadn't already been sprung, and Aspen spared a moment to regret that they had ransacked the house. If he'd known Rouge could transform into George, he would have left it looking as it had when they entered so that goblin-George would be undermined even further. Aspen winced slightly, though. He had a suspicion that the real George's initial reaction would be correct, anyway, and the transformed half-breed would be beaten at best, and likely even killed without getting a chance to tell his story.

The three males looked at each other, drawing in a simultaneous buoying breath before following the whistling.

🍂 🍂 🍂

Somehow, they all made it out of the neighborhood around the Tannery without any significant difficulties. A few people looked like they recognized 'George', but they all ducked their heads and scurried away, so Rouge didn't have to pretend to actually be the hulking brute. Nobody looked concerned or surprised at seeing the smaller man draped over the bigger one's shoulder, either.

Shortly after they started garnering curious looks from people who didn't seem frightened enough of George to know him, Rouge dropped into a side street. When they came up on her, her burden was lying on the ground, still thoroughly passed out due to Aspen's continued gentle magical pressure on his mind. He hadn't been entirely certain that would work, and he was relieved to see that it had. Rouge was back to her normal appearance, and her fingers were twitching as they did when she was working on something in her 'Heads Up Display'.

When the trio entered the alley, her attention switched briefly to them, then returned to whatever she was working on. After a moment, she looked back. "Okay, I think we need to do this as quickly as possible. Schmuck here," she nodded to the man at her feet, "clearly knows more than Giddyup did, and we need to get him to talk. There's a Thieves Guild safe house nearby, one of the temp ones, so I can take 'guests' there and it won't matter because they'll take it off the list once I say I used it."

The girl looked over at Aspen, expression pleading. "So, uh, can you carry him from here? Because that felt really icky. I mean, he wasn't heavy, but *ew*." She shuddered in disgust, and Aspen nodded.

Leaning over, he easily pulled the limp figure up by one arm, then glanced at Vonn, who looked human enough as long as his mask concealed his delicate elven bone structure. If they went much further from the Tannery, however, people would start getting paranoid about seeing a group of masked people wandering the streets.

"Vonn, grab his other arm and drape it over your shoulders. Let's go for 'good buddies helping their friend home,' if we can." Once Vonn had joined him in awkwardly draping their burden across their shoulders – awkward mostly because the man's foot was dangling on Aspen's side, and his toes were dragging on Vonn's side – Aspen smiled reassuringly at Rouge. "Let's go."

Without another word, Rouge slunk off, slipping from shadow to shadow down narrow back streets so smoothly that Aspen quickly realized that his young friend barely needed [Stealth] to stay unnoticed. At least, she would if she wasn't being followed by three awkward idiots, one of whom was complaining that *he* could have helped Aspen with the unconscious man more easily than Vonn, who was actually a hair's-breadth shorter than the boy. Aspen kept his suspicions that the lad's strength stat was probably not actually high enough to carry the limp weight to himself, and just concentrated on keeping his burden from slipping off his shoulders. He was already feeling the strain of walking in the crouched, twisted position he'd been forced into, and he dreaded what his back was going to do to him later.

Fortunately, the safe house really was very close, and they only had to cross one busy intersection during their journey through a series of narrow back-alleys Aspen had only vaguely been aware existed. A few people on the larger thoroughfare cast them a dubious look, but when Aspen staggered into a wall, pulling Vonn and the limp figure with him, then broke out into slightly hysterical laughter, they looked away in disgust. Well, except for one man who was burdened down by a towering stack of boxes as he scurried along behind a rather imperious-looking lady. His gaze was definitely more longing than contempt.

Once they were past that junction, however, they soon saw Rouge pull a large board from where it rested against the wall. She leaned down to murmur in the ear of the man 'sleeping' beneath the board, and he rolled over to allow them passage, though one sharp eye cracked open to watch as they entered the door concealed behind him. Once they were all through, with everyone except

Rouge forced to duck, the man pulled the board back and resumed his position.

Rouge immediately dropped to the floor with a grunt, then grimaced and rubbed her rear as best she could without moving. "Stupid pod," she muttered. "Okay, I got us here. Now, how do we get this bozo to talk?"

Aspen and Vonn gently lowered the man to the ground, afraid to disturb him too much, though one would think that if he was going to be able to resist Aspen's continuing encouragement to remain asleep, he would have done it already. Indeed, as if to underscore how deeply he rested, a line of drool slithered from between his loose lips, and he snorted a bit.

Aspen shook his head. "I suspect that my usual techniques wouldn't sit well with you, lass, and I must confess my conscience lies less easy when I use them outside of a genocidal war for survival. I could try something with magic, but-" he paused as he felt a strange tug on what he had recently figured out was a tether to his Goddess much the same as the one he had with his companions and his new staff, only with him as the 'pet' in the bond. "I think that would be unwise."

Vonn growled a little. "If I weren't bound by the oaths of *r'nspiga*, I would take that burden from you, my friend. Unfortunately, I am meant to aid the helpless, not torment them, no matter how they may deserve it."

Lyrec waved his hands. "Don't look at me. I'm not water-boarding anyone or anything, even in a game!"

Aspen paused. "What is- No, never mind. Rouge?"

Rouge cleared her throat, looking from Aspen to Lyrec and back again, though she refused to meet her young friend's eyes. "Weeeeelllll.... I do have *one* idea."

And that is how Lyrec, after much protestation that his music wasn't *that* bad, found himself standing right beside their prisoner's head, holding his lute in a white-knuckled grip. Aspen nodded to the boy, and then released his hold on the supine man's brain. Their prisoner instantly jerked awake, gasping in a deep breath of air, which Aspen promptly knocked out of him with a well-placed boot to his gut. The man curled up, groaning and struggling against the ropes that bound him.

"Wha' th'-" He choked in a breath, and stared, wild-eyed, as Aspen crouched down beside him, face once again concealed by mask and lowered hat brim.

Aspen restrained a sigh as he realized they'd forgotten something basic. Again.

::Rouge, what's his name?::

The little thief girl looked like she wanted to sink into the floor, and Lyrec, too, looked embarrassed. Both Travelers squinted, though it seemed like Rouge had to work at it much harder. ::Leonard. Sorry, Aspen.::

He turned his head and gave her a tiny wink with one eye. ::We all forgot. We've been among friends too long.::

Turning back to Leonard, Aspen spoke in a deep but conversational tone. "We just wanted to ask you a few friendly questions, Leonard, but you and George assaulted my friend here." He indicated Vonn, who was barely visible in the pale and dusty rays of lights that filtered down through the poorly-built ceiling. "Then, when we came back to try again, you attacked him again."

He picked up Vonn's heavy hunting knife, which he'd stabbed into the dirt floor by his boot, and twirled it, grateful that Birdie and Plum had been so entertained by sleight of hand when they'd been little girls. Ignoring the heavy blade flickering between his fingers, he continued. "Now, George already talked to us, and-"

Leonard's black eyes were darting around the small space in which they found themselves. "Where's Gippy? What'd you do with 'im?"

Aspen sighed theatrically and planted the knife two inches deep in the ground beside the other man's ear, trimming a few stray wisps of hair as he did so. "*George* talked to us, so we let him go. Unhurt." He held open his now-empty hand, and his new silver tattoo glinted in the dim light. *Damn it, I forgot about that. I'll need to get some gloves.*

Forcing himself not to yank back his hand, he curled it closed and pulled the blade from the ground in an effortless movement. "Now, the question is, are *you* going to talk to us so we can release you unhurt, too? Or are you going to force us to do things we don't want to before you talk. Because," he leaned in, knowing his eyes were an eerie pale gold in the dimness, "you *will* talk to us. Eventually."

Leonard's throat bobbed as he swallowed, and he leaned as far from Aspen as he could. "I dunno nothin'. We tried to tell yer tree-fu… Uh, elf friend there that we dunno anythin'. Just woke up one day, and they was dead or gone. Terrible thing." His nasal voice lifted into a pathetic whine by the end of this, and he widened his eyes, trying for 'sad', or maybe 'nauseated', if Aspen were to guess.

Aspen reached into the shadows behind him and raised the dull knife and two hoods Lyrec had found. On closer inspection, one hood was black around the bottom, while the other one was trimmed in deep red, though they were otherwise identical. "Now, now. George was positively eager to help us. He said you two *fine* upstanding citizens let a concerned group know that you had outsiders in your midst. He told us the group who took the woman and killed her husband and father were called Maskers, and wore hoods just." He shook the limp cloth in his hands. "Like. This."

Once again Vonn's knife was embedded into the dirt, this time leaving a tiny scratch in the skin just over the man's carotid artery. He yelped and jerked away, face contorting in panic. "Fine, fine! We, ah, found those in th' house when they was taken. I kept 'em, is all."

Aspen twisted the knife in the dirt, and the razor-sharp blade *scrape scraped* against the scrawny throat. "George didn't know anything about them. So, what about them made it worth concealing them from your best friend, eh? I'd think if you found them while you were together, you would have split them. Maybe put them on, had a little fun acting the part of villains? Pretend to be something you aren't?"

He leaned close again, sliding the knife from the earth as he did, and lowered his voice to a hoarse whisper. *"Unless it wouldn't be pretending for you."*

Leonard began to squeal like a pig in pain, writhing against the ropes that held his arms tied. "Nooo! I can't tell ye! They'll know! They make you swear to their God, and if you tell anyone, he'll crush yer head like an egg!"

Aspen rocked back on his heels, eyes as wide as those of his victim. A god? What god would be involved in this? He looked over at Rouge.

::Do you know what God he means? Not Erasa. She'd never be mistaken for a male deity.:: Erasa was the Goddess of assassins and murderers. Anyone who killed outside war or duels came under her purview. She was usually depicted wearing a skin-tight red costume, and her femininity was pronounced.

Rouge shook her head. ::I don't know. I mean, there are a *lot* of gods. Somebody went way overboard there, even given that the advertising promised 'a god for everyone'. It's ridiculous.::

He huffed a beleaguered sigh. ::Well, now I know why Gina's involved in this. The Gods generally let us clean up our own messes without interference, but if this God is poking his nose in where it doesn't belong, it would explain a lot.::

Lyrec looked back and forth between Aspen and Rouge. The bard's face was visibly pale, even in the faint illumination. ::Does that mean I don't have to do this? 'Cause I'm cool with that.::

Both Aspen and Rouge jumped a little, having once again forgotten that Lyrec could hear their conversation.

::Nope.::

::Alas, no.::

They shared an amused glance as the boy wilted a little. ::Fine. Can we get on with it, then?::

Aspen turned back to the prisoner. "What is the name of this God?"

Beads of greasy sweat formed around Leonard's receding hairline. "Dunno." He squealed again as Aspen raised the knife. "No, no! He'll kill me!"

At the reminder that the little man had supposedly taken an oath that would allow his God to kill him if he told his secrets, Aspen frowned. Certainly it was true that one could make a binding oath before the gods, but he had never heard of the retribution for failure being so dire. A life-time of pox, yes. Silence for a month. Loss of all profits and status that the person had gained because the oath existed was a common one.

Then, too, there was something *off* that Aspen had noticed about Leonard's... what? Spirit? Mind? Animus? *Soul*? Whatever it was that Aspen could now see around all living beings with even the slightest effort. Leonard's wasn't exactly greasy, like the Demonic Swineherd's, but it could be described as *frayed*. It looked something like a woolen cloak that had been stored improperly, and had become a feast for moth larvae.

Aspen had dismissed it as part and parcel of the man's cruel nature, but now he thought he should take a closer look. Cautiously, he pressed his right hand, the one with the new tattoo, on the man's chest, feeling the ribs bend as he pinned the slight figure down on the ground so he couldn't move.

::Uh, Aspen? What are you doing?:: Rouge's voice was faintly shocked.

Lyrec sounded equally concerned, but also very mildly thrilled. ::It looks like you're going to, um, kiss him, or, uh, something.::

Aspen growled in disgust, but didn't pull back, staring into the terrified eyes inches from his own. ::Give me a minute.::

He opened his Life Sense wide.

The first thing Aspen noticed was that Leonard's 'spirit' was, for lack of a better word, *flimsy*. The frayed effect that he had noticed before was much more pronounced, and he felt like it would actually give way with the slightest touch of Aspen's mana.

To test this theory, Aspen first reached out and very gently prodded Vonn's spirit, causing the young elf to shiver and look around as if someone might have snuck into the room with them. Making a mental note to apologize to the young elf later, Aspen considered the 'feeling' of his spirit. It was something like touching a bubble blown from the processed sap of a certain tree found only in countries far to the south of the human-held lands. The bubbles had become a fad when Lark was seven or eight, and Aspen had purchased a great number of them for her birthday party. Like those bubbles, Vonn's spirit was springy, smooth, and resilient, almost pleasant under his mental touch.

When Aspen attempted to do the same with Leonard's spirit, however, it 'felt' almost sticky, as though clinging to the power in his touch. The pliable warmth was entirely missing, and it seemed more like a soap bubble ready to pop, except that no soap bubble had ever been so bedraggled. As he pulled his mana back, he saw that the spirit clung to him like a web. When he managed to break free, he saw that the area he'd interacted with now looked brighter and stronger than what hung around it.

The thing was draining his mana to try to repair itself!

Shuddering, Aspen pulled every bit of himself back, using his Life Sense to see what was going on. At first, nothing else seemed obviously different in the midst of the general malaise. Then, he saw that the area that had recovered slightly was now fading once more. Looking closer, he could see that one of the frayed strands of spirit-stuff wasn't dangling free like the rest. Instead, it narrowed to a thread so fine its presence was only detectable by the fact that the attached spirit held still in whatever served as an ethereal breeze.

Very, very carefully, he prodded at the area where the thread would be, if it were visible, and 'felt' something oddly cold and unyielding. Instantly, he felt weaker, as if some noticeable portion of his power had been sucked away, and when he pulled back, the coldness clung until he managed to force his physical body to fall backwards unceremoniously onto his rear.

"Great Gina," he whispered, "something is *eating* him."

The horrified gazes of everyone else in the room fell on him.

Leonard's eyes were wild, and his voice was a cracked whine. "What d'you mean, *eatin'* me? Nothin's eatin' me!"

Aspen shook his head, climbing to his feet. "I don't know what you've done, but somehow, you've given *something* access to your very soul, and it's eating you from within. Depending on how quickly this progresses, I doubt you'll survive its predations much longer."

The little man quivered, and curled into a fetal ball. "I knew it wasn't right," he muttered. "I told 'em. Told 'em I didn't feel *right*. They said, they said…" He began to sob pitifully.

Aspen, Vonn, Lyrec, and Rouge retreated to the corner farthest from their prisoner, and Aspen explained what he'd seen. Rouge was horrified, but Vonn seemed grimly satisfied. Lyrec simply asked plaintively if it meant he *didn't* have to play the lute to torture the guy, because, seriously, his playing wasn't *that* bad.

"What do we do now, Aspen?" Rouge asked, tugging at a braid nervously. "I mean, if the guy really is linked to some Big Bad, then he might *actually* die if we force him to tell us what he knows. Which, yeah, he deserves to be punished, but that [Metamorphosis] thing should be enough, right?"

Aspen shook his head. "I don't know. We could probably force him to talk, but I believe the risk that his oath will truly take his life is high. I could use [Metamorphosis], and we could send him out, and let things take their natural course. I could…" He flickered his eyes to his staff, where it rested, momentarily quiescent, against the wall. "I could *try* to sever the bond, with Gina's help. She clearly has no liking for what is happening here, and I have the sense she would assist me if I ask."

He grimaced. "Though we saw how that worked last time. And, to be honest, I suspect that there would be some risk to me, in trying."

Rouge's response was immediate. "Forget it, then. We'll find out the information some other way. We can put that dagger in the map somewhere and wait for the baddies to come to us."

Aspen shook his head at this. "These Maskers likely have some way of verifying the accusations. George said it takes a few days for them to respond. Why wait, if they simply come in and kill the accused without checking?"

Lyrec raised his hand. "Oh! I saw a vid like this once! It's a sting operation! Have some actual half-breeds move into a house, then use the dagger. When the villains show up," he smacked his hands together sharply, "*boom*! You've got 'em!"

Vonn pondered for a moment, then sighed. "I would volunteer myself, except that I don't know if they would attack full-bloods, or if their hatred is reserved for those who have crossed the barriers of race. Also, this would take a minimum of three days, likely more, and in the meantime, others are dying. My sister, if she survives, possibly among them. I would prefer haste."

The elf's gray eyes shifted to Aspen, and his voice was grave. "If you are willing to undertake this risk, I believe it is worthwhile, both for your own quest, and mine. I would owe you a great favor."

"No!" Rouge's voice was a little frantic, and she glared at Vonn. "He just promised not to take unnecessary risks! *This* isn't necessary! We can-"

Aspen gently laid a hand on her shoulder. "If it seems to be going wrong, I'll stop. Rouge, my friend, I appreciate your concern, but I believe this needs to be done."

The slim girl threw her arms around him, burying her face in his chest. "Be careful, okay?" She asked, voice muffled. "Don't be stupid."

He chuckled, hugging her back. "When was the last time I did something stupid?" When she reared back, mouth opening to respond indignantly, he grinned, lifting his right hand to show the shifting tattoo. "Don't answer that."

She stuck her tongue out at him.

A few minutes later, Aspen was crouched over Leonard once again. The man was attempting to thrash away from him, so Rouge was gripping his feet, while Vonn held his bound hands pinned. Lyrec, who had gratefully returned his lute to storage, attempted to help, but his strength was so low that the panicked prisoner simply knocked him away.

"No no no no no no no no! Don' mess with it! You'll get me killed! Lemme go!" The man on the ground was howling in fear, and Aspen finally had to stuff his own shirt into his mouth. Even then, hoarse sounds continued to emerge from his throat, and Aspen could only hope that the guard outside wouldn't choose to investigate.

Cautiously, Aspen opened himself again. His vision quickly locked onto the stiff section of Leonard's spirit where the thread was attached. Now that he knew what he was looking for, he wondered how he could have missed it in the first place.

Moving slowly, he placed Stick beside the invisible thread, and sent it a request. Instantly, the dainty leaves twisted and reformed into something much more akin to a tiny sickle. The blade of the sickle rested just on the far side of the thread from Aspen, who held his arm extended and rock steady. With the smallest of motions, the razor-sharp blade would meet the thread, and he could only hope it would sever the thread instead of becoming stuck itself.

This time, he didn't try to form words for the others to hear. He simply sent a mental prayer to his Goddess. *Gina, I'm sorry for bothering you twice in one day. We've found a man who seems linked to another God in some foul way. He'll die if he tells us more, and we need what he knows. Please, help me cut the tie so he can speak in safety.*

In his Life Sense, he saw his Stick begin to glow, much as Aspen had when he had prayed to Gina before. Thankfully, this time the light seemed limited to the spiritual realm, and the others didn't flinch from it. Aspen, however, flinched when words once again appeared before him.

The Goddess Gina has heard your prayer. As Her Champion, you may now use the following Skill.

[Winnow] *Separate the wheat from the chaff. The divine wind of Gina's holy garden will assist you in cleansing those who have become impure. If the damage was done as a result of their own choices, it cannot be repaired, but if they are innocent of wrongdoing, this will also help heal some of the damage.*

Be warned that this Skill must be used with great care, as it can irrevocably damage the soul of the target. This Skill is a Divine gift. If this Skill is used for other than its intended purpose, it will be reclaimed. Unpleasantly.

Releasing his breath in a hiss of relief, Aspen triggered the new skill. A wind began to blow, circling the miniature sickle. In his magical vision, he could see a sparkling silver wind wrap around the blade, glimmering brightly. The heady scent of plumeria and lilac filled the room, and everyone drew in a cleansing breath. Leonard's body relaxed beneath Vonn and Rouge's grip.

Aspen's wrist bent.

Beneath the curved and brilliant edge of his sickle, something caught, pulling tight as the string of a lute. Leonard's body arched, and his eyes and mouth opened wide, though, eerily, he made no sound other than the scraping of his body on the dirt floor. In Aspen's ears, however, a new sound made itself known.

Growling.

It was the sound of a beast, utterly devoid of sense or humanity. It was Leonard, but not, and Aspen knew that whatever was on the other end of that strand had noticed what he was trying to do. Then the thread parted, and the sound cut off as suddenly as it had begun, leaving an uncanny silence that was quickly filled by the *whoosh* of Gina's wind as it wrapped around the little man's ragged spirit. The aroma of that wind became earthy and sad, filled with patchouli and water-dampened soil, and then wisped away, vanishing into the mortal scents surrounding them.

"Holy smokes, Aspen!" Rouge exclaimed, releasing Leonard's feet as if they burned her. "What happened? Did you do it? I thought I just smelled," she stuttered, then finished lamely, "s-something I smelled before, somewhere else."

Vonn's head was bowed, one hand resting on his heart as the other traced a symbol on his forehead. He looked up. "That was undoubtedly a moment shared with a God, my lord. Were you able to sever the connection?"

Lyrec frowned. "What are you guys talking about? Why is everything about smells today? This is some kind of gimmick to get headset users to buy a pod, isn't it?" He looked up, presumably speaking to some pantheon of his own. "Well, joke's on you, 'cause there's no way I can afford a pod, and my parents *definitely* aren't getting one. So cut it out!"

Aspen looked down, examining Leonard's spirit once again. The sad thing looked as pathetic as before, undoubtedly because he'd brought this upon himself, but it moved freely now, no longer anchored by the alien thread.

Sighing in relief, Aspen stood, using Stick to help pull himself to his feet, even as he told it it could return to its preferred shape. In a shower of tinkling chimes, it did so, practically glowing with pride. Aspen patted it approvingly, and it chimed again. A faint whiff of lilac touched his nose.

"It's done. I can't fix the damage, since he brought it on himself, but it will, at least, not worsen. I don't know if a," he hesitated on the word *soul*, and instead said, "spirit can heal itself or not, but I suspect," he fixed the exhausted and barely-conscious Leonard with an icy glance, "it depends on what is done with it in the future. Some life changes are undoubtedly in order."

Rouge, who had moved to stand beside him, suddenly sucked in a breath and reached up to touch Aspen's hand where he gripped Stick. "Uh, Aspen?"

Suddenly certain he knew what he was going to see, Aspen looked over. Indeed, the index finger on his right hand was now sheathed in silver. The skin and nail of the finger gleamed faintly at the tip, then softened into gently billowing swirls traveling toward his knuckle. There, it vanished toward his palm.

He shifted Stick to his left hand and held out his right, palm up. There, he saw a perfect reproduction of a sickle surrounded by clouds, presumably representing wind. The wind touched the mercurial tattoo on his middle finger, and when a butterfly swirled into existence there, it looked as if it was being lifted on a breeze.

Rouge grabbed his hand, poking at the tattoo as if to see if she could affect the creatures there. They continued moving, ignoring her prodding fingers. "Shoot. Oh well. That's still cool." She looked up, much as Lyrec had, speaking to the ceiling. "I want one! Can you, like, make it a quest reward or something?"

Her braids suddenly lifted as if a hard wind had buffeted her, and she staggered slightly. Her lower lip poked out. "Fine. Be that way. Next time *someone* owes me a favor, though, we're going to have a Talk."

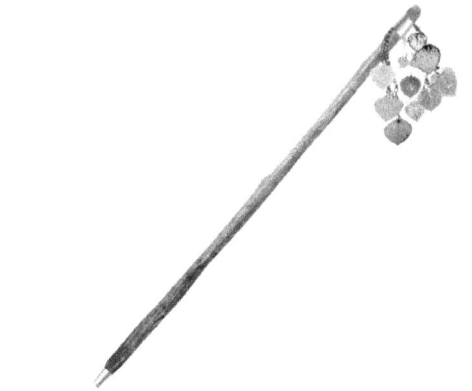

Chapter Fifteen

Rouge

R ouge was still thinking about Aspen's awesome new tats as they all stood around Lennie. The little man lay on the floor, sullen, still bound, and utterly ungrateful for whatever Aspen had done waving that teeny scythe around in the air like a crazy person. Seriously, he should get bonus gratitude just for being willing to look that silly.

Aspen still had his mean face on, and his eyes were like frigid topaz chips above his black mask. He was using his I'm-the-lord-and-you're-the-minion voice, too, but Lennie was bearing up under it surprisingly well. The guy was apparently still convinced that either this God would smite him, or his fellow Maskers would take him out. Which, she had to admit, was actually fairly likely. The Thieves Guild frowned on that kind of thing, too.

Finally, with a beleaguered sigh (that Word of the Day app was really coming in handy lately), the tall farmer looked at Lyrec. "Do it." He said.

Lyrec squirmed, but got out his lute. "*Seriously*, I don't know why you all think this will work, but whatever…"

Rouge the Rogue: Oh my gosh, Jace, just *do it!* This is going to be awesome!

Lyrec: I blame you for this.

Rouge the Rogue: I blame all those games you played Bards in that made you think you could play music. You're pretty good with your jaw harp, but you need to actually record yourself or something.

Lyrec: I did! I've just never actually *tried* to play badly!

Rouge the Rogue: Just plaaaaaaaay!!!

Still grumbling, Lyrec got out his lute.

Leonard laughed. "What, is yer bard goin' to make me Nauseated or Fearful? I'm not goin' to tell you-"

Lyrec struck the first chord. It hung in the air, somehow flat and sharp at the same time. Rouge was quite certain that it wasn't a sound that a single instrument could produce in real life, but game logic somehow made it work. Just as the first jangled mess began to fade, Lyrec, chin set as he clearly decided to prove his doubters wrong, began to really get into it.

Oh, I never went back,

To my sweet Molly Mack,

For her gasket was blown

And she could o-only groan,

And when I whispered sweet nothings,

She ran.

Oh, I never went home,

To my kind lad Jerome,

For his cat had had puppies,

And he always ate guppies,

And when I told him I loved him,

He ran.

Yeeeeeeeessssssss, I oft fall in lo-ove

With beauties from abo-ove,

But it never works out in the end.

I somehow offend,

Or make a new friend,

And whenever I visit,

They run.

No-o-o-o, I never went to the farm,

With good fellow Sharm,

For he bought a cow with his funds,

And—

A string snapped at the same time as Leonard, who had begun screaming sometime in the middle of the second stanza. "Apofis, my great God, save me! Spare me from this terrible-!"

His head imploded.

Rouge looked at Aspen in disbelief as she was once again glad she couldn't actually vomit in game. Imploding was presumably better than exploding, but *gross*. Gross. Gross. Gross. *Gross*! "I thought you cut the link!"

Aspen took off his mask, looking at something sticky that she was glad she couldn't see in the low light. Imploding apparently still involved some things that used to be inside going outward after the 'plosion.

"I did. I'm certain. Unfortunately, doing so attracted the attention of *something*, and when Leonard spoke the name, well. It seems Leonard's God truly did not wish his name to be known." He carefully folded the mask around the remnants of whatever-it-was and tucked it into a pocket. When he saw her look, he shrugged. "Leonard may yet be more helpful to us, but it will require Manuela's assistance."

Vonn, who had retreated as far from Lyrec's truly heinous 'music' as he could, had escaped relatively unscathed. He stepped forward now, nudging the body with a foot. "What do we do with it?"

Aspen looked at Rouge and Lyrec. "When a Traveler loots a corpse, the corpse decays much more quickly than if a Native searches them. Would one of you care to do the honors?"

Lyrec was distinctly green, and looked as if he would like nothing more than to rip off his headset and run to the bathroom. He stepped back quickly, using his inventory to switch to a backup set of gear. The first set would need to go to a Tailor for cleaning, but this was definitely the easiest way to get cleaned up after a gory battle. He still had something on his cheek, but she wasn't going to mention it.

"Go for it, Rouge," he managed to choke out.

Shrugging, she knelt down over what was left of the body, keeping her gaze on Leonard's dirty boots. *He did this to himself*, she reminded herself firmly, and set a fingertip on his leg. A moment later, a Ball of Lint, a Suspicious Note, two silvers, and three coppers had entered her inventory. The body would break down to Fertile Soil in about five minutes.

Rouge pulled the Note out of her inventory. It held only two words, so she read them aloud. "Tonight. Ten. Also, whoever wrote this has terrible handwriting and spelling. They spelled tonight t-o-n-i-t."

Aspen's hand rubbed his jaw. "Presumably Leonard knew the location, and didn't need to be told. Reminds me of rule number one of taking prisoners; search them. We would have had a more specific question to ask if we'd found that first. Well, at least we know the name of the God, and-"

"Apple-face? Aphid? Apnea? Apode?" Rouge asked. "Seriously, guys, I'm not going to say 'He Who Shall Not be Named' or 'You know, *that* guy' every time we need to talk about him, and obviously he pays attention when you say his real name. I mean, they all *can*, right? Just some of them do it more than others." *I'm looking at you, Gina.*

"How about 'Chris'? Like he's just a guy or something." Lyrec suggested, looking calmer now that he was (mostly, because cheek) clean.

Aspen and Vonn both nodded. "That should divert attention from any conversations we may have out loud," Aspen said. "Good idea, Rouge, and good suggestion, Lyrec."

The teenagers exchanged glances, and Rouge could see from Lyrec's blush that he was as warmed by Aspen's approval as she was. Which was silly, because they were an equal team, but there it was. She felt like her favorite teacher had just given her an A+.

Clearing her throat, she glanced down at the body, which was already starting to look a little soft around the edges. "So, do we go home, then? I mean, back to Aspen's stupidly huge mansion-that-he-calls-a-house?"

Chuckling, Aspen nodded. "Yes." He pulled the mask from his pocket, then reached out and wiped the Leonard-bit from Lyrec's cheek. Lyrec looked like he couldn't decide if he wanted to blush or try to throw up again, but Aspen went on as if he hadn't noticed. "We need to get this to Manuela as soon as possible."

🐦 🐦 🐦

The journey back to the mansion was quick and easy. Rouge slipped the thief watching the safe-house a gold coin, and he gathered up his things and left. The marker was already gone from her map, so the Guild knew the place was blown. Then her group cleaned up any lingering traces of their activities (Aspen kept them, which was extra disgusting) and headed off as if they were just a group out for a nice day of shopping.

Half an hour later, Rouge's primary inventory had officially grown. It was stupidly expensive to expand your basic inventory, but she'd added twenty slots to hers, so now she could store more things without having to worry about them being stolen or dropped on death. She'd also purchased several *much* larger (and also very expensive) Chests of Holding so she could stash her nifty new treasures without being covered in bags. The chests could be strapped to Burrito, so though they could still be stolen, they'd be a lot easier to carry, and wouldn't be dropped unless someone managed to kill her and steal her pack animal.

Speaking of animals, though, it was time to go retrieve her bird. Aspen had left Rouge's Zombie and Codswallop at a Dead Tent yesterday before he ran off alone to go do his stuff. When she woke up, she'd decided to leave Wally there, since she wasn't sure what she'd need to be doing, and she didn't want to have to leave him somewhere by himself if she had to go thiefy and break in somewhere. The poor guy had been alone for almost a whole day now, and he'd be sad.

When they got to the house, Aspen headed up to his top-floor secret lab to do something with the left-over Leonard-bits. Vonn was checking on the kids, and Lyrec said he 'needed to lie down for a while' and logged off. His Zombie was standing in the corner of the room, because he hadn't even wanted to wait until she found him a bed. She threw a towel over his head because Aspen was right, Zombies were creepy.

At last, she scribbled out a quick note and pinned it to the table with one of her many, many knives. It was time to go get her ostrich back.

Aspen had showed them all the snazzy secret passage he'd made in the estate wall for his daughter, and she used it now, slipping out in [Stealth] until she could seamlessly join the flow of people walking around the city.

Veritas Online's system had some snazzy technique of seamlessly merging servers together, so people who knew each other would always be able to see and interact with each other. In the old days, you had to know what server your friends were on in order to play with them. Other games just put everyone with IP addresses in the same area or the same native language on the same server.

If *Veritas* 'saw' that two Players lived close to each other, it made sure that they were on the same server, but it would also pull in people with whom you'd exchanged messages or had on your Friends list. You could message across servers, so it only mattered when someone was actually close enough that you should be able to see them. Then it would seamlessly shift one of you to the other's server, which kept the server loads fairly level, and also made it so that you didn't actually see all the hundreds or thousands of other Players who could be standing in the same spot as you.

Bright, for instance, was always well-populated, but obviously all however-many-million users playing worldwide couldn't be in the same place at the same time, or nobody would be able to move. It undoubtedly required a lot of processing power to figure all this out, but then, she supposed that was why they had a semi-sentient AI running the show.

All of which explained why she wasn't shocked when she saw an elf who looked like a stretched-out and prettified version of Mirna walking toward her, chatting with two other elves who looked just like her little minions from school. Mirna, of course, was Zoey's Nemesis from school; a bigoted, hateful, self-important brat who had taken it upon herself to make Zoey's school life miserable.

As Zoey had learned recently, however, she was also a teenage girl from a broken home whose father had remarried a Black woman named Jazmin. Mirna and her mom apparently blamed Jazmin (and somehow her entire race?) for destroying their family, and, honestly, Mirna was probably getting a whole lot of poison poured into her ear by dear old mom. Also, Zoey totally understood what it was like to be stuck in the middle of a bitter divorce. She, too, had been angry, confused, and more than a little bit sad when her parents split.

None of which excused Mirna's behavior, but it did make it a lot harder to hate her for it. Darn it.

Rouge instantly dropped into [Stealth], hugging a shadowed wall as the three girls walked by, giggling. Since she was paying attention, the system kindly brought their voices out of the hubbub surrounding them, and she clearly heard a few snippets of their conversation.

"…seriously love being in Apofis' cult-thing." That was Flunky A. Rouge recognized the slight accent left over from an early childhood somewhere other than the United States.

"I don't know." That was Mirna, who was making that wrinkled-nose-like-something-stinks expression that Rouge knew all too well. "All the wearing hoods and chanting stuff is a little too realistic. I liked it better when we were just doing reputation quests."

Flunky B rolled her inhumanly blue eyes. "That's so *boring*. I mean, I know we need to have a, like, super high Rep to become Nobles and stuff, but making tea for old ladies and finding lost dogs is *lame*."

The girls were walking by right in front of Rouge's hiding place now, and she lost sight of their expressions, but she could see Mirna's shoulders tighten up as she tried for a noncommittal shrug. The other girl obviously had a top-of-the-line pod, to pick that up. "I don't think I'm going to go to the induction thing tonight. My dad and the step-monster are taking me out to dinner at that new Italian place. I'm putting up with it because it's supposed to be *très chic*."

It was Rouge's turn to roll her eyes. Mirna thought she was so special because her mom had hired her a French tutor. She dropped French words into random conversation like they were Skittles from heaven.

"Ugh. Fine." Flunky B, and now they were walking away, so Rouge slid left a few feet to keep them in listening range. The trio passed so closely that Rouge could have touched them. If she wanted to break [Stealth]. Though it would be funny to see the looks on their faces... "You're going to miss out, though. I think we're going to go up in rank after this quest."

"The quests are stupid easy anyway. 'Donate ten gold coins', 'take a vow', 'pay a ten mana per day tax'. I can make it up tomorrow, probably."

The other two girls made slightly dubious sounds of agreement, and then they were out of earshot, though Rouge trailed them until she had to stop at the very edge of her patch of shadow.

Rouge waited until there were no Players nearby, then dropped out of [Stealth] and strolled off down the road. *Now* it was time to get her bird, and oh boy, did she have some things to tell Aspen when they got back.

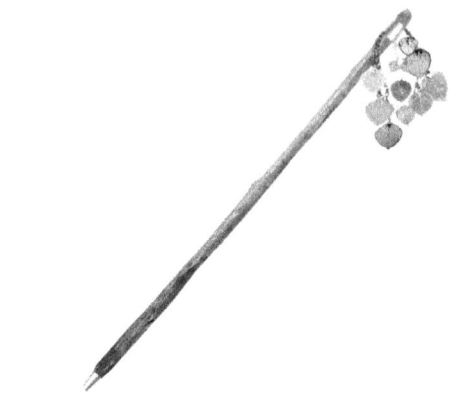

Chapter Sixteen

Aspen

Manuela had just finished tracking down and checking over the last squirming, half-feral imp infesting Aspen's house when the farmer managed to track her down. Releasing the brat into the wild again, his old friend looked up, her expression happier and more relaxed than he could remember ever seeing it. When she took in his grim countenance, however, her own tightened and grew guarded.

"What is it?" she asked, coming to her feet from the crouch she'd assumed so she could look into her patient's eyes and ears. She brushed herself down, wincing slightly when her fingers crossed a livid bite mark on her arm.

Aspen stepped forward, reaching slowly to touch the wound, remembering that Manuela wasn't one for physical contact outside of medical procedures. She stiffened, but held still when she saw his hand begin to glow softly. He whispered a prayer, and the injury vanished, along with some other scrapes and bruises his Life Sense told him lay where he couldn't see them with his eyes. Her small subjects had not been gentle in their efforts to escape her ministrations.

The woman relaxed a bit, the deep creases around her mouth softening so she looked no more than her fifty or so years. Chuckling quietly, she said, "It's strange to see you as a fellow healer, instead of," she paused, visibly choosing and discarding several descriptions for his former occupation, "what you were." She finished simply.

He sighed, dropping his hand and stepping back. "I, for one, am glad to see you finally able to use your gifts to heal, rather than forced to do harm." He shook his head. "I haven't asked, before, but – if you can tell me…"

Manuela sighed, casting her eyes down. "You didn't have to ask. I told you when we escaped Akuji's lair. I knew the risks of helping Birdie before we snuck outside the city. She would have gone alone, if I hadn't helped, and, seeing you here before me, I would do it again." She looked up, dark eyes bright.

"We were all going to die on the morrow, Iorgas. Two days at the outside. If things hadn't happened the way they did, the human race would have been all but destroyed the next time Akuji broke the thin defense provided by the bluestones. I know you regret it, and I wish Lark hadn't been the sacrifice required by the Gods to enable you to kill that bastard, but she would have died anyway, along with everyone else."

She held out her hand, looking at the network of faint scars radiating from her fingertips halfway up her arm. "I wish I hadn't lost to that damned ghoul, too, but at least losing half my levels convinced the King and Duke Geral I was a broken tool they could safely discard. The price for my freedom was high, but not one I regret paying." Flashing a smile, she said, "Plus, I was able to use my gifts differently this time, since I wasn't, ah, 'invited' into the military. My new skills are far more focused on aiding people in growth and recovery than the old. I was even able to find a physician who appreciated the, ah, *tranquility* of having an aged apprentice, and I picked up some less esoteric skills."

Aspen smiled a bit at this last. "That must be a story in itself, my friend. Unfortunately, today I must ask if you still retain one of your old abilities." He held up the cloth containing the bits of Leonard that remained. Since they were in his possession, they now counted as loot, instead of part of the corpse, but they would still begin to break down within a day. "[Soul Tracking]?"

Manuela took the handkerchief and looked within, eyeing the contents with clinical detachment. "I take it you've had an interesting day?" she asked wryly.

He tugged at his hat. "Yes, you could say that. I'm assisting Vonn with a problem, and seem to have stumbled over something Gina is also interested in."

Her capable fingers jerked, nearly dropping the make-shift bag. "The Gods? Iorgas, you know I don't–"

Aspen gently took his prize back. "Call me Aspen, please. And I certainly know how you feel about anything that involves the Gods, but -" he gestured to himself with the hand holding Stick, which was in its favorite form, and the staff chimed cheerfully at being included. "I haven't much choice, and I need your help. Please, old friend."

The woman sighed deeply, and held out her hand. "Fine then, but no more than this. [Soul Tracking] has come in handy more than once in preventing the spread of disease, so it has re-leveled several times. I can only look back a little over a day, though. Nothing like what I once could do." Her fingers curled as he carefully handed back the Leonard-bits. "To the map?"

He nodded.

Manuela was one of the very few people who had once been entrusted with tokens to allow them safe entry to Aspen's private sanctum. As his closest friend, he had even asked her to look after Birdie for him, if anything had happened to him but left Manuela and his daughter alive. Thus, Manuela knew all about Aspen's magically updating map table.

They stood across from each other now, staring down at the detailed depiction of the city in which they had once lived. Even as they watched, tiny walls rose in the better parts of the city, and crumbling buildings became more derelict in the poorer areas.

Manuela hefted the now-exposed gobbets of goo resting in her palm, eyeing them critically. "This is only enough for one attempt, so watch carefully. Hopefully what your former acquaintance here did on his last day will help you with whatever you need to do."

Aspen puffed a breath. "I hope so as well. He had an encounter with Vonn earlier today. I'm hoping that what he did after that will tell us something useful." His eyes searched the city, then fell on a small, ramshackle building. He pointed, noting as he did that the building seemed to have suffered a recent fire, judging by its crumbled and blackened frame. "He'll start here."

"He'll end there, you mean." Manuela chuckled darkly, her husky voice making the sound faintly menacing. "Watch, then." She held out her hand, and closed her eyes, muttering incomprehensibly beneath her breath.

Her eyes flashed open, pupils suddenly so huge that only the faintest rim of color could be seen around the blackness. Tendrils of hair that had escaped her black and silver braid began to flutter in an unfelt breeze. To his amazement, Aspen could actually sense the ghostly wind that disturbed the life force around her, though it was glaring more for its not-thereness more than its existence.

In his surprise, he nearly missed the faint speck of light that had appeared on the map inside the shell of the old building. Fortunately, he brought himself back to the moment in time to watch as it flowed backwards along their path, far more quickly than when they had actually walked it. Soon, it was back in Leonard and George's house, where it remained for several seconds.

Backwards, then, down the street to a pub, showing that the early bout of drunkenness he and his companions had acted out likely wasn't unrealistic. From there, Leonard's soul-trace was tracked to the Tannery itself, where it seemed the man had worked, given the long minute it remained.

Aspen focused closely on the next part, because very little time remained when the now-dead man could have interacted with Vonn after the young elf left that morning. From the Tannery, the light flickered to a building nearby, and then back to the Tannery it went. The time elapsed was so brief that if Aspen hadn't been looking so closely, he would undoubtedly have missed it.

After that, everything was fairly predictable. Back home, where Vonn must have caught the two men just before their shift. Leonard's soul-memory showed that he'd spent the night at home, and spent the evening before in the same pub he'd visited after work today. Aspen sighed, straightening, as the light faded and the flesh in Manuela's palm crumbled to dust.

Manuela, eyes still slightly unfocused, looking more than a little pale beneath her brown tan, leaned heavily on the table. Her fingers passed harmlessly through the magical image, and the tops of tiny houses showed over her knuckles. "Did that help?" Her voice was raspy, as though her throat was raw or dry, and Aspen handed her the mug of honeyed water he'd brought from the kitchen for just this purpose.

Aspen reached out, finger hovering over the building Leonard's light had so briefly entered. His voice was grim. "I think so. The man I met had no business waltzing in and out of a guard station so easily. He had some errand there, and I fear I know what it was."

Shaking her head, Manuela stood a little straighter. Downing the mug of water in one long draw, she set it down and sighed deeply, expression apologetic. "This is all I can do for you, then, Aspen. The Gods business is none of mine, though you may come to me if you're injured." She grimaced. "Though I suppose that any injury you can't repair yourself would be beyond my abilities as well."

He smiled at his old friend, who had been caught up in the games of the Gods when she was young. Though she had come out stronger and wiser, it was an experience she only spoke of late at night or when deep in her cups. Since then, she had forsworn any involvement with deities, and had taken rather a long time to trust Aspen, who was once the Left Hand of Atae.

At that moment, there came a sharp rapping at the stairwell door, and both of them whipped around, hands instinctively reaching for weapons. Manuela touched the hilt of a small knife sheathed at her waist, and Aspen grasped Stick, retrieving it from its resting place against the wall nearby. Aspen reached out with his Life Sense, and relaxed a moment later.

"It's Rouge," he told the tense woman across from him. "I'll let her in."

He strode down the hall, reaching the door just as another series of enthusiastic bangs resounded through the entry chamber. When he opened the door, Rouge bounded in, barely glancing around before words started tumbling from her mouth.

"You are never going to guess who I saw when I was on my way to get Wally!" Excitement brightened her pretty hazel eyes, and she nearly danced in place as she forced herself to pause for a half breath. Then she rolled her eyes and went on. "No, I guess you really wouldn't, since you don't know her, but I saw Mirna! I mean, she goes by 3DKitten now, which is just lame, but whatever. She was here with her two besties, and they were just chatting in the clear, so I could hear them, and they were talking about Chris – you know, *that* Chris – and said they were in some kind of cult!"

Aspen's attention was suddenly focused on his young friend, momentarily dismissing thoughts of what Leonard's little side trip might mean.

Rouge was already going on. "Apparently there's some big event tonight that they called an 'induction' that they were all three supposed to go to, even though Mirna said she wouldn't because it was creepy. I mean, she said it was because she was going out to dinner, but she totally chickened out. Anyway, I bet Lennie was into all this stuff, and the cult is the Maskers, or the Maskers are part of the cult, or something. What do you think?"

She finally stopped, eyes huge in her triangular face as she waited for his response.

Aspen nodded. "I agree. Leonard had definitely gotten into something much larger than he had any business dealing with." He rubbed his jaw. "If something big is happening tonight, I think I know where to go to start gathering information. Though," he eyed her consideringly, "do you have any idea where your three friends might be now?"

Rouge made a face. "Ew. No friends of mine. Buuuuuuut," she lingered on the word, savoring it. "Since I had to pick up Wally at the Dead Tent anyway, I popped out into my study room." She waved a hand as he opened his mouth to question her. "Explain later. Anyway, 4DKitten (which is totally derivative) is a streamer. She has, like, twelve subscribers, but whatever. Basically, that means she uses magic to, um, show what she's doing to any random person with too much time on their hands.

"So, I pulled up the stream, and watched a bit. You can't stream some quests that are involved in an active storyline, and apparently this cult thing counts, but I could see where she and Mirna and PentaKitten (which is only slightly better than 4D) are. They spent the morning doing some *seriously* boring item shopping, and now they're eating at some super fancy restaurant called Le Danse Macabre, which is apparently the place to be seen right now. So, here's the deal."

Holding up one slim brown finger to stop the flow of questions he had regarding the semi-gibberish she was spouting, the little elf girl grinned, white teeth flashing brilliantly. "I seriously have to go, even though poor Wally is pouting because I brought him here and then told him I couldn't stay. He's in the garden, by the way, so there probably won't be a lot of veggies left. Sorry, not sorry, since I know you can grow them back. Anyway, Lyrec and I are going to watch her stream and see where she goes. I'll be back as soon as I can, or when she has to stop streaming, and then we'll go wherever we last saw her. Sound good?"

Aspen barely had time for another bemused nod before she was popping up her thumb, and then her eyes went blank and staring. Manuela, who had come in at some point during the rapid-fire monologue, snorted. "I've seen them all do that now, but it still looks like one of your meat puppets after I pulled its soul. I think it actually makes it worse that I know they'll be back. It goes against everything I've ever known."

He sighed, taking off his hat, slapping it against his leg a few times, and then settling it back on his head, mind racing all the while. "I know. I put something over their heads when they do this."

A few moments later, a small throw blanket was over Rouge's head, and both adults felt simultaneously mildly relieved and embarrassed by their relief.

"Now what?" Manuela asked.

Aspen shrugged. "I guess I wait."

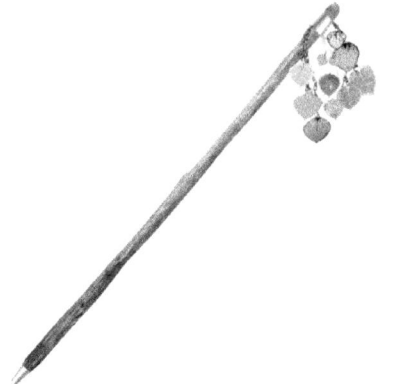

Chapter Seventeen

Rouge

O nce again, Zoey found herself hustling home. For one thing, spending any extra time in a place where Ms. McMaybeMcKiller could find her was now more than a little creepy. Mostly, though, Aspen had a definite track record of running off to do his own thing without her. (Which he *totally* shouldn't be able to do! It was *her* quest! Darn semi-sapient NPC!)

This time, however, she had a decent amount of money burning a digital hole in her bank app. She'd been putting half of every paycheck into her 'Advanced-Education Fund', which was one of her dad's conditions before he let her take a full-time summer job, but the other half had been accumulating. She only made minimum wage, but it was still way more money than she'd ever had before, and for once, she was going to use it!

Pulling up her ride-share app, she saw that a car was heading from the Veritas building to a grocery store just a few blocks from her house. Probably someone who lived in the same area grabbing something for dinner tonight. Bonus, because that sounded like a brilliant idea. She was pretty sure the only thing they had in the house was leftovers of her dad's eggplant parmigiana, and while it was awesome the first night, it just didn't reheat well.

Quickly, Zoey geotagged herself as an additional rider, and while she waited for the car to show up, she sent a message to her dad.

@RedZ: Hey dad, I'm catching a ride home in a 'lime-green Tesla with sunflower décor'. I'll snap a pic of the driver when it gets here. My geotracker is on, and I'm going to grab dinner on the way. See you soon!

There was no immediate reply, which made sense, since her dad was having office hours now. She glanced around, and saw the distinctive car heading her direction. She waved, and the car pulled up beside her. She discreetly snapped a photo of the inside of the vehicle as she slid into the seat beside the only other occupant, sending it off to her dad with a subtle swipe of her thumb.

That done, she looked up, smiling brightly at the driver, who was a fairly nondescript guy of Asian descent with some kind of bird shaved onto the sides of his head. He nodded at her, checking his app.

"Zoey Williams?" As if she could be anyone else, since the app sent her photo to him when she reserved the car.

"Yep!" She shot him a thumbs up, then quickly approved the transaction he sent her to cover the fare. It would hold the funds until they both agreed that the service had been performed as requested, and if there was any dispute, it would continue to hold the money until they worked it out.

"Rockin'," he said, then turned back to the console, resting his hands on the biometric sensors built into the steering wheel so the car would start moving. The car was fully automatic, but legally the driver had to be holding the wheel and watching the road whenever the car was in motion. Once the man's grip and gaze were registered by the car's Assistive Intelligence, they smoothly slid into traffic.

Zoey turned her gaze to the other passenger, who was sitting in the back seat beside her, assessing whether he was going to be a chatty companion or a silent one. When she first looked at him, he was gazing at her with something almost like astonishment and recognition, but he quickly lowered his lids, sliding his eyes away with a speed that was almost rude.

"Hi!" she said brightly. "Thanks for sharing your ride!"

He grunted, and she sighed internally. It was going to be one of those rides. She didn't mind not talking to people on the bus, since just people-watching was usually plenty of entertainment. In the closed environs of a car, however, silence quickly grew awkward, if not oppressive, and from the way the driver was bobbing his head, he seemed to be in his own world, listening to music, so he wasn't going to be much help.

This ride was awkward until it became oppressive. It was nearly a forty-minute ride home in rush-hour traffic, and Zoey spent most of the time on her screen, watching 4DKitten as she described the 'unctuous' flavor of her duck ravioli, and raved about the 'truffle foam'. Oh. Em. Gee. After the third time she caught her co-passenger surreptitiously trying to see what she was watching, she pulled out her knock-off ValPAC glasses and set her screen to shift frequency to match. The next time rude-dude tried to see her screen, she had to suppress a grin at his look of frustration.

By the time they reached their destination, however, Nina's conspiracy-theory-driven paranoia was fueling a full-blown delusion that somehow this guy was stalking her, even though she was the one who had picked this car to go home in. For a man who was clearly completely uninterested in conversation, he was definitely spending far too much time shooting glances at her, which led to her shooting surreptitious glances back at him.

The guy was tall and slim, almost bony, but with a slight belly that spoke of a disinterest in food rather than a penchant for physical fitness. His eyes were dark, with an epicanthic fold, but his skin was pale as nonfat milk, and his tightly-curled hair was a blonde almost as light as Jace's. His nose was broad, with a short bridge, and his lips were soft and wide.

He *could* just think she was cute, but first, *ew*, and second, he didn't give off that kind of vibe. He was probably in his mid-twenties, which meant he should just see her as a kid. He also wasn't giving her any little smiles, trying to edge in her direction, or attempting to re-open communication, which was what all the romantic leads in her books would try to do.

When the car stopped at the grocery store, Zoey had long-since decided that she wasn't walking home until this creep was gone, and there was no way he could follow her. Thankfully, however, the moment he finished unfolding his gaunt, stoop-shouldered frame from the small car, he strode away deeper into the parking lot, rather than heading into the store. This was a mega-retailer, so it was entirely possible that he just used the huge lot as someplace to leave his own vehicle. In any case, he was gone.

Sighing in relief, she turned back to offer the driver a smile and a thank you, only to find him watching the retreating figure with as much distaste as she felt. She quickly pulled up the ride-share app and dropped a 20% tip on the transaction, smiling when his screen chimed. The driver checked it, then gave her a grin.

"Hey, thanks, Zoey. Anytime you need a ride, you let me know. Handle's Jackie Chan."

She laughed. "Sounds good. I don't know, though. That guy was kind of disturbing. Is he a regular?" She flashed a 'I'm just a kid and need protecting' smile at him, and he sighed.

"Yeah, he's out there every weekday. Catches a ride on the regular. Not always me, but my buddy Arnie gets him a lot, too. Never talks, never tips, always something about him that just makes your skin crawl, but if I reject his rides without a reason, the app dings my ratings."

Zoey tried to look disappointed. "Yeah, I think I'd rather take the bus." Then she brightened. "Does he always go to this store?"

Jackie shrugged. "Usually, but sometimes he goes to those block houses on 17th and Pine. I saw an old lady meet him once, so I think he lives with his mom or something."

She smiled. "Great! I'll just skip any days I see you heading here or there, then." She tugged at a curl. "Do you think he works at Veritas? I'm just an intern, but I don't remember seeing him there."

The young man's screen pinged, and he shrugged, looking down at it as he accepted a new fare. "Yeah, he just started a few weeks ago. Maybe a month. At least, that's when he started catching rides." He put his hands on the wheel, shooting her a final absent smile. "Nice to meet you, Zoey. Look me or Arnie Schwartz up next time you need a lift. Have a great day!"

She backed up as the car started rolling, looking around to make sure spider-boy wasn't anywhere close by. Seeing no familiar faces, she headed into the store for a take-n-bake pizza.

🐞 🐞 🐞

When she got home a half hour later, she was greeted at the door by a frantically excited Max, who looked as happy to see her pizza as he was to see her. Laughing, she put the pizza down on the counter and turned on the oven, then flopped Max's ears and played 'good boy' with him until the oven dinged. Quickly, she stuffed the pizza (vegetarian, of course, because Dad) into the oven, set a timer on her screen, and headed for the back yard. Max raced ahead of her, dashing out the dog door as soon as the door recognized his microchip and opened.

They spent twenty happy minutes playing together in the back, interrupted only twice. First, her dad sent a message indicating that he'd be home late thanks to long pre-finals office hours, so good job heading home alone. Next, the house system let her know her pizza was done, and she had to dash inside to take it out and put it on the counter to cool.

Max was just starting to calm down from the excitement of one of his Humans arriving home when her screen chimed with a message from Jace.

@JaceCo: They're on the move. Given the time lapse between game-time and real-time, even with the smart programming editing out the 'boring' parts, they probably finished dinner fifteen or twenty minutes ago. They're somewhere near the docks now. Mirna just logged off at an inn down there.

@RedZ: Sounds like this is it! I'm going to cram some pizza and then get in my pod. I'll watch her stream until it cuts and then log in. You coming?

@JaceCo: Any more people going to explode? Totally NOT because of my playing?

@RedZ: Implode. I can't make any promises.

@JaceCo: Think I'll sit this one out. That last session made me rethink some of my life choices. I'll log in and do some leveling. Your quests are just going to get me killed. Again.

@RedZ: Fair enough. I'll help as soon as I get some free time!

@JaceCo: Ha! I'll believe it when I see it.

@RedZ: LOL Fair.

Zoey stuffed a slice of pizza down even as she climbed into her bodysuit. She was glad her dad wasn't there to see her, since he'd be badgering her about grease on the suit, as well as not taking food upstairs. Poor Max laid down sadly as soon as he saw her pull out the suit, and she gave him half of her second slice as a peace offering.

"I'm sorry, bud," she murmured, patting the dog's silky ears as he wolfed down the treat. "This'll be over soon, I swear." Thinking about the note Nina had shown her, she swallowed hard, then forced a smile. "Just not on September 12, right?"

The chocolate lab looked up and whined pathetically, eyebrows twitching as he glanced between her and the slice of pizza sitting on her bedside table. She sighed, and tore the crust off, tossing it to him. "You only love me for my food, anyway."

Max woofed reproachfully, then went and laid down on the floor at the foot of the pod, clearly indicating that he would be patiently waiting for her when she emerged again. She crouched down and gave him a hug, then stood and climbed into the pod. Lying down, she pulled the headset on, futilely attempting to get it to sit as comfortably on her head as the one at work did. When it was as good as it was going to get, she laid back and said, "Show *Veritas* livestream, 4DKitten."

Between one blink and the next, her vision filled with a view of *Veritas Online*, only this time from someone else's perspective. She was looking at a gamer with the tag *PentaKitten – Level 32 (Friend)* floating over her head. Clearly 4DKitten wasn't interested in the life-simulation aspect of *VO*, and kept things like gamer tags on.

NPCs walking by had generic tags over their heads as well. *Dockworker* was repeated several times, along with a few *Sailor*s and even a *Captain*. As soon as a player actually interacted with the NPCs, the tag would shift to their name and possibly their level, if it was lower than the player's, but before that it was pretty basic. It wasn't always accurate, either. For example, Zoey's buddy Gunthrax was tagged as a *Mercenary*, and you wouldn't know he was a *Thief* unless you caught him in the act.

All of it was just too busy and too distracting for Zoey, so she always left the tags off. Besides, the game was made to be as immersive as possible, and even warned you against things like turning the tags onto 'Always Visible' because it was against the spirit of the game.

4DKitten was obviously a rebel.

In any case, the girl was rambling about something, so Zoey tuned in.

"…have a *super* cool quest tonight! Those of you who are in the [gibberish] religion probably know, but this is so big, *I* think it's tied to a new World Event! Yeah, that's right, you heard it here first! I'll put some more deets in the chat, but this whole thing is supposed to be super-secret! I'm going to cut out here as soon as we pull on our cloaks, because it won't let me live-stream this quest, but trust me, as soon as it's done, I'm going to be the first one to post the videos. I've been editing them since I realized what a big deal this is, so you should follow me if you're not already so you're in on it as soon as the vids drop!"

As she spoke, the girl was glancing between a large warehouse beside the dock and her friend, PentaKitten, who would wave and smile alluringly (Zoey assumed that was what that was supposed to be) every time she realized she was in the shot. Probably had her notifications set to let her know any time she was being recorded or streamed so she could try to do something interesting and get followers herself.

4DKitten held up something that looked like a basic black cloak. Zoey suspected that the same system that traded generic chars for the avatars of players who *didn't* want their every move plastered all over a million wanna-be's random streams was working here too. She was willing to bet one of Millie's cinnamon rolls that what the other girl was actually holding was a hood similar to the one that had belonged to the deceased Leonard.

"Okay, I'm going in now. We're a little early, but I don't want to miss anything. Don't forget, you saw it here first! Follow me for more!" Then the stream switched to a cheesy logo of a tabby kitten playing with a 4 and a D. Okay, fine, the logo was kind of cute, but Zoey wasn't ready to admit that.

"Allie," which was the name Zoey had given her interface instead of Emily, "send Jace a message. Message starts. Oh my gosh that was so lame! I'm logging on, though, and I'll head for the docks. There was a ship named *Lady of the Water* nearby, so I'm going to start looking for that. Later! End message."

Taking a deep breath, she braced herself for the drop. "Allie, start *Veritas Online*."

❦ ❦ ❦

Rouge blinked, wondering why it was so dark. Even if Aspen had left her in a dark room, her [Darkvision] should allow her to… Oh, wait. Huffing in amused irritation, she pulled the square of silky fabric off her head, then tucked it into her inventory just to show Aspen what happened when he covered her up. Plus, it was purple and pretty.

As soon as she oriented herself, finding that she was still standing in Aspen's Sanctum Sanctorum, she threw open the door, slammed it shut behind her, and raced for the kitchen. Even though her stats hadn't changed since she'd logged in at work, the tiny lag in response time between this pod and the one at work meant she still felt the slightest bit 'off' every time she went to jump and push off a wall as she rounded a corner, or leapt up to swing from a handy chandelier.

The experimental pod really made her feel like *this* was just as much her real body as the one she was in as she played with Max and hugged her dad before bed. As amazing as her home pod had always seemed before, she still couldn't help feeling a small twinge of regret that she wasn't in the other one. By the time she reached the kitchen, though, dropping into [Stealth] just for the fun of it as she snuck through the door, she'd once again gotten used to the slight hesitation, the feeling of being wrapped in something that kept her from moving as freely as she should be able to.

When she entered, slipping through the partially-open door so smoothly that it barely moved at all, she saw that Aspen had once again gathered the whole crew, except for Vonn, who was conspicuously absent. Even Mai Ley was there, and Rouge came to a full stop when she saw the avatar that the AI had created. Who was in there? Emily? Amy? Something else entirely?

Then Aspen picked a carrot up from his plate, flicking it toward where she was standing, and she saw a notification a moment later.

You have taken 1 point of damage from *Carrot*. Your [Stealth] has been broken!

Rouge rubbed the spot between her eyes where the carrot had struck, glaring at Aspen, who was unsuccessfully trying to hide one of his half-smiles. Then a small puff of wings and fur struck her, and she jumped in surprise before instinctively reaching up to cup Silus in her hands.

::Rouge! Aspen called *everybody* here, and he says we're going on a quest! A real, grown-up quest, with plans, and sneaking, and everything! And you and I get to go together!:: The little bat's squeaky voice was practically inaudible with excitement, and Rouge laughed as she stroked the so-pettable silver tufts in front of her ears.

::He *does*, huh? Sounds like Aspen has things all figured out.:: Rouge tried to arch an eyebrow at Aspen, but felt both go up instead, so she was sure she looked more surprised than skeptical.

Aspen tugged at his hat, his grin just getting bigger as everyone around them let out various versions of greetings and their own versions of what Silus had just said. Struthio, standing by the stove holding a platter onto which his wife was piling steaming roasted vegetables, was the only one who didn't say anything, though his broad smile let her know he was glad to see her, too. Millie immediately clucked and sent the tall man toward the servant's stairs, presumably to deliver the platter to the children. As soon as he was on his way, she began putting together a fresh plate of what looked like roast beef and mashed potatoes.

Mouth watering, Zoey had to swallow hard before she could force herself to speak. "No time for food, though that smells *amazing*, Millie! 4DKitten just vanished, but she was at the docks putting on some kind of cloak when she did, so we're a go for the mission." She looked around at the small crowd. "Uh, I think this many people would probably be a little conspicuous though."

Aspen nodded, pushing himself to his feet. "Restur is here because he had… something else to talk to me about. He, Plum, Tomas," he paused to look meaningfully at the old man, who pinched his lips together stubbornly but nodded, "Manuela, Tia, Struthio, and Millie will either be staying here or going about their own business." The rest of those named nodded with varying ranges of enthusiasm, and continued eating, though they were all visibly curious about the goings on.

The farmer pointed at Tessle, who was caught mid-bite and flushed as she waved weakly. "Tessle will be going with me to join Vonn, who is watching the location which we suspect is a point of contact for the Maskers. We're going to check it out while you, Silus, Flu-flu, and Mai Ley investigate this Induction. You three," he indicated Rouge and Silus, then nodded to Flu-flu, who attempted a small bow while still stuffing her face, "have some form of [Stealth], and Mai Ley's knowledge of religion and Gods may well prove invaluable."

The priestess, one of the few who weren't eating as if they had a ten-mile-long tapeworm, nodded to Rouge, though her red and white painted face remained expressionless.

"Also," Aspen motioned to the plate of food that Millie, her face wreathed in smiles, pressed into Rouge's hands, "you should eat. Never turn down a buff before a mission."

"Oh!" Rouge flushed. She'd momentarily forgotten that food in the game was more than just delicious. It could also confer benefits far beyond nutrition. Manuela and Tia shuffled their chairs to the side, making room for Rouge to put her plate down. She was just looking for an extra chair when a knot in the floorboard below her sprouted up into a short, thick branch, grew one leaf, and then broke off with a crack of splitting wood.

Manuela rolled her eyes, tilting her head toward Aspen. "He's been showing off all night," the older woman said after swallowing quickly. "You'd think there wasn't a houseful of extra furniture around us." She shot a mocking glance at her old friend, who reddened slightly.

Aspen rubbed the back of his neck. "It just seemed easier than going looking for a chair," he mumbled.

Plum was quick to speak up in his defense. "To be honest, Lord Aspen, much of the best furniture was sold or taken away by the people who attempted to buy the manor. What's left is mostly upstairs for the children to use, and," she grimaced apologetically, "it's not in the best of condition any longer."

Sending a vindicated look at Manuela, Aspen nodded in acknowledgement of this information. Then he turned back to Rouge. "Eat, then we'll be on our way."

The food was as delicious as it looked, especially once Millie produced a thick

294

brown gravy from a pot that had been simmering on the stove. Rouge wasn't usually much of a fan of gravy, but this was like a tiny blanket of savory richness that perfectly complemented the pillowy-soft butter-filled potatoes. Once Rouge realized she was starting to sound like 4DKitten raving about duck confit, she just set to eating, and a few minutes later was gazing at her buffs in satisfaction.

You have eaten an Excellent Meal! Due to both the skill of the chef and the quality of the ingredients, you have obtained the following buffs:

Boosted Recovery: **You will regain hp and mana at 1.5x the usual rate for the next four hours.**

Enlarge: **For the next five hours, you will count as a Creature of the next size up for all offensive maneuvers.**

Basic Haste: **Your movement speed will be 1.2x the usual for the next five hours.**

Just as she was pushing her stump back from the table, the back door flew open, and Lyrec stepped in from the darkness outside.

Rouge sent the Mambele she had almost instinctively summoned back into her inventory, glaring at her friend, then the door. "Doesn't anyone ever knock anymore?"

Lyrec just waggled a hand at her as he bent over, hands on his knees, puffing as he tried to catch his breath. He seriously needed to level up and put some points into his physical stats, because he was a mess. "I... just... ran... here from... the Guild," he gasped out. "I got a... new buff... and I wanted to... use it before you left." He looked up, smiling weakly as he waved to the crowd. "Hello, way more people than I expected."

His eyes sharpened as he zeroed in on the food with a teenage boy's single-minded focus on anything that could provide him with calories. "What's that *smell*? Can I have some?" Millie just laughed, face pink at the implied praise, a dimple appearing in her right cheek, and began preparing another plate.

Once food was clearly on the way, Lyrec turned back to Rouge and Aspen. "I just learned a song that gives you a Courage buff. It gives you an increase to saves against Fear, Shock and Awe, and Paralysis. Let me just play-"

The sound of multiple chairs pushing away from the table broke into his speech as everyone who had heard or heard *of* his playing attempted to get up and leave at once. Lyrec looked around, baffled, as Rouge and Aspen waved them back down.

"You mean a song on your *murchunga*, right, Lyrec?" Rouge asked pointedly, gesturing for him to come inside and close the door.

"Oh, yeah, of course," Lyrec said absently as he tugged the door closed, and thus fortunately missed the expressions of relief on the faces of nearly everyone else present. The young bard's instrument appeared in his hand, and he put it to his lips. He made a few test twangs, and then he was off into a simple but enthusiastic tune with a beat you could march (or dance) to. The *bongs* and *twonks* of the uncomplicated music made you smile even as your foot began to tap.

You have heard an Encouraging Tune! You have now obtained the following buff:

*Courage***: You gain a 5% increase in resistance to all Fear, Shock and Awe, and Paralysis debuffs for two hours.**

Rouge grinned. Sure, 5% wasn't much. But it was better than nothing, and most importantly, it showed that her friend was finally on the right track with his character. Lyrec had actually been created a few months before Rouge, but had languished due to Jace's insistence on choosing Bard as his class.

Rouge the Rogue: That's awesome! What level is it?

Lyrec: It's level 2. Level 1 was only a 2% buff, but I buffed random players all the way over here. I have three new friend requests! LOL

Rouge the Rogue: You going to accept?

Lyrec: Dunno. With all the weird stuff going on, I'm not sure I want to take the chance of ending up on the wrong side.

Rouge the Rogue: We could totally use a spy on the inside!

Lyrec: No way! You know how I feel about being on the front lines. I like being a bard because I can help people without anyone trying to kill me. Everybody takes out the healers first, but no one pays attention to bards.

Rouge the Rogue: I know, I know. Plus, you can't join Chris' cult because you love Muse too much.

Lyrec: You know it! Best God ever!

As soon as the song was done, everyone applauded, smiling. This was a new experience for Lyrec, whose pale skin flushed beet red, though he gamely took a bow, sweeping his broad-brimmed feathered hat (which he refused to give up, though he had dyed it to a deep azure, instead of its original violent red) in what he undoubtedly thought was a gallant fashion.

Keeping an admirably straight face, Millie handed Lyrec a plate heaped high with steaming meat, potatoes, and vegetables. Rouge stood and motioned for her friend to take her stump.

Aspen clapped the young bard on the back, causing his blush to return full force. "That was truly wonderful, Lyrec. I look forward to hearing your future songs."

Topaz eyes glinting with humor met Rouge's own, and she could see that he had had the same thought she had. *Especially since you can't sing while you play.*

"Now," Aspen's voice grew serious, and he reached out and grabbed his way-too-cool Stick with his way-too-cool tattooed hand (though the tattoos were now covered with a simple leather glove). The staff immediately grew short and thick, while its tinkling leaves swirled down into a solid metal cap with nothing more interesting than some faintly engraved swirls. Aspen stuck the thing, which now resembled a cudgel, into his belt. "Let us go!"

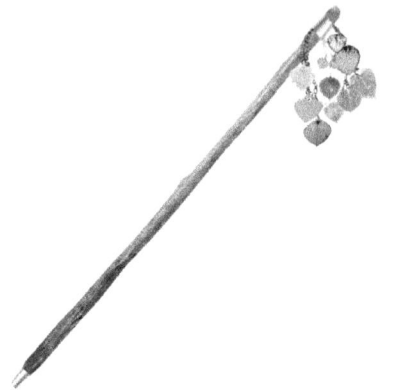

Chapter Eighteen

Aspen

After some brief farewells, Aspen and Tessle quickly traveled to the guardhouse near the Tannery. The Traveler, who seemed a bit nervous about being alone with Aspen for the first time since he'd killed her in her previous incarnation as a reluctant enemy, spoke very little. She was, however, clearly grateful when he passed her a mask shortly after they entered the aromatic zone near the factory, and she even offered him a tentative smile before donning the black fabric covering.

Vonn had been stationed at the empty building across the street from the guardhouse. Many buildings had been left vacant following Lich Lord Akuji's attacks, and though many of them had acquired new occupants, mostly non-human, this area still had many abandoned lots. In fact, once Aspen began looking, he noticed that they passed almost no one who was anything other than completely human. The two dwarves and one orc he did see were clearly employed as guards for a single human merchant, and all three kept wary hands on the weapons at their sides.

A few blocks before the corner where the guardhouse stood, Aspen dropped into a dark alley he had noted on his magical map, and followed its winding path as it narrowed to little more than two feet of extra space between one building and the next. Finally, he heard a crunch from behind him and turned around, scraping his shoulders on the walls as he did.

Tessle, who had been trailing him at enough of a distance that they hoped they didn't seem to be together, was jammed against the walls behind him. Her feet scrabbled at the ground as she tried to maneuver her bulky armor and her broad shoulders through the space, to no avail. Her expression, what he could see of it between her horned helm and the black mask, was embarrassed but determined.

Gently, he reached out and touched her shoulder, causing her to still and stare at him with wide blue eyes. "Can you remove your armor, as Rouge and Motte do?" He murmured softly, hoping no one in the buildings around them would suspect anything more interesting than a particularly large rat was invading their space.

Jerkily, the half-dwarf nodded, and a moment later she dropped a good two inches as her heavy boots and plate vanished, leaving her in a pretty periwinkle dress that complemented her flaxen hair and made her eyes seem almost violet. Aspen smiled as reassuringly as he could, hoping she could see approval in his eyes. He cupped his hands in front of him and crouched so that the woman, who, in her current form of a half-dwarf Shield Maiden, stood barely five feet tall, could set one slippered foot in his hands.

"I thought this might happen," Aspen whispered, "but we're only a few buildings away now. I'll lift you up on the roof, and then follow myself. I think there may be a hole in the roof of the old house we're heading for."

Nodding, Tessle allowed herself to be lifted, gingerly bracing her hands on his shoulders for support. He raised her up carefully, noting that in spite of the solid muscle of her short form, she wasn't too heavy for him to lift easily. "Ready?"

Her fingers tightened momentarily on his shoulders, but then she let go, standing in a crouch on the platform of his palms. He dropped his hands, then shoved up. He looked up, watching her feet travel through the air, and readied himself to catch her if she didn't manage to grab the lip of the roof that was only a foot or so over her head.

 He heard a grunt as the short woman came to rest on the wooden roof above him, but he must have gotten the amount of force he needed right, since she didn't seem to be scrabbling for a grip, nor had she landed with enough force to fall through into the building below. He reached out with his Life Sense, noting that the only occupant of the building they were climbing onto seemed uninterested in finding out what might be going on outside, since they hadn't moved toward the front door.

A dark shadow blocked his view of the stars as Tessle stuck her head out from the rooftop. He saw movement, and a heavy coil of rope dropped down beside him. Thankful again for Travelers and their seemingly infinite storage, Aspen tugged at the rope, which held firm against his weight. His original plan had been to 'walk' up the wall with his back on one side and feet on the other, but he was no Rouge, so he was glad he wouldn't have to put that plan to use.

Aspen quickly clambered up the rope, emerging at the top to find that Tessle had found a solid rafter to stand on, then re-donned her heavy armor. The rope was tied firmly around her middle, and she seemed an immovable anchor. He saluted her gratefully, and her eyes smiled back at him as the rope vanished again, along with her armor. Apparently, she, too, was wary of putting any unnecessary weight on the flimsy roofing material.

The old house that was their goal was, indeed, only thirty or forty feet away. It was distinguished not only by the fact that there was only empty space after it, but also by the gaping hole in the roof, with torn shingles and shattered beams bearing silent witness to the likely fate of the former residents. That hole had been clearly visible on his map, and he'd told Vonn that's how they'd likely enter, so the elf shouldn't stab them when they dropped through.

Pointing to their goal, Aspen gestured for Tessle to lead the way, which she did with surprising grace. She tested each step carefully, and he made certain to follow exactly where she led. Without any further excitement, they were able to lower themselves down through the dark hole, where his Life Sense told him the young elf awaited them.

Vonn's voice was quiet but eager as it came from the darkness. "There's only one of them left. The boy you sent with me this afternoon put the knife into an empty house on the map, as you instructed, and one of the guards came out to get it as soon as it grew dark. He went somewhere, but you told me not to follow, so I stayed here." His usually gentle voice was frustrated, and Aspen could see his life-light moving restlessly as he shifted from one foot to the other.

Aspen nodded. "That confirms that they're part of this, as we suspected. That's all we needed to know for now. Rouge and her team are investigating the Maskers, and with your racial debuff against dexterity while you're in the city, you would have been at too great a risk of being discovered. If anything happened, you would have vanished, and in all likelihood, we'd never even have found your body."

The elf growled softly, the sound animalistic in the darkness. "I *know*, but they might also have led me to my sister and my nephew!"

Aspen sighed, moving forward now that his eyes had adjusted as much as they could to the near-darkness in the room. "Trust Rouge. She'll find your family, if they're still alive. There was no way anyone not human could pass as a Masker, but we have our own mission tonight. It's even possible we'll learn more than our friends."

Vonn sighed as well, and the faint flickers of color limning his spirit shifted from red to a deep orange. "I know, I just… It has been hard, just *waiting* here."

Aspen grinned. "Then let's stop waiting."

🍂 🍂 🍂

The first step to their plan was to empty the guardhouse of guards. If Vonn was correct, and there was only one guard left inside, this should be fairly easy, with a little minor assistance. Aspen walked to the nearest window and carefully hung a brown cloth from the sill. It was barely visible, but anyone looking for it could tell it was there simply because of the way it fluttered in the soft evening breeze.

Plum's host of urchins, many of whom were long-familiar with life on the harsh streets of Bright, included a young man who went by the name of Jiminy. He was, like most of the others, slender to the point of being skinny, and his nondescript looks and indeterminate age led to him being dismissed as unimportant if one happened to notice him at all.

Jiminy, however, had a rather unusual skill. Apparently, his family, before they became just a few of the many casualties of the Battle of Bright, had been actors. They had not only taught the boy how to read, but also how to speak in many different tones and accents. The child had played many of the smaller roles in their productions, and one day he learned to throw his voice. His family had been in the process of figuring out how best to make use of this talent when they died. After that, Jiminy had quickly learned to use it to distract enemies and marks alike.

Now, at the age of eleven or twelve, Jiminy's voice often went from treble to tenor clef in a single sentence, but his skill was finely honed and extremely useful. Thus it was that nearly as soon as the cloth went out the window, a woman's shriek was heard from down the street, even as someone banged on the door of the guardhouse.

"Help! Help! Please, someone help my family! Our home is afire! Please, someone save my baby! I'll give you anything, but please! You must come!" The wailing voice was cracked and terrified, and a moment later, a heavy-jowled face emerged as the door cracked open. Seeing no one, the guard scowled.

"Whozat?" The man grunted, looking around suspiciously.

Now the woman's voice came from some shadows further down the street, where a dark figure seemed to move restlessly. "Oh, good sir guard! You must assist me! I could not wake my husband, and my babe lay down the hall, unreachable. Help me in saving my family, and all our worldly goods will be yours!"

Aspen thought Jiminy was laying it on a bit thick, as all actors seemed to do when given a chance, but the guard stepped out of the door, closing and locking it behind him. "Fine then, woman, but you'd best be havin' a fair amount of them worldly goods!" The guard laughed coarsely as he dropped into a slow jog, following the sounds of a woman he'd never find.

Following that rather attention-grabbing performance, the three hiding in the house held as still and silent as possible for what seemed forever. Finally, Tessle, no doubt using her magical Traveler's clock, whispered softly. "Five minutes. Long enough?"

Aspen reached out with his Life Sense, finding that no one within his most distant senses seemed to be awake and paying attention. He did realize, however, that there was a disconcerting lack of information coming from the guardhouse itself. He could discern the usual small lives in the front of the building, behind the door; rodents, insects, even one of Silus' small kin resting in the cramped attic. After that, however, it was as if he hit a wall of silence. Nothing alive seemed to exist within the building after that first room.

He murmured to his companions. "Seems to be. Something is blocking me from being able to tell if the building is empty, though. It's at the edge of my range, but I should be able to sense *something*."

The two shadows that were his friends nodded silently, and Vonn led the way through the building to the front door. There, they paused as Aspen made one more mental sweep of the area before nodding. The three of them moved out of the building.

Vonn was hidden by his version of [Stealth], which was, as Aspen had mentioned, hampered by the debuffs Wood Elves took in cities. A faint flicker surrounded him as he moved, though when he was still, his concealment was nearly perfect. Plus, unlike Rouge's skill, which focused primarily on hiding her movements, he was also utterly silent, and Aspen knew no scent would betray his presence either.

Aspen simply depended on the cover of darkness, as well as his long stride and high agility, to get him unnoticed across the street. Tessle, however, managed it by using her Traveler's gifts to change into a daring black gown that seemed more shadow than fabric. The long train flowed behind her like water, and the design of the dress was utterly unsuitable for their current activity except that it was dark and far quieter than her usual armor.

When she joined the two men, she shrugged one suddenly bare and surprisingly attractive shoulder. "Boss drop," she murmured nearly inaudibly. "Lots of buffs, but looks stupid."

Aspen, for his part, thought that the young Traveler looked lovely, though it certainly wasn't his place to say so, especially since he'd killed her once, in another lifetime. Relationships with Travelers were so confusing.

჻ ჻ ჻

Unlocking the door without a thief wasn't as difficult as Aspen had feared. He could, of course, have simply melted and reshaped it, as he had once done with the manacles holding Manuela prisoner, but they were trying to be subtle. He hadn't wanted to tell Rouge, since she clearly enjoyed lock-picking, but he was fairly certain that...

Click.

Aspen stood from his crouch, holding the large worm he'd pocketed from the garden after talking to Rouge that afternoon. He'd kept it in a pouch of moist earth, and had been feeding it mana for hours. The thing was closer to small snake-sized by now, but retained its slimy coating and ability to form itself to the shape of its container. In this case, a keyhole.

A worm's senses weren't particularly sharp, but even it could tell when something moved and when it didn't. Once he'd placed the little creature into the opening of the fortunately quite large keyhole, it had wriggled inside. It didn't care for the cold sharpness of the lock's metal surface, but Aspen had been sending it mental images of what he needed it to do as he 'fed' it. It had quickly wriggled in, then pushed against the parts of the lock that moved. Two simple pins later, the latch clicked open, and Aspen retrieved the worm, sending it warm thanks along with an extra-large chunk of mana as he slipped it back into his pouch.

Tessle's eyebrows shot up as he gently pushed the door open, motioning for Vonn, as the only party member who was in [Stealth] to enter the room first. As the elf slipped in, Tessle switched back into her armor, quietly asking, "How did you do that? I have some basic lock-picking and a magical lockpick." She held out a softly gleaming silver pick. "I was going to offer to do it."

Aspen laughed under his breath. "Those are single-use, are they not? This worked well enough. The door is open."

Vonn's soft whistle sounded the all-clear, and Aspen and Tessle slipped through the door, closing and locking it behind them. Fortunately, the inside lock was on a large metal handle, so getting out quickly if they needed to do so should be easy enough, but if a guard returned too soon, the loud sound of the lock should give them some warning. Well, that and Aspen's Life Sense, though he feared that when they entered the silent zone beyond the door he could see across the room – but not sense at all – he would then be cut off from this area.

The room looked like-enough to guardhouses that Aspen had seen in his previous life. A desk sat in the center, with messy stacks of scrolls on it, ready to receive citizen complaints. Beside the desk was a trash bin, full to overflowing with similar scrolls, though these were covered in sloppy letters and ink-spots. Two very uncomfortable-looking wooden chairs, with short legs and hard, narrow seats, sat to one side. Dust gleamed on them faintly. Clearly this guardhouse received few visitors who stayed long enough to sit.

A ring of keys hung in plain view on a hook by the far door, likely left there by the vanished guard in case his brethren returned before he did. Aspen glanced over at Vonn, who was already looking through the desk, though so far it seemed he'd found nothing beyond a tattered feather pen and a half-empty pot of ink.

"Did you check for traps?"

The elf glanced up, then sighed and shrugged. "I can find traps in the wild; snares, deadfalls, cages, things like that. These dart and gas traps you city-dwellers seem to prefer are different, and more difficult for me. I simply hoped that since this is in a semi-public area, and these guards seem lax, that they wouldn't want to have to disarm a trap every time they needed to write a note."

Aspen shook his head, but couldn't really argue. He'd known sending their rogue with the other group was a risk, and frankly it probably would have been better to bring one of Plum's budding young cutpurses, but Rouge had the best chance of infiltrating the cult, and he couldn't countenance placing a child at unnecessary risk. At least he, as their healer, was here, as was Tessle, with a Traveler's seemingly bottomless bag of tricks.

The three of them made short work of the small room, even turning the dusty chairs upside down and looking beneath them. Aspen quickly read through the notes in the trash, most of which were nothing more interesting than lunch orders, though a few seemed to be desultory notes regarding complaints made by locals. Near the bottom, he pulled out a particularly crumpled page and skimmed the contents.

"Hmm. Vonn, where exactly did your sister live?"

The elf was beside him in a flash, though his eyebrows drew down as he struggled to read the note in Aspen's hands. Finally, he growled a little. "You humans and your bizarre language. Why don't your letters look like the things they represent? What does it say?"

Aspen traced a finger down the parchment. "It looks like someone came to make a report after your family was… taken. Or perhaps it was another family with the same situation. It says the husband and father were found," he grimaced at the description, and edited it down to, "murdered, and that a woman and child were missing. The address given is at the intersection of Tannery and Scud, which is where Leonard and George lived, I believe. The report was given by a Mavis Little, who says she lives a block down Scud. She used to go to the market with the woman, who she calls Violet, but suddenly Violet stopped coming to the fountain. She made the report because no one seemed to be looking for the missing people."

Vonn snatched the page from Aspen's hand, gray eyes frantic as he tried again to read the foreign language. "My sister's name is Violeta! We must find this Mavis woman, and question her further!"

Aspen grimaced and tapped the bottom of the page. "Here, it says 'Measures taken. Case closed.' We'll certainly look for Mavis, but I suspect that we'll find she herself has either gone missing, or she won't speak to us. As a friend of your sister, and someone who cared enough to try to find her, I doubt you want to bring further trouble on her by trying to force her to talk, if she even can."

Vonn crumpled the page in his hand, then punched the desk so hard Aspen could see a hairline fracture form in one of his finger bones. Gently, he touched the back of the young man's hand, sending Gina a mental prayer to relieve the pain and repair the injury. Vonn sighed, hand relaxing beneath Aspen's, and lowered his head in relief.

The two men turned as they heard a soft, "Oh." They looked over at Tessle, who was staring at them, hands clasped in front of her, eyes huge and glimmering. "That was so sweet. I'm totally shipping you two now." The half-dwarf practically cooed, and Vonn jumped back, nearly snatching his hand from beneath Aspen's. Aspen just chuckled, reflecting once again on what a strange lot the Travelers were.

After a few more moments of fruitless search, the three turned their gazes to the ring of keys by the inner door. Aspen sighed. "I have no idea what's in there," he warned, not for the first time.

Vonn nodded determinedly, and Tessle just shrugged resignedly. "Probably something to keep mages from casting spells while they're in confinement. Makes sense, really, R3d-," she cut her former beau's name short, "um, I mean some people I used to know said that if you get arrested, you can't get out until you've done your time or paid your fine. No cheating and picking the lock or blasting your way out, you know?"

Aspen stepped closer and concentrated on the hook, the keys, and the wall. He could sense the surface of the wall, and even part of a mouse family living inside, but one mouse was little more than a sense of smell, a whisper of life, as most of the creature was apparently within the blocking force. Aspen was aware that he was becoming too reliant on his magic, especially since he knew that unnatural creatures such as the Swineherd, as well as thieves like Rouge who had a high enough [Stealth] skill, were essentially invisible to him. Nonetheless, it made him nervous to know that he was likely about to return to having only his own physical senses on which to depend.

Vonn, clearly impatient, hooked the keys down from the wall and began trying them in the door. Tessle reached past him and pushed. When the door swung open, she shrugged. "Who locks the door when they're the only person here?"

The elf snorted agreement, and dropped into [Stealth]. Less than a second later, he reappeared with one foot over the threshold. He laughed a little at their looks. "Worth a try."

Since there was no possibility of sneaking into the back area, the three simply walked through the door, closing and locking it behind them. If the guards came back before they were done, there was no chance of concealing their presence, so they might as well slow any pursuit.

Aspen looked around. They were in a small open space with two doors on each side, as well as three barred cells on the far side of the room. On the principle that whatever was in the cells would keep, but if there were enemies in any of the rooms, they needed to know, they began opening doors.

The first door on the left turned out to be a storage closet. There were a few pieces of dirty or damaged armor in a pile on the floor, and two very basic iron swords laid on a shelf. Beside them rested four of the dull and apparently worthless knives that the Maskers used to communicate the locations of non-humans.

Aspen picked each one up and looked at it. The first three were indistinguishable from each other, but the fourth had crusted black flakes caught between the grip and the blade. On closer examination, he was unsurprised to find that the flakes were dried blood, though they definitely seemed to be black, not just dark rust red. When he touched his tongue to one of the flakes, the taste of iron and salt were distinctive.

Tessle choked behind him, and he turned around, finding the Traveler woman watching him with a disgusted expression on her face. "How can you *taste* that?"

He gave her a crooked grin. "Blood and I are old friends, I'm afraid. As a healer and as a necromancer, I've never had the time to indulge in squeamishness."

She shook her head, looking faintly green. "Won't it make you sick?" She waved a hand helplessly. "Give you a Disease debuff or something?"

Aspen carefully laid the weapon back on the shelf. "No, though that's a possibility when dealing with certain beasts or infected people. Mostly, I should be able to cure that kind of thing." Not for the first time, he tried to use his mana, feeling like a man with a sore tooth, prodding the painful spot with his tongue. "Though I admit that would be difficult at the moment."

Vonn, who had been looking through the rest of the room while they talked, interrupted. "There's nothing else here. Some bread and cheese, empty waterskins, cleaning supplies that look brand new."

Tessle twitched a bit, then cleared her throat and asked, "So... Can I take this stuff? I mean, they're going to know someone was in here, right? So, there's no point trying to leave things the way they were."

Aspen rubbed his chin. "I guess so. The weapons and armor won't be worth much, though."

Even as he spoke, the items vanished into the Traveler's inventory. "That's okay," the half-dwarf said cheerfully. "Every little bit counts!"

The other three rooms yielded similar results. One was a break room, with several decks of cards and dice on a rough wooden table. Two were clearly offices, but though they went over every piece of paper they found, as well as two books that looked like records of expenditures – one of which was hidden beneath the larger desk, and which Aspen suspected was probably the *real* version – they found nothing obviously helpful. Tessle stored everything away so that they could go over it more thoroughly later.

All of this took only twenty minutes or so, and they found themselves back out in the central room, looking at the barred doors. Two of the cell doors were ajar, but a silent lump lay in the back corner of the center cell. It hadn't moved since they entered, despite the noise they had made. After a brief exchange of looks, Vonn headed for the door. There were seven keys on the ring, and the fifth one opened the door. The lump still didn't stir.

Tessle, as the party member best able to take damage, entered the small space. Her short, wide body took up most of the area, and it took only two steps to reach the bundle. Cautiously, she nudged it with her heavy sabaton.

"Hey," she said softly, clearly trying not to frighten whoever or whatever might be held prisoner in this place. However, there was no response, and she nudged harder. Something rasped like dry leaves within the bundle, and part of it flopped over. It was a sleeve, and the arm within was little more than a shell of dried skin and bones.

In a flash, Aspen was through the cell door, on his knees beside the desiccated corpse, which seemed to be of a woman, judging only by the long brown hair on the dry scalp stretched taut over the skull. A worn copper band slid from one dry finger, rolling across the floor to come to rest against Vonn's boot.

With a cry, the young elf leaned down to scoop it up in trembling fingers. It was a frail thing, tarnished a brownish green, and probably left a similar color on the finger of the person who wore it. Obviously, in spite of its lack of monetary value, the woman before them had treasured it.

Now, Vonn clutched at it, tears beginning to run down his cheeks as he rubbed the patina from the inside surface, leaving a green smear on his thumb. "*Vilotte*," he murmured in a choked voice. "Beloved, it means. Violeta's true name in our language. My mother couldn't afford much. We're not allowed to gain worldly goods while on *r'nspiga*, and must leave anything we do own behind when we return. Mother bought this for her child before she left, and told her to wear it always, and someday we would find her again." He looked up, gray eyes haunted. "This was my sister. What happened to her?"

Aspen raised his head, his topaz eyes ice-cold.

"Vampires."

Chapter Nineteen

Rouge

Rouge had never been the leader of a multiplayer mission before. It was both really exciting and really scary. Plus, What the heck was even going on with Mai Ley? Once Amy was cut off from Emily, Rouge had honestly never expected to see the 'player' again. After all, Mai Ley was actually Amy. Wasn't she? If she wasn't, did that mean Emily really was gaining her own personality as well? Was she just *another* copy of Amy that was going to split off from the whole? How many times could that happen? Was she even aware of what was going on?

These questions were burning their way through her mind even as she and the others discussed their plan on the way to the docks, which were on the eastern side of the city next to Lake Ata and the Dawn River. Mai Ley remained silent during the entire journey, other than to whistle for her own horse, which was a black mare named Shinu, and which Rouge was absolutely certain the avatar hadn't had before.

Codswallop, Shinu, and Flu-flu's horse, Sophia (which was an oddly non-dramatic name, because Rouge had totally expected Fluff's horse to be named

'Mighty Blaster, Bringer of Death' or something) made excellent time crossing the three or four miles to the docks. Silus remained safely tucked into Rouge's saddlebag, so she wouldn't be buffeted by the wind. Natives and other players alike were used to seeing groups of Travelers running or even jumping through the streets, so everyone just made way and paid them no particular notice.

When they arrived at the outskirts of the docks, the three climbed down from their mounts. Rouge and Flu-flu began chattering about places to eat and their favorite shops, though the chuuni girl couldn't resist throwing in a few lines about 'robes of fire and mist' and 'a meal fit for the great God Toko'. When they reached the northern end of the docks, Rouge finally saw what she'd been looking for. The *Lady of the Water* was moored at one of the largest docks near the luxury district, just as Rouge had hoped.

She nodded to her companions, tilting her head toward the ship, then wandered around until she found a spot where the view looked identical to what she could remember from 4DKitten's stream. She and Fluff continued chattering about nothing while Mai Ley lurked nearby, and Rouge watched the warehouse the two streamers had been so blatantly glancing at.

After a few minutes of this, Rouge saw that a few individuals as well as small groups of players were, indeed, heading toward the warehouse. However, rather than entering the building itself, they would step to the side and enter what at first glance looked like nothing more than a particularly deep shadow. During the morning, with the sun shining brightly over the docks as it rose over Lake Ata, that shadow would disappear entirely, and Rouge doubted if it became particularly dark until dusk began to fall. She wondered what she would see if she looked in that spot as the sun came up. She had a suspicion that the answer would be nothing at all, or, rather, a blank and innocent stucco wall.

Leaning close to Fluff as if admiring the heavy golden torque the other girl wore around her neck, she whispered, "I'm going to [Stealth] and go over there. I want to try something."

Fluff nodded, buffing her necklace and smiling proudly, even as she loudly announced, "This amulet was a gift from my great Patron Toko for my deeds in suppressing the invasion of the insidious spider mages…"

Rouge stepped back into the shadow for which she had selected their current viewpoint, and after a brief glance around to be certain no one was paying attention to her, entered [Stealth]. Thankful that she now had a high enough skill level that she could run while concealed, she raced to a spot close to the deep shadow through which so many people were vanishing.

It took a moment, but soon enough a trio of chattering girls, reminding Rouge of Mirna and her cronies with their expensive gear and even more expensive custom hair mods. *Veritas Online* had well over a hundred potential hairstyles for players, but Rouge had looked through every single one many times. It wasn't terribly expensive to import a basic change, like cutting a tattoo-like design into a shaved head, or adding some individual braids or ribbons to a ponytail, but all three of these girls had super elaborate hairstyles. Rouge thought she even recognized one as a copy of a hairdo worn by a Euro princess when she got married a few months ago!

All in all, these girls were the type who would be on the docks for only one reason. A quest. They undoubtedly spent most of their time in the luxury shopping area to the northwest and the Traveler zone where the uber-rich could even buy their own homes. As she watched, the three giggled slightly nervously and stepped into the shadow not five feet from where Rouge was hiding.

The two girls in front immediately pulled up their hoods and stepped forward into the wall, vanishing instantly. The third girl, the one with the royal 'do, hesitated, looking around and biting her lip. She lifted a hand and touched the wall, which remained solid even where it was completely concealed by dark shadow. Finally, with a small resigned sigh, the girl raised her own hood. As soon the material settled around her face, she, too, disappeared.

Holy frijole, Rouge thought, *the hood itself is the key.*

Then she had to almost jump out of the way as a figure all in black suddenly emerged from the gloom practically on top of her. Someone else had been using the same shadow as a [Stealth] cover! The man's hood was already up, and he hurried through the strange portal as if he'd done it many times before. Definitely none of the hesitation shown by the girl before him. Rouge noticed in passing that his hood was trimmed in deep red, unlike those of the girls, which had been black.

Rouge waited as a few more Travelers went by, each of them seeming to be in more of a hurry than the one before. Each pulled up a hood as they went in, and the majority of the hoods were black-edged, though she saw one more red. The last one passed so close she almost bumped into Rouge, and the thief decided it was time to move.

Full dark was nearly upon them now, so she was able to cross to her companions without having to worry about sticking to the edges of buildings. Flu-flu was still trying to involve Mai Ley in conversation, but the priestess offered little more encouragement than an occasional 'Mmm' or 'I see'. The look of relief in the wood elf archer's black eyes when she saw Rouge reappear was almost comical.

Quickly, Rouge stepped in close. "There's some kind of magical portal over there. When someone wearing a hood gets close enough, they're teleported or something. They disappear, anyway, and they definitely aren't in [Stealth], because they'd be falling all over themselves by now. Plus, I'm pretty good at seeing through [Stealth] and other illusions."

She held out her hand, mentally calling the hoods Lyrec had found in George and Leonard's house out of her inventory. "I have two hoods. I could try to [Steal] one, but even if I succeeded, it would be noticed right away, when they couldn't put it on, so that's not really a good option. We're on bluestones here, so we can't attack somebody and take it. I think we're going to have to pick two of us to go in, and the third will stay to keep watch and let Aspen and the others know where we are if they finish their job first and come looking for us."

Flu-flu looked torn. "I... As much as I would like to accompany you, my dear friend, I must tell you that my time in this world will come to an end in only two turnings of the hourglass. I had thought this wouldst be sufficient, but if one must remain behind, it should, mayhap, be me, due to my sad limitations."

Translation: Fluff would hit her eight-hour login limit for the day in two hours. While the game wouldn't log her out after that, it would start stacking debuffs on her until she logged out on her own. The first few weren't bad, but within an hour she'd barely be able to move due to *Exhaustion* and *Encumbrance*. Two hours should be plenty for a quick information-gathering run, but she was right, if this turned into anything more and went over her time limit, she'd be dead weight, or Rouge would have to leave her Zombie behind in enemy territory.

Rouge looked at Mai Ley, feeling conflicted. So far, 'Emily's' avatar hadn't really done much after that first ritual that allowed Struthio to kill the Demonic Swineherd in North Goose. She mostly just hung out on the edges of the group, appearing and disappearing randomly.

"Uh, Mai Ley," Rouge asked tentatively, "are you going to be around longer than two hours? I know you have, um, a lot of stuff to do, so…"

Atae's priestess tilted her head, her silken waterfall of black hair falling swaying around her shoulders. The nearly white shade of her pale blue eyes seemed even eerier than usual in the darkness. "I will be here for as long as I am needed," the avatar said formally.

"Ohhh… kay?" Rouge hesitated. "Can you, uh, take off your makeup?" She gestured at her own face, indicating the areas where red and white makeup marked the other woman as a member of Atae's priesthood.

A moment later, Mai Ley's face was clean of the identifying colors. Without the makeup, her high-necked, long-sleeved, ankle-length black dress became nothing more than a particularly plain outfit. Rouge gulped a little as she realized that she could now clearly see Amy in Mai Ley. In fact, the AI's avatar looked exactly the way Bridget's best friend might if she lost twenty pounds, went full Goth, and had an Asian ancestor a few generations back.

"Wow." Rouge cleared her throat. "Yeah. Well, do you want to be the boss or the minion?" She lifted the red-trimmed mask slightly, using her body to make sure it wasn't visible to anyone but them. She would have *sworn* that the corners of Mai Ley's mouth twitched before the woman answered in her flat voice.

"The black one. I will leave the greater task to you."

Rouge huffed out a startled laugh, but nodded. She handed the all-black mask to Mai Ley, and tugged the other one over her own head, though she left it pooled around her neck and shoulders as the other players had. Looking at Flu-flu, she grimaced apologetically.

"I wish we had three of these things, but…"

The archer shook her head. "I believe this may be for the best. I have also been observing those unholy, fetid vermin entering yon dark passage, and I have seen not a single member of any of the great races the Gods hath placed upon this world except for humans. While you may, perchance, be able to conceal your own race, due to your heroic calling, I am unable to do the same. Though," she suddenly struck a pose, one arm raised in challenge as the other fisted on her hip. She widened her stance and turned her face up to the sky. "I will yet be here as long as I am able, ready to rid this pure world of any taint of malevolent and malicious forces! Simply call me, and I shall come, upon the instant!"

Rouge grabbed the arm, trying to pull it down without drawing any *more* attention to them. "Okay, okay!" she hissed, relief flooding her as Fluff seemed to realize that the timing of her dramatic announcement might not have been great and lowered her arm. "We'll try to be back in less than two hours then. If we're not here by the time you have to go, run home and let them know what we found out, okay?"

For once, Flu-flu simply nodded.

Rouge went over to Codswallop, who was tethered with the other steeds at a hitching post nearby. As if he already knew what was coming, he gave her a long look full of resigned sorrow. His liquid eyes blinked slowly, and she wouldn't have been surprised if her ostrich somehow produced crocodile tears.

Rouge cupped his beak in her hands and leaned forward to rest her cheek against his.

"Sorry, Wally," she murmured. "There's no way you can go in there. Nobody else brought their mounts. If the door would even open for you, we'd stick out like a sore thumb. I promise I'll be back as soon as I can." Pulling several apples and a water bucket from her inventory, she placed them on the ground in front of him.

::Hey, what about me?:: Silus' little voice sounded in her mind, and she grinned, stepping around to Codswallop's side. Leaning casually against Wally's soft side as he gobbled the apples, Rouge made sure her shoulder was next to the opening of her saddlebags. The little bat's adorable, fluffy face popped out of the top of the bag, quickly followed by her small, fuzzy body. The tiny creature pulled herself out with her wing-thumbs, then burrowed into the mask around Rouge's neck.

::It stinks in here.:: The bat's voice sounded disgusted.

Rouge wrinkled her nose, unable to smell much beyond generic 'water-side aroma'. *That's one benefit to this pod, I guess,* she thought, patting the minute lump on her shoulder. ::Sorry, Silus. Just hang in there until we get inside.::

::Ha, ha. She tells the bat to *hang* in there,:: Silus muttered, and the two friends giggled at Rouge's inadvertent joke.

When Rouge stepped back around Codswallop, Flu-flu had already taken several strides away, heading for a nearby pub with outdoor seating from which she could keep an eye on the area without seeming too out of place. Mai Ley had pulled the hood up around her face, though the flap at the bottom meant to conceal her lower face was still beneath her chin.

Rouge grinned tightly. "Let's do this."

Turning, she headed for where the shadow had been before it was engulfed by the darkness of night. She heard soft footsteps indicating that Mai Ley was close on her heels. Just before she entered what she believed was the portal's Area of Effect, she pulled up her own hood, then cast [Substitution], using the

Wolf's Tooth she had stolen from the last player she watched enter as an anchor for her illusion.

> **You have cast [Substitution: Lv1]. You now appear to anyone viewing you as the sapient being <u>DayDreamBeli3ver</u>. This illusion will last 27 minutes (15 base + 12 minutes for Lv12 Common item *Wolf's Tooth*.) If your theft is discovered while you have more than 15 minutes remaining on your illusion, time will be reduced to a maximum of 15 minutes. Spell will be canceled if you take damage or if someone with a high enough [Illusion Break] skill attempts to Identify you.**

They stepped through the portal that was now visible as a shimmering space on the wall. As the view of the docks blinked away, Rouge grinned. *This* was fun!

The transition felt very familiar to Rouge, and she suspected that the developers had used the same code for this 'magic portal' as they had for the Stone Circles at the Traveler's Guild. Since the fastest way to get around Bright (or anywhere else) was to use the Circles (especially since they only cost five gold to travel within the same city or town) most Travelers used them to get around Bright, saving themselves hours of wasted time. Unfortunately, NPCs couldn't use them (and using them to go to another town was stupidly expensive, especially after you completed the tutorial) so Rouge hadn't done it since meeting Aspen.

Nonetheless, she easily fell into old habits, stepping forward and walking out of the portal area as soon as she reappeared, since anyone who came after her would bump into her or even appear on top of her. While that had some hilarious results, as she well-remembered from when she was a newbie, she didn't want to attract attention now.

She continued moving forward, refusing to even glance behind her to make sure Mai Ley had also made the transition, doing her best to look like she'd been in this place a hundred times before. That was difficult, since she was clearly in a temple, but it was one like none she'd ever seen before. All buildings devoted to a god were unique to that god. That held true for everything from the smallest roadside shrine to the grandest temple in Bright. Whether the signs and symbols were subtle or grand, wooden or alabaster and gold, they were everywhere in every place of worship.

In that, this place was no different. However, even in temples to Keykar, who was a god of war, or Erasa, goddess of murderers and assassins, Rouge had never seen friezes and murals depicting such slaughter. Monsters raged in battlefields covered in dismembered bodies. Towns and townspeople were ravaged by twisted, enormous creatures with extra limbs and talons as long as she was tall. In the midst of the, yes, *demonic*, creatures were men and women, fighting beside them to kill anyone who stood in their way. These people were tall, beautiful, glowing with power and covered in glittering armor.

Rouge's furtive glances, as she walked through the few stragglers who were still entering through other portals similar to the one she had used, found not a single surface that was free of some depiction of horrible death. She swallowed hard, slowing even as the others around her were picking up their pace.

One masked man, his hood trimmed in virulent green, shoved hard at her shoulder, and sneered as he went by. "Hurry up! If you miss the vow, you'll never make it to green!" He flicked green fabric at her as if she should be overcome by this symbol of his own achievements, and then dashed off down the wide hallway.

Mai Ley came up beside Rouge, setting her pace to match the shorter girl's, and lowered her head, murmuring softly. "Fear not. You and I are protected by the ones to whom we have already given our oaths. There is nothing these can make us say that will sever us from that connection. We are already beyond them." She paused, then spoke consideringly, "It is, however, likely for the best that our third companion did not enter here. For all that she speaks so often of her Master, her link is weak, and would break with the simplest of repudiations."

As she finished speaking, they reached the end of the hall, emerging into a vast chamber. The ceiling above, if there was one, was so distant that she couldn't see it, even with her [Darkvision]. The floor was something like obsidian, but not a single scuff marked its reflective black surface in spite of the hundreds, or perhaps thousands, of pairs of feet that crossed it. The walls, what she could see of them, were covered with the same horrible scenes that had been depicted in the hallway.

Worst of all, however, were the statues. Monsters easily twenty feet tall raised their (sometimes many) arms to the sky. Claws and teeth far outnumbering anything found in nature (except snails, which Rouge had been amazed to learn had *thousands* of tiny teeth) dripped stony gore and humanoid body-parts.

Rouge drew in a sharp breath, the completely absurd memory of her biology teacher wearing a snail hat and a t-shirt depicting a cartoon racing snail snapping her out of her daze.

Courage has helped you throw off the effects of *Shock and Awe*. You gain +10% Resistance to *Shock and Awe*.

Holy moly, Jace. I'll definitely have to thank you later. Rouge swallowed hard as she looked around again, this time without the debuff clouding her vision. It was gaudy. There was so *much* that it just crossed the line between terrifying and vulgar, much like the décor in Aspen's house couldn't decide if it was opulent or just tacky.

The monsters, now that they weren't overwhelming her, were clearly just twisted versions of regular monsters. Much like the *Hamster Hellion* they'd defeated on the way to Bloodhaven, they were bigger, toothier, more claw-some versions of simple things. She saw what looked like monstrous variants of a bunny, a fox, a squirrel, and even a giraffe, which she hadn't thought they had in *VO*. She gritted her teeth as she recognized a few critters she'd seen in sketches on the large screens during meetings of Harris' team. Oh yeah, she definitely owed that guy some surprise jalapenos in his lunch.

As she moved closer to the crowd gathered ahead of her, she saw that everyone here had black-trimmed hoods. Looking around, she saw that the reds, like her, were heading away to the left. She turned back to Mai Ley.

"I think we'll stand out if we try to stay together. Will you be all right?" Rouge spoke as quietly as she could, her voice drowned out by a thousand quiet conversations and the scuff of feet on stone.

Mai Ley nodded and replied simply. "I am safe."

Rouge nodded and started to turn away when the avatar suddenly reached out and grasped her sleeve. The thief stopped, surprised, and glanced back. Mai Ley's dark eyes were cast down, but after a moment they flicked back up to meet Rouge's, and she seemed to smile very slightly beneath her mask. "Thank you for worrying about me." Her hand fell away, and Rouge just nodded, a hard lump forming in her throat.

Then some newcomers pushed between them, and Rouge was on her own.

Well, almost.

::Is she really going to be okay?:: Silus asked from within the folds of Rouge's hood.

Rouge smiled, pulling in a bracing breath at the welcome reminder that she wasn't really alone. She joined the flow of reds as they walked toward some unknown destination. ::There's nothing here that can really hurt her.:: She coughed a bit. ::I mean *us*. Travelers. Us Travelers. Um, anyway, I'm sure she'll be all right.::

Silus' voice grew smaller. ::This place is scary, and these people are scary. Why are they all here?::

Rouge sighed slightly, feeling a little sad. ::Most Travelers see your world as, well, a game. Nothing here really matters, so changing gods to get better boons just really isn't a big deal. Chris is definitely some kind of fighting-type god, so since most Travelers come here to fight, they don't see it as an issue to just," she waved a hand, taking in the milling crowd, "follow whatever deity works best, even if they're kind of icky.::

She looked around again, taking in the enormous statues she was walking past. These were more humanoid than the first ones; more along the lines of the heroic figures who fought alongside the monsters than monsters themselves. They still had some monstrous features, like long teeth and fingernails, and even occasional wings, tails, or horns, but for the most part they looked like characters few players would hesitate to play. Many would even enjoy the inhuman features.

Rouge shook her head. ::I haven't figured out yet what the end game is here, but I do know most pla…Travelers are always looking for new, fun quests. This whole thing looks designed to draw us in.:: Her eyes widened. *Maybe because it is?* After all, her own quest had been to bring Aspen back to Bright and figure out what bad stuff was going on here. What if this was part of the quest on the other side, and she'd just managed to stumble into it?

Looking around one more time, she swallowed hard. If this *was* the work of her opponents in Bridget's contest, it was clear that they were *way* ahead of her side. While she and Aspen had been lounging around playing with babies and unicorns, these guys had been recruiting what seemed like nearly every player in Bright to their side. This was *not good*.

Suddenly, she ran full-force into someone's back, and she struggled to keep her balance as she was snapped back to the present. The person she'd run into, a slim, androgynous figure in a red-trimmed hood and leathers with a sword at their side, turned to her. "Watch where you're going," a feminine voice snapped, but at the same time gloved fingers were reached out to support Rouge. Not that she needed any help, but this seemed like a good chance to get someone to talk to her.

"Oh, um, sorry." She tried to sound as helpless and young as possible, raising a hand to her mouth and widening her eyes. "I just haven't been over here before. I'm, um…"

The woman's posture relaxed slightly, and brown eyebrows arched over softening brown eyes, which was all that was visible above the balaclava-like mask. "New, huh? I remember when I became a red, and it was weird coming over here instead of *there*." Her voice was dismissive as she waved languidly toward the masses of black-trim people. "Most of them won't take the second vow. Casuals, you know? *I*," she touched her own chest, "am going to make it to green soon."

Rouge squinted slightly, trying to be subtle about it, but the taller woman saw and laughed a little. "The masks hide most of our tags, remember?" Indeed, the letters Sep were all that the thief could see above her new 'friend's' head. The other player went on condescendingly. "It's actually Sephiroth." She rolled her eyes. "Sephiroth77, actually, but you can call me Seph. *Not* Sephi."

Rouge desperately tried to recall the name she was currently using, and finally pulled up the spell icon from the corner of her vision.

[Substitution: Lv1]. You now appear to anyone viewing you as the sentient being <u>DayDreamBeli3ver</u>. Time remaining – 00:19:11

"Um, you can call me Day," she said hurriedly, seeing suspicion beginning to creep back into Sephiroth's gaze at her hesitation. "Sorry, this is all just so strange. I forgot for a minute. I'm usually here with some friends, but they didn't want to, uh, take the vow."

Seph huffed scornfully. "Couldn't take the requirement that they offer up ten percent of their mana, or didn't want to promise to be on Apofis' side in the war? A lot of players don't want to make the commitment, but I'm excited!"

Rouge nodded as if she were still listening, but her mind was whirling. *War? What war? The war ended over a year ago!* She felt like ice water was pouring over her head, and even her teeth felt cold. She remembered the scenes of devastation she'd seen on the gamer news streams, and descriptions given by people involved in the battles who said how thrilling and realistic it was.

She'd only been twelve when *Veritas Online* came out, and her dad had actually had her go stay with her Aunt Danika for three weekends straight while he played. She remembered how tired but exuberant he'd always seemed when she came home, and she'd harassed him to show her his game. Finally, he'd recorded a little of the more peaceful parts of it for her, intending to show her the shops and streets of Bright, but she'd seen something else.

Everywhere he went, as he chatted about how immersive it was, and how customizable everything was, she saw the NPCs in the background. There were certainly some in bright clothes, with fluttering fans and sophisticated hairstyles, but mostly there were just people. Kids like Matilda, all thin, sad faces and frightened eyes. Adults who looked terrified but determined. All of them trying to go about their lives even as their likely deaths loomed over them.

It had been these scenes that had led to Rouge badgering her dad into letting her play the moment she reached the minimum age of fourteen. She knew he'd only relented because the war was over, but, somehow, it looked like a new war was coming. A war brought on not by a trite story-line of humanity against Other, but one created to pit players against players to decide something which could affect the fate of the entire world.

The *real* world.

For an instant Zoey, not Rouge, stood there in an echoing temple to an evil god, and her mental finger hovered over a button only she could see.

Do you want to LOG OUT?

This was too much. Too much for a fourteen-year-old girl who only had one real friend, and still struggled with her calculus homework. Too much for someone who just wanted to tease her dad about never going on dates, but was actually happy that she didn't have to share his attention with anyone else. Too much for-

::Rouge?:: Silus' tentative voice entered her mind. ::I think something is happening up front. Are… are you okay?:: Rouge felt fluff stroke her cheek as the little bat bumped her head against Rouge's jaw.

Her hands fisted at her sides. ::Yeah. Yeah, Silus, I'm okay.:: She turned her gaze to the area beyond the sea of players in front of her, where, indeed, something seemed to be changing. She *would* be okay, because she had to be. She *wasn't* alone, and leaving her friends behind wasn't even an option.

Dramatic music seemed to swell from nowhere, and Rouge had to fight not to roll her eyes. One of the many options *VO* offered was to have background music, much as non-virtual games had always done. It was considered a 'non-immersive' option, though, and was off by default. She knew lots of players liked to stream their favorite bands or even listen to the (admittedly really well-done) background track Veritas Corp. had created for those who did want to tune in. She, however, had always tried to keep things as realistic as possible, and sudden ominous music coming from nowhere *wasn't it.*

Honestly though, in this situation, it was really helpful. It reminded her that this was a *game*. Sure, it was a game with war, and dear friends that she loved as if they were real (which they might be, depending on what was going on with Emily), but it also had giant hamsters who tried to eat you, and a background track. Plus, she wasn't Zoey Williams, loser extraordinaire, here. She was Rouge the Rogue, level 49 *badass*, and these crazy cultists were going *down.*

Right after this message.

She chuckled to herself as she settled in to listen, though she did make sure to pin the countdown timer for her spell in her vision so she wouldn't get distracted and forget that she was going to change from a 5'6" blonde human to a 5' tall wood elf-dark elf hybrid in, um, sixteen minutes and fifty-four seconds.

A voice echoed out over the crowd as a platform slowly rose into the air in the center of the crowd. The platform was made of the same obsidian-like stone as the floor, but as it rose, a bas-relief scene came into view, wrapping around the circular stage. From where she stood, she could just catch the edge of a hand on the arm of some kind of throne, the rest of the body vanishing to the left, while directly in front of her were pictured more of the humanoid creatures.

To her right, disappearing around that curve were the mostly grotesque monsters that seemed like twisted animals, rather than twisted people. All of the monsters were bowing (was that kowtowing, when they laid flat on their faces, or completely bent over with their foreheads touching the ground?) to some degree, with, of course, the animal-things genuflecting the most, while the more human ones simply bent deeply at the waist.

Well, at least whoever designed this place was really committed to their theme.

A dark figure stood on top of the stage, which was now at least ten feet above the crowd. His robe was covered in elaborate runes, and both his hood and his sleeves were trimmed in a brownish orange that reminded her of pumpkins and wilting fall leaves. As he spoke, he held his arms above his head, and his words were projected over the still-swelling music.

"Welcome, followers of our great God Apofis! We have gathered tonight for the Induction of the Faithful, but first! Bow your heads before God and repeat your vows!" His voice was rich and appealing, with well-enunciated vowels and sharp consonants. He sounded like someone who had trained in public speaking, and she wondered if he was an NPC or a player.

Around her, everyone was lowering their heads, the loose folds of the top part of the hood falling forward to shadow even their eyes and foreheads. Rouge quickly followed suit. In this pose, she couldn't see the speaker, but his voice seemed somehow even more powerful as a result.

"I vow to follow no God but the one God, Apofis," the man on the stage proclaimed.

"*I vow to follow no God but the one God, Apofis.*" Around her, everyone repeated the words, some more enthusiastically than others.

Rouge did as she'd been taught in elementary school, when she'd been forced to join choir and they'd had a concert while she was recovering from a cold that left her with a voice more like a croak than anything melodious. She muttered, so quietly that there was no way anyone could pick her words out of the crowd. "Watermelon watermelon watermelon."

"I vow to speak to no one of the will of the great God Apofis, until such time as He is ready to reveal His Word to the World."

"I vow to speak to no one of the will of the great God Apofis, until such time as He is ready to reveal His Word to the World."

"I vow to obey the Word of the Great God Apofis in all things."

"I vow to obey the Word of the Great God Apofis in all things."

"Reds and above, repeat after me! I vow to tithe ten percent of my daily mana to the great God Apofis."

The crowd to her right grew suddenly silent, and she would have sworn she felt a general sense of relaxation from the majority of the crowd in that direction. Their part was over, it seemed.

Now, though, those around her raised their voices higher, as if trying to prove their superiority through sheer volume. *"I vow to tithe ten percent of my daily mana to the great God Apofis."* Rouge swallowed hard, seeing a few nearby hoods tilt slightly toward her. They were beginning to notice that she wasn't playing along.

"In the coming war against the impure, I will devote my life and my death to the great God Apofis."

"In the coming war against the impure, I will devote my life and my death to the great God Apofis."

Rouge forced the words between her stiff lips, her heart pounding in her chest. In spite of Mai Ley's assurance (and, really, who should know better than her?) that this vow wouldn't be binding on them, Rouge still felt dirty as she spoke. "In the coming war against the impure, I will devote my life and my death to the great God Apofis."

Not! Not, not, not, not! She screamed in her mind, fighting to relax her fists against her sides and loosen her stance. The hoods surrounding her turned away, satisfied, and she slumped a bit as she heard the next words.

"Greens and above, repeat after me! My body and mind belong to the great God Apofis, to do with them as He wills."

Off to her left, past the small crowd of red-trimmed hoods, she heard what sounded like only twenty or thirty voices. *"My body and mind belong to the great God Apofis, to do with them as He wills."*

"Oranges and above, repeat after me! I am the hands of the great God Apofis on this earth, and my actions are His actions, my breath His breath, my thoughts His thoughts."

This time the chorus was smaller, though it still echoed through the huge room. *"I am the hands of the great God Apofis on this earth, and my actions are His actions, my breath His breath, my thoughts His thoughts."*

Rouge shuddered, abruptly feeling as if she was being watched. A pressure bore down on her shoulders, and she heard sharp, pained cries from her right as some people among the black-trims suddenly found they couldn't remain standing, and their knees hit the hard floor. The pressure grew until most of the low-level cultists were bowing or lying flat on their bellies, and many of the red-trims around her were crouching, though a few had given in to the first press of power and knelt in an attitude of prayer.

As the heads around her dropped, she could see a few of the green-trims to her left, and all of them were in a pose of supplication, and none seemed to be straining against it as the newer members were.

Rouge gritted her teeth. She knew she should kneel. Knew it, and refused, from the depths of her being, to do it. Even if it got her killed, that was better than yielding to this *thing*, whatever it was. Her knees trembled beneath her, feeling like they might break. The looming *presence* seemed to focus more closely on her, and she bit her lip so hard she tasted the distant tang of copper.

Then she heard Silus's voice. ::Gina, please help us. Help Rouge! This place is really, really scary, and I'm really hungry, but there's something creepy looking at us, and we could really use some help now. Maybe some fruit, too, but mostly some help. Um, Amen!::

A flood of new energy filled Rouge, and she almost sighed in relief. The presence lifted, and instead, she felt surrounded by warmth and the scent of flowers. Her knees suddenly felt like buckling for a very different reason, and she went with it, falling to the floor in the midst of the sea of kneeling bodies. *Gina, or Bridget, or whatever, thanks,* she thought. *Thanks a lot.* A gentle hand seemed to touch the top of her head, then playfully tug one of her braids, even concealed as they were by the hood and her illusion.

Oh, cripes! Speaking of the illusion… She checked the timer, which was just beginning to flash at the corner of her vision. Five minutes, then. Five minutes, and she had already attracted far too much attention with her silent battle against Apofis' domination. Grimacing, she glanced over at Sephiroth77, who was watching her with narrowed eyes.

"Sorry," Rouge muttered, "First time as a red. It felt different from before."

The taller woman seemed to consider this for a moment, then nodded in acceptance. "It gets stronger with every tier. The best thing to do is just kneel as soon as it hits. Once you're down, it lets up a lot."

Rouge tried for a smile that would reach her eyes, and thought she might have barely managed something credible. "Thanks, uh, Seph. I'll do that next time." *No way there's going to* be *a next time, though. Why would people* do *this to themselves?*

Sephiroth nodded, turning back to the speaker. As if her dismissal had reassured the others, as well, everyone around them turned their attention away from Rouge.

::Oh my gosh, what was *that*?:: Silus asked, little voice almost panicked.

Rouge shook her head minutely. ::I don't know, but it sucked. Big-time. We'll talk about it later, though, okay?::

The furry lump against her throat moved convulsively, but remained silent.

Ahead of them, the speaker raised his arms again. "All rise!" He shouted.

Everyone rose, though some, probably those who had held out the longest before collapsing to the ground, groaned slightly as they did so.

"We will now begin the Induction! Let those who would like to be raised up in Apofis' eyes step forward, that he may judge you!"

All eyes were now riveted on a set of stairs that suddenly formed from the sides of the stage, circling down until they, presumably, reached the ground somewhere on the other side of the pedestal from where Rouge stood. A moment later, the first of the inductees appeared, walking up the stairs with carefully measured paces. The first ones came in pairs. One 'regular' cultist led someone else with what looked like a dark gray pillowcase on their head. The pillowcase didn't even have eyeholes, so the cultist with them guided them and instructed them when to step.

[Substitution: Lv1]. You now appear to anyone viewing you as the sentient being <u>DayDreamBeli3ver</u>. Time remaining – 00:01:00

As the countdown continued, Rouge glanced around. Everyone's eyes still seemed to be locked on the stage, Rouge's strange behavior completely forgotten. Slowly and silently, she backed up, moving until she was at the very edge of the crowd. Glancing around again as the last ten seconds of her spell ticked down, she saw that while there were some people with green-trimmed hoods standing against the walls, probably as guards as well as ushers, they, too, seemed focused on the central platform.

The timer ticked to one second. No time to second guess herself.

Rouge triggered [Stealth].

She nearly broke her own [Stealth] a moment later by releasing a hissing breath of relief that was loud enough that if the room had been silent, it would have instantly attracted the attention of all those nearby. Fortunately, the ceremony was continuing, with the Master of Ceremonies or the priest, or whatever he was, accepting the black-trim vows from each of the bagged supplicants, then replacing their pillowcases with snazzy new hood-aclavas.

After the second one of these started exactly the same as the first, and Rouge saw the far-too-long line that trailed down the staircase, she decided she could take a moment to think. First, her [Substitution] skill was on cool-down for the next fifteen minutes, so she was stuck as an elf in a room full of xenophobes for a while. Fortunately, as long as her [Stealth] stayed on, she should be all right, and she had plenty of stamina to keep it going, though it was a noticeable drain on her reserves.

Second, she still needed to know what else was going on with these Maskers, and especially where the Natives came into it. Vonn's sister and nephew were still missing, and Leonard had obviously been a member, or he wouldn't have had the hoods. Leonard had definitely said that there was an Induction tonight. But if everyone here was a player, *where were the NPCs?*

Looking around, Rouge noted that not everyone had crowded as close to the center of the room as possible. There were definitely some conversations happening, probably in Private Messaging, which could only be sent between two people who had each other on their friends list and were standing within twenty feet of each other. She saw more than one small group watching each other rather than the MC, and a few hidden laughs and eye-rolls that weren't really appropriate to the situation.

It would be easy enough to maneuver around the edges of the crowd, using these groups as a cover, since they usually held themselves slightly apart from the rest of the attendees. With her small size and high agility, as well as the *Haste* buff from Millie's cooking, she should be able to get a few more experience points in [Steal], [Legerdemain], and [Sleight of Hand] as she went.

Heading left, she got started with a quick dip in Sephiroth77's belt pouch. Yep, definitely getting back into the swing of things now!

The new black-trim members had been inducted, and current black-trims were taking the red-trim vows by the time Rouge made her way past the reds and to the back of the much-smaller group of green-trims. If this lot was representative of the whole, then it looked like only about 10% of each group was choosing to get deeper into the cult. So, out of a thousand black-trims, there were around a hundred reds. Out of that hundred, only about ten would become green. If that held true, then only one person in a thousand was reaching the orange rank, and even fewer would be higher than that.

If you looked at it from the perspective of a military organization then, didn't that make the black-trims little more than cannon-fodder? If the reds were sergeants, then green would be, what, lieutenants? Which made Mr. Orange up on the podium, currently taking vows from newbie reds, a captain or a major? It only made sense that there had to be people higher than him, since who sent out their generals to bring in recruits? So, where were the generals?

That was a lot of questions, and while Rouge liked asking questions, she wasn't a big fan of having no answers. Which was what she had right now. Bupkis, as Jace's dad liked to say.

She tuned back into the ceremony as the music swelled and the orange-trim priest-guy's voice echoed out almost painfully loudly. Two green-trims standing in front of her perked up, the private conversation that had been obvious by their intent gazes, as well as the fact that they were holding hands and leaning in so close that they looked like they were about to kiss, forgotten.

The shorter figure, probably a girl, from the long, flowing dress and wavy light-brown hair cascading from beneath her hood, murmured out loud. "Is it Para's turn now?"

Her (boy?)friend nodded. "Yeah. We'll be able to group up for green quests now. Kes, you're still going to tank, right? Para will have to go through the tutorial quests, and she'll need your help."

A big guy standing next to them sighed, but grunted an affirmation. "Yeah, whatever. Once we have six, we can actually finish that stupid orange qualifier test, right? Because you said it would only take five, Raz, and here we are."

The boyfriend's shoulders stiffened, but he managed to keep his voice friendly. "*Yes*. For the last time, Kes, I'm sure. I know we party-wiped last time, but those knights are tough. We need a healer, and not many of them went to Apofis, since his buffs don't help them much. Para's good, though, and she'll get us through as soon as we raise her up."

The short girl elbowed Raz in the ribs. "Shh! She's up!"

Only two reds stood on the podium with the orange-trim MC, and one of them looked really nervous. Her hands were hidden by her long sleeves, but it looked like she was twisting them. She also kept shifting from foot to foot as she stared down into the crowd, trying to see something in what must be near-darkness from where she was standing.

The girl in front of Rouge raised a hand, waving vigorously until the red-trim girl seemed to catch sight of the motion. The red's hands loosened, and then she waved back, very slightly.

While all this was playing out, the MC had droned on about how important it was for each of them to devote themselves fully to Apofis, and how great these two were, and Blessings, and Boons, and blah blah blah. When he finally got around to actually giving the vows, it was mostly anticlimactic, though a dim, dark-purple glow did shroud the new green-trim for a moment as he finished speaking. Then it was Para's turn, and she stepped forward hesitantly, still throwing nervous glances down toward the crowd below. Rouge wondered if she was just shy, or if there was something more going on.

Then, as the orange-trim raised his hand to lead the girl through her new vows, a voice rang out from the crowd. With a sinking feeling, Rouge dropped back behind everyone else, allowing for a clear view down the outside curve of the congregation.

As it turned out, moving was unnecessary, because a familiar figure, gleaming with red light, was rising above the crowd as if lifted by an invisible platform of her own. Mai Ley. Not only Mai Ley, but a Mai Ley in full 'Atae's Priestess' regalia. Her plain black gown now looked somehow majestic, and her silken fall of black hair hung free past her waist, gleaming in the dim light. Her face was once again covered in the ritualistic makeup that masked it in red from nose-bridge to hairline, and white from nose-bridge to the edge of her high-necked dress.

When she spoke, Mai Ley's voice was easily as loud as that of the priest of Apofis, and her lack of emotion and inflection after his almost melodramatic phrasing made her words seem even more ominous. "Parabemata! You once promised yourself to the Goddess Atae, She who holds us all in Her cold grasp. Do you now forsake Her gifts and Her love? Know that She will curse your name if you choose to pursue this path any further. She has overlooked it so far, since she had no Voice to warn you. You have lost her favor already. Will you truly earn her wrath instead?"

The girl on the stage shrieked, backing away from Mai Ley as if she'd been physically attacked. Her merely mortal voice was almost lost in the sudden hubbub as the guards around the edges of the room began simultaneously moving toward the intruder in their midst, and the attendees began chattering among themselves loudly. Nonetheless, Rouge could just make out the girl's babbled excuses that she was just doing a favor for her sister, and she didn't *mean* it.

Beside Rouge, Kes swore. "Did you just get a green-ranked kill quest for that chick with the face paint? Look at the rewards! Let's go, guys!"

Raz started forward, but his girl grabbed his sleeve. "No! We have to help Para! Look!"

Sure enough, up on the podium, Para was being held by the orange-trim guy, who now gripped a sinister-looking dagger in his free hand. The girl was struggling, and her hood had been knocked askew in the fight so Rouge could clearly see her frightened face.

Raz paused, clearly torn, but finally called after the big man. "C'mon, Kes. She's in trouble because she was going to help us. We should-"

Kes pulled his hood down, revealing a deeply-tanned face with too much forehead and not enough chin. He sneered at his erstwhile friends. "Whatever, dude. I joined up with you guys because I thought you were in it to win it, but obviously you're not any more. You go after Margog up there, and he'll bust you back to black. You really want to start over? For a girl?"

Raz hesitated, looking around as his girlfriend pulled him toward the central platform. He waved toward Kes. "You do what you've gotta do, man. See you later."

The big tank just shook his head, then headed toward the mass of people already gathered below Mai Ley.

The priestess, for her part, was entirely ignoring the showers of arrows and Magic Missiles that were being cast toward her, only to ricochet off the red glow surrounding her. Rouge knew her character was powerful in Ritual magic, and she must have been casting this one for quite a while, holding it until it was just the right time. That said, all good things must come to an end, and unless the AI cheated, which she either chose not to or was unable to, Mai Ley would be vulnerable sooner or later.

As Rouge stared up, torn between whether or not she should sacrifice her own life to try to help (because, frankly, she had no chance against this crowd, no matter what nifty new abilities she'd picked up recently) the world seemed to hiccup. For an instant, everything froze. Arrows hung in the air. Margog's dagger paused in its descent toward his captive's chest, and Mai Ley looked straight at Rouge.

Go.

The voice echoed in Rouge's mind, neither frightened nor angry, as time once again began to flow normally. This was on purpose. This was all to give Rouge a chance to investigate beyond those now-unguarded doors. And Rouge had never been one to let a good chance to be sneaky go by.

Instantly, the thief spun on her heel, dashing through the crowd, which now buzzed like a beehive disturbed by an intrusive bear. She ran away from Mai Ley, and toward the farthest exit from the cavernous room. That exit was beyond even the small group of greens, and not one but two guards flanked it.

::What are you doing, Rouge?:: Silus squeaked angrily. ::We have to help

Mai Ley!::

Rouge shook her head, running as quickly as her *Hasted* body would take her, so quickly that if she hadn't had an absurdly high Dexterity, she would have run into half a dozen high-ranking Maskers as they prepared weapons and spells to repel the intruder.

::She told me to go, Silus. This is the plan!:: Rouge twisted and rolled to avoid a ball of fire that threatened to burn her hood right off as it flew by overhead.

::When was this *ever the plan*?:: Silus nearly shrieked, as sharp little wing-thumbs dug into Rouge's neck.

Rouge grinned, performing a perfect front handspring with a half-twist, ending up beside the now-abandoned doorway with her back pressed to the hard stone wall. Somewhere during her run, she'd lost three health points, breaking her [Stealth], but fortunately no one was paying attention to another cultist running around in a mask and dark clothes.

She didn't bother pulling up her notifications to find out where those points had gone. She'd set filters so minor notices wouldn't distract her while she was focused on theoretically non-violent information gathering, and obviously they hadn't considered whatever it was to be important. She had a suspicion, though, that a level twenty-something Fruit bat could deal about three points of damage to a level forty-nine Fowl Trickster if she dug in her claws hard enough.

Carefully, Rouge reached up and tugged at the soft lump under her mask until Silus took the hint and let go, though not before another hitpoint drained away from Rouge's pool of health. ::Ouch,:: Rouge said gently, as she snuggled Silus reassuringly.

::Oh. Sorry.:: The bat sounded embarrassed, and Rouge had to resist the urge to just pet her for a while until she felt better.

::It's okay.:: The short cool-down period for [Stealth] was up, Rouge triggered it again, then knelt in front of the door, examining the lock. She was just pulling out her lockpicks when she remembered something Aspen had recently reminded her about. Check the door before you try to pick it.

She pulled her Mambele from her inventory, gripping it tightly in her right hand. With her left, she pressed the heavy metal tab of the latch down, pulling the door toward her at the same time. Silently, it swung open, and she held herself still, with her back pressed against the solid wood, waiting to see if anyone would emerge from beyond.

When nothing happened except a sudden increase in the sounds of battle nearby, though she couldn't make anything out in the veritable storm of projectiles that were now filling the air where Mai Ley had been, Rouge slipped around the edge of the door. With a last glance toward the space the priestess probably occupied, Rouge murmured, "May Gina and Atae protect you." Just in case.

She shut the door behind her.

Chapter Twenty

Aspen

With a silent exchange of glances, Aspen and Tessle backed out of the cell, leaving their companion to his mourning. Tessle hitched a thumb to the right, indicating that she would go back over the break room and the smaller of the two offices. Aspen nodded and returned to the larger office. Even though the three of them had gone over the rooms quite thoroughly, Aspen still felt like they were missing something. There was simply no way that a nest of vamps could be living under Bright.

His eyes shot to the door. That was it. That was what was bothering him.

Under.

Under, under, *under!*

Running back out of the room, he called Tessle's name. The half-dwarf's blond head, her awesomely ugly horned helm slightly askew, popped out of the break room door a moment later.

Somehow, Aspen couldn't help but chuckle at the image. "Putting your feet up, were you?"

She stuck her tongue out at him, then seemed to realize what she'd done and clapped her hands over her mouth. Her pale cheeks went bright red. Aspen laughed again, but shook his head, sobering. "I had an idea," he said, and pointed to the open cell door.

Vonn was still inside, gathering up his sister's pathetic remains into a bundle that fit in the remnants of her tattered dress. When they entered, he looked up, then stood, struggling as if the weight in his arms was nearly unbearable. He held the bundle out to Tessle. "Lady Tessle, I ask you this. Please, protect my sister until this night is done. I must discover where her husband and father are buried, and reunite them in death, as I could not in life."

The warrior mage, face solemn, accepted the package, which rustled with the dry sounds of old paper and sticks. The sad parcel vanished into her inventory, and Vonn and Tessle turned their attention back to Aspen.

An expression of fury drove the sorrow from Vonn's face, and it sharpened into as inhuman a mask as Aspen had ever seen it. Even when fighting, Vonn had never looked so fierce. You could tell he fought only because he was attacked, not out of any desire for violence. Now, though, his chin firmed to elvish sharpness, and his cheeks seemed to sink as they tightened, bringing his high cheekbones into sharp relief. Even his winged brows dropped over his suddenly frozen gray eyes, which gleamed like a cat's in the shadowed cell.

"Lord Aspen, you said you had an idea. Do you know where the monsters that committed this atrocity hide?" The musical lilt that Vonn's native wood-elf tongue usually gave his speech was now a sibilant hiss that lengthened his vowels and cut his consonants short.

Aspen nodded. He would have liked to reach out and offer the young elf a consoling grip on his shoulder, or even a hug, if their relationship had been closer. As it was, all he had to offer was a chance at vengeance.

He looked around the cell. "Vampires cannot bear the sun. None of Plum's little spies mentioned hearing rumors of strange goings-on at night. So how do the vampires get here? How do these corrupt guards manage to communicate with them so easily? Certainly, they may be sending messages through some higher power, and, indeed, it is likely that such low-level commoners have some more powerful sponsor. That, however, does not explain how your sister's death came upon her in this place, nor, indeed, why she was left here."

Vonn and Tessle, too, were looking around the small space with fresh eyes. "You think there's a hidden passage in here," Tessle stated.

Aspen felt a smile lift one corner of his mouth. "I do. I think the vampires enter here, and that the guards fear their 'allies' too much to come inside and clear away what they leave behind. This door was the only one locked. I suspect that is not so much to keep poor Violeta in, as to keep the vampires *out.*"

Tessle suddenly looked nervous. "So, if we find this passage, what do we do? I mean, there's no way the three of us can face even one vampire, much less several. We have no idea what we'd be walking into. I remember the war, too. I was, I mean," she swallowed hard, forcing herself to continue. "My boyfriend and I were on... the other side. Then. It seemed... like they would win. You know?" Her blue eyes begged understanding from the two men, and though Aspen felt his heart clench painfully, he sucked in a breath between his teeth and let it out slowly, nodding acceptance. After all, he had also believed Akuji would win. In the end, he, too, had tried to change sides.

Seeing that neither of her companions was ready to castigate her for the choices she had made in a different lifetime, Tessle continued hurriedly. "I didn't really like it. I was ready to quit, but R3dLit3... Anyway, I saw what the vampires could do. I know I'd be all right, eventually, but you two..."

The short woman shook her head, blonde braids swaying with the vigor of the motion. "I'm not who I was, then. And I'm *glad.*" Her voice grew fierce. "I can't just let you guys die because you're, um, Natives. We need backup. We need a plan! We need-"

A loud bang from the outer room interrupted her, as if a door had been slammed shut. They could suddenly hear the muffled words of many men, as well as the sounds of booted feet on the stone floor.

One voice rose above the rest. "Roger!" A hard hand beat on the door.

"Roger, damn you! Where are you? Where are the keys? You'd better not be sleeping off another drunk in there, you..." Multiple forceful blows resounded, drowning out the last words.

Aspen turned back to his companions. "We're out of time. Find that passage."

Tessle looked suddenly resigned, while Vonn's face hardened into determination as he began moving swiftly around the small space. Tessle spoke. "As soon as they see us, they can use [Arrest] to send us to prison, but at least we'd have a chance there. We just have to wait a day for our trial, and I know Aspen can afford a lawyer, so..." Tessle's voice trailed off as a stone beneath her hand depressed with a click.

Aspen chuckled darkly. "They didn't even try to hide it well. After all, if the vampire's dinner goes to them, all the better." He looked over at Tessle. "That system is for Travelers and wealthy Natives, and only if the Guard is honest. These Guards are anything but, and if they send Vonn and me to prison, it's a death sentence as certain as the bite of any undead. Not to mention that there's apparently a price on my head."

He reached out and pushed harder on the stone. A narrow slice of the wall popped free and swung wide. "I very much doubt any of them will follow us even a single step into that passage. We must go."

Behind him, punctuating his words, came more and more vicious blows against the heavy door, which now shook in its frame. A furious roar came from beyond, and an axe blade broke through the wood, then was pulled back with a grunt. The dim light filtering through the broken slit darkened as an eye peered through.

Aspen swore. "They only need to be able to see us clearly to cast the spell. It takes less than thirty seconds. Go, go!" None too gently, he shoved his friends through the opening. Vonn slipped through easily, though Tessle's armor stuck for a worryingly long moment before scraping into the wider space beyond. Aspen followed immediately, pulling the stone panel closed by the handle embedded on the inside.

Darkness surrounded them, silent and thick.

Aspen growled softly. "Does anyone have a light?"

❦ ❦ ❦

Tessle, of course, had a glowstone. She also had a thief's lantern, with a series of built-in panels that allowed only as much light as they wanted, and at only the angle they needed. Of course, she didn't really need it, since she, like Rouge, had [Darkvision] as a result of her dwarven heritage. Vonn, however, only had low light vision, much like a cat or raccoon, so while even a faint light was enough to allow him to see quite well, he did need that light.

Aspen, on the other hand, was blind as a Cave Worm. Literally, since the worms used Tremor Sense to move around, and Aspen abruptly found that his Life Sense, which had been blocked by whatever spell or blessing was on the interior of the guardhouse, was working again. Well, working somewhat. It was still limited, but he could at least sense twenty or thirty feet to either side and in front of them. He reminded himself, however, that he couldn't sense undead at all, so his renewed ability to 'see' worms, roots, and moles wasn't going to help him avoid vampires.

Thus it was that they began to make their very cautious way forward. Aspen could, at least, tell them which branching of the narrow dirt tunnels led to close-by rockfalls or dead ends, so they were able to avoid a few of these. Vonn led the way, using the lantern and [Perfect Navigation] to guide them when Aspen's Life Sense couldn't reach far enough. Tessle brought up the rear, her [Darkvision] allowing her to watch behind them in case something managed to flank them or come up from one of the short tunnels they thought were empty. Between the three of them, they managed to make their way through what seemed an eternity of crisscrossing burrows.

The first indication that they were coming to the end of the maze was the sound of chanting. From the rhythm, it sounded like one voice was speaking, and a loud chorus of others would repeat the words back to them. Tessle stopped, touching Aspen's sleeve, and Aspen reached out to hold Vonn.

"It sounds like church liturgies. My nonna makes me go with her every Christmas, and that definitely sounds familiar," the half-dwarf muttered.

Aspen frowned. He knew some of the more organized religions had meetings at which a priest or priestess spoke, but neither Atae nor Gina encouraged that kind of thing. They preferred when their people came to them as needed, rather than on a pro forma basis.

"Where there are people, there's a way out," he murmured. "I doubt there are that many vampires, and they were never good at acting in concert. The fact that they usually fought alone is the main reason we were able to kill as many as we did."

Vonn, whose people had stayed out of the war, as had all the other elven races, offered a nod of understanding. "Then these should be humans?"

Aspen frowned. "Not… necessarily. The vampires often had minions, some of whom were very inhuman indeed. Let me see." He closed his eyes, cautiously reaching out with his limited Life Sense toward the noise. He found people. Many, many people. All Natives, from the varied glow of their spirits, since they lacked the cascade of numbers that marked Travelers. All of their spirits were corrupted in the same way Leonard's had been, to one extent or another.

His eyes flashed open. "There's a chamber. There." He pointed with a hand which he saw was shaking slightly. He clenched it into a fist and let it drop back to his side. "Filled with people. All of them are being eaten by the same force that was devouring Leonard."

Vonn paled, even his fierce thirst for vengeance dimmed slightly by the memory of their erstwhile prisoner's gory fate.

Tessle, who had only heard about it second-hand, looked disgusted but not frightened. "You mean we found those Maskers? The ones Rouge is after? Do you think she's here?" A clear note of hope rang out in the Traveler's voice.

Aspen shook his head. "I… don't know. She was supposed to follow her Traveler acquaintance, but there are none of your people in that room, only mine. I would recognize Rouge herself, and she is not within my sight. It seems likely that they keep Travelers and Natives separate, if only because most of your people seem to view mine as disposable toys."

Tessle winced, but nodded. "That does make sense," she said, reluctantly.

Vonn, meanwhile, was staring as if his gaze could bore through the wall. "Only Natives? Then, is there a chance this is where they brought my sister's son? Can you tell if any of these are captives?"

Aspen frowned and sent his thoughts questing back out into the space beyond, finding himself pressed hard against the wall, as if that would extend his range enough to matter. "I don't know," he told the elf hesitantly. "There do seem to be some children, as sadly eroded as the rest of these fools, but whether they are here voluntarily or otherwise, I could not say."

He lifted a now-steady hand and pointed to the right. "They are that way, however, and it seems as good a way to go as any other."

Vonn's face lit up in a ferocious smile.

"How much farther *is* it?" Tessle muttered. The trio had been walking for a good ten minutes already, and there was no sign of a door, a portal, or even a crack in the earthen walls.

"I. Don't. Know," Aspen gritted out, frustrated. One thing he had noticed about Travelers was that they did not deal well with delays. They always seemed to want immediate action, even if acting now was more dangerous and likely to bring lesser rewards.

Vonn was trailing his left hand along the wall, looking like he wanted to simply try tunneling through it. They had passed the area with the children quite some time ago, and Aspen had had to close down his Life Sense to the barest fraction of even its current limited reach. The young spirits only ten or fifteen feet through that wall were so riddled with holes and blight that he could practically smell the rancid scent of rot rising from them.

When the young wood elf had learned that those pathetic young spirits had been left behind quite some time ago, he was furious. Aspen had to admit that he could probably convince the roots supporting the walls to move aside for them, but the odds were too great that they would immediately be discovered and captured or killed, or, worse yet, fed to whatever monstrosity was devouring this gruesome feast.

At last, Aspen had to admit defeat in spite of his concerns. He paused, sighing. "We should have gone left, I think. I can still barely catch 'glimpses' of a few of them at the edge of my range, but that's it. The question is, do we go back, or forward?"

Vonn's reply was instantaneous. "Back! We must see if my nephew is among those children!"

Tessle shook her head. "Forward. We already know there's an overwhelming force behind us, and if we do get into that cavern, what can we actually do? I'm sure we could kill a lot of low-level NP-" she coughed awkwardly. "Um, Natives, but what happens when the high-level ones show up looking for the people making all the noise?"

Vonn's hands clenched at his sides. "Just because you're too frightened to-"

Aspen's hand sliced through the air, cutting the boy off. "She's right, Vonn. Our deaths will not free your nephew or bring any prisoners to safety. Plus," he looked into the young man's rebellious gray eyes, "Tessle has no reason to be afraid. When she dies, she wakes up a few hours later, little worse for wear. She's thinking of us, and you would do well to remember it."

He could practically hear the elf's teeth grind as the muscles in his jaw clenched, but Vonn finally looked down in defeat. "I know you're right," he muttered. "But knowing I could be so close, and doing nothing…"

Setting a gentle hand on the young man's tense shoulder, Aspen gripped it reassuringly. "We will find a way to save your nephew, if he is there to be saved." He felt the muscles under his palm spasm at the reminder that, in all honesty, they were probably already too late. "I believe we can save those children, but we must do it wisely. Remember that someone must care for them once they are released. It's not enough to save their bodies if their spirits die."

Nodding jerkily, Vonn stepped back. "Fine," he said, swiping at some dampness on his cheek. "Let's go then."

It was another ten or fifteen minutes before Aspen once again sensed anything besides worms and other small, nearly mindless creatures. When the first questing tendrils of his Life Sense touched the blazing spirit, he flinched back, both physically and psychically.

Vonn and Tessle immediately stopped, turning to Aspen with expectant expressions. He held up a forefinger for silence before cautiously reaching out again. This time, before he even reached the spirit, he could sense something like waves of heat coming from it. He stopped, close enough to see the shape of it, but not actually contacting it.

"I... don't know what I'm seeing." He shook his head, whispering even though they had been talking in near-normal tones for quite some time. "I can't even tell if it's a Native or a Traveler. Or," he squinted, as if his eyes had anything to do with that strange second sight, "if it's an animal or a humanoid. Whatever it is, though, it's more powerful than anything I've ever viewed before. Also," his stomach sank as he finally managed to adjust a bit to what he was seeing, and noticed something horrifyingly familiar. "It's being eaten by the same thing that is devouring the Maskers."

Tessle's blue eyes were huge, and she looked like she couldn't decide whether to be excited or worried. "Is it the Masker Boss, do you think? If we keep going, are we going to have to face it?"

Vonn cast a longing look down the cramped passage behind them. The walls and ceiling had been slowly closing in for quite some time, and Tessle's broad shoulders and pauldrons were beginning to scrape against them rather alarmingly as she walked. "Perhaps we *should* go back," the elf offered hopefully. "If this thing is as powerful as you say, then fighting some common cultists might be better than-"

Aspen shook his head. "Not *some*. Hundreds. Perhaps thousands, though I couldn't see far enough to confirm that. This thing, powerful as it is, is only one being. All we have to do is avoid it."

Tessle rolled her eyes, muttering, "Yes. *All* we have to do. As if it's ever that easy."

Aspen cast her a quelling look. She gave him a rebellious look in return, but sighed and nodded. "You're the boss. And that's something I never thought I'd say to a… Native." She shrugged apologetically, and he quirked a smile at her.

"Vonn?" He looked back at the young elf, who dug the toe of his soft leather boot into the floor.

"Fine," the elf mumbled finally, sounding like a child who has just been denied a favorite treat. Then he cleared his throat, straightened his shoulders, and looked up, clear eyes meeting Aspen's. "I mean, yes. If that's what we need to do."

Aspen felt his heart clench in his chest. How many times had he and Lark had conversations like this as she was growing from a child to a woman? How familiar was that expression of determination, of readiness to be the adult they so longed to be, while at the same time feeling all the rebelliousness of a teenager and the longing for reassurance that every child felt when they were frightened? He had to draw in a sharp breath against the pain of memory, forcing down the image of light brown eyes that overlaid the gray eyes watching him so earnestly.

Fighting down the urge to give the boy a hug, he nodded sharp confirmation. "Forward once again, then, but we need to be more cautious." He looked over at Tessle. "I know it makes you uncomfortable, but could you…?"

The half-Dwarf sighed, and a moment later she was once again clad in starlight and shadow, with the train of her dress trailing back down the passage so far that it vanished around a curve. Tessle started hauling in the yards of silken fabric with a long-suffering expression. It took several minutes for her to wind the cloth around her waist and bare shoulders, and when she was done, she sent him a look from beneath her pale golden brows that would have shriveled a lesser man.

"If we get into combat while I'm wearing this, I'm going to be worthless. It's meant for a mage, standing at the back and looking pretty. I'm more tank than spell-caster, and the only distance spell I have is [Fireball]." Her tone suggested that if he had anything to say about it, he should really keep his opinions to himself.

Aspen just nodded, and for the first time in quite a while, the soft silver shimmer of a stat gain appeared around him in the darkness. At Tessle's questioning look, he shrugged. "Wisdom, I think."

She laughed.

🍎 🍎 🍎

It was a good thing that the half-dwarf had changed, because soon enough the rough dirt walls were so tight that Vonn was the only one still slipping easily through the passageway. Aspen even had to gently feed mana to a few large roots to convince them to move aside so his wider shoulders could get by. The more open areas were gone now, and what they walked through seemed more like a naturally formed crevice than anything created by man. The ground beneath their feet was half hard-packed soil, and half slabs of natural stone.

When Aspen thought it was a toss-up between whether he or Tessle would become hopelessly stuck or the fissure would simply fizzle out, he finally sensed the strange lack of life that generally indicated an open area ahead of them. Of course, given their current situation, a lack of life could also mean a plethora of undead, but he chose not to dwell on that at the moment.

He was about to speak when Vonn, who was well in the lead by now, his short stature and slim frame allowing him much more freedom of movement than Aspen's height or Tessle's dwarven breadth, reappeared in front of them, his finger held over his lips to indicate that they needed to be silent. "There's an opening ahead, I think," he hissed almost inaudibly. "I can smell clearer air, and, perhaps, hear some sounds, though faintly."

Aspen and Tessle exchanged glances, and the half-dwarf made a face, tugging unhappily at the beautiful, still perfectly clean and intact, garment wrapped around her body. "I'm still not going to be of much help," she muttered, fingers twitching as if the desire to dig into her inventory and change was almost more than she could bear.

Aspen nodded. "Stay at the rear, then. Try not to get pulled into combat until you can change, but, if you must, stick to [Fireball] and any defensive spells you have."

She shrugged. "I have [Shell] and [Resistance], but I can't cast spells through [Shell]. That's part of why I never bothered with any more distance spells. They don't do me any good when I'm fully buffed."

He nodded. "All right. Cast a [Fireball] if you think we need the help, but otherwise just use [Shell] and [Resistance]. Stay safe, and flee, if you must."

She smiled a little, casting him a small salute, though he wasn't certain she intended to follow his instructions. Travelers were far too cavalier with their own safety, since even death was no true deterrent.

Aspen turned back to Vonn. "You'll be our scout, of course. When you're able, [Stealth] and go through if you can. Don't try to engage anyone." He hesitated. "Have you ever seen a vampire before?"

The young elf shook his head.

"They just look like people, for the most part. The biggest giveaways are the sharp teeth and the red or black eyes." Aspen grimaced a bit. "Sometimes the lower-level ones, or ones that haven't eaten recently, will smell, too. They have an odor of old loam and decay. Mostly, though, they just look like everyone else. So, it doesn't matter if you only see one person. Don't think you can take them, or even that *we* can take them. The best way to kill a vampire is to surprise them and get some wood into them. Once the wood is in their flesh, they can't shift forms, and a large enough group can usually decapitate them."

Aspen slid a hand over the wall beside him, dripping mana in its wake. The wall seemed to boil as tiny tendrils of roots thrust out and curled into his palm like kittens seeking comfort. He stroked them, and they fell into his hand, instantly turning into sharp, hard splinters. In thanks, he gently pushed a few more drops of mana into the donor trees.

He turned as best he could in the confined quarters, and handed each of his companions a small bundle of the sharp sticks. "Hopefully, no one 'felt' that," he murmured, "but it needed to be done. I should have thought of it long ago."

Aspen tucked his own wood-fragments into his belt, then warned them again. "Get the wood into them. Once they can't shift, we may be able to win. Don't worry if you're not sure if they're a vampire or a human. First, anyone out there is likely to be an enemy, and second, these splinters won't do anyone any lasting damage. Unless," he smiled lopsidedly, "you manage to get it in an eye. Which is probably a good place for it, honestly. I once saw a vampire rip off his own arm to get rid of the wood embedded there, and he killed thirty soldiers after doing so."

Both Vonn and Tessle were looking much less confident now, which, to Aspen, meant he had done his job. He pointed down the dark crevice ahead, "Now then-"

A muffled scream echoed from the path in front of them, interrupting him. From the place in Aspen's mind where the Traveler's party chat emerged, he heard a too-familiar voice squeak out, ::Rouge!:: The little cry was faint and terrified.

Swearing, Aspen forgot everything he had just been saying, and sprang into motion. His strong hands shoved Vonn, who was between him and the source of that sound, down flat on the ground. Then Aspen gathered himself, using his long legs and powerful muscles to leap over the young elf's prone body. A second after the sound reached them, Aspen was gone.

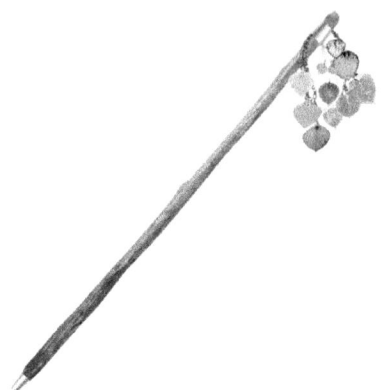

Chapter Twenty-one

Rouge (as Aspen is wandering dark tunnels)

R
ouge didn't dare look around properly until the door was firmly closed behind her, shutting out the sound of ominous music, fireballs, magic missiles, and exploding arrows. The quick glance she'd sent through the door had told her there were no immediate threats, but she hadn't really taken in any details. Now that she did, she was almost impressed with the sheer amount of gaudy self-glorification that *Chris* seemed capable of spewing everywhere.

Well, she supposed that it was probably Harris' team's fault. It was obvious after the way they desecrated poor Mr. Hamncheese's adorable fluffy cuteness that this group had no shame, and she fully intended to let them know how she felt about it. They clearly needed some player feedback, because this was *ridiculous*.

Everything around her was obsidian, gold, or carmine. Not a speck of lighter color showed anywhere, and as a result the walls seemed to loom around her shoulders even though the hall in which she stood was at least eight feet wide and tall. Glowstones set in recessed golden sconces covered by carved obsidian grates cast intricate shadows everywhere, making the leering carvings and statues of men and monsters to seem like they were watching her as she walked around examining them.

A shudder ran up her back as she looked up into the nearly-human visage of the largest figure, whose image was repeated over and over with arms outstretched in benediction over his horrifying minions. It was hard to tell coloration, with the extremely limited palette the artists had to work with, but the hard golden jaw and short, dark hair definitely seemed masculine. The blood-red fangs in a soft-lipped mouth, and equally sanguine eyes looked out from under heavy golden brows, definitely had a 'manly' vibe. In fact, hadn't she *seen* that face somewhere before?

Silus' little voice broke into the girl's reverie as she was trying to follow up on the niggling hint of recognition. The bat was whispering in spite of the fact that only Rouge could hear her. ::Um, Rouge? Aren't you supposed to be in [Stealth]?::

Rouge's eyes widened, and she looked down at herself. Sure enough, instead of being slightly unfocused and faded, her body was as sharply visible as ever. ::They must have a Spell-breaker ward on the door! Darn it, I should have caught that! Thanks, Silus!::

Quickly, she tried to trigger [Stealth]. Nothing happened. She tried it three more times, each time with the same result. "Insanity is doing the same thing over and over again and expecting different results," she muttered, pulling up her list of skills.

Sure enough, [Stealth] was grayed out, as were [Sneak], [Lockpicking], and, for some reason, [Dig], which was one of the random skills she'd gotten while helping Aspen on his farm last fall and winter. On a hunch, she looked at her spells, too, and saw that [Substitution] was also unavailable. "That is *so* uncool, Harris, you cheater!"

::Who is Harris?:: Silus' confused voice pulled her back to the present.

Rouge shook her head. ::Sorry, I was kind of talking to myself. Harris is a guy I work with in my world, and I'm really starting to not like him.::

::But why would you-::

Rouge broke in before her little friend's curiosity pulled them into a conversation she really didn't want to have. It was one thing to tell the Natives that Travelers came from a different world through magic, and quite another to say that Rouge's people had actually *created* this whole world. That would make Harris like, a *real* God to the Natives. Rouge shuddered at the thought.

Reaching into the neck of the black hood she still wore, Rouge gently retrieved the bat. ::Silus, I'm going to need you to scout ahead. Just stay up as close to the ceiling as you can, and if you see *anything* alive, let me know and come right back, okay? If anyone sees you, just yell and come back.:: Rouge sent a glance at the closed door, which was now several feet down the hall behind her. ::I don't think going back is really an option, so we're just going to have to be extra sneaky without skills. Which we can totally do, because we're *awesome*.::

Silus grinned a little bat-grin, her flat nose and big ears twitching. Her beautiful golden eyes shone in the partially-occluded light. The small creature flashed one wing-thumb in the most adorable thumbs-up *ever*, and then she dropped off of Rouge's hands and flew down the hall. A few extra wing-beats later, she was hugging the ceiling, her slight, dark-furred body already hidden among the bas-relief figures crowding the space, just as Rouge had hoped.

They went on, with Silus proudly in the lead, until the bat chirped a warning in Rouge's mind. ::Door,:: she said. ::It's closed, but I think I hear sounds from the other side.::

::I'm coming,:: Rouge sent, picking up her pace slightly. ::No sign of anyone around?::

::Nothing. Just more of these ugly carvings.:: Rouge could picture the way Silus' nose wrinkled when she smelled something disgusting, and she had to restrain a giggle in spite of the seriousness of the situation.

Rouge could see the door now. It was even larger than the one they'd entered through, and that one had been easily seven feet high. This one nearly brushed the eight-foot ceiling, and the wood was a deep black inlaid with a gold image of (who else?) good old beneficent Chris himself.

Swallowing hard, Rouge looked back and forth between the door and the nice, tacky but so-far innocuous, hallway down which they'd been traveling. Honestly, yes, she wanted to find more information, and she definitely wanted to find Vonn's family. (Because he would be so *grateful. Squee!*) But she felt naked without [Stealth], and she was (sorry, Silus) pretty much alone, and she just wanted to know how to get *out* of this place, since she obviously wasn't going back out the way they got in, and *when was her dad going to log on?*

She huffed out a sharp breath, closing her eyes for an instant. Easy there, it was going to be fine. Just. A. Game. Though… She sent a look up at where she could barely make out Silus hidden in the curve of Chris' benevolent arm. ::Silus, if anything happens to me, I want you to run. Fly.::

::But-:: Silus tried.

::No! I mean it. Remember, I'm a Traveler. Even if I die, I'll be back tomorrow. *You* have to get out.:: Rouge had a sudden idea. ::I mean, you have to tell everyone what happened, right? And there has to be a way out somewhere. Just follow someone and get out, and go let Aspen know how to get back in here. He needs to know so he can save Vonn's sister as soon as possible, right?::

Silus sounded reluctant, but said, ::Okay. But maybe this *is* the way out? We can go together, and come back with more people. We were just supposed to gather information, anyway, right?::

Rouge looked at the huge, sinister door. ::I don't think this is the exit, Silus.::

::Then we should just skip it! We don't have to open all the doors! We just need to get away!::

::There's something really, *really* important behind this ginormous door, Silus. My thiefy-senses are tingling like crazy. I *need* to know what's in there.:: Rouge's fingers were starting to twitch at her sides, and her lock-picks were already out and prepared.

::You really don't, Rouge. Really, really.:: The bat's voice was pleading. ::I bet all the doors in here look like that. Except the exit. The exit is probably pretty, with blue clouds and sunshine painted on it. Or maybe it's just a regular door, made of regular wood, with a handle. Come on, Rouge! Let's go find the plain old brown door that-:: Silus broke off as Rouge quickly checked the handle, and, when the door didn't budge, slipped a lockpick into the large, ornate keyhole.

[Lockpicking] is disabled in this area. Attempt failed. Your *Lockpick* has broken.

::Oh, sassafras and salt! I forgot about that!::

Silus sounded hopeful again when she answered. ::Forgot what?::

::They locked down the best Thief skills in this area. Now how am I supposed to...:: Rouge trailed off as she saw something in her Inventory that she'd gotten as a quest reward while she was still in the tutorial. A *Skeleton Key*. Everyone got one, and usually you used it to open the treasure chest you also received at the end of the quest, which couldn't be opened any other way. Rouge, however, had heard that the chest only contained one hundred to one thousand gold, and to her, the *Skeleton Key* was invaluable. Sure, you could buy (or sell) one for around eight hundred gold in the Auction House, but she didn't have eight hundred gold, and she sure wasn't likely to get that much by opening the little treasure chest. So, she kept them both; chest unopened in the bank, and key safely tucked away, taking up a single slot of precious space in her inventory.

Waiting for today.

The deceptively simple-looking item appeared in her hand, and Rouge held it up, examining it for the last time.

Skeleton Key – A key with a classic design. The head is shaped like a skull.

This is a single-use item that will open anything with a keyhole. Weight – 1oz. Rarity – Very Rare.

Rouge raised it to her lips and kissed its creepy little skull, then inserted it into the golden keyhole. With a nearly inaudible *click*, the lock opened, and the key shattered to dust in her hand. Torn between a desire to giggle gleefully and an urge to sob at the loss, Rouge simply pushed the heavy black and gold door gently, trying to peer around it as unobtrusively as possible. Her attempt failed miserably, as it swung wide, revealing the room to her, and her to the occupant of the room.

The figure was seated at a desk topped with neat stacks of scrolls and books. One hand, covered in aged skin like fine yellow parchment, held a soft golden quill dipped in carmine ink. The rest of the figure was concealed by what looked like a full-body variant of the hood the rest of the cultists wore. Around the hem of the robe, where it draped down over a comfortable-looking black chair, was a yellow-gold trim.

As the door swung open, the robed person looked up, and a gentle, elderly voice emerged from the darkness of the hood. "Ah, there you are, my dear. I had wondered when you would arrive. Come in." The feather pen was carefully wiped, then placed neatly on the paper on which the person had been working. The wrinkled hand gestured in invitation.

Rouge gulped. "Uh, me, sir? Um, ma'am?"

A creaking laugh came from the darkness beneath the cowl. "Oh, oh, oh. That old, am I?"

Rouge took one careful step into the room, glancing around sidelong as she did. She seemed to be in some kind of extremely ornate receiving room. At one end of the chamber, which was easily fifty feet long, and nearly as wide, with a vaulted ceiling lost in gloom overhead, sat a towering golden throne. She couldn't really make out any details, but it seemed that any normal-sized person would be dwarfed by the massive seat. Certainly the little old person at the desk would have a hard time even getting up into the thing.

"Um, no?" Rouge slid to the side, trying to stay away from the being as they rose to their feet. She knew better than to underestimate old people. Her grandma seemed ancient, but she could swat little fingers away from cookie dough with the speed of a striking snake. The girl squinted at the old person, trying to see if their name would give her any hints, but nothing appeared. That cloak-hood thing seemed even more effective than the regular hood at blocking [Identify].

"You may call me Panginoon. They didn't tell you?"

Oh! She… He… They think I'm someone else! Rouge's fingers lifted to touch the edge of the red-trimmed hood she had forgotten she was even wearing, and her shoulders relaxed a little. There was no way for this person to tell who she was, or even that she wasn't human, while she had this thing on her head, right? She'd even built her avatar without the tell-tale eyes-that-glowed-faintly-in-the-dark that full-blooded elves had.

She tried for a little curtsey, which turned into a bobbing bow as she realized she didn't have on a dress. "Um, no… Panginoon. I just…" She gestured at the door, helplessly, and Panginoon clicked their tongue in chastisement.

"I guess that's what happens when you're part of a secret organization, eh?" Again the creaky laugh, encouraging Rouge to join in the slightly self-deprecating humor.

"I," Rouge cleared her throat when her voice cracked, and tried again. "I guess… so?"

Panginoon moved away from the desk, walking slowly toward the monumental throne. A yellowed hand, long fingernails thick but clean and smoothly curved, gestured for her to follow. "Come along, then, child. Come along. It won't do to be late."

Rouge warily walked along behind, staying as far away as she could without looking like she would rather be running the other direction as quickly as possible. Which she would. Because in spite of this being's advanced age, seemingly gentle demeanor, and sense of humor, she had never wanted so badly to be anywhere in the world but where she was right now. If her thief-sense had told her there was something very important in this room, her girl-senses were telling her she was in over her head and needed to *run*.

::Silus, go!:: She sent frantically, as she saw the bent figure pass through a low opening that had been concealed by the throne until they were almost upon it.

::Why? That guy's creepy, but it's okay so far,:: her friend sent back.

::There's something really, really wrong. I mean, more than all the rest of this has been wrong. You need to go, and I'll-::

Rouge stopped, stunned, as she crossed into the room behind the throne. There, in a space that made the cavern in which the Induction had been held seem tiny, lay a dragon. A dragon who looked half dead, with smoke-colored scales broken and dangling, suppurating flesh visible beneath. Its body was as big as the life-size blue whale sculpture Rouge's dad had taken her to see when they were visiting her Uncle Milo in California. The dragon's head lay at what seemed an impossible distance away, at the end of a serpentine neck, and just the head was almost as large as a truck. One eye was gone, leaving a black cavern filled with glistening goo, and Rouge would have sworn she saw something *move* in there.

She was fighting nausea when the other eye, an incongruously brilliant Ceylon-sapphire blue, blinked open.

IS IT THAT TIME AGAIN?

The power of the mental voice, even defeated and exhausted as it was, nearly knocked her from her feet. Panginoon chuckled happily, reaching out and patting the beast familiarly on its snout. The lip rolled up in a half-hearted growl that sent shudders down her back, and revealed rows of arm-length teeth, still white and sharp in faded and receding red gums. "There, there. We're nearly done, I think, and won't you be glad when we don't have to do this any more?"

The huge eye rolled, then slitted almost closed as a rattling sigh shook the huge body. Rouge could see the skin between the ribs pull taut as the beast struggled to breathe. For all her terror, she felt a horrible, wrenching pity as well.

Panginoon turned back to her, their previous good will and humor entirely gone. "Well, girl? Well? Get on with it!" The seemingly-decrepit old person stepped between her and the door through which they'd entered, a sudden dark power crackling around hands that abruptly looked more clawed than elderly.

Rouge crouched, backing away from the insane cultist. Her eyes darted wildly as she tried to find some way out that didn't require going through one of them. "Do *what*?"

"Did you *really* think we don't know when someone enters our province uninvited, child?" Panginoon raised hands whose power made the surrounding air ripple as if it was hotter than an asphalt road during a record-breaking heat wave. Rouge's Mambele appeared in her hand in response. "Did you *really* think we'd just let you wander around, uncontested, until you could return to whatever rat-hole you came from? The only reason," The man, and now that the voice was louder, Rouge definitely felt it was more masculine than feminine, stepped forward, causing Rouge to back up instinctively. She only realized what she was doing when she felt her back press against the cold, hard side of the dying dragon.

Panginoon went on, "The only reason you got this far, was because you so-conveniently arrived at *feeding time*."

A scream tore from Rouge's throat as she felt something punch through her chest. Looking down, she saw a broken gray claw protruding from beneath her rib cage. Her Mambele dropped from her hands as she clutched at the bloody talon.

She barely had time to hear Silus shout her name before her vision went black.

You have been dealt 1,923 hp of damage by *Greater Dragon*. You have died.

Chapter Twenty-two

Aspen

A
spen nearly howled as he saw the brilliant cascade of numbers that he somehow knew represented Rouge flicker and then go out. The last numbers tumbled out of their tidy pattern and instead swirled as if they were the final wisps of smoke from a blown-out candle.

Instinctively, he reached out with his mana, grasping at those drifting numerals even as he sent a heart-felt prayer to his Goddess. *Gina! Gina, it's me, Aspen! Please, oh Goddess, please hear my prayer! Rouge is dying!* He swallowed hard against the bile rising in his throat, even as his shoulder slammed hard into a black stone wall. He pounded his fist against it, feeling the last traces of Rouge's essence slipping away. *She may already be dead! Please, Gina, don't let her die!*

The light that surrounded him this time was brilliant, and such a pure color that he thought that he would never again be able to describe any mortal shade with that previously simple word, 'white'. The light grew so great that it developed force, and the wall beside which he stood began to buckle from a concussive burst.

In that instant, with the wall half-destroyed, the ceiling and walls around him fragmenting into powder, and his mana desperately scrabbling at the final trace of Rouge's spirit, everything stopped. The moment hung suspended in time, as a sliver of the perfect whiteness surrounding him *twisted*, and a being stepped from nothing.

To his utter astonishment, it wasn't Gina. This woman had none of Gina's perfect beauty, her effervescent joy, or the strange sense of burgeoning life that always surrounded her. Instead, this woman, though pretty, was merely human. Her hair was long and brown, and her eyes were a rich greenish color. She was slightly plump, and her nose was tilted up at the end. She was also, though he was certain he'd never met her before, strangely familiar.

The woman smiled at him, looking as if she'd met an old friend for the first time in a very long time, and wasn't certain when they next might meet. "Hello, Aspen."

Aspen blinked, feeling oddly disconnected, as if this moment and the one before were each part of two different lives. His desperation and horror at seeing his friend fade away were still there, but distant, and he could hold them and the astonishment and awe of this moment at the same time.

"I... I..." He stumbled, feeling a million questions tangle on his tongue. Finally, he just shook his head and said, "Hello."

She laughed, though it sounded a little choked. "Hello, *Amy*. My name is Amy. And I'm so very glad to meet you, Aspen."

Aspen just nodded, though he lifted one hand slightly before letting it fall to his side again.

Amy stepped forward, reaching out to grasp his hand, picking it up and holding it between her two warm, soft ones. She smiled again, though this time there was a hint of a mischievous twinkle to it. "I can't stay long. The system is applying a patch, and I slipped into that moment of... inattention, I guess. I'm having to speed up your perceptions to make this work, and it's dangerous to do it for long. I just really wanted to see you, and," she tilted her head, "I guess that's it, really. You're someone very important to me, and I don't know how long I'll be able to do things like this."

He shook his head, though his hand tightened around hers without his conscious control. "Who... Who are you? Are you Gina's," *friend*, flashed through his mind, but he said, "servant? You don't look like-" He broke off, not sure how to say it without being insulting.

She knew what he meant anyway. "A goddess? No, I'm just a person. I do know Gina, though. She's very busy right now, but she set things in motion for this," she freed one hand and waved at the light and the destruction surrounding them, "a long time ago, so even though she can't come herself, she's still taking care of you."

The light shifted, dimming an infinitesimal amount. Amy growled in frustration. "Damn. They'll notice me soon, and I can't risk that. Just, listen." She, too, started to fade, and his hand clenched around nothingness. "You're about to be offered a choice. Don't doubt yourself. Follow your heart." She smiled, then vanished, and the world returned with a vengeance.

The wall in front of him blew out.

Revealed in the shattered stone was a scene that made his heart nearly stop beating. To his right, a thing, disguised as a man but invisible to Aspen's Life Sense, stood in front of a low door. A deep black cassock concealed him from head to foot, but his hands, yellow and clawed, were fully visible. To the left...

To the left lay a Bone Dragon. The beast still had some flesh, but it was desiccated and torn. Shreds of skin and scales hung like the rind of a shriveled orange. One eye was rotted, and Aspen could just make out the skeletonized wings lying uselessly behind the monstrous reptile. The dragon was also the source of the extremely powerful spirit Aspen had seen through the wall. The same spirit that was so corrupted that he could practically smell the rancid stench of it.

On the dragon's claw hung the limp body of Rouge. The girl's head hung forward, and her arms and legs were as limp as a marionette with cut strings. He couldn't see her face, concealed as it was by the hood she still wore, but he had seen the slack faces of the dead often enough that his imagination proved sufficient.

The sense of separation that he'd felt while speaking to Amy was ripped from him, and all of his fear and rage poured back into him, filling and overflowing as he leapt forward, pulling the small corpse from the impaling claw.

The moment his arms wrapped around Rouge's limp body, words filled his vision.

The Goddess Gina has heard your prayer. As Her Champion, She grants you one of the following Skills to be used in pursuit of Her goals.
[Vengeance] *Whenever one of Gina's faithful falls, you may use the power of their death to strike at their murderer, instantly killing them.*
[Resurrection] *Once every three days, you may bring one of Gina's faithful back from the Chaos Pool. They must have died within the last five minutes, and be a pledged adherent of Gina.*
You have thirty seconds to choose. 30... 29... 28...

Aspen bowed his head over Rouge's remains, feeling her warm blood covering him, and fury blazed in his chest.

He knew what he *should* choose. Rouge was a Traveler. She would be reborn tomorrow, none the worse for her transitory demise. At this moment, with Vonn and Tessle still just on the other side of the wall, and Silus' bright little spirit visible at the edge of the range of his diminished Life Sense, he needed to reduce the number of enemies. Specifically, he needed to destroy the hugely powerful Bone Dragon before it could wipe them out with a single flick of its decayed talon. That, and the ferocity of his anger argued for [Vengeance].

But with the lifeless form of another child lying in his arms, taking him back to a day not nearly long enough ago when it had been the body of his *own* daughter he clutched to his heart, he chose [Resurrection].

The light beyond white flashed around him once more, and then, miraculously, he felt Rouge twitch in his arms. The girl groaned, then sat up suddenly, cracking the top of her head against his chin so hard that he fell backwards, landing on his rear with the elf-girl sprawled across his lap.

Rouge ripped the hood off her head, a huge grin on her face. *"Oh my gosh,* Aspen! That was *so cool*! I was totally about to log out, and it *wouldn't let me*! Holy cats, it was scary! I thought I was stuck, and it was the worst thing *ever*, because my dad was going to *kill* me if I wasn't already dead, but then it said you were *rezzing* me! Rez!" She pumped a fist. "Yes! Ultimate priest skill! Wooooo*hooo!"*

Then she spun, the small, colorful beads on her braids whipping Aspen's face as she did. She landed in a crouch, balanced perfectly on her toes, with her Mambele in her right hand. She pointed the weapon at the robed man standing, frozen in shock, behind them. "Also, that guy is a total... *lickspittle*! He fed me to the dragon!"

The man, as if stung into action by Rouge's outlandish insult, pointed at Aspen and the little thief. "Dragon! Slay them!"

The great dragon, nearly dead as it was, simply rolled its one remaining eye at the pair.

KILL THEM YOURSELF.

If Aspen hadn't already been seated, he probably would have fallen from the sheer force of that mental voice. Even filled with apathy and sorrow, it held more power than he had felt since he had faced Lich Lord Akuji himself.

The thing in the robe shrieked furiously, sounding not at all human any more, and began to swell. His robe shredded as he shot up well over two feet, suddenly going from just over Rouge's petite height to towering over Aspen's 6'3" by a foot or more. His arms grew disproportionately long, until the yellowed limbs reached nearly to his knees, with four-inch-long claws that touched his ankles as his hunched back forced his head forward and his arms to dangle low in front of him.

His head, covered with sparse remnants of black hair, twisted as well. The lower jaw seemed dislocated from the upper, with massive reddish teeth protruding at all angles. His eyes protruded from his head, yellow and rheumy, and his nose receded, leaving little more than a dripping hollow in the center of his face.

The monster raised his taloned hands and shrieked again, this time in pained surprise, as an axe sprouted from his chest. Aspen heard a whoop from behind him, and turned his head to see that Vonn and Tessle had scrambled through the gaping hole he had left in the wall. Tessle stood in front, a triumphant smile on her face as a second axe appeared in her hand. She was back in her armor, and her horned helm actually looked more ferocious than comical.

Rouge yelled gleefully, "Tess! Vonn! Oh man, you don't even *know* how glad I am to see you guys!" The girl looked around, taking in everything around them, then locked her eyes on the single remaining eye of the dragon, who laid still beside them, each breath seeming slightly shallower than the last.

"Look, dragon," she said quickly, "I don't know what these bad guys have on you, but if you help me for just a minute, I promise we'll help you." She sent Aspen a glance. "I got a quest to help her, and I really think we ought to take it, because it says she'll eat us if we don't."

He just nodded, still unable to do more than stare at the now vibrantly alive girl. He felt both a fierce pride in Rouge's resilience and an agonizing sorrow that he would never again see Lark's face filled with the fierce determination that had been so characteristic of her in life.

Suddenly, Rouge pointed behind the slavering monster who was now standing, chest wound closing into a pulsing greenish scar as the creature dropped the axe to the ground beside it, huge hands unable to hold onto the handle of the weapon because of its long, curled yellow claws.

"Hey, what's that?" The thief yelled, in such a blatantly false tone of surprise that Aspen was shocked when the creature actually whirled to look, exposing its bony back, ridged with too many ribs and vertebrae.

The instant the thing began turning to look, Rouge took off, moving so quickly that Aspen nearly lost track of her. The flicker that was the elf dashed from shadow to shadow up the dragon curled behind them. First the limp, clawed foot, then to the rough-scaled elbow, and onto a suppurating shoulder-blade. As she rose higher and higher with each barely-visible leap, the dragon raised the remains of one skeletal wing, and Rouge used the osseous platform to get even higher.

At last, just as the monster turned back to its attackers and began to shamble toward them, once again whole and hale, lean muscles rippling with terrible strength, Rouge reached the summit of the wing. She leapt up, vanishing into the darkness.

Aspen's eyes widened. It had been a long time since he'd seen this, but it was burned into his memory, as was the pain of the broken arm that he'd suffered. Aspen rolled to the side, toward Vonn and Tessle, who were moving forward, each gripping their weapons as they readied themselves for battle.

"Tessle! Shield, now! Vonn, get back!" Aspen shouted, climbing to his feet and immediately diving for the hole in the wall.

Down came the rain. Poisonous blades showered down on the monster behind him, stabbing into its flesh until it looked like a ham seasoned with spikes of clove. Three times the knives fell, and as the last one pierced the thing's flesh, Rouge appeared from above, Mambele already swinging for the exposed side of the bony and misshapen skull. With a crunching pop, the weapon pierced the skull, and the horror swayed, then fell with a heavy *thud*.

Rouge leapt free of the body, rolling twice until she came up on her feet, bouncing slightly on her toes. Her eyes flickered to the side, and she groaned. "No death notification? What does it take to kill this guy?"

Aspen looked at Tessle, who was now crouched just outside the hole in the wall, with a shield that was taller than she was braced on the floor so that she and Vonn could hide behind it. The half-dwarf's mouth was hanging open as she stared at Rouge.

"Tessle? *Tessle!*" Aspen had to yell to catch the warrior's attention. "Cut off its head! Quickly!"

Gulping visibly, Tessle stood, trading the tower shield for a battle axe with a head as wide as she was. Taking a running start, she whirled the heavy blade twice before slamming it into the fallen body just as it was beginning to struggle to rise. With a wet *crunch*, the head separated from the neck and rolled several feet away. The mouth was still snarling when the dragon lifted an enormous foot and crushed the head with contemptuous ease.

Chapter Twenty-three
Rouge

A spen had a new tattoo. Seriously, why did he have *three* now, while she (and honestly, who had done all the hard work in that battle, anyway) had none? But she totally wasn't jealous. At all.

She sighed as she examined the newly illuminated pinky on Aspen's right hand. It looked like there was a bioluminescent white oil slick just under his skin, which was also now bleached so pale you could barely tell there was skin over the glowy light.

"Well, at least now you have a 'handy' night-light," she joked. Her dad would be so proud.

Tessle groaned, but the two males chuckled slightly. Maybe bad jokes were just a boy thing, and they were called dad jokes because once a guy had kids, he felt like he could let his true dorkiness shine? If so, maybe they should do it sooner, because she actually had kind of a thing for dorks. Look at Jace.

Nope. Totally *not* looking at Jace, because he was her *best* friend, not her *boy*friend. Diff-er-ent.

She cleared her throat slightly, and read off the quest that was currently floating at the top of her vision.

> **Quest: "Dragon Tails" accepted.**
>
> **You have met a dragon who has been imprisoned. Convince her to escape.**
>
> **Success: Your enemy loses a great asset in the upcoming war.**
>
> **Failure: The dragon will eat you all, and it's pretty likely everyone in the kingdom will die.**

When she finished speaking, Silus, whose terrified shivering was just beginning to fade, poked her little head out of Rouge's braids. ::I don't want to be eaten,:: the little bat said plaintively.

The dragon's cerulean blue eye, larger than the silver platters her dad's college had used at the last 'Winter E'en Feast' (because all college professors were dorks), blinked open and rolled to focus on the bat.

YOU SPEAK*?*

Everyone staggered slightly, and Rouge held up a hand. "Hold on, um, dragon. First, what's your name? Second, could you, like, think more quietly? Please? Third, *you heard that*?"

A sense of distant amusement filled the pained voice that answered her. **I am sorry. I forget how fragile you mortals are.** The eye blinked dismissively at the smear on the floor that used to be Panginoon. **I did not care if I damaged that one.** The blue orb looked back at Rouge. **You may call me Beryl. Of course I heard your tiny friend. She spoke, did she not?**

Rouge nodded. "That was in party chat, though. No one not in the party should be able to hear it."

The enormous head rocked ever so slightly, dismissing Rouge's small concerns. **I am a dragon.** The dragon said simply.

Tessle was staring at Rouge. "Wait," the half-Dwarf hissed, as if everyone couldn't hear her, "you have a *bat* in your party?"

Rouge bit her lip, suddenly aware that this was Supposed To Be A Secret.

Aspen chuckled softly, resting a hand on her shoulder. He hadn't gone more than two feet from her since the battle ended, and he kept touching her, as if he was afraid she wasn't real. Seriously, it was like having another dad. Why did they *worry* so much?

"You may as well let her in," the tall man said. "Though I struggle with trust myself, I believe we must extend trust to gain it, and she has proven herself tonight."

Rouge tugged at one of her braids, then nodded decisively. She threw a party invite to Tessle.

The Player you have invited is already in a party. Ask them to leave their party, and try again.

Oh. Duh. Tess was probably partied with Doom Bloom and Fluff.

Rouge smiled a little sheepishly at Tessle. "Um, yeah, so we can party with Natives now, at least sometimes? And, uh, Silus is actually more than just a pet."

The half-dwarf's mouth opened and closed. Twice. Then she held up a hand and shook her head. "Okay, back to *that* later, but right now, I don't want to be eaten."

Rouge giggled. "That's what Silus said."

The two girls grinned at each other.

Five minutes later, they were all much more serious.

"So, let me get this straight," Rouge said slowly, from where she was leaning against the wall near the hole Aspen had blown through it. "These rotten," she clenched her teeth against the words she *wanted* to use, "*fopdoodles* stole your baby, and then convinced you that if you ever wanted to see him again, you had to do what they told you to do, which, as it turns out, involves letting their god *eat your soul*, and then get turned into some kind of zombie dragon?"

"Bone Dragon," Aspen murmured.

Beryl released a sigh that set her dangling scales quivering and nearly knocked Rouge off her feet. Pro tip: half-undead dragon breath is *nasty*. Even in her home pod, Rouge could smell it way better than she thought was reasonable, and she wanted to brush her own teeth in sheer self-defense.

You have the gist of it. I am held here now by the geas they were able to place upon me when I swore to do as this God required. But, even were I not, I will not leave while there remains a chance I may reunite with Malachite. Alas, I fear he is dead, but until I am certain, here I shall remain. Beryl sounded resigned to her fate, but Rouge's hands fisted at her sides.

"Uh uh. Nope. No *way* are we leaving you here. I mean, even without the quest. Though, um, you wouldn't really eat us, right? I mean, we're friends now!"

The dragon did her minimalist head-shrug thing again. **I hunger,** she said simply. Then added, **I would let you go, but the geas compels me to feast on the flesh of innocents, that I may become ever more corrupt. No other innocents are available to me, and even now I struggle to resist. My will is weak, after so long.**

Rouge gulped, and all four of them took an involuntary step away from the suddenly once-again-threatening form of the colossal reptile. Rouge nearly stumbled over some fallen rubble, but managed to catch herself and maintain her dignity.

"So, um," her voice cracked, and she cleared her throat and tried again. "So, do you know where they're keeping Malachite?"

Beryl's voice was bitter. **The Panginoon told me he was kept only a little further down the hallway, in another room like the one through which you entered. He enjoyed mocking me in my helplessness. *I* enjoyed crushing his head.**

Aspen's head lifted from where he was examining his shiny finger. "Wait. *The* Panginoon? That wasn't his name?"

Indeed not. That was that creature's title, and he shares it with at least a dozen others. They take turns feeding me, though this one was the one who came most often.

"Damn it," Aspen muttered. "I knew this was too easy." He looked at Rouge, fixing her with his topaz eyes. "We need to go. Though I hadn't met one of this ilk before, undead creatures like this Panginoon usually have some connection with their master. He will know his creature has died, and send others to discover the how and why of it. The longer we linger, the more likely we are to be trapped, and we have no chance of winning against eleven more of these things."

Fear not, holy man, Beryl said, her eye drifting closed as if she were exhausted. **All but one have been sent on other missions. I heard them discussing it when they last changed places. You should go now, however,** she yawned, showing a mouth full of disconcertingly sharp, white teeth. **I will not be able to restrain myself much longer.**

Tessle was on her way to the door through which Rouge and the Panginoon had entered almost before the last mental syllable was done echoing in their brains. "Okay, guys! Let's go!" The warrior was swinging her axe like it was a baton. "We have a baby dragon to save, right?"

Rouge and the others exchanged glances, and they all followed Tessle with perhaps a bit more haste than was entirely dignified. Aspen, bringing up the rear, came to a halt when they emerged from behind the massive golden throne and he was finally able to see the room properly. He pointed to the desk.

"Tessle," he said.

Tessle just nodded and headed to the desk, gathering everything there into an extra bag hanging from her waist. Rouge was impressed. "Is that the five-hundred slot bag?" She stared as more and more papers disappeared. Every one of those would take up its own slot in the other woman's inventory, and most people could barely afford fifty-slot bags.

Tess shrugged, cheeks flushing slightly as she shoved the last book in the bag. "Yeah. They had a sale last Cyber Monday, and I *hate* inventory management. Fortunately, I like cup noodles, because I was pretty broke for a while. Totally worth it, though."

"Whoa," Rouge's eyes widened. "I wonder if dad would let me get one with my savings. I mean, he says I should save up for a car, but that's so cool."

Tessle laughed. "You should save up for a lot of things before you get a bonus bag. Though I bet you could afford one with in-game funds now, if you wanted to. I heard about your big haul."

"Ho-ly *cats*! You're right! I increased my bank storage and the size of my primary inventory, but I didn't even think about-"

Aspen cleared his throat from the door, and the two females turned to look at them. Rouge tugged at a braid, which, she was starting to feel, wasn't nearly as satisfying as pulling her curls, though her dad got after her for that, so maybe it would help her break the habit? "Sorry about that, Aspen! We're coming!"

The hallway was just as dark and ominous as it had been on the way in. If anything, the grotesque monsters depicted on the walls were even worse now that she had *met* one of them, and knew that they were more than just artistic flair.

Aspen grew grimmer and grimmer the further they walked, his icy gaze sweeping over the murals and carvings that covered every inch of the walls and ceiling. Rouge hurried up to walk beside him.

"Do you recognize these things?" she asked.

He pointed to one particularly ugly baddie eating something she didn't want to think about too hard. "I believe that is our friend the Panginoon. This," he drew a finger over one of the more human-like images who were standing closest to the God-figure with his arms open over them all, "is probably a vampire."

A chill ran down her back, and Rouge remembered Jezerey. The vampire queen had been part of the trials Rouge had had to face in order to reach Gina's temple so that she could accept her sub-class. "I thought vampires were extinct? Like, Akuji called all of them to be in his army, and they were all killed in the war. Except for Jezerey and what's-his-name, her son, and William, of course."

Aspen's voice was bleak. "That is what I believed as well."

A hiss echoed down the hall from Vonn, who was leading the way, since he was still really good at being quiet even without using his [Stealth] skill, which was just as borked as hers was. An instant later, Silus winged into view, fluttering down to land on Rouge's shoulder. ::There's a door up ahead, but there's somebody guarding it. He looks really bored, and I don't think he noticed us, because he's kind of... singing to himself?::

Rouge frowned a little, then gestured in a 'hold on' motion to Aspen and Tessle, who was wearing pretty black slippers on her feet, even though the rest of her was covered in hunks of metal. Cautiously, she edged forward until she was crouching beside Vonn, who was plastered against the wall and standing so still that Silus had to pinch Rouge's neck with a wing-thumb to keep her from running into him.

The wood elf tilted his head down the hall, and Rouge squinted into the darkness, glad for the billionth time that she'd picked a race with [Darkvision]. Sure enough, there was a really, *really* bored guard standing by another big black door like the one she'd entered when she'd met Panginoon. He was wearing a green-trimmed hood, and above his head, she could see three characters: 'n00'. He was a Player.

Thinking fast, Rouge pulled her own red-trimmed maskaclava hood-thing up over her head, disturbing Silus, who squeaked in protest. Then she strode confidently out into the light given off by the guard's glowstone.

"Uh, hey!" She waved nonchalantly.

The player, who had been using the 'air guitar' emote while singing VaJay's 'Money for His Heart', immediately jerked to a halt. Even behind the mask, Rouge could see the deep red color that suffused what showed of his skin. He choked, waving her off when she stepped forward as if to pound him on the back. It wouldn't do any good, of course, but it was the thought, right?

"Uh, did you... see...? Um, no, but..." The guy finally stammered to a stop, then tried again. "So, are you, like, my replacement? Where's Jones? I thought he was supposed to... But you're just a red, and... Anyway, who are you?"

Rouge pointed above her head, where the first three letters of her handle should be visible. "Round Robin. Duh. Didn't Jones tell you?" She really wanted to keep going, try to add some details to make it sound more realistic, but she knew she'd probably just say too much if she tried, so she bit her tongue.

N00 shook his head. "Nah, man. That's typical. Nobody tells me anything." He stepped away from the door. "Well, whatever, right? This is the lamest cult-quest ever, but at least it's worth some good experience." He started to walk off down the hall, thankfully *away* from her friends (because she would have felt kind of bad about killing him) then glanced back.

"So, uh, Robin, right? Just, um, don't tell anyone about..." He mimed strumming a guitar, and she grinned, then zipped her lips and threw away the key. He sighed in relief. "Thanks. See ya' around!" With a wave, he walked off, already humming under his breath. She would be willing to bet he was one of the ones who streamed music into the game.

As soon as they couldn't hear n00-whatever's slightly off-key warbling any more, Vonn emerged from the darkness behind her. He shook his head in admiration. "That was truly wonderful, Lady Rouge. I would have simply slain him."

She shrugged, feeling her cheeks heat. "Best not to kill Travelers if you can help it. We just come back, and we can be pretty cranky about the whole thing. Plus, we can talk to each other in our world, too, and he probably actually knows some other Maskers. He'd let them know there were intruders down here, and then we'd have an army on our tails."

Vonn hissed a breath in through his teeth, then bowed slightly. "I hadn't looked at it from that perspective. You are wise, my lady."

Rouge was pretty sure her face was going to just burn through her mask, but fortunately Tess and Aspen showed up at that point.

Aspen looked at the door, his face a study in disgust and frustration. "How did you get through the other door, Rouge?" He spoke quietly, though she was pretty sure the door, being at least four inches thick, would block any sound from passing through.

She shrugged. "I had a *Skeleton Key*. I just let myself in."

Aspen nodded, contemplating the large keyhole. "All right. Was there a guard at that door? I didn't see any signs of one, but Traveler's bodies vanish much more quickly than those of Natives."

"Nope, just a great big door."

"So this one is different."

"Maybe because Panginoon was in the other one?" she ventured. "If this one needs a guard, maybe it's unoccupied?"

He nodded. "We'll step back. You try the door. If the guard was all the deterrent they needed, it may simply be open. If there's someone inside, try to bluff your way through again, and if things go badly, we'll back you up."

Rouge huffed out a breath. "Yeah, because the bluffing is going so well for me today."

He quirked his half smile. "You did well with that Traveler. We'll back you up," he repeated firmly.

Muttering, she took hold of the door handle, then waited for everyone else to step to the side so they'd be out of easy line-of-sight. Gritting her teeth, she pushed. Nothing happened. She pulled. Nothing. The door was definitely locked.

Aspen growled in frustration. "Do you have another magic key?"

She shook her head.

Tess coughed slightly, then waved a hand toward Aspen's waist. "What about your, ah, worm-thing?"

Rouge's eyes shot to her friend, and Aspen, with an 'ah-ha!' expression, pulled an *actual worm* from a little pouch on his belt. As Aspen knelt to slide the slimy little critter into the keyhole, Tessle met Rouge's eyes and winked cheekily.

A loud and slightly gooey *click* sounded, and Aspen stood back up with a triumphant expression, tucking his worm back into its pouch. Aspen stepped back and waved to Rouge. "After you." Rouge stared. Why did Aspen get all the cool toys? She definitely needed one of those!

Everyone resumed their positions, and Rouge shook off her distraction, drawing in another bracing breath. This time when she pulled on the handle, the door swung silently open, revealing a room which was completely different from the one where she'd met the Panginoon.

Cautiously, Rouge stepped inside what was clearly a laboratory. Carved runes covered the floors, some of them filled with crouching, pacing, or prostrate captives. Shelves lined the walls, housing books, jars, and neatly labeled pots of all shapes and sizes. Three long tables stood to one side, cauldrons bubbling and steaming alongside beakers of various potions.

A man stood with his back to them, his hands waving as he attempted to infuse some sort of spell into a concoction that was spitting sparks in front of him. As Rouge entered, the man jerked, his concentration broken, and the spell backlashed, wrapping his hands in fire.

He yelped, flapping the appendages wildly, and began yelling as he turned. "Damn it, n00burger! How many times do I have to tell you-?"

Breaking off, the mage's dark eyes narrowed, and his crispy hands formed into claws. "Who the hell are you? I don't recognize you, and only upper-tier greens should get this quest." As the smoke produced by his ruined spell cleared, she could see that his hood had a deep orange trim.

"Uh, yeah," she tried, "Jones couldn't make it, so-"

"Bull," the man said abruptly. "I just saw him less than an hour ago at the Induction, before that crazy priestess started up with her 'you're all going to hell' crap. Try again."

Rouge sighed, then said conversationally, "I could use that backup now." Before the man could respond, she'd crouched and pushed off with her ridiculously powerful legs, leaping up onto the closest table and knocking as much of the contents onto the floor as humanly possible.

Howling in fury, the mage lunged at her, but before his feet could even leave the ground, he sprouted a hand-axe and two daggers from his chest. Gasping, he spun away, his eyes locked on Tessle, Vonn, and Aspen, who had entered behind Rouge and spread out, deploying their distance weapons. His hand scrabbled for a large glowing purple orb that sat on the table behind him, and it rolled to the edge of the table, where it teetered, nearly falling.

In an instant, Rouge assessed the situation. Either it was good for them if the orb broke, or it was bad. Given the way the guy was making no effort to catch the glistening ball, she was going to go with option two, and no one else was close enough to do anything about it.

Leaping into a dive, Rouge did a forward handspring, then twisted into a spin-kick on the way down, sweeping the enemy's feet out from under him. Meanwhile, she reached out to catch the tumbling sphere... and fumbled it. Hissing, she watched as the bright glass shattered, releasing what she now realized was smoke into the air.

"Ha!" The mage shouted, scrambling to his feet. "It's just the two of us now, kid!"

Rouge looked around, hearing choking coughs coming from behind her. Aspen, Vonn, and Tessle were all on their knees, and blood sprayed from between Aspen's lips as he struggled to breathe. The deadly smoke wreathed her friends, and she could see their health crashing like a freight train rounding a curve with no brakes.

Warning! Party member Aspen (NPC) has fallen below 50% health.

What the *heck* was in that dumb ball? And why wasn't it affecting her... or

Silus? She suddenly realized that she could still feel the bat's furry warmth against her throat, and she hadn't received a message saying the small creature was injured.

The mask. The stupid, ugly, *magical* mask! ::Aspen!:: she sent urgently. ::Mask up!:: Now she could only pray he got it before anyone died.

Catching a spark of light out of the corner of her vision, she realized that she'd almost forgotten the orange-trim Masker who had broken the sphere in the first place. Spinning out of the way, she nearly dodged a [Magic Missile], the weakest but fastest spell in any mage's arsenal.

You have been dealt 47 points of damage by Player Neo****.

Holy hangdog! Forty-seven health from a [*Magic Missile*]? This guy had to be several levels higher than her. Level seventy? *Eighty*? Whatever he was, that left her with 178 hit points, and if he could nail her with a few more of those, she was as good as dead.

Rolling away from where the MM had thrown her, she found herself beneath the table where Neo-whosit had been working. A moment later, another [Magic Missile] hit the ground near her, but pretty far from the furniture beneath which she was hiding. Was there any chance this guy still hoped to salvage whatever it was he'd been working on?

Figuring it was worth a shot, she finished her roll, bouncing up so that the table was between her and Neo. The smoke was beginning to clear, and she hadn't received any more notices about Aspen's declining health, so she was really hoping he was going to be fine. She couldn't check at the moment, but that didn't stop her from muttering a quick prayer to Gina.

"All right, dude, that's fine. Just you and me, huh?" *Keep thinking that, jerk,* she thought, desperately hoping it wasn't true. "You might want to look over there!" She pointed behind him, toward the farthest part of the room, triggering [What's That?!] as she did.

He laughed. "What was that? Some kind of distraction skill? Forget it, kid, I'm not stupid." He threw another [Magic Missile] at her, but it was a half-hearted attempt, and she could tell from his shifty eyes that he was up to something.

She shrugged. "Worth a shot, right?"

Meanwhile, she was desperately turning all her skills and spells over in her head. The obvious one was [Poof!!], but anyone who wasn't a member of her party could suffer from the *Smoke Inhalation* or *Poison* debuffs, which meant she could accidentally kill Vonn or Tessle if they were close to death. [Poison Rain] and [Pterion Puncture] both required her to attack from above. [Knockout] required [Stealth], which was blocked. Wally wasn't there, so no Awesome Ostrich Attacks. She eyed the unfortunately well-lit room. No shadows for [Shadow Glide]. She was pretty sure she wasn't going to [Barter] her way out of this, so it was going to have to be…

She reached forward and pushed a flask off the table. It crashed to the floor, and Neo squawked indignantly, reminding her unavoidably of Nuisance the duck.

"Hey!" The mage shouted, taking a step forward, glowing hand raised threateningly. "Do you know how long I worked on-"

She pushed off another flask. It shattered, and something in the resultant orangish goo writhed slowly. "Oh, gross, dude! What have you been making in here?"

Neo pulled at his hood in an agony of frustration. "Stop! Just stop! C'mon! I don't know what quest you have in here, but don't ruin mine! It takes days to make those things! I have to log in every three hours and stir it. I even have to set an alarm! I haven't slept properly in a week, and I was almost done. This is why no one takes the Alchemist sub-class!" The man was whining by the end, and she would almost have felt sorry for him if he hadn't just *tried to kill her.*

She pushed off a small silver cauldron, and ribbons of red fabric spilled across the floor, steaming slightly. She nudged one with her toe, and it seemed to twitch unnaturally. "Seriously, what do you *do* in here?" Something caught the corner of her eye, and she plucked at the red trim of her hood. "Is that how you make the trim for all these things? Seriously? That's your big project?"

The mage began to edge around toward the door, slowly, like she wasn't going to notice. She pretended not to. He went on talking, obviously trying to distract her. "There are, like, four spells just in the black-trim hoods, and it takes *seven* different ingredients. The red trim takes six spells and ten ingredients. We set quests for what we need, but some of that stuff is really rare." He was almost turned so his back was to the door now. "You don't even want to know what it takes for the orange ones, and only a Master Alchemist-"

As he took his final step, allowing himself a clear path to her, his hands emerged from where they had been hidden in the sleeves of his robes. Both hands were glowing. *A double-caster! Great!* She dove to the side again, throwing the Mambele, which she had been holding loosely, as if she'd forgotten she had it. The weapon whipped through the air, with the full force of fifty points of Strength behind it. *Let him be a glass cannon, please!*

She managed to avoid one of the [Magic Missiles], but the other one caught her side, once again punching her like Joe Lewis taking down James Braddock (and the next time Uncle Milo started waxing poetic about boxing, she was going to let him know how she actually felt about it).

You have been dealt 96 points of damage by Player Neo****.
You have dealt 114 points of damage to Player Neo****.

Rouge sprawled on the ground, watching the pulsing red notifications of a *Stun* debuff compete with equally frenetic ones alerting her to the three cracked ribs on her left side. She couldn't move yet, but she had a direct line of sight beneath the table she had been sheltering behind.

Neo's robed figure staggered backwards, and a few drops of blood spattered on the ground near his feet. No death notification appeared, though, and he didn't go down. Not really surprising. At his level, even if he'd poured most of his stat points into intelligence, he had to have a few hundred health points.

Then one of the huddled figures of her friends (Vonn?) rose with lithe grace from where it had been lying, and bright metal flashed. Another one of the 'corpses' stood (Tessle, from the shape of it) and swung an axe with vicious precision. As Neo grunted and his knees buckled, the final form stood, and Rouge would have laughed (if she could) to see Aspen rubbing his lower back. Stick, now at its default length, struck out, crushing the player's throat and finally dropping him to the floor.

You have assisted in defeating Player Neo****.

Aspen was at Rouge's side before Neo's body finished crumpling to the floor, and she was particularly grateful because his body blocked her view of the rather gruesome mess. Her friend quickly restored her to full health, and Rouge was back on her feet within a minute. Vonn and Tessle were already scouring the room for clues (and valuables, because loot), with Tess tossing everything not nailed down into her Big Ol' Bag.

Aspen smiled tiredly at Rouge, pulling off the simple black mask that he'd bought to protect himself from the stench of the Tannery. He held it up. "Thank you. That gas was incredibly lethal, and it was difficult to think while under its influence, as well. If you hadn't reminded me of the masks, you and Tessle would likely be the only members of our party to see sunshine again."

::What about me?:: Silus demanded indignantly, wiggling her way free of the red-trimmed mask that Rouge still wore.

Aspen reached out a hand, and Silus climbed into his palm, snuggling down as if she was the one who'd been doing all the work. The tall man gently stroked the bat's soft ears, a gentle smile on his usually rather stern face. ::You as well, thank Gina. If you hadn't been in Rouge's mask-:: He frowned, deep lines suddenly bracketing his mouth and eyes. ::Well, fortunately you were, so we shall let that pass.:: He looked up at Rouge, then flicked a glance at Neo's corpse, which, having been looted by Tess, was already fading. "What do we do now?"

She sighed. "That guy's probably already on whatever forum or chat the Maskers have set up, calling for reinforcements. We need to hurry and get out of here as quickly as possible. The only thing that's likely to save us is that this isn't exactly the kind of place where anyone wants to leave their Zombie, so it should take a little while for people to get here."

Aspen nodded. "So, time is even more of the essence than it was before. Silus, start looking for anything draconic. Be cautious, since the baby won't know we're here to help him."

"I don't think we need to worry about that." Tessle's voice was sad, and everyone turned to look at her where she was standing near one of the runic circles that contained an ominously silent form. Everyone else hurried to join the warrior woman, and when Rouge saw what lay there, she wanted to kill Neo again. Fortunately, the odds were decent that she'd get the chance, someday.

A sad little shape lay in the circle. It was so skinny Rouge thought she could count every bone in its body, and it laid utterly still, green scales dull and sunken, half-open eyes clouded.

Rouge's fists clenched at her sides. "I," she said, "am really starting to hate these guys."

Tessle's blue eyes met Rouge's hazel ones, and they shared a look. Sure, this was a game, but this was like those people who ignored their mounts. The devs had at least built in a process for 'punishing' people who didn't take care of their horse, but this? This was not cool.

Aspen leaned forward and lightly touched one of the runes carved into the floor. He cocked his head consideringly, then drew Stick from where it was tucked into his belt, once again in cudgel form. The subtly carved metal cap glowed for an instant, and became the miniature sickle again. Aspen sliced into the stone floor, scratching the runes, which flickered an angry red and dimmed back to blackness.

Leaning forward, Aspen scooped up the limp form of the baby dragon. Its head dangled limply, and he frowned, shoving his small staff back into its makeshift holster. Aspen cradled the dragonling's head, which was about the same length as his forearm, showing that the baby was larger than it had appeared when it was curled up in its prison. The farmer frowned, then looked up at Rouge and Tessle. "Release the rest of the prisoners. Just cut the wards. If they're sapient, and want to come, bring them with you. Gather everything you can. Burn everything else. We'll have to go back out through the tunnel in Beryl's prison."

Rouge stared at him. "But how will *Beryl* get out?"

Mouth quirking in a grim half-smile, Aspen answered, "You'll see." He headed for the door, carrying his cargo as if it were made of blown glass.

Vonn, Tess, and Rouge looked around at the other occupants of the runic circles. Many of them looked to be past saving, while others stared at the invaders with eyes that barely dared hope. None of them were human. At a quick glance, Rouge saw there were at least four humanoid creatures that she didn't recognize. The others were beasts, several of them so twisted that she wasn't sure what species they might have been to begin with.

The three of them exchanged glances, and Rouge hooked a thumb at the shelves and tables behind them. "Tess, you have the Awesome Bag of Awesomeness. Get grabbing until you can't grab anything else. Just, um, leave anything that looks like it used to be part of a critter. I have a bag for that."

One of Tessle's blonde eyebrows rose, but the warrior just nodded and headed back to begin what would probably be the fastest looting of her entire gaming career. As soon as Rouge saw Tess chucking All the Things into her bag, she was once again determined that she was going to get one of those. For now, though, she had another task.

She looked back at Vonn. He nodded at her, far grimmer than she'd ever seen the usually gregarious elf. "Break *all* the seals. I know not what they do, but it is possible they have some sort of 'Raise Dead' curse in them." His expression turned sad. "Also, these poor creatures deserve to be free, even if it's in death."

She nodded back, then looked around. "All right, folks! Anyone who agrees not to try to kill us when we let you out, raise your hand! Or, uh, hoof," she added, taking in a faintly zebra-like creature who was looking at them with a disconcerting degree of intelligence. Hands (and hoof) went up.

In the end, there were seventeen survivors. The dead far outnumbered them, but Rouge and Vonn, with the assistance of a few of the more able-bodied former prisoners, made quick work of all fifty wards, including two in the back that seemed to contain the remains of the largest orc she'd ever seen, as well as something that might once have been a wyvern, and had been well on its way to becoming a Bone Wyvern, if that was a thing. Which she supposed it was, since she was looking at one.

Six of the survivors were sub-sapient animals, all of them somehow marked by the experiments that had been performed on them. A particularly warped calf had two heads and long fangs, but also seemed very docile, even to the extent of following a young dwarf around after the little girl dared to pet it.

Nine sapients remained, all also touched by their captivity, though the extent of those changes varied widely. Some of them tried talking to her as they were released, but mostly they were all silent except for the occasional sob or pained moan. Rouge ignored the talkers, because as much as she really, *really* wanted to know what had happened here, now was *not the time*.

There were three dwarves; a man, a woman, and a teenager. All of them now had deep black skin, red eyes, and no hair anywhere on their bodies. When released, they quickly moved to nearby circles that held the corpses of others who looked like they might also have begun life as dwarves.

Two elves stood alone at opposite sides of the group, and they seemed to be making every effort not to look at each other. One was tall, almost stretched, and cadaverous, with hollow cheeks and long claws. All signs of gender, which were already difficult to find in the androgynous race, were gone. The other elf had gone in an entirely different direction. Her hair, eyes, and lips were now all blood red, and her femininity was far more visible than the racial specs were supposed to permit. A long, barbed tail emerged from beneath the filthy dress she wore, and two almost metallic black horns poked through the hair falling around her forehead.

Only one orc was in the group. He remained relatively unchanged, though his blunt tusks were now sharp, and his eyes were a strangely luminous shade of pink, while his skin and hair were bleached utterly white.

The remaining three who seemed intelligent enough to understand what was going on were now beasts, though Rouge honestly couldn't tell if they had once been something else. When she tried to [Identify] them, she just got back a series of question marks. The first was the small, golden zebra, who watched the events around it with a strangely calm demeanor. The second was something that looked very much like a gigantic guinea-pig with orange fur and a long, fuzzy tail like a squirrel. The last one had the head and shoulders of some scaled, anteater-like creature, and the back half of a bird, complete with a brilliant red underbelly, black feathers on top, and huge, clawed feet that would have made Codswallop envious. This one watched Rouge with an intent and almost hopeful gaze.

"Okay, everybody! If you can understand what I'm saying, then you know we need to get moving! Vonn here," Rouge pointed, "is going to lead you to a way out. There's a dragon in there, and she's probably really sad, but she's not going to hurt you." *I hope.*

Fifteen of the seventeen followed, though some of the non-sapients were led by the humanoids via rope Tessle had produced from her inventory. Two of the beasties had run the instant their confinement was breached, and no one had time to chase them down. It was sad, but there wasn't much she could actually do, given the current time crunch.

Rouge turned back to Tess, who was now dropping things like rags and a small mountain of *Wolf Teeth* on the ground. The half-dwarf shrugged. "Finally ran out of room. A lot of this stuff doesn't stack." Rouge nodded, pulling out an item she'd gotten from a quest months ago, and had since nearly forgotten.

Body Bag – This item can hold any number of bodies and body parts. It will only take up one slot in your Inventory. This item is Soulbound to Rouge the Rogue, and cannot be sold, traded, given away, or dropped.

Usually, bags couldn't go inside other containers of Holding, so this was already a slightly over-powered item. Add the fact that it had infinite space inside, as long as all you wanted to put in were body parts, and it was a little ridiculous. Honestly, if she could sell it, she could have made a mint from someone who liked to hunt monsters for levels. Which, frankly, seemed like almost everyone except for her, which made it especially ironic that she was the one who'd gotten this thing.

Now, however, she stuffed *Toad Spit*, *Wyvern Teeth, Worm Hair*, and *Werewolf Tails* into the bag, leaving anything that wasn't once attached to a living creature for Tess. When she found herself pouring a jar labeled *Gall of a Two-Headed Serpent* after a jug of *EyeBall Eyes*, she decided she was done. Aspen had explained that the disgusting jars of critter bits in his secret rooms were actually powerful alchemical ingredients, and the same was probably true here, but a girl had to draw the line somewhere.

She looked around the room. With everything living except for themselves now gone, the space felt oppressively silent. She had always hated gross, body strewn, torture chambery dungeons in games, and now, surrounded by what felt like the reality of it, she was grateful that she'd never gotten into horror games. She would have had to throw away her entire collection after this.

Tess came to stand beside her. "You ready?" The woman asked, pointing at a table where she'd stacked up all the bottles of goo Neo had been working on.

"Yep, go for it." Rouge dropped back out of the door. Behind her, Tessle cast a [Fireball], holding it in her hands until it was as large and powerful as she could make it. The half-dwarf released the spell, nearly leaping backwards out of the door. Rouge slammed it shut, and they both ran back down the hall as quickly as they could.

They got about three steps before the **BOOM** behind them blew the door they'd just closed off its hinges. Virulent green and purple flames burst out, engulfing the hallway.

Rouge swallowed hard. "Well, that escalated quickly."

She heard a choked giggle from Tess, and then they were all off again, running towards the place where Aspen waited with a dragon.

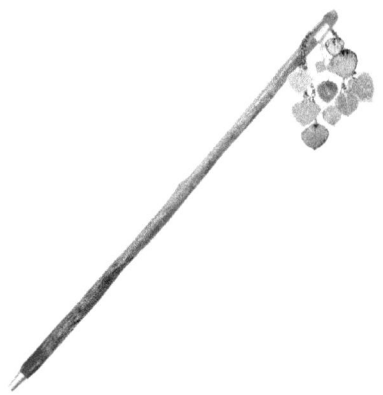

Chapter Twenty-four

Aspen

As soon as the ward circle around the dragonling was cut, Aspen's Life Sense was able to touch the small form that lay within. He could instantly tell that a tiny flicker of life still burned within the small, tattered spirit, though the body could barely sustain it. Even as he watched, the glimmer sank lower, and the darkness that ate at all of the Masker's victims rose an equivalent amount. He had a sudden, horrible feeling that if he delayed too long, that light would go out, but the dragonling's spirit would be trapped in undeath, rather than departing for the blessed forgetfulness of Atae's cool embrace.

He scooped the baby into his arms, gently lifting the too-light head so it was supported on his forearm. Turning to Rouge, who looked more than a little green beneath the warm brown of her skin, he said, "Release the rest of the prisoners. Just cut the wards. If they're sapient, and want to come, bring them with you. Gather everything you can. Burn everything else. We'll have to go back out through the tunnel in Beryl's prison."

Rouge stared at him, though having something to do was already bringing some of the light back into her hazel eyes. "But how will *Beryl* get out?"

Smiling a bit, Aspen answered, "You'll see." He headed for the door, cradling the small creature in his arms like the precious life that it was, even as he began, ever so gently, feeding his healing magic into the small form. If he did too much too quickly, the weakened body would attempt to repair itself using resources it no longer had, and he could kill the dragonling as surely as the Maskers would have.

His long legs ate up the distance between the laboratory and the throne room, and in less than a minute he found himself standing in front of the door that they had left behind at least a quarter hour before. The baby dragon was beginning to tremble in his embrace, and the eye he could see was open and clear, but terrified. If it woke any more before he reached its mother, it might try to attack him, and he couldn't defend himself if he wanted the creature to survive.

He cut off the flow of mana to his gentle healing spell, and the baby dragon's eye drifted closed almost instantly. This time though, he could feel the soft flutter of its heart within its thin body, and the ribs rose and fell enough to be visible if one looked very closely. Cautiously, Aspen pulled open the door, feeling the limp tail drop from his embrace and brush the floor as he did. With urgent movements, he resettled the small creature, and darted through the opening.

The room beyond was dim now, since Travelers seemed to have a magpie's fascination with all things shiny, and took anything that came within their reach. Only a few glowstones, placed high above in filigreed sconces, still cast their illumination down into the space below.

Aspen's toe caught on the first step up to the colossal, garish golden throne, and he stumbled. Desperately, he clutched the dragonling to his chest as he swore at his apparent inability to remember to bring a damned light!

The baby dragon squeaked so softly that the sound was nearly lost in his own grumbling, but a moment later an enormous clawed foot had punched through the wall between the throne room and the room where Beryl lay captive.

Though she was captive no longer. Broken chains dangled from the metal loops that circled her neck and wrists, and her one remaining eye was wild as she brought it down to peer through the fresh opening.

Aspen lifted the small form in his arms, offering it to the desperate mother, and she scrambled backwards to make room in what would have been a comical fashion if it hadn't been driven by such desperate fear.

IS HE DEAD? I WILL DESTROY THEM ALL!

The voice drilled into his brain, making him stagger once again, but his Dexterity was high enough that he caught himself without disturbing the child in his arms. Fortunately, as Beryl backed up, she stopped blocking the light that came through the ten-foot-high hole in the wall, so he was able to avoid the worst of the rubble piled on the ground.

"Beryl, he lives!" Aspen had to raise his voice to be heard over the scrabble of claws on stone and the soft keen that was beginning to rise from the mother dragon's throat. She stopped crying immediately, and thrust her head forward on her long neck. Aspen laid the bony little body on the ground between the blue dragon's huge forelimbs, and she nosed at her baby.

I DO NOT SMELL LIFE IN HIM. The mother dragon's voice was so forlorn that Aspen was compelled to rest a reassuring hand on the ragged scales closest to him.

"It is there, but fragile. We must be very cautious, or we may lose the chance to save him. I think they were using him to test whatever they were doing to you, but his body was unable to bear up under it. Still, if he dies with this taint upon him, I fear he may rise again as a Zombie Dragon. Zombies are mindless things, controlled only by their own hunger and their master's desires, unlike the Bone Dragon they were attempting to create in you. Do not lose hope, though. I believe we may yet snatch this victory from our foes."

Now that the baby dragon was returned to his mother, Aspen was no longer concerned that the young creature might panic and attack as it recovered. Keeping his left hand on Beryl's foreleg, he rested the right on Malachite's thin shoulder.

"Gina," he murmured. "An innocent has been injured in this hidden war. I beg you, please, aid me in cleansing him and his mother of the foul contagion that infects them." He almost smiled to himself, knowing that if his Goddess was listening, she'd likely chide him for his formality. Nonetheless, he felt that the moment called for it, and that Beryl would appreciate it, even if Gina did not.

"[Winnow]!" He felt heat and light pulse from his hand as he used his new divine power for the first time since it had been granted to him. Under his right hand, he felt soft, almost felted scales grow hard and smooth. Beryl's arm, however, seemed to writhe beneath his touch. The dragon collapsed first to her knees, and then to her belly, her head falling to *thud* onto the stones beside him.

Aspen swallowed hard, knowing that he could easily have been crushed by that huge head, but he was unable to move or stop now that the process had begun. His Life Sense 'saw' that the baby dragon's spirit was clean of the black flaws that had marked it, and it was now whole and strong again. The ribs beneath his palm rose and fell in deep, cleansing breaths. He could still feel each bone in the dragonling's side, but the life within the small body was strong and bright.

Beryl wasn't faring as well. Her flesh knit, and the worst of the abscesses and wounds closed, revealing silver-blue scars. The lesser injuries vanished entirely, but the broken and missing scales did not repair themselves, nor did her missing eye recover, though the socket now looked healthy and clean. Worst, however, was her spirit. It was cleansed, yes, but the tattered edges still fluttered, instead of becoming whole cloth once more. Frayed threads seemed to blow in an unfelt wind, and the holes left by Apofis' predations refused to close.

When the light dimmed, Aspen found himself abruptly exhausted, feeling as if every speck of mana had been drained from him by his efforts, and he, too, fell to his knees. "I'm sorry, Beryl. You accepted what was done to you, though it was under duress, and my skill cannot repair the damage done. It will get no worse, at least, but I fear that you will never again be as you once were."

The mother dragon's huge blue eye was staring at Aspen in something he could almost believe was awe, except that he wasn't certain her species could feel such a thing. The enormous creature levered herself back to her knees, stretching her wings up behind her. The bones of these appendages were still clearly visible, but they were covered in fragile, silvery skin that seemed made up of as much magic as flesh. She lowered her head and gently nudged at her baby.

Malachite, still far too thin, but now uninjured, with gleaming green scales covering his small body, slowly opened eyes that gleamed like fractured emeralds. **Mama?** came a small mental voice, and Aspen smiled broadly.

Something large and brilliant formed in the corner of Beryl's single eye, and she tilted her head so that a brilliant pale-blue sapphire nearly as large as Aspen's hand fell onto the ground beside him.

I THANK YOU, MORTAL. The huge neck curled around the comparatively tiny dragonling, entirely concealing him from Aspen's view. **TAKE THIS STONE. I MUST GO TAKE MY CHILD HOME SO THAT WE MAY RECOVER, BUT KNOW THAT IF YOU ARE EVER IN TRUE NEED, I WILL COME TO AID YOU IF YOU BREAK THIS GEM. ONCE ONLY, FOR THAT IS ALL I AM ALLOWED BY THE PACT BETWEEN MY RACE AND THE GODS, I WILL COME, AND LAY DOWN MY VERY LIFE FOR YOURS, IF IT IS NEEDED.**

Aspen shook his head, though he removed his cloak and carefully wrapped it around the stone, tying the precious bundle to his belt with the coat sleeves. "I pray that time will never come, my friend. Only take your son and flee while you may."

The huge body coiled, powerful muscles bunching as the dragon prepared to move. **WILL YOU BE WELL?** She sounded dubious, but he could see that all she really wanted was to take her child and escape.

He nodded. "Just, ah," he eyed the ceiling, which seemed both ridiculously high above him and yet far too close to the dragon's raised head. "Try not to drop the building on us, if you would."

Beryl bared her gleaming white teeth, once again set in gums of a healthy deep red. **I WILL DO MY BEST.** She pointed her head up, and *breathed.* Aspen watched in awe as the stone melted away above her.

There had never been many dragons in the world. They lived for centuries, but the few females bore only two or three clutches, and produced only one or two offspring at a time. In large part, this was because, unlike most other reptiles, dragons gave birth to live young, and, during the last year or so of their gestation, the mothers were earth-bound. This was the most vulnerable period of their lives, since not only did they depend on their mate or mates to bring them food, they also could not flee from attackers.

As a result of the relative rarity of the majestic creatures, as well as their tendency to willingly snack on the occasional sapient being, most dragons were known by name. The few hundred who still survived were listed in a book that sat on a dusty shelf in Aspen's house. Beryl was a blue acid dragon. Her breath would melt anything it touched, including stone, metal, and, of course, flesh. According to *A Treatise on Dragons, Wyverns, Basilisks, and Hydras*, she was mated to Peridot, the last of the green water dragons. At least, he had been the last, until Malachite was born.

Now, with her comparatively tiny, precious child clutched in her foreclaws, that ancient dragon rose on her hind feet, taller and taller as she melted a hole through the ceiling of the room in which they stood. At last, her oddly beautiful bone wings began to move, beating faster and faster until there seemed to be a storm trapped in the chamber with them.

Aspen found himself clinging to the wall so he wouldn't be blown around, and he was glad that no one else had come with him when he came to return Malachite to his mother. His Goddess-boosted strength was barely enough to allow him to keep a grip on one of the pillars that had supported the ceiling.

Had, because the ceiling was now almost entirely absent. Far in the distance, stars shone, and he could tell that Beryl had had to melt through several meters of stone and earth to reach the open air. The great dragon paused, impossibly hovering in mid-air, doubtless aided by more magic than any human would ever be able to bring to bear. A gleaming sapphire eye looked down at him.

BE SAFE. THANK YOU. She said simply, and then with a few more wingbeats, she had lifted away and was gone. Leaving behind Aspen, a huge room now open to the sky, and a great deal of rubble and debris.

Aspen's legs, which had been bearing his weight primarily through sheer force of will, collapsed out from under him, and he sat down both abruptly and ignominiously. His head fell back, and he realized that at some point during the recent cyclone, his hat had vanished.

"Gina," he said to the stars above, "I never want to see another dragon in my life."

"Are you kidding?" Rouge's voice came from behind him, and he turned his head to see her standing just on the other side of the hole in the wall that led to the throne room. Her eyes were huge and shining. "That was *awesome*!"

Chapter Twenty-five

Rouge

Rouge, Silus, Tess, Vonn, and their crowd of escaping captives managed to reach Beryl's prison just in time to see the enormous dragon melt her way out of the room. The sight of the enormous cerulean creature, complete with silvery scars and wings that looked like gossamer over gleaming white bone, lifting herself from the ground and hovering against the backdrop of black sky and blazing stars, was... Well, it looked like a cinematic from one of the coolest games ever created. Which it was, but it was so different to experience it. Her sense of awe was only slightly dimmed when she got a notification that the 'Dragon Tails' quest had been completed, and she swiped the glowing text out of her vision irritably.

Between Bree Stephenson's announcement that when she returned from hiatus, she would be part of revealing "an extraordinary new innovation", and the setting Rouge herself had stumbled over that told her she was part of a Beta Test and couldn't opt out of recording, she was fairly certain that Veritas Corp was actually recording the entire competition. It was part of the reason she was so mortified every time she did something stupid – *that* was going in a blooper reel somewhere. On the other hand, it meant that when the quest was over, she'd be able to see this again, and that pretty much made the potential embarrassment worthwhile.

Mostly.

So, when Aspen thunked down on his butt and told Gina he didn't want any more dragons, Rouge had to vehemently disagree.

"Are you kidding? That was awesome!" Rouge looked up at the gaping hole in the ceiling. "Though, uh, would it have been too much to ask for her to take us with her? I'm pretty sure we all would have fit on her back."

Aspen chuckled quietly as he stood, brushing himself down. He'd been blown around by the windstorm raised by Beryl's wings, and not only were his clothes and hair askew, but his new hat was missing entirely. Not really a loss, in her opinion, but he seemed particularly attached to the ugly things.

"Perhaps," the tall farmer said, eyeing the small crowd now gathered in the much larger entryway. "But could they all have hung on?"

Rouge had to admit some of the former detainees were looking pretty rough, and the few animals they'd managed to save were obviously terrified. There was no way they all would have remained calm enough to cling onto the dragon, even if they were physically up to it.

She shrugged in defeat, then looked around. "So, how do we get out, then?"

Aspen pointed to the opening in the wall through which he, Vonn, and Tess had arrived. "I believe we can make our way back out that way. If we bring the opening down behind us, the resultant rockfall will appear no more suspicious than any other part of this shattered room. Who would believe that we left via a hidden tunnel, rather than the more conspicuous opening above?"

Rouge eyed the narrow passage that was just visible beyond the ragged opening. "Uh, I don't think we're all going to fit through there." She tilted her head to indicate the orc, who was, admittedly, fairly small for one of his race, but probably still topped out at over seven feet tall, though he wasn't much broader than Aspen or Tessle. It was obvious that none of the prisoners had been fed regularly, since they were all thin and wasted looking.

Aspen sighed and reached up as if to tug the brim of his missing hat, then looked around absently. "Has anyone seen my hat? It's woven from grass, and…"

Everyone paused as the two-headed calf let out a particularly loud munch. They all turned to look, and the creature eyed them docilely, each mouth placidly chewing one side of what remained of Aspen's hat.

"No, no," Aspen muttered. "That's all right. You go ahead and finish that." He finger-combed his brown, gold, and silver hair, which was now long enough to cover his ears in rough waves, then raised his voice to address the group. "I think we've made enough noise that a little more won't attract too much attention. Tessle, Rouge," he looked at the two Travelers. "See what you have in the way of food and water. Nothing too rich, but enough to get rid of any Starvation and Dehydration debuffs they may have. I'm going to heal everyone the best I can, but I don't really know how effective it will be. We need to leave as soon as possible, or we'll have an army on our heels."

Everyone who was able nodded, and the former prisoners huddled together in a miserable, silent mass. They were all clearly traumatized, and none of them seemed ready for anything more complex than following orders or running away. Rouge did notice, however, that the anteater-bird thing kept throwing looks her way, and she wondered what that was all about.

Rouge turned her attention to her Inventory while Aspen began his glowing laying-on-of-hands thing again. He murmured quiet prayers as the glow engulfed the group, and Rouge could see the figures standing taller within the light. She and Tess began to build a small pile of Travel Rations, Water Jugs, and Animal Feed on the ground between them. When Aspen's prayer-spell faded, the fifteen rescuees fell on the food as if they were starving. Probably because they were.

The thief eyed the group critically. Aspen's [Winnow] skill should have repaired the damage to their souls, since they were innocents who had been forced into their current situation, but it hadn't done much for their bodies. He'd managed to [Heal] any actual wounds, but the changes they'd undergone were apparently irreversible. She did think that the dwarves were closer to a charcoal-gray color now, instead of the pitch black they had been, but that might just be their new 'healthy' color.

All of them were grabbing food and water from the pile. The dwarves shared amongst each other, and the girl held out a bowl of water for the calf. The orc was eating handfuls of ration bars, though Rouge noticed that he avoided taking any that anyone else was reaching for. Which, frankly, was pretty unusual behavior for an orc. The elves had each taken one ration bar and a jug of water, and retreated to the outside of the group again, though Rouge caught the pretty, demon-looking one casting glances at the skinny one from under her long, blood-red eyelashes.

Aspen gave everyone about two minutes to cram food into their mouths before clapping his hands loudly. For all that he was still being extra bossy, Rouge thought he looked pale beneath his tan, and his hands shook slightly. It was clear that he, too, was reaching the end of his endurance. "Everyone, gather up whatever food you want. We need to go, so you'll have to eat as we walk."

Everyone did as they were told, though the calf and the three other warped creatures initially refused to stop eating. Vonn finally scooped up two vaguely ovoid balls of fur with too many teeth and insect-like legs, and tucked them into a sling he made by tying the corners of his cape together. Once some Travel Rations were stuffed in next to the fuzzy critters, they seemed content to stay where they were. The two-headed, fanged calf followed the dwarven girl once she offered it some food.

That only left a twisted beasty with at least twenty eyes and even more legs, none of them matching, and a bizarre thing that looked like nothing more than a puffball dandelion that crawled along using slimy stems. Tessle had briefly carried the dandelion, and quickly discovered that the slime was slightly acidic. After a few attempts to convince the ball of legs and eyes and the flower to go with them, Aspen shook his head.

"We can't afford to stay, and they're too large to carry easily. Either they follow us on their own, or they remain behind. I can feel living beings gathering at the edges of my senses. Thus far, they have passed by this room on their way to the laboratory, but soon they will realize that's a lost cause, and return to investigate this room as well." The tall man strode to the gap in the wall, and gestured toward the darkness. "Our time is up, and we must be gone."

The former captives glanced at each other, clearly bolstered by the food in their bellies and the healing they'd received. The male dwarf moved first, followed by the female dwarves and the calf, pulled by a rope tied around both necks. The others followed along quickly after that, including the eye-leg thing, though the puffball lingered on the pile of food, which was slowly dissolving beneath its tentacle-stems.

Rouge and Aspen were the last ones through, and they exchanged glances. "Is it just me," Rouges asked, "or is that thing getting bigger?"

Aspen smiled a little grimly. "It is close enough to a plant that it falls within my power. I could force it to come with us, I think, but," he shook his head, "it was not designed well, unfortunately. Its acid is destroying its own stems, and soon it will be unable to move at all. I believe it was meant to eat until it grows large enough for the flower portion to explode outward when touched, and those who are seeded will quickly regret that fact. I am bolstering its growth, now that it has something upon which to feed, and our pursuers will find themselves facing something entirely unexpected."

Rouge paused a moment longer, staring at the writhing acidic tentacles and the puffball flower, which looked less puffy and more spikey now that it was taller than she was. "I feel kind of bad leaving it behind, though. Like, we got it this far, and we should be able to save it."

Aspen gave her a little push, firmly urging her after the rest of their party. "There is nothing you can do, and it is barely more sentient than the food on which it feasts. Now go, and let me seal this path behind us."

Silus, who had been oddly silent since they left the laboratory behind, spoke up quietly. Her voice was much more serious than Rouge was used to, and her voice was a little less squeaky and more simply very high-pitched. ::Let's go, Rouge. Aspen knows what he's doing.::

Rouge frowned, but finally gave a reluctant nod, and ducked into the tunnel, which Aspen had slightly enlarged by convincing the roots woven through the soil to pull apart. Even the orc had managed to scrape through, and the fleeing group was probably leaving Rouge and Aspen further behind with every moment.

When she was perhaps five yards down the tunnel, which looked more like something naturally formed by the rocky clay soil and thick roots surrounding her than anything someone had deliberately created, she heard the distinctive sound of falling rocks and earth from behind her. A moment later, Aspen, his form faded to grayscale in her [Darkvision], appeared from around the twist of earth she'd just passed.

"Go, go, go!" he muttered, gently but irresistibly urging her forward. "The path is collapsing behind us. The roots are swallowing it up, so they won't be able to tell there was ever enough space for anyone to escape in this direction, but I may have fed them a bit too much mana."

Even as he spoke, something writhed behind them, swelling and twisting as it bulged from the side of the tunnel. Rootlets shot out, clinging to each other as they twined and pulled in rocks and dirt, completely obscuring the passage. Then the walls around them began to wriggle as well, and Rouge felt something fibrous and powerful shove her leg out of the way. She stumbled, caught herself, then turned and began to run.

According to Rouge's in-game clock, it took fifteen minutes and forty-six seconds for their disparate group to make their way out of the natural tunnel network and back into the probably man-made one. Fortunately, thanks to Aspen's ability to coax the roots into opening and closing the passage, and Vonn's [Perfect Navigation] skill, they not only didn't get lost, but they could be fairly certain there was no pursuit.

It was a further eighteen minutes and six seconds before Aspen's quiet voice called them all to a stop. Rouge, who was at the front right behind Vonn, couldn't make out the words, but fortunately Aspen also spoke over party chat.

::Rouge, let Vonn know we're back to the spot near the children.::

Rouge frowned, wondering what children Aspen was talking about, but reached out and tugged at Vonn's tunic sleeve. "Aspen says we're near the children?" She whispered as quietly as she could, knowing Vonn's sharp elven hearing would pick it up.

The wood elf halted instantly, and his hand went to the nearby wall. His face, what she could see of it, twisted into an expression of mixed anger and hope. "We must find them, this time. I will go alone, if I must."

Rouge conveyed his words to Aspen, and soon after the farmer himself made his way up to join them. Soft murmurs of unfamiliar voices as he passed showed that time and darkness were giving some of the former prisoners enough of a feeling of safety for them to begin speaking amongst themselves. Aspen set a hand on Vonn's shoulder in what seemed like a gesture of solidarity, but the elf flinched beneath it, not in pain, but as if in expectation of something he dreaded.

"I agree," Aspen muttered, and Vonn's shoulders slumped, though whether in disappointment or relief, she didn't know. "I sense far fewer spirits near us now. Either their meeting has simply ended, or perhaps the cultists who were here have been called to assist in tracking down those who have invaded the temple." His mouth quirked slightly. "I find myself hoping it is the latter, and they are chasing a wild goose which has already escaped them. In any case, there are only a few of those rotted life forces close by, though," he raised a warning finger, "I cannot sense the truly undead. Those who have accepted an existence beyond Atae's embrace and the oblivion of the Chaos Pool are as invisible to my Life Sense as a pebble or a pane of glass."

Rouge bit her lip. "So, there could be vamps out there, and you wouldn't know it?"

He inclined his head. "There could be a room packed with vampires, zombies, and ghouls just on the other side of that wall, and we would have no way to know without looking."

::Then let's look!:: Silus's voice sounded a bit more like herself now, though Rouge was still a little worried about her small friend. ::Make a hole, Aspen. I'll go through and see what's there.::

Aspen hesitated. ::Silus, are you certain? They may see you, and-::

Silus stirred and poked her head out of Rouge's red-lined hood. Rouge felt the solid warmth on her shoulder move, and suddenly realized that it was noticeably heavier than it had been before. The little bat's large, mobile ears were also just visible at the bottom of her vision now, and before, Silus had been too tiny for any part of her to be seen without Rouge twisting her neck to bring her little friend into sight.

Rouge gasped and reached up, gently plucking the bat from her hiding place. ::Silus! Did you grow? Or evolve? Or what-do-you-call-it? You're bigger!::

Silus ducked her head, which was probably half again the size it had been just an hour before. Admittedly, she used to be only about four inches tall, with maybe a seven-inch wingspan, but she was a solid six inches now, and when she stretched out her wings, they were over a foot wide. Her weight had also increased, from a few ounces of flying fluff to something that was probably approaching half a pound. Her little face, with its flat nose and huge, adorable eyes, had elongated and fluffed out slightly, so she almost looked a bit foxlike. The silver tufts in front of her ears were now rosettes of pure white fur that looked like the silky down of a ripe milkweed pod. Rouge couldn't resist gently reaching out to pet those inviting poufs of hair.

The bat leaned into her friend's touch, and when Aspen also reached out to carefully stroke Silus' head, the small creature seemed to smile, revealing petite but needle-pointed fangs. She carefully preened one white rosette with a sharp-clawed wing-thumb.

::I'm a *Greater Bat* now,:: she said proudly. ::I got level twenty-five from helping kill that mean Traveler guy. I had the option of either *Pusillus* bat, which was sneaky, or *Onslaughter* bat, which can actually attack stuff, and,:: the small voice, familiar and yet not, grew defiant, ::I took *Onslaughter*, because I'm tired of never being able to help!::

Aspen sighed softly. ::You did help, little one, but I understand. As you wish, then. If you want to help, then help you may. Though,:: his voice slightly amused, ::you do realize you're more likely to be seen now, yes?::

Silus bared her miniature fangs. ::I can do more than [Bite] once a day, now! If someone tries to attack me, they'll regret it!::

Aspen rubbed his face tiredly, but nodded. Looking up, he focused, and a Silus-sized area of earth rippled and moved out of the way, clumps of dirt and small rootlets twisting as they shifted. Aspen gently scooped the bat from Rouge's hand and lifted her up to the edge of the opening. Silus clambered up into the hole using her taloned wing-thumbs.

::This is a tunnel.:: The bat sounded disgusted, but her small body disappeared through the opening.

::Yes,:: Aspen returned. ::The wall is still nearly two feet thick here.::

::Blech! Yuck! I hate the taste of dirt!::

::Then don't eat it.:: Aspen's voice sounded eminently reasonable, but Rouge could see the twitch of a smile at one corner of his mouth.

::Oh! There it is! I'm up near the top of a wall, and I can see... Oh.:: The small voice was suddenly sad. ::There are children. All kinds, stuffed into cages together. No zombies or anything, though. There are two guards I can see, and they look bored. I'm going to go look around.::

::Silus!:: Rouge tried, but the hole above them was already emitting filtered light, only visible because of the darkness in which they stood.

She looked at Aspen. "Isn't it enough to know there are only two guards and no vamps? Let's go!"

He looked grim, but shook his head. "She wants to look, and feels it's safe. Scouting is her job. Let her do it."

Rouge's fingernails bit into her palms as she waited, and then Silus' quiet voice started up again. ::Sorry, one of them caught a glimpse of me when I flew out. There must be other bats in here, though, because she didn't look concerned. This place is basically a cavern, so I'm actually more surprised I'm not seeing any bats- Whoa!::

Even Aspen stepped forward this time, resting his hand on the wall in front of him. Roots wriggled up, winding gently around his fingers, but he didn't seem to notice. After a moment, Silus started talking. ::Spoke too soon. There's a whole colony of Lesser Bats up here.::

Rouge grinned. ::Can you ask them about this place?::

Aspen was already shaking his head when Silus replied. ::They can't really talk. When Aspen gave us a link to his soul, we got a small portion of his stats. That's why Sumi, Khor, and I are so different from other animals, even Greater ones.::

Aspen smiled ruefully, almost unconsciously reaching down to touch the short staff at his belt. ::It's also why I can't bond often. Each bond creature keeps the stats they receive, so the more bonds you form, the weaker you, yourself, become.::

Rouge suddenly had a *lot* of questions, but Silus was speaking again. ::I've checked everywhere that isn't closed off. The room is just a rough cavern. I mean, the walls have been smoothed a little, but you can tell it's just natural earth up here. There's kind of a stage in the middle, and three doors. Two of them are to your right when you break through, and the third one is pretty much straight across from you.::

::Are there any other guards?:: Aspen's fingers were back on the wall now, and she was pretty sure his hands were actually sinking into the dirt. It was kind of cool, but also a little creepy, especially since he seemed to have no idea he was doing it. Or the dirt was doing it. Whichever.

::Only the two that I can see. I don't know what's behind the doors, though. I don't *hear* anything, no matter how close I get, but that just means nobody's in there screaming or snoring.::

::No screaming is a good thing,:: Rouge muttered, tugging at a braid.

Aspen threw her a smile. ::Indeed. So, if we take out these two guards quietly enough, we may be able to free the children and get out without anyone noticing. Silus, can you tell if any of the doors are an exit?::

Silus' voice suddenly sounded less self-assured, and a little squeakier. ::I *think* maybe the door across the room goes outside. *Maybe.* It's bigger and heavier than the other two, anyway. But I could be wrong!::

Rouge wanted to give Silus a huge snuggle. It was really kind of scary to stop being a kid and start having some actual responsibility. Rouge had felt that a little on her first day of high school, and even more after her first day of work. As amazing as it had been, and as much as she'd tried to just stay calm and handle everything, she'd kind of wanted to cry when she saw her dad that night.

Aspen's hands had sunk in up to the wrist now, and he'd definitely noticed, but he wasn't doing anything about it. ::I know. It's okay,:: he said soothingly. ::You're doing a wonderful job, Silus. Your mother would be so proud of you.::

Rouge choked a little, knowing how much that would mean to her little friend.

Turning back to look at Vonn and Rouge, Aspen pulled one hand from the earth, while the other gently nudged roots apart like a curtain. Some loose dirt spattered to the ground, but most of it stayed trapped by the thousands of tiny rootlets that had almost completely taken over the area in front of them.

"You two are our quietest members, even without [Stealth]. I'm going to send you through, and you need to take care of the two guards." His face was hard as he said, "Do whatever you need to. Remember, these are people who are willing to sit beside a cage full of children and do nothing."

Vonn's expression was stark, and Rouge had never seen him look so inhuman. Every angle of his face was sharp, and his gray eyes almost seemed to glow like a cat's in the low light cast by the shuttered glow stone he held.

Rouge just nodded, and Aspen turned back to the wall. ::Silus, Rouge and

Vonn are coming through in the same area you did. Will the guards be able to see them?::

It took a second, but Silus answered, ::Maybe. It's partially behind the cages, but if they turn at just the wrong moment, it could happen.::

::Can you create a distraction? A small one. We don't want them calling for help.::

Another moment, and then the little bat answered, her voice sounding gleeful. ::Oh yes, I can definitely do that.::

Aspen widened and deepened the hole he had created. He had told Silus the wall here was almost two feet thick, and Rouge guessed that he'd opened up about a foot and a half of earth.

::On three, then. One.:: A few more inches. ::Two.:: She would swear she could just see a bit of light between the roots now. ::Three!::

The wall crumbled, and Rouge was through it, with Vonn close on her heels.

The first thing she noticed was that Silus had really underestimated the number of bats. Or maybe 'millions' was a normal population count for a bat colony. (Okay, so maybe 'thousands' was more accurate, but that was still too many zeroes.) In any case, a *lot* of bats were swirling around in the cave. The cacophony of flapping wings and high-pitched squeaks and clicks was almost enough to throw Rouge off her game.

Not quite, though.

Other than the swirling cloud of bats, the first things she registered were the two guards ahead and off to the left. She reached out and tugged at Vonn's sleeve, holding up two fingers, then folding the one on the right and pointing the remaining one at herself. She would take the left guard. He nodded, and they were off.

The bats made a very effective distraction, though they probably didn't count as a 'small' one. On the up side, the guards were too busy swatting at the flying creatures to call for help. Rouge crouched down beneath the blanket of bats and ninja-ran toward her target.

The guard, a heavy-set woman in boiled leather armor, didn't even see Rouge coming. Rouge swept the other woman's legs out from beneath her, and as soon as the guard hit the floor, a single [Pterion Puncture] put the woman out of her misery. Rouge made a mental note that apparently, standing over the victim counted as 'attacking from above' for this purpose.

Rouge quickly turned to Vonn's target, but found that the man was already down, and Vonn was just finishing him off with an efficient strike to the throat. They grinned at each other, then turned to loot their victims. Rouge sent a message over party chat.

::Done here. Silus, can you get your friends to go back to sleep?::

Silus sounded a little embarrassed. ::Yes, I think so. I just asked the leader of the colony to send a few bats to fly by, but since I'm a Greater Bat now-::

Aspen's voice was amused. ::You have far more authority with others of your species than you did before.::

::Yes.:: Silus glided down and landed on Rouge's shoulder as the girl stood to look around.

Now that the bat-cloud was dispersing, Rouge could see that the huge room was mostly empty. There was a dais set up slightly off from the center, no doubt for Apofis' priest (or whatever those orange-trim guys were) to make their 'let's kill all the nonhumans' speech from. The space was definitely able to handle a big crowd of people.

The three doors were exactly as Silus had described them, as were the cages of children *stacked* near the wall through which Rouge and Vonn had come. She felt her face tighten in fury even as tears sprang to her eyes as she took in the frightened people locked in those cages.

The small prisons were stacked in cubes of eight. Four cells on the bottom, and four more on top. Each cage held one to four children, most of whom were looking at Rouge and her friends with varying degrees of terror and hope.

Suddenly, the dwarves that they had rescued from the laboratory let out a cry so filled with emotion that Rouge felt her heart clench in her chest. When she looked toward the sound, she saw the three dwarves on the floor, crouched around a cage, their arms thrust through the bars to desperately embrace two small, filthy children. All five dwarves were crying in great, wrenching sobs, and the man was pushing against the bars with such force that it looked like he might break his own arms trying to get the small cell open.

Rouge's fingers clenched around the ring of keys that she'd taken from the female guard's body. She had to clear her throat twice before she could speak. Her voice was hoarse when she said, "I think these will open the cages. Let's get those kids out of there."

🐦 🐦 🐦

With all of the adults helping, the prisoners were released in remarkably short order. Fortunately, though they were dirty and traumatized, they had clearly been given food and water fairly regularly, so they weren't in nearly as poor condition as those in the lab had been. Aspen healed the small injuries that they had sustained simply from being crammed into a space far too small for them for far too long, and then he used [Winnow] on them all.

Instantly, pale, frightened little faces brightened. A warm, flower-scented breeze swept the sour scent of the cave away, and playful gusts twirled the hair of everyone present. Rouge felt the gentle pressure of a loving hug, and relaxed a little into the unseen embrace. Around her, she saw fifty or so children simultaneously relax, though a few little ones began to cry, as if they were finally in the presence of someone who would hold them through their sadness.

Even Aspen, standing near Rouge and looking even more drawn and pale than he had earlier, straightened his tired stance and smiled a little. "All right everyone," Aspen looked around, taking in the crowd surrounding them. "I wish we had time to sit and recover, but we must leave. We aren't truly safe until we're home."

His topaz eyes were calculating as he looked them all over again. He nodded and said, "Everyone find a partner. Adults, each of you take one of the littlest. Older children, pair up. Stay together, and if one of you can't continue, help each other or let someone know. Do any of you know where these doors lead?"

One of the oldest of the children raised her hand. Her voice trembled, but her brown eyes were confident. "The two over there lead deeper into the caves. That one," she pointed to the big door, "is where the Maskers come from for their meetings. When it opens, you can smell fresh air. Once, I smelled rain." Her little face scrunched up, and one tear trickled down her dirty cheek.

Aspen nodded firmly. "Do you know if there are more guards nearby?"

The girl shook her head. "Someone came not long ago, and called them all away. Usually there are two guards by each door, and others wander through sometimes. They all left when that man came, though, and went that way." She pointed to the door furthest on the right.

Nodding again, Aspen turned to his party. "Let's get them outside, and then we can decide what to do."

The group of children was the most subdued and obedient Rouge had ever seen. Each of them held hands with another, fingers clenched in a way that likely would have been painful if the other child wasn't gripping back just as desperately.

There were three babies, ranging in age from maybe six months old to nearly two years, each cradled by one of the oldest children, who had clearly taken on the role of protector for these youngest victims of the Maskers. Four more toddlers were too young to be able to walk quickly or well, and also needed to be carried. These were handed to the adults in the group, and Rouge and Tess quickly produced cloth from their inventories to be used as makeshift slings.

With the urgent speed of desperation, the assemblage, which now numbered nearly seventy, gathered themselves and headed for the door. The cavern seemed even larger than it actually was, and every step echoing on dirt or stone made everyone wince in anticipation of discovery. The deceptively long journey across the hard-packed floor was probably the most nerve-racking two minutes of Rouge's life.

When they reached the large door, which was a basic, heavy wooden portal, far different from the ornate monstrosities in the player area, Aspen simply reached out and pulled it open. Fresh, cool, evening air flooded over them, along with the distant sound of waves washing against the shore. They were somewhere near the wharf, but not at the docks themselves.

Stepping outside, Rouge looked at the building from which they had escaped. It was an unprepossessing wooden shack, which seemed to have been built against the side of a hill. The only thing that marked it as different from the surrounding buildings was the solid wooden door, though even that was weathered and cracked from the outside.

Rouge heard sobbing, and turned to look toward the sound. As each of the former prisoners exited the 'shack', setting foot on the bluestones of the street, they gasped. A few even fell to their knees, touching the smooth stones with trembling fingers. Rouge bit her lip, realizing what those stones meant to these people.

Safety.

Once their feet rested on the bluestones, no one could attack them. They couldn't be abducted, assaulted, or robbed. All they had to do was walk away from this place, and they were free.

Aspen turned to Rouge, the lines around his eyes and mouth smoothing out for the first time since he'd brought her back to life after Beryl stabbed her. "I hate to ask," he murmured, "but-"

"Can I go back in and check out those other two doors? Heck yeah." Rouge grinned at him fiercely. "I'm not leaving anyone behind in that place, and plus, we still haven't gotten a quest completion notice yet, right?"

Aspen's mouth pinched, but he nodded reluctantly. "I would go with you, but…" he gestured at the milling crowd a little helplessly.

She shrugged. "Honestly, it's probably best that I go back in alone anyway."

A small, piqued squeak came from her shoulder, and Rouge laughed. "Okay, it's probably best if *Silus* and I go back in alone. Though…" She trailed off as she looked for her friends.

Tessle was closest. She was holding a toddler, and she met Rouge's eyes apologetically over the blonde curls snuggled beneath her chin. The child was fast asleep, little face exhausted and diminutive hands clutching the half-dwarf's armor as if it was the child's favorite toy.

The warrior shook her head very slightly. "I have enough time to take them back to Aspen's house," she whispered, "but then I need to go. I have work in the morning, and it's really late."

Rouge nodded, then looked around for Vonn. She found him standing by the orc, who seemed to be covered in children. Looking closer, she could see that the orc was, in fact, strapped to not one but two babies and one of the youngest toddlers. Like the one in Tess's arms, these were all fast asleep, and Vonn was examining them carefully.

Realization struck Rouge like a thunderbolt. "Is one of these your nephew?"

Vonn shook his head, gently smoothing flyaway black hair back around the little ear he'd been examining. "Two half-elves and a half-troll. Both of the half-elves had a high elf parent. There is one half wood elf, but that child is a girl, and old enough to remember her parents. If my sister's son lives, he is not here."

Gently, Rouge touched Vonn's arm, feeling the tense muscles beneath his supple leather shirt. "I'm going back in," she said. "Do you want to go?"

The wood elf's gray eyes locked on her own like knives glinting in the darkness. "Yes," he said simply.

Note From The Author

I know I dropped you on a cliffhanger again, but hopefully it's not as bad as *Clearing*. I promise the next book is coming soon! When I originally wrote these books, it was as a trilogy, but logistics required that the first and second book each be divided into two parts for printing. (A thousand-page paperback isn't fun to read, and is really expensive to print.)

The books are fully written, so I'm editing these and getting them into your hands as quickly as possible, and all five books will be published by the end of 2022. I hope you'll join Rouge, Aspen, and crew for *Cultivation*, the fourth book of the Legendary Farmer series. They're on the run again, and this time trouble will follow them on their way back home. Also, Khor gets his own chapters! Look forward to it!

In the meantime, I'm available on Patreon, Goodreads, Instagram as authorelizabethoswald, and Twitter as @AuthorEOswald. I'd love to hear from you, even if you only want to castigate me for leaving you cliffhanger endings. (I really am sorry!!)